TENNIS
NOIR

TENNIS NOIR

CRIME FICTION ANTHOLOGY

EDITED BY
JOHN SHEPPHIRD

Contents

Introduction

Over a steak dinner at Smith & Wollensky's in NYC, I shared an idea with fellow crime writers Scott Adlerberg and Jason Starr (contributors here) for an anthology of crime fiction set in the world of tennis. We all play and brainstormed for contributors. Many crime fiction anthologies are themed by cities, regions, recording artists, or nostalgia. Very few are devoted to sports.

Jason Starr had co-edited the star-studded collection *Bloodlines: A Horse Racing Anthology*, but horse racing is entirely different. Fans may follow (and bet) on racing, but they don't compete. There may be money at stake, but no sweat equity. Tennis is unique in that most fans have played tennis at one time or another. Players sweat. Game. Set. Match.

Besides—love means nothing in tennis, so ripe for noir.

This is a handpicked collection of authors I've known for many years—friends, colleagues, and even family. More than a few I've come to know from attending the Bouchercon World Mystery Convention over many years. Contributors feature a tennis instructor, tech lawyer, hybrid graphic novel and print novelists, a teacher, audiobook director/producer, several film professionals, and other established authors. My cousin is a lifelong tennis player. She writes cozy mysteries, so I asked her to contribute.

Thanks to Scott and Jason for encouraging me to pursue this anthology. Much gratitude to Shawn Reilly Simmons from Level Best Books who showed great enthusiasm and followed up when I pitched the idea. And many, many thanks to all the authors that contributed herein.

It was a thrill to put this all together. Enjoy.

The Summer Tournament

By Jason Starr

Borg hit a deep topspin forehand to Connors' backhand and Connors hit an awkward, bottled-up shot into the net.

"Yes, yes, baby!" I shouted and hugged the person nearest to me, Marilyn Ziskin. "Incredible! Unbelievable!"

A group of about ten of us had been watching the Wimbledon final all morning, huddled around the small black-and-white TV with fuzzy reception in the lobby of Chaits, a resort in upstate New York. I'd been rooting for Borg, of course, since I'd modeled my entire game after him. I used the same Bancroft racket, strung my racket to the same eighty pounds, and I even curled my index finger on my left hand to track the ball when I hit my topspin forehand, exactly the way the master did. I loved how Borg used strategy and skill to win points rather than sheer power. It was like he was playing a chess match, outwitting his opponents because he was always at least two or three steps ahead.

"Wow, I really thought Connors would pull it out," Marilyn said.

"No way," I said, still hyped from the victory. "I knew after he beat Gerulaitis that nobody can beat Borg in a long match. Even after Connors won that fourth set, I knew Borg was toying with him."

"He might win the Open too," Milton Cohen said.

Like me, Milton was a psychoanalyst, though Milton was stuck in academia—he taught at Queens College—while I had a thriving practice in

Greenwich Village.

"Definitely," I said. "If Borg can beat Connors on grass, he can beat him on any surface."

"I think McEnroe's gonna be tough at Forest Hills," Stevie Wasserberg said.

Stevie was sixteen years old and a pretty good tennis player. I'd beaten him in the round of sixteen in last year's Chaits summer tournament in straight sets, but the last set went to 7-5; he'd grown a few inches since then, and now he was playing starting singles on his high school team in Rockland. He'd be stiff competition this year.

"*McEnroe?*" I said, like it was the name of a disease. "That spoiled brat'll be lucky if he even qualifies."

There was more discussion about Borg's big win, then everyone gradually dispersed. Some returned to their bungalows or hotel rooms; others went to the cafeteria for lunch. I stuck around in the lobby and had a cup of coffee while reading an article on Chrissy Evert's backhand in *Tennis*. I was already dressed to play—tight white shorts and a white Izod shirt—and I had my racket with me because I had a court reserved for one p.m.—doubles on the red clay, my best surface.

For eight years now, my wife Bev and I, along with our kids Danny and Shoshana, had been spending summers at Chaits. It was around a forty-minute drive from Monticello, the heart of "The Borsht Belt", in a sleepy town with a general store and that's about it. The owner, Max Feinberg, advertised in *The Village Voice*, and this attracted arty, eccentric guests, especially Jewish, lefty intellectuals, hippies, and mixed-race couples. Julius and Ethel Rosenberg, the Communist spies, used to come to the resort and there were rumors that the FBI was still bugging the premises.

Unfortunately, Max didn't spend anything on upkeep—much of the place was falling apart. There was a small hotel and lobby on the top of a hill, and bungalows down the road below. Every year we stayed in the same rickety, shanty-like bungalow, across from a dilapidated, bat-infested barn. All the bungalows were in horrible shape with uneven flooring, torn window screens, and decades-old appliances. One year, we arrived and discovered that the Board of Health had posted a warning about contaminated water, but we stayed, as did pretty much everyone else.

For us, the pros of summers at Chaits outweighed the cons. We'd made lots of friends over the years and so had our kids. The free day camp was saving us a ton on sleepaway camp—money that I'd invested in an up-and-coming cable TV stock—and it also worked out very well for us schedule-wise. Bev, a special ed teacher at a public junior high school, had summers off so she could stay alone with the kids all of July while I came up on weekends. In August, I always stayed at Chaits full-time, as August was the universal vacation period for psychoanalysts. As I often joked with friends and colleagues, if you were planning to go nuts in New York City, you'd better make sure it was after Labor Day.

But, by far, the greatest thing about Chaits was that everyone was as obsessed with tennis as I was.

Every summer, in early August, a tournament was held to determine the Chaits singles champion, and I loved the build-up as much as the tournament itself. Throughout the year—including during dull therapy sessions—I fantasized about the seeds, and to stay in top form I played tennis twice a week at the Murray Hill Racquet Club. I was undoubtedly one of the best players at Chaits, but I knew I had to keep raising my game, physically and mentally, if I wanted to stay on top. There were always up-and-comers, especially teenagers like Stevie, who were trying to dethrone me. I'd won three summer tournaments, including the last two, and this year I was going for three in a row.

My doubles match today was me and Gary Greenberg versus Ron Weissman and Kenny Brody. Gary and I complemented each other well. He had a strong, consistent serve and I, of course, had a big Borg-esque topspin forehand, as well as a deep, slicing backhand. We both kept the pressure on, hitting with pace, and when we got to the net we were nearly impossible to beat. Kenny, a waiter at the hotel, was in his twenties, a solid player with nice strokes, but he wasn't nearly on my level or even Gary's. Ron was a good player, but he was forty-eight, seven years older than me, and he had one major weakness—a lack of agility. Because he was tall and stiff, due to an old back injury, I'd heard some teenagers refer to him as "Ron the Robot," which, admittedly, made me chuckle. Despite his physical issue, Ron had a strong serve-and-volley game, rarely made unforced errors, and was always a top ten seed in the summer tournament, and he'd even won it all five years ago, though that was a year I couldn't compete because of tennis elbow. Today would be an easy, casual doubles match, a nice warm up for serious singles matches later in the summer, though it always felt awkward to play with Ron, or even interact with him, since, for the past two years I'd been fucking his wife, Joan.

The affair really wasn't very serious—at least not for me and Joan. We weren't in love; we were just using each other to fulfill our needs, and neither of us felt any sense of attachment. I'd been very honest and open with her from the first time we got it on, telling her:

"I'm only interested in your body, that's it."

Joan said that Ron had lost interest in sex years ago—I suspected that he was impotent, and that Joan felt corresponding shame over this, which led to passive-aggressiveness toward him—and, while Beverly and I still had good, regular sex, I'd been open and honest with her about my need for multiple partners. Joan and I got together mainly during summers when Ron was home in the city—he had a dental practice in Park Slope—and Ron and Joan's kids were in day camp. During the rest of the year, Joan occasionally visited me at my office off Bleecker Street on evenings when I told Beverly I was "working late."

"So your guy Borg pulled it off, huh?" Gary said as I joined him on the red clay.

"Two in a row," I said. "You missed a great one."

"Yeah, I wanted to watch but I got caught up with Cathy and the kids, you know how it is."

I noticed that the lines were dirty, especially the baseline, so I grabbed the roller broom from the corner of the court and began cleaning. Kenny and Ron were seated on a bench, getting ready to play, Ron having trouble bending over while he wrapped an ace bandage around his gimpy left knee. I made a mental note to myself to hit a lot of drop shots today to force Ron to hustle—I was a competitor, always looking for an edge.

As I passed them, I said. "It's a hot one today, huh?"

It was already over ninety and extremely humid and it was supposed to get even hotter.

"Yeah," Kenny said smirking, "you better take it easy on us. I'm already hungover from last night."

"Don't worry, I will," I lied.

Ron avoided eye contact with me. As far as I knew, Ron didn't know, or even suspect, anything about me and Joan. But, on some subliminal, *primal* level, I could tell he felt uncomfortable around me, perhaps because he perceived me as "the dominant male" whom he had to defer to, and he wasn't at peace with this.

The first set wasn't very competitive. I held my service, then we easily broke Kenny's. Gary and I both held, then we broke Kenny again, and I breezed the rest of the way, taking the set 6-1. I was playing okay, not great. I missed an easy volley that I made ninety-nine out of a hundred times—I blamed it on the heat and early summer rustiness. It figured that I wasn't in top form yet, but I was naturally hard on myself. In the second set, we were tied 3-3 and I was serving. At deuce, I hit a deep first serve and attacked the net, but Ron got to it with his forehand and whipped a passing shot by me. I glared at him, but he was still avoiding eye contact. It was ad-out, but I wasn't going to give in and spin in an easy first serve, so I unleashed my hardest serve of the day and attacked the net again. The serve was perfectly placed, right on the line, but somehow Kenny lunged and hit a short lob. It should have been an easy overhead slam, but—maybe the heat's fault again—I somehow mistimed it, and the ball hit the rim of my racket and caromed off to the right.

In my case, the adage "your true personality comes out on the tennis court" was fitting. While I was usually steady and pragmatic—a rational thinker people often told me—I was also hard on myself, especially when things didn't go as planned, and I could easily lose my temper.

"Damn it, Alan, you fucking suck!" I screamed at myself, and then I threw my racket against the fence as hard as I could.

The other players, and a few people watching, weren't surprised. My tennis tantrums were well known at Chaits; I often threw my racket and screamed at myself, or hit balls far over the fence into the woods when I was upset or just extremely frustrated. I'd been working on these issues with my own therapist back in the city.

I retrieved my racket, happy to see that it wasn't damaged as I'd broken several rackets in the past. We lost the second set, but went on to win the third set easily, 6-2. At the net, when we all shook hands, Ron was still avoiding eye contact with me—he definitely *knew*.

Ron left the court first. I hung out with the other guys for a while, shmoozing, then headed down the hill to my bungalow where Bev was serving lunch to the kids.

* * *

I took a shower and when I came out Danny and Shoshana were gone.

"Ron Weissman's taking them and his kids to see *Saturday Night Fever,*" Bev said. "It's rated R but I guess that's okay, right?"

I didn't care what movies my kids saw, as long as it wasn't *Deep Throat*—though they'd probably seen that already without telling us, which was fine too—so I said, "Sounds great. When do you think they'll be back?"

"I don't know. Guess around dinnertime."

Interesting—Ron and all the kids would be away for a few hours. If I could just get rid of Bev, Joan and I could have some time alone to fool around.

"What about you?" I asked.

"What about me?

"What're your plans for the rest of the day?"

"Not sure." She was collecting the kids' dishes from the table and putting them in the sink. "I really want to finally finish that Harold Robbins novel I've been reading, but Harriet Stern asked me if I want to go antiquing in Rhinebeck."

"Oh, you should definitely do that."

"Yeah? You won't mind?"

"No, not at all." I was trying not to sound too excited about the prospect of being a free man for the day. "I was up so early watching Borg, I'm kind of zonked now. I think I'll probably take a long nap so I have energy later on. Go. Have fun. Maybe you can find a console table for the foyer."

"Oh, maybe I can."

When Bev left—I made sure I actually *saw* her get into Harriet's Chevy station wagon—and then I sprayed some Brute onto my chest and pubic hair, then strolled over to Joan's bungalow.

As I approached, I gazed through the kitchen window and saw her.

"Joaneeee," I said. "Oh, Joannneee."

Me saying her name in a sing-songy way was sort of our mating ritual.

She came out onto the screened-in porch and said, "Heyyyy there, Alan," already sounding flirty, excited to see me.

She was in a flowy light-green dress—similar to other summer outfits she often wore. Although I didn't think she looked particularly sexy in the dress, or sexy at all really, I was excited to see her too, and I already felt a hard-on pressing against the zipper of my shorts.

I knew from many sessions with cheating spouses—and contrary to popular belief—that people often chose partners for affairs who were less attractive than their significant others. While the rule didn't hold up all the time—for example, I was much sexier than Ron—there was no doubt that Bev was much prettier than Joan. I knew I was turned on by the espionage, the thrill of averting disaster, and feeling like I was "getting away" with something, probably related to my abandonment issues as a child and my awkward first dating experiences in high school, but I had no interest in altering my behavior. I believed that to be truly alive, you had to embrace your needs and desires, not run from them.

When I opened the porch door, she immediately dragged me into the bungalow, through the kitchen, toward her bedroom in the back. We rarely kissed or even talked very much. I didn't like her personality at all. She had a grating Long Island accent and was one of the most oppositional people I'd ever met, always disagreeing for the sake of disagreeing, and we didn't have any common interests.

But I still liked screwing her.

I pulled off her dress—she was bra-less as usual—and as I pulled off my shorts and sandals she inserted her diaphragm. I tried to focus on her face rather than her body. She was heavyset with too much cellulite, and I preferred thin women like Bev. Joan didn't have a pretty face either, though from some angles she looked quite a bit like Barbra Streisand.

She climbed onto the wobbly bed with the springy mattress and got onto all fours.

"I need this so bad," she said.

Before we had sex she always said this, or some variation of it, but I never responded. I wasn't a big talker in the bedroom, especially with Joan. This affair wasn't closeness; it was about sex, and I preferred to stay in my own head, focused on my *own* fantasies.

I mounted her from behind, which was perfect because it allowed me to close my eyes and fantasize more vividly. I was thinking about the photo of Barbra Streisand on the cover of her *A Star is Born* album that I kept in my office.

I'm fucking Barbra Streisand, I'm fucking Barbra Streisand, I kept repeating in my head, like a mantra.

As my orgasm built, I was thinking about the way Streisand looked at Kris Kristofferson, imagining that *I* was Kristofferson, then, right as I was starting to come, I opened my eyes and saw Ron's Wilson T-2000 tennis racket in the corner of the room near the window, propped up against the wall. The racket could have dampened my passion, reminding me that I was committing adultery with a friend's wife, but instead it reinforced the huge risk I was taking, which made me harder and my orgasm more intense. As I ejaculated, I was so lost in my *Star is Born* fantasy that I muttered, "Oh fuck Barb…" but I managed to cover it up with my usual loud grunting.

"Alan…*Alan*."

I'd heard Joan say *something* while I was orgasming, but I'd been so absorbed that it hadn't fully registered.

"Yeah, what?"

"Didn't you hear that?"

"Hear what?"

"There was a noise…outside the window. Someone's out there."

"It was probably an animal," I said, already antsy. After I orgasmed, Joan always wanted to lie in bed and go into a long monologue about whatever minutiae was going on in her life, and I always wanted to get away as fast as I could.

"It wasn't an animal, I'm telling you, Alan."

To placate her, and also as an excuse to get out of bed, I got up and looked out the window.

"No one's there," I said.

"Check out front."

"Okay, okay."

I grabbed a moist towel that was dangling from the doorknob, probably the one that Ron had used after tennis, and wrapped it around my waist. When I went on to the screened-in porch, I didn't see anyone immediately in front of the bungalow, but I saw Stevie Wasserberg, jumping over a narrow stream that sliced through the property as he rushed away toward the road.

"Who is it?" Joan was on the porch in a pink house robe.

"We shouldn't be out here," I said.

"Is that Stevie Wasserberg?"

I went back to the bedroom and began getting dressed.

"What was Stevie doing out there?" she asked.

"We don't know if he was there."

"What do you mean? I heard him in the bushes. I know what I heard."

God, that whiny voice.

"We don't know if he was there or not. He was just walking away."

"More like running."

"It doesn't mean anything." I already had my boxers and shorts on and was putting on my shirt.

"What if he saw us, Alan?"

"There's nothing we can do."

"I knew it was too risky to get together here. We should've stuck to the city."

"You seemed like you were happy to see me."

"This is awful." She looked like she was about to cry. "What if he tells Ron? My marriage'll be ruined. My *life*'ll be ruined."

"He won't tell Ron." I slid my feet into my sandals. "He has no reason to do that and he probably didn't see anything anyway. Besides, Ron already knows."

"What?" She looked horrified.

"Relax, relax, Jesus Christ. I don't mean he *literally* knows. I mean, on a subconscious level, he senses a dynamic between you and me."

"You *told* him something?"

"Of course not. I just mean that I have a lot of experience dealing with these situations in my practice, and I don't think Ron would be shocked if he found out. He might actually feel relief."

"How can you be so…so…so *casual*? Do you think Beverly knows, too?"

"Absolutely not."

"Then why does Ron know on this *unconscious level* and Beverly doesn't?"

"I didn't say Ron actually *knows* anything." Jesus, how did Ron put up with this twenty-four, seven? "Okay, let's just drop it. If you want to just come to my office the next time we're both in the city and have sex there, let's do that. Or if you want to break it off, that's an option too."

"Who's Barb?" She was glaring at me, not blinking.

"What?" Though I'd heard her and knew exactly whom she meant.

"When you were coming, you said, 'Oh fuck Barb.' Are you fooling around with somebody else? I don't think there are any Barb's up here, but maybe there's one staying at the hotel, or maybe you have another woman in the city or something."

I did have other women in the city, but as I advised my patients—you don't have to be truthful all the time in relationships; secrets are okay.

"I don't know anyone named Barb," I said, "and I didn't say Barb. But even if I did say Barb or some other name, that would be between me and Barb or whoever, because this is just about sex, remember? Physical release, that's it."

She still seemed upset, but I wasn't in charge of other people's emotions.

"So, what are we supposed to do now?" she asked.

"Nothing." I kissed her quickly on the lips, imagining she was Barbra Streisand. "Just go on with your day."

* * *

Back at my bungalow, I showered, then I took a long nap and woke up refreshed and energized. It was still blazing hot, probably 100 or close to it, but I went to one of the hardcourts and practiced my serve, especially my second serve, working on getting it deeper with "more kick," like Borg's. When I returned to my bungalow, the kids were back from the movie, and a little while later, Bev arrived from antiquing. She didn't find a console table, but she bought a mirror and some other knickknacks.

We had dinner—burgers and pasta—and then the kids ran off. I usually had no idea where the kids were or what they were doing. Sometimes they had "sleepouts" in the woods and didn't come back till morning, smelling like pot, which was fine with me. If they wanted to spend the entire summer in the woods, I wouldn't have cared.

Bev and I got dressed for the Saturday night cocktail party at the hotel lobby. She put on a sexy purple sequin jumpsuit with bell-bottoms, and I was wearing my favorite floral shirt with the top buttons undone, exposing my bushy chest hair.

Holding hands, we headed up the hill.

The cocktail party was already hopping. Bernie Shore was playing the piano—*Sunny Side of the Street*—and Alice Goldstein was singing. Dozens of other guests were walking around mingling as Kenny, Richie, Joel, and the other waiters were bringing around hors d'oeuvres. Some people, like Frank Ziskin—a civil rights attorney—and Stevie's father, Herb Wasserberg—a defense attorney—were already tanked. I went to the bar and got a Scotch on the rocks, then left Bev with a few of her friends and started to mingle.

The hot topic, as usual, was tennis. Everyone was still buzzing about Borg's big win and about the matches today. Everyone knew that I'd won the doubles match, and there was also buzz about Stevie who'd won a singles match against Derek Fine, another top young player.

"That Stevie's really somethin' else this year," Eddie Lepidus said. "He's gonna be tough in the summer tournament."

Eddie was an old-timer, in his seventies, who was in charge of determining the seeds and brackets for the tournament, so I tried to stay on his good side.

"Yeah, I saw some of it," some bearded guy I vaguely knew said. "He was really on fire out there. He looked like Borg."

It was hard enough for me to hear about how good someone else's game was when I was the reigning Chaits champion, but comparing him to Borg?

"Okay, now you're going way too far," I said. "The kid has a good forehand, okay, but I know Borg, I've studied Borg, and he's nothing like Borg."

The conversation suddenly stopped. It seemed like the music stopped too because all I could focus on were the faces staring at me. I couldn't tell if they were jolted or incredulous, but I realized I'd raised my voice louder than I'd intended.

To break the ice, I held up my glass, grinning, and said, "To Borg!"

And everyone toasted, "To Borg!"

A few minutes later, I noticed Ron and Joan at the other end of the lobby, in the sunken area near the fireplace, chatting with some people. At one point, Joan looked over at me and I could tell she was worried, but Ron seemed normal, talking in an animated way.

Then Stevie entered the lobby with his usual crew of teenage friends—Joey, Jonny, and Josh. They were laughing, engaged in conversation, and Stevie didn't look over at me and wasn't acting unusually.

Later, I was at the bar getting a refill when Stevie came over to me and said, "I heard about your doubles win today. Nice going."

"Thanks," I said, "and I heard you had quite the performance today in singles. Good for you."

Then Stevie rejoined his friends, and they headed down to the basement, probably to play ping-pong.

I joined a few other conversations, and when I saw that Joan was alone, I went over to her and said discreetly, "Coast is clear."

"How do you know?" she whispered, fake smiling to pretend we were talking about something else.

"Spoke to Stevie briefly," I said. "He seemed totally normal."

"Well, that's a relief," she said. I guess you were right. Sorry for causing so much mishigas."

"Never apologize for emotion, Joan," I said, and then went to join Bev.

I finished my drink, then cut myself off. I had a seven a.m. court time reserved for my first singles match of the summer, and I wanted to be at the top of my game.

When the party wound down, some people stayed to watch a movie screening in the dining room—a 16mm print of Chaplin's *The Great Dictator* shown by Al Greenberg, movie buff who was a guest at the hotel—but Bev and I returned to our bungalow. The kids weren't home, and their sleeping bags were gone, so we assumed they were on a sleepout.

Bev and I made love. As always, it was sweet and enjoyable.

I wished that was enough for me, but it wasn't.

***

After I whipped Mo Feldman's ass 6-1, 6-0, I drove back to the city for my work week. I had patients stacked up, but I still had time to hone my tennis game. On July Fourth, I could hear the Macy's fireworks from my apartment while I re-read Gallwey's *The Inner Game of Tennis*. On Wednesday, I had a tennis game in Riverside Park with Carl Rosen, one of my city friends. I beat him two out of three, but I was disappointed I didn't sweep him.

As the summer went on, Joan and I weren't intimate. It was okay with me. We'd probably pick it up again in the fall, but if we didn't, I was okay with that, too. I was a happening, successful guy—finding sex partners outside of my marriage wasn't difficult for me. There were women in the city I could call—even a couple of ex-patients—or I could always bop around the Village and pick up women at bars and jazz clubs. Having an affair-free summer would be better for me anyway, as it would allow me to focus on what was really important—winning the summer tournament.

All in all, I was happy with how I was playing. Although I was making some annoying unforced errors with my backhand, my forehand was rock solid, and my net game was strong. I hadn't lost a match all summer, and I felt like, if I kept it up, winning another championship was pretty much a certainty.

In early August, I was staying at Chaits full-time, when the big day came—Eddie revealed the seeds. Word spread quickly around the bungalow colony. I was actually having breakfast at my kitchen table when I heard some chatter about it outside, and I rushed up to the lobby to see for myself. This was by far the highlight of my year.

Eddie had set up an easel in the lobby with a big piece of oaktag with the tournament bracket written in magic marker. About ten people were there, huddled around the easel, including Stevie and Ron. I thought it was given that I would be the one seed—I was more curious about the other seeds and whom I'd be playing in the early rounds—so I was shocked to see that the number one seed was Stevie Wasserberg.

Ron had his arm around Stevie's shoulders, saying, "Number one, wow, you're moving up fast, kiddo."

Everyone else was congratulating Stevie too, as if he'd won something, when actually the only thing he'd done was stole my seeding. There was absolutely no basis for this—none at all. I was the reigning two-time Chaits champion and Stevie had never beaten me head-to-head and now he was the *one seed*? Gimme a fucking break.

I was caught up in such a furious haze that I hadn't even checked the other seeds. I was the number three seed—fucking *three*—, and Ron was two.

Without saying anything to anyone, I stormed out of the lobby. Kenny Brody was on his way in and said, "Hey, Alan, what seed are you?" I didn't answer, but as I was rushing off I shoved him a little and he stumbled into a hedge of bushes.

"Man, what the fuck's wrong with you?"

I ignored him and ran down the hill.

It took a while—maybe an hour—but my calm, steady, analytical mindset finally returned and I decided that I couldn't let my ego control me. Yes, it had been a huge kick in the balls to make me the three seed, but instead of raging against this injustice, I had to use it to my advantage, to motivate my game, and have my greatest tournament ever.

For the rest of the day, I was in a zone—stretching, doing push-ups and sit-ups, and hitting some balls with Gary Greenberg, the twelve seed. I wanted to get more practice on the hardcourts—where the tournament would be played—but I didn't want to push myself too hard physically. I was much more concerned with preparing my mental game. Obviously, I knew I had the talent to win it all, but, like Borg, I had to make sure that my mind was ready to dominate as well.

* * *

My first-round match was against Stephanie Ribman—a sixteen-year-old who had some potential, but she only won six points total, and I destroyed her 6-0, 6-0. The following day, I won an easy second round match against Martin Rabinowitz, a non-serious player, and then I played in the quarters against Derek Fine. I thought it would be an easy match versus Derek because, although he was young and athletic like Stevie, he had just recently taken up tennis. But he broke my serve twice in the first set and beat me 6-3. I buckled down and grinded out some long points in the second set and evened it up one-one. It was annoying how the crowd—well, ten-or-so onlookers—were pulling for Derek to upset me, but my serve came up big in the third set, and I beat him 6-4.

I'd made it to the semis, but my match against Derek had been a struggle, and my biggest, toughest matches were coming up. Stevie had been breezing through his bracket, and I was set to face off against him in the semis tomorrow morning. Then, assuming I won and Ron won his semis match—which he probably would—Ron and I would meet in the finals.

I entered my bungalow, looking forward to a long shower, pasta for dinner, and a great night's sleep, but Bev was waiting for me on the porch, glaring at me with her hands on her hips.

"So is it true?" she said. "Are you really fucking Joan Weissman?"

* * *

My first thought—*Well, the timing of this is extremely curious, isn't it?* The day before my match against Stevie Wasserberg, Bev suddenly finds out about my affair with Joan?

Of course, I wasn't going to fess up to anything, especially without knowing any facts, so I said, "Where did you hear this?"

"Please, Alan. Just tell me it isn't true."

I was confused. Why did she seem so devastated? Was the affair really such a shock to her?

"I asked you where you heard it."

"What difference does it make?"

"I need to know."

She glared for a few seconds—it felt like a minute—then said, "Okay, if you really want to know—from Danny."

She'd heard about the affair from our *son*?

"*Danny*? Where did Danny get that idea?"

"All the kids were talking about it, apparently, and now the whole bungalow colony knows. So, tell me, Alan. Is it true or not?"

Then it hit me—Stevie Wasserberg, the sneaky son of a bitch, had been playing the long game all summer. He *had* been outside Joan's bungalow that day, spying on us like a delinquent pervert, but instead of spreading the news right away, he'd saved it for the optimal time, when he could get an edge over me in a big tennis match. I had to hand it to the kid—it was a clever, calculating move, exactly the kind of move I would've made if I were in his position.

"Does it really matter if it's true or isn't true?" I asked.

"Excuse me?"

"Oh, stop it with this fucking theater, Beverly." I was raising my voice, my frustration building. "Acting like this is some kind of catastrophic event when I told you about my sexual needs, and you said you understood. We've been in an open marriage for years."

"*Open marriage*? What the hell's that supposed to mean?"

"Oh, stop it, Beverly. You don't remember that discussion we had in Washington Square Park? On that fucking bench?"

"I remember you going on about your needs, yes, but I never said anything about an open marriage, and I certainly never gave you permission to fuck my friend."

"I don't like your tone right now."

"My tone?" Bev's face was pink. "Are you serious?"

Deciding to take the higher road, I said very calmly, "Look, I understand that you're feeling like there might've been some kind of miscommunication or—"

"I can't believe this—"

"But," I spoke over her, "I know what I said, and I know you heard me. I mean, for Chrissake, Bev, I was respectful of your wishes when you told me you didn't want to go to orgies with me or wife swap anymore, wasn't I?"

"I think orgies are disgusting and I never wanted to fucking wife swap, or husband swap…those were all *your* twisted ideas."

"Well, you seemed to enjoy it. Or was that another Beverly Waldman I watched orgasm with my friend Jerry, moaning 'Oh my God, Jerry. That feels so amazing, Jerry?'"

"You son of a bitch. I never wanted to sleep with Jerry. I never felt so degraded in my entire life. I just wanted to have a normal life, for *us* to have a normal life…but you have these sick narcissistic desires, and now you did this to me, humiliating me in front of everyone."

"All right, that's enough, Beverly. Let's discuss this another time."

"You're damn right it's enough. I want a divorce."

"Oh, stop it with that nonsense."

"I'm moving in with my parents in Woodmere, and I'm taking the kids too."

My pulse was throbbing—she was pushing me too far.

"You know," I said, "this is all extremely passive-aggressive."

"Oh, really? Who's being passive-aggressive? Me or you?"

"I have a big tennis match tomorrow. You know how important the summer tournament is for me, how much I look forward to it, and yet you choose this time to confront me with this ridiculousness?"

"Oh, who cares about your stupid tennis tournament?"

I stared at her, stunned. Threatening to leave me to make a dramatic point was one thing, but attacking my love of tennis?

I couldn't hold back.

"Shut up, Beverly!" I yelled. "Just shut up, or I'll slap you silly!"

Then I looked over and saw Danny and Shoshana standing on the porch with the door to the bungalow open. I didn't know how long they'd been there, but I sensed they'd heard most of it.

"Hey, kids," I said, grinning, trying to compensate for the awkwardness. "How're you guys doing?"

They turned and ran out of the bungalow.

"See what you did now," Bev said. "You traumatized them!"

"*Me*? *You* were the one screaming about divorce."

"I don't want to see your face anymore, Alan. You disgust me."

She went into the bedroom and slammed the door so hard the flimsy bungalow shook.

I wasn't worried about Beverly leaving. She'd been making the same threats about leaving me for years during arguments; she just needed some time to settle down. She'd been right about one thing, though—I *was* a narcissist, but this was one of my best qualities, actually. It meant I was in touch with my needs and desires and had the courage to love myself. What was so wrong with that?

* * *

I slept in Shoshana's bed, and Shoshana slept with Bev. I had a restful night's sleep, doing my best to block out all of the conflict at home, and focusing on my most important goal—winning my third consecutive Chaits championship.

In the morning, Beverly wasn't speaking to me. Great, the silent treatment. I can't say I was surprised—while Bev was a great mother and had other wonderful qualities, when it came to emotional maturity, she had a lot of room for growth.

After my usual stretching and self-love talk, I headed for my match with Stevie. Approaching the court, I felt like Borg, strutting onto the center court at the All England Club. I had the white headband with blue stripes; all I was missing were the long blond locks.

Stevie arrived with his entourage—Joey, Jonny, and Josh. They were all smirking, looking over at me occasionally, obviously getting a big kick out of my affair with Joan. But I wouldn't let this blatant attempt at mind games get to me—I was way too savvy for that.

Before the match, when I met Stevie at the net, I said, "That was clever of you, kid…keeping your mouth shut till the night before our match."

Pretending to be confused, he said, "I don't know what you mean."

"Nice," I said, "keeping the act going. Well, I guess you'll have to learn the hard way."

I came out of the gate strong. My first serve was so good, I barely needed my second serve, but when I did, my time practicing paid off—it was deep and had a big kick. He was playing well, too; he could certainly cover the court, and it was hard to win the long points. But I got to the net often enough to keep the pressure on, and I broke him late to win the first set. In the second set, he played better and made some big shots. Although we were even, one set to one, I still felt in control of the match. I detected cracks in his game, like his inability to hit deep shots with his backhand and how he wasn't placing his second serve well, so I exploited these weaknesses and prevailed, 6-4.

As we shook hands, he looked clearly disappointed—his grand plan of dethroning me had fallen flat, and he didn't even make it to the finals.

"Can't beat me at my own game, kid," I said, and left the court without looking back.

* * *

Entering my bungalow, I immediately noticed a lot of stuff was gone, including all of the kids' toys and sports equipment, and then I saw the note on the kitchen table, written in pencil:

Got a lift back to the city and took the kids.

You will hear from my attorney promptly.

I was surprised that Bev had actually followed through on one of her threats, but I was determined to not let her acting out affect me.

After a shower, I returned to the courts to watch Ron's semifinal match.

Milton Cohen came over to me and said, "I heard Bev left with your kids. How're you holding up?"

Gossip sure as hell spread fast at Chaits.

"Doing okay, thanks."

"Are you planning to resign from the tournament?"

"*What?* Of course not."

"I guess you heard about Ron and Joan, huh?"

"No, what?"

"They had a huge fight last night. I heard they're splitting up, too."

"Huh, well that's unfortunate," I said, wondering how Ron would react in this situation. Would he even show up for today's match?

As if on cue, my question was answered as Ron marched onto the court. He was always stiff and serious, but today he seemed even more robotic—walking with long clunky strides, staring straight ahead. He didn't acknowledge me or anyone else.

"Playing tennis when your marriages are falling apart," Milton said. "I don't understand how you guys do it."

Thinking, *And that's exactly why you'll never win a summer tournament, my friend,* I said, "C'mon, Milt, you of all people know that tennis is a cathartic sport."

Ron's opponent was a dark horse in the tournament—some guy "Phil" who was a guest at the hotel this month. No one had played against him or knew his game, so he got a corresponding low seed for the tournament, but he'd breezed through his earlier matches and had made it to semis, and there was chatter that he could go "all the way." I knew this was ridiculous because no one was beating me, but I was interested in studying Phil's game. If I ended up playing him in the finals, I needed to know what weaknesses to exploit.

But after the first few points of the match it was clear that Ron was going to crush Phil. Phil wasn't bad—he actually had good strokes—but Ron was playing with a ferocity I'd never seen before. His first serves were monstrous, and he was attacking the net every chance he got. His return game was just as dominant, and Phil had no counterattack. Ron won easily—6-1, 6-2—and then he left the way he'd arrived—marching off the court robotically, without talking to anyone. A man with a different personality might've confronted me, tried to punch me in the face for destroying his life, but obviously Ron wasn't interested in an ego boost and fleeting satisfaction. No, he intended to settle his issue with me on the tennis court, and I was up for the challenge.

* * *

My quiet bungalow was a blessing. It allowed me to relax, get a great night's sleep, and I woke up thinking about my topspin forehand. I'd put so much work in—spent so much time and energy to get to this point—and now I just had to finish the job.

There were about thirty spectators—on the benches outside the court and just standing around—but to me it felt like thousands, like I was arriving at the West Side Tennis Club for the US Open Final. The drama was intense—everyone wanted to see who would win, the cheater or the cheated on. I imagined a tennis broadcaster telling the audience: "The two men, embroiled in an epic scandal, were now facing off in an epic finale!"

Ron didn't say hi or shake my hand—I didn't expect him to—but I wasn't going to let anything get to me.

Like versus Phil yesterday, Ron came out firing—blasting serves and unleashing forehands. But I was ready for the onslaught. I weathered the attack, playing a measured, defensive game that I knew he hadn't anticipated, and he was clearly thrown. I won the first set handily, 6-3.

In the second set, I had to give him credit—he adjusted his game. He played a finesse game with longer rallies, deeper and more targeted serves, and he even incorporated dropshots. I counter-adjusted, but not quickly enough, and lost 7-5.

Now this was it—do or die; the definitive third set.

We both played well, making difficult shot after difficult shot, garnering lots of applause from the crowd. We were on service, but he was up 5-4, but after my first double fault of the set, I was serving down love-forty. I didn't lose any confidence in myself, though, because I knew in my gut that I was the best player at Chaits and no one could beat me, especially not Ron. I battled back, uncorking three consecutive aces, saving all the match points. He won the point at deuce and had another break point. I hit a great first serve to his backhand that he barely got to. Then I hit a dropshot and attacked the net to cut off his angle. He hit a weak shot to my forehand side. I could have hit an easy winner down the line—that was the high percentage play—but at the last moment I switched up and hit a cross court slicing volley instead. He lunged to his right and hit a weak stab volley that dribbled over the top of the net. I got there an instant late and the ball bounced off the frame of my racket into the net.

Ron dropped to his knees and shouted, "Yes! Yes! Baby! Yes!"

I was stunned, in "another place," unable to fully process what was happening. This was impossible; this wasn't the way this was supposed to go. *He* was Connors, and *I* was Borg—I was supposed to be celebrating right now, not him.

"What the fuck is *wrong* with you, Alan?!" It sounded like my devastated voice echoed throughout the Catskills.

Then, driven by rage and total disgust, I flung my racket as hard as I could. I wasn't trying to throw it at him, or even in his direction, but a moment after I released it, I knew it was headed toward the side of his head. His body was so stiff that he tipped over, like a tree after a lumberjack slices its trunk, and he fell head-first onto the court with a loud, cracking thud.

Blood leaked out of his right ear; he wasn't moving at all. For the first time all summer, he was looking right at me.

Marilyn Ziskin was screaming, "Oh my God, oh my God, he killed him, he killed him!"

I was in shock, I guess. I couldn't believe how, after just one bad decision, my life had gone to hell. If I'd just hit the winner down the line, Ron never would've had a chance to hit that stab volley.

Watching the growing pool of blood around his head, I knew I'd be replaying that idiotic decision for the rest of my life.

* * *

Jason Starr is the international bestselling author of many noir crime novels, thrillers, and graphic novels. His latest books include *The Next Time I Die*, *Casual Fling*, *Silicon Bandits*, and *Supermax*. He played on his college tennis team, and he still has a mean topspin forehand.

The Right to Lose

By Wil Medearis

"At the Zoo, he was glorious. You were glorious Millar, just splendid, a sight."

"And this was juniors?"

"The 18s, of course. Two points away from winning the whole thing. An automatic ticket to the US Open. Tell her who you would have played. You're going to die. Tell her."

Eloise Waxman's friend didn't seem impatient or antsy to start hitting, but she didn't look particularly interested either. They never are. They ask because there's nothing else for them to do.

"Roger Federer," I said.

Eloise put one hand on me and one on her friend, as if the name carried a current that must be grounded. "Two points away from playing Roger Federer in the US Open. Can you imagine?"

* * *

His name was Ethan Hakami, and I guess it's some consolation that you've never heard of him either. We faced off at the USTA Junior Finals in Kalamazoo, the winner of which, as Eloise correctly noted, receives an automatic entry into the US Open. I had two match points on my own serve. I botched the first one and the second clipped the net twice before we settled into a rally that ended when I blasted a forehand—my shot—at the corner. It felt like a winner when it left my racket, but it struck the ground a half inch past the baseline, and I lost the next two points in quick succession. We played two more games before we shook hands, but that miss was the end, not only of that match but of my peak, the height of my narrow glory.

Ethan Hakami went to Flushing and lost to Roger Federer in the first round 6-0, 6-1, 6-1.

That was ten years ago. How different would my life be if, instead of losing to Ethan Hakami in Kalamazoo, I had lost to Roger Federer in Flushing Meadows. Sometimes I mouth the words, under my breath, to see how it would feel.

* * *

"You seem anxious." Angie struck her zippo and dipped her face toward the flame. "Or distracted."

"Eloise brought a friend today."

"So, what, you're having second thoughts because she likes you?"

"She doesn't like me." I plucked her cigarette from her hand, took a drag, and gave it back. I still considered myself an athlete, and athletes don't smoke. "She likes that she happened to be there when I lost the junior finals. She likes the coincidence. I'm only a detail, like the weather."

The bartender dropped off our second round. We never had more than two when Angie met me here at this dingy pool hall at the base of the mountain. We took separate cars even though we came from the same place—Blue Glen Country Club.

"You know they're talking about building a gate?"

The club was a ten minute drive up a curving road that led nowhere else. Occasionally people went up to gawk at the views and the houses, but to play the course you had to be with a member and to be a member you had to own property on the grounds, so strangers were easy to spot, and anyway the sprawling homes all had their own security systems so no one seemed to worry that much about keeping people away—until this summer.

"They'll never build a gate," Angie said. "It's too overt. A gate means you can be touched, and the entire idea of a private club is that you're past touching. That you've transcended the need for physical barriers and can live among people without any but the minimum of physical contact. Like the spirit realm."

"The members are rich, not dead."

"The rich are alive only to each other."

"So what does that make you?"

She thought about it while she smoked. "A wandering ghost. Condemned to roam for betraying my class." She reached for her bag, pried it open, and tilted it toward me, so that I could see what was inside.

A rope of black pearls.

I punched her bag shut before anyone else could see. "Are you crazy? Why do you have that here?"

"When else was I going to give them to you? And besides," she offered a teasing grin, "I thought you might want me to wear them later."

"This might surprise you, but when we're together, I try not to think about your family."

I nearly added *I kind of hoped you did the same,* but I knew better, knew where I sat, what our time together was for her—a gratification of the same mutinous impulse that compelled her, three months ago, to start stealing jewelry from her parents' friends.

* * *

Blue Glen was a golfer's dream, plotted by a star designer high in the Blue Ridge Mountains, where the thin air lets rich sixty-year-olds imagine they can drive like Tiger.

I was the tennis pro.

The courts were decent enough, tucked away from the clubhouse in a grove of red maple and scrawny pines, but the status of my preferred sport was clear, third in line behind golf and single malt scotch. My job was to give the wives something to do while their husbands roamed the fairways and greens. It was vital only in the sense that a janitor or a dishwasher was vital—someone had to do it, and that someone didn't need any particular talent other than a willingness to set aside their pride.

In that regard, at least, I was overqualified.

I took the job after I'd gone straight through rock bottom to whatever was below it. I spent the final three years of my playing career in the red—travel expenses, hotels, food, and trainers—living on credit cards and personal loans, my credit score plummeting faster than my ATP ranking, both of them crashing to roughly the same number. I didn't have bad habits, didn't drink too much or gamble—I went broke from only one bet, the big one I had already lost, the foolish wager on my own talent, good money piled on top of bad, month after month, city after city, thinking—what—that a single tournament would turn it around? That I would get hot and rattle off wins, assemble a streak long enough to touch real prize money again? There's stubborn, and then there's delusional.

By the time I gave it up and retreated to Blue Glen it was too late for a steady income to turn things around. I'd tried. I rented a room above a garage, copped free meals from the clubhouse chef, cut every corner, sent my paychecks to the collection agencies and banks whose threats, politely masked in stark white envelopes, choked my mailbox. I'd been working steady for two years and couldn't get ahead—couldn't even keep from falling a little further behind.

My dad had taken out a second mortgage and was going to lose the house.

In late May, Angie appeared at the pool hall where I shot twice a week, my only indulgence. She had freckles, brown hair, a sharp wit. I made her laugh the first night and took her home the second—there was never any sign that it could turn serious, but I told her my life story anyway, the lonely pressure of my debt seeking any escape, any release, like howling steam. In return, she told me her last name.

The club only had a few hundred members, so I recognized *Bellinger* right away. I'd never coached either of her parents, but they'd been on the courts a few times. Angie said they were clubhouse regulars, active in Blue Glen's bridge nights and happy hours and golf socials (and also, crucially for what would come later, close friends with Eloise and Henry Waxman.) There wasn't a rule in the employee handbook about sleeping with a member or the family of one, but that didn't make it any less certain that I'd be fired if it came out. Angie was living at Blue Glen for the summer—she'd been out west with a guy and it had gone bad, and she was using the time to reset. At thirty-one, she was a little old to move home with her parents, but who was I to judge? She had her own reasons for hating her decision to come back. She said she loved them but despised who they were, their indifference to their own privilege—at first I wondered if she only said that because she thought it was what I wanted to hear, but as the summer progressed I came to believe she really meant it.

When she told me she was behind the robberies, she'd admitted it was personal, a petty revenge. An act to distance herself from people whose values and lifestyle she couldn't accept. To Angie, it was all psychological, or political, I couldn't keep it straight, her smoldering resentment. It didn't matter to me. I didn't resent the members, didn't really think about them as anything other than the source of my too-meager income—my reason for saying yes, when Angie asked me if I wanted to help her with one final summer heist, was much more straightforward: I really, really, really needed the money.

* * *

After the bar, Angie lay on my bed with the necklace draped across her fingers. She was wearing my T-shirt and nothing else.

"They look even better than I imagined," she said.

The Chilston Strand was named after some royal someone or other—thirty-eight Tahitian black pearls, dark as storm clouds, each the size of my middle knuckle. Seven years ago, it went for 1.2 million dollars at Christie's—to Henry Waxman, a gift to his wife, Eloise.

The necklace in Angie's hands was made of glass.

"You sure they'll pass?" I said.

"They better. They cost enough to make."

She'd had the beads hand-blown by a forger in China, strung by a Penland hippie too granola to care that she was assembling a fake. The Chilston pearls were too valuable to simply steal, the way Angie had stolen Laura Gardner's diamond earrings or Nora Bagwell's ruby bracelet, losses describable in four or perhaps five figures, enough to sting when bundled with the inevitable sense of violation and vulnerability that their loss provoked, but not high enough to warrant a sustained investigation. When the disappearance of the Chilston Strand was discovered, there would be real heat, the kind that went much further than sending the local cops to the Mexican trailer park where the club sourced most of its cheap labor.

So Angie thought—why not delay that discovery? Eloise wore the necklace at most a few times a year—the only reason she'd brought it to Blue Glen was for her daughter's wedding, which the clubhouse had hosted at the beginning of the season. Otherwise, it was sitting in its case, where it would remain until the next gala or reception or formal dinner party, long after the Waxmans returned home to Atlanta.

"It might take a year or more for them to notice," Angie said when she laid out her plan to me, on a night not unlike the current one, in my bed after a few rounds at the pool hall. "Maybe until the next time she updates her insurance policy. By then, the trail will be ice cold."

At a dinner party with her parents, Angie convinced a tipsy Eloise to take her downstairs to show the Chilston off, and noted the combination for the case. She sussed out the alarm code for the house. She already had a fence, an underworld contact she'd cultivated while rebelling from her privileged inheritance. By mid-July, she was ready.

But her plan had a flaw. Eloise's mother had come to Blue Glen for the wedding and was staying all summer. Her health was fragile—she was mobile but tired easily, and rarely went out. There was no way to make the switch because the house was never empty.

Until this weekend.

The Glen Cup was a members-only golf tournament that marked the end of the season. The winner earned a gaudy trophy and bragging rights, which was all they cared about anyway; the rest of their concerns retired along with their lucrative careers. The event lasted for four days, capped by a party at the clubhouse—the largest and most indulgent of the year. Everyone would be there—including Eloise, her nurse, and her ailing mother. The pearls would finally be left alone. They didn't fit the dress code, and she'd never wear them twice in the same season.

It was the opportunity Angie had been waiting for—except that her own parents insisted she attend the party with them, which meant that she couldn't take advantage of the Waxmans' empty house.

But I could.

Maybe I always had larceny in my heart—maybe it was planted there by grinding failure. The fence would pay maybe a third of the value, which Angie said she'd split with me 60-40, in my favor—more than enough to get me right. The only things I stood to lose were the things that only stealing that necklace could save—and anyway, you can't think about the consequences of a miss when you see an opening for a winner. One night, one act, to turn my life around. If she hadn't asked, I would have begged.

But now that the weekend was here, I felt a hard knot in my chest. Seeing Eloise that morning had humanized the crime in a way I wasn't prepared for.

"So you have no guilt at all?" I asked. "You've robbed three families this summer, and you don't feel anything?"

"Four." Angie rested the fake on my nightstand. "The Macleods either never noticed the missing rings or didn't report them. It made them easier to fence."

"I know the insurance company isn't going broke. I know the Waxmans can afford to lose it, but I feel, I don't know what exactly." It was a sense of foreboding, not for the consequences but for my conscience, an anticipation of regret.

She slid toward me and rested one bare leg across my lap. "Eloise doesn't deserve that necklace."

"And we do?"

"Her only claim is what, that her husband bought it? And how did he get the money for it?"

"He started some kind of company." I had a vague idea from the time we'd spent together on the courts. "That takes some kind of talent or hard work or something."

"And talent and hard work entitle him to…?"

"To success, at least, and what comes with it."

"Success is a lie." She raked her fingers through the dark hair across my chest, spoke tenderly. "Who's that guy you would have played, if you'd made it to the US Open? The famous one?"

"Roger Federer."

"And you said there was no way you would have beaten him?"

"He was the best in the world. And I wasn't. Sports are fair in that way. Cold, but fair."

"Fair is a word invented by winners so they don't have to feel bad for losers. It's all luck of one kind or another. Why was this guy so good? Did he work harder than you?"

"No. Guys like me, on the fringes of the tour, we have to grind just to hold on. No one outworked me."

"But he was still better than you, because of, what, talent?" I shrugged because there wasn't a better answer. "And why was he born with that talent and not you, or me? That's luck too. Even working hard, self-discipline—you inherit those qualities from your parents, if not from their blood, then from their example. There's nothing fair about rewarding people for being born a certain way."

It seemed repellent, cynical. It stripped even losing of meaning.

"I think you get what you deserve," I said. "Success has to have a reward."

She lay back—I thought because my answer was too shallow and she was bored—but she was only reaching for the fakes. She lifted them up to the light. "It doesn't have to. But it does."

* * *

On Saturday, all the employees were asked to park at a distant lot, near the administrative offices, to make room for the cars of the members and their guests. I ignored the request and took my usual spot near my office, a small outbuilding beside the courts. Eventually, one of the valets was sent to ask me to move. By then the admin lot was full and I drove instead to a small lot by a maintenance area deep on the property, walked the half mile back to the courts, and made sure to grumble about it to the valets.

By sunset, the partygoers had all arrived. I locked up my office and started toward the maintenance area and my car.

About halfway there, I passed the Waxmans' house.

Because of the club's strictly enforced building codes, all the houses were permutations of fieldstone and blonde wood, as if constructed from a shared kit. The Waxmans' was a split-level, the back end climbing down the green slope of their rear lot, capped by a wooden deck that accessed all three floors. There were no other houses in sight. Other than the properties with views of the course, each home at Blue Glen was nestled in privacy, a swaddled treasure. I circled toward the back, through the woods. The porchlight winked between the trees. I climbed the deck to the main floor, the wooden stairs swollen and fragrant in the humid evening. There was a glass door, large windows, drawn curtains. I removed a pair of nitrile gloves from my back pocket and put them on.

I used a screwdriver to pop the sliding door from its track, hurried through the twilit room to the front entrance, and cut the alarm. I returned to the back, fit the door into its groove, and tested to make sure it rode smoothly before I moved toward the bedroom. The decor was English countryside filtered through Appalachia, a pastiche of someone else's aristocracy. All the paintings were of horses. I went downstairs, switched on my penlight, entered a closet that was half the size of my apartment. It was messy, like she didn't let the help inside, and smelled of clean laundry and the remnants of perfume. Past the rows of haphazardly hung dresses was a wooden bureau— in the top drawer I found a hard black case roughly the size of a notebook. It had handles and latches, a combination lock. I entered the code and opened it.

Angie had made a mistake. There was no way the necklace she gave me would pass for this.

The Chilston pearls caught the light of my penlight and absorbed it, sending back not flashes or glints but revelations of a dusky, mercurial depth. Each orb was flawless and rich, one in a series of perfect worlds.

The glass frauds were wrapped in cloth in the front pocket of my khakis but I wondered if I should even bother—Eloise would know as soon as she saw them. I undid the plush fasteners that clasped the Chilston in place, took the fakes out, and placed them beside it. I arranged both necklaces on the pale cushion, ran my penlight across them.

There was someone else in the house.

I left the box where it was and stepped out of the closet. I heard a floor creak, wood shift, footfalls so faint that had there been any sound in the bedroom, any at all, I would have missed them.

No. Not in the house—outside, on the deck's second level.

Someone had gone up while I was in the closet. I waited to hear the slide of the glass door—I hadn't locked it back or reset the alarm. Who was it and why were they here? The mother, too sick after all for the party? Eloise's husband, sent back to fetch some forgotten essential? Why take the back door? I imagined another thief, on the same mission, the same night.

They weren't coming in. The bedroom had French doors that opened onto the deck's lower level; I gently cracked one open, placed my ear to the gap. The humid evening slipped in, with voices.

"God, this house."

"Right?"

"You think I can convince them to adopt me?"

"And have to put up with Mrs. Waxman? Not worth it."

Two speakers, one male and one female—both young.

"I could do it," the boy said. "For this house, I'd be whatever she wanted."

"Don't be gross," the girl said, and there was a light smack, a shoulder playfully hit. "Or she's gonna be all you get."

The boy laughed. "I'd sneak you in when she wasn't around."

The faint musk of marijuana drifted down. I listened a little longer, until I was sure who they were—waitstaff from the clubhouse, taking advantage of a lull after dinner service. There was a storage shed near the maintenance building where my car was parked—they must have been sent on an errand and stopped to smoke. They probably knew the house and its secluded deck from a private function—the members frequently paid staff to work their parties.

I considered my options. Even if I could get out of the French doors without being spotted, I'd be leaving the alarm off and the back door unlocked. I could sneak upstairs and leave through the front, set the alarm on my way out—but it was twilight, not pitch dark, they'd see movement in the house.

There was nothing for it but to wait them out. They'd have to be back to the clubhouse soon. I sat in the dark until I saw their shadowed bodies descend the deck stairs and retreat into the woods.

I returned to the closet. The fake and the Strand were lying beside each other in the box where I'd left them, arranged in identical fashion. I took out my cloth to wrap the original, which I had placed on the right.

Or had I placed it on the left?

Before I walked away the difference had been so apparent, so obvious, that I hadn't bothered to pay attention to which one was where. Now they seemed identically lush and seductive. I shined the penlight close. I picked them up, one at a time. There must be some vital distinction, some testament of their worth, of the vast, obscene gulf between their value. I had felt it—hadn't I?

Only I couldn't see it now. Whatever it was, I couldn't see it.

I remembered pushing the Strand to one side to make room for its imitation, from left to right—I was a lefty, it was a forehand motion. I stood over them and repeated the gesture. Maybe it had been a backhand. I tried that one too. I closed my eyes and replayed the moment. I conjured the sensations, the strangeness of entering someone else's empty home, the sense of transgression, already fading. The way the fake looked in the handkerchief was like a toy. The way the original had seemed to contain some essential lesson.

Right or left. Which one was it?

I took the necklace from the right, wrapped it in cloth, and slid it into my pocket. I fastened the other into place, returned the case to its drawer, turned out my light, and left the closet.

I set the alarm, locked up the house, and left.

* * *

Angie was coming over Monday night to pick up the necklace and take it to her fence. I left it wrapped in the handkerchief and stuffed the bundle into my sock drawer. I was afraid to unwrap it, to see it in the pure light.

But as the day progressed, my confidence began to return. I'd hit it clean and true. I'd come out with a prize to turn my life around. My mind drifted away from its usual bleak shores, away from the unpayable debt, the serves lost, the advantages squandered, away from my father's house, away from my failures and my inexhaustible shame. Away, even, from the match that never happened, the one I thought of the most: the prestigious loss that I was denied.

It was a mild afternoon, nearly cool, the way late August can be in the mountains.

After I'd paid everything off, there would be some left. Wasn't North Carolina beautiful? Maybe I'd buy a place, something modest, pick up clients at other clubs, do more private coaching—hell, there were colleges all over the state, maybe I could get a position somewhere. To be free of debt was to be free to make choices that didn't hurt.

My optimism carried into the morning, and I drove to work humming, the engine of my old beater growling up the switchbacks and curves. I passed through the entrance—Angie was right, they'd never put in a gate, it would be too garish, but who cared. I'd escaped with my plunder. I turned left onto Club Drive, toward the courts.

Police cars lined the roundabout in front of the clubhouse entrance. Three cruisers, plus a plain sedan with the officious air of an unmarked car. My throat caught. I crept past them on my way to the courts—I could see figures inside the clubhouse, but nothing else.

I parked and walked to my office, went through the minor routine of opening up the courts, the lockers where members stored their gear, all of it done by rote, by my zombied body while my mind was far away, racing. How? Had Eloise noticed the difference? Had those kids seen something, heard something? Were they spotted, blamed? I thought about what I would say if I were asked. Sure, I'd passed the scene, but I was only walking to my car; the valets would verify where I parked. I could say that I saw a light on in the house, that I thought nothing of it. I could say I heard something. Did I remember the exact time? Would an innocent man remember? I needed to sort my meager facts. Lies were revealed through inconsistencies—I had read that somewhere, or seen it. I thought about the pearls in my drawer, beautiful bombs that could blow my life to pieces.

I waited and waited, and no one came.

I had my client in the afternoon, but I didn't ask her about the police. We weren't on those sort of terms. Other than that hour, I spent the day alone, stewing—it wasn't safe to call Angie.

With an hour remaining, I heard women's voices outside. I looked out to see Eloise approaching with another friend, one I hadn't seen before. I gathered her rackets and some balls and went out to meet them.

"I don't have you on my schedule." My chest and throat were tight, but my voice sounded level.

"No lessons today," Eloise said. "We just want to hit a few." She took one of the rackets from me. "Settle us down after all that excitement this morning."

"Excitement?"

"Didn't you see the officers when you drove in?"

"Oh, the police. Right. I did see them." I swallowed so hard I thought she might have heard it. "Something happen in the clubhouse?"

"No, they were just interviewing the staff. They got her at home."

"Her?"

Eloise and her friend exchanged looks. "You mean you haven't heard?'

"Other than Mrs. Gordon, I haven't seen anyone all day. It's always quiet after the Cup."

"It's not really our place," her friend said.

"Better to hear it from us instead of a rumor." Eloise's momentum wouldn't be halted. "It's the Bellingers' daughter. You've probably never met her, she doesn't know a thing about tennis."

"But you might have seen her around," her friend said. "She's young. Quite pretty too, I'd say."

Eloise made a skeptical face. "If she took better care of herself, she might be. She's never been right, that one. The Bellingers are dear friends of ours. We go back years—I couldn't even say how long. But that daughter, no matter how much they love her." She sighed, as if recalling a tragedy. "Still, we never imagined this."

"This what?" I heard myself say.

The women took a step toward me, like they were afraid the sound would carry across the hilled grounds to the clubhouse and homes. "The robberies this summer. The Bellinger girl is behind all of them. One of Laura Gardner's housekeepers came forward and said she saw her in the bedroom, where the earrings were. She didn't say anything before because she was scared no one would believe her, but her conscience wouldn't let up. You know how religious they can be. The Gardners didn't want to believe it, but you just have to check, in that situation, no matter how awkward—and it's not like the Bellingers don't know about their daughter, why do you think she's here—so they searched her bedroom, and there they were."

"They?"

"The earrings, of course. And Nora Bagwell's bracelet and two other pieces besides. Everything that's been taken this summer."

"She had it all in her bedroom? She didn't…you know…fence them?"

"Fence? You mean sell? How would she know how to do such a thing? She'd be caught the moment she tried. There was nothing to do but hold on to it." She leaned forward conspiratorially. "And not to be crude, but she doesn't need the money. Her father takes very good care of her. I think she did it just to make some obscure point—she's always been overflowing with obscure points—but who could really say for sure. That girl lives in a fantasy."

Eloise's friend put a warning hand on her arm.

"Oh, I know I'm saying too much, but you'll hear it all in the clubhouse anyway, and besides, we have a bond, don't we?" She turned to her friend. "I watched him nearly win the 18s at Nationals. Tell her who you would have played if you won, Millar. Tell her how close you were. Tell her how incredibly close."

* * *

A native of Jacksonville, Florida, Wil Medearis is the author of Restoration Heights (Hanover Square Press, 2019), named a *CrimeReads* Best Crime Book of the Year and deemed "an instant New York fiction classic" in a starred *Booklist* review. He holds an MFA in painting from the University of Pennsylvania and lives in Brooklyn.

Lady, Get Some Balls

By Jen Conley

I was at the gym, walking on the treadmill while listening to my 1990s playlist, when I saw him: Lydia Myers's husband, Christopher. And yes, Lydia always called him Christopher, not Chris. I had never met Christopher in person, but I knew him from Facebook and Instagram, as Lydia frequently posted about him. I knew his love of football, the Yankees, and sports in general. Lydia took photos of Christopher showing off his small gun collection, which he needed for family protection. She posted pics of his "cute man cave," a room in the finished basement decorated with historical sports posters, like "Murderers Row," and antique sports equipment that hung on the walls. And there were more pics—Christopher grilling on his five-star barbecue, mowing the lawn, fixing the deck boards because he was such a good man. She also posted about how wonderful a father he was to their ten-year-old twins, Luna and Loki, which seemed to be names you would give pets, but I was fifty-six years old, old enough to have seen Nirvana live and drink from a garden hose, out of touch with the younger crowd and their creative baby name choices. And, of course, there were many photos and videos of her pet-named children being perfect at whatever they were doing. They seemed like good kids, but I found Christopher more interesting—as if deep down, he felt miserable and oppressed, and any day now, he'd lose it and blow his life up.

Then I thought: *Maybe it isn't Christopher? Maybe he has a doppelgänger?*

Yet when I looked at him closer without trying to be a weirdo, then checked Lydia's Facebook on my phone (she kept everything Public), I realized it was definitely him.

As I walked on the treadmill and listened to music, I watched Christopher lift weights via the Smith machine, wondering why he was at my gym. I knew he and Lydia lived at least forty-five minutes away south, and surely there was a Planet Fitness near his beautiful home. I also knew he worked even further south, near Atlantic City, so this was a real trek up north for just the gym.

He must've changed jobs, I concluded, then turned my eyes to the fifteen TVs in front of me—I had my choice of cable news, sports, and HGTV. I was over HGTV. It made me feel like a loser because my house hadn't been updated in years. I wasn't into sports, and I was sick of politics, so I looked back at Christopher Myers. He wasn't a bad-looking guy: normal weight, normal height, a bit over-sculpted in the arm muscles, receding brown hair, fair skin—your average dad-man at the gym. I estimated his age to be around forty years old because Lydia had turned forty on May 3rd. They'd thrown a party in her beautiful backyard, celebrating her milestone, complete with family, friends, drinks, and cake—details I gathered from Facebook and Instagram. There was even a video of Lydia blowing out the candles while flanked by her adoring parents, her cheering pet-named children, and Christopher, super-husband, lurking in the back, until she turned around and he kissed her. I don't know why—I didn't hate Lydia— but this video irked me. (Maybe because it felt so staged. Or maybe because I wished I had Lydia's life.) Whatever I felt, I realized her entire Facebook and Instagram bothered me, so after the party videos and photos, I unfollowed her on both sites. That was two weeks ago. I preferred my other coworker's page, where she posts videos of her dogs.

Thinking about Lydia and how I didn't hate her but didn't love her, suddenly I noticed that Christopher was smiling, just glowing, not at me, but at a woman with a ponytail bopping toward him. She approached, they hugged, and I think he kissed her. Soon, they were laughing and appeared to be flirting. He then changed the plates on the Smith machine so she could do a set of lifts. I was sweating and had only fifteen minutes to reach my 30-minute mark on the treadmill, but I found Christopher and the mystery woman intriguing. No, not intriguing, but fun. This was fun.

Lydia and I taught at the same middle school, so I scolded myself for finding Christopher's betrayal fun. Lydia was a good person, a happy person, and she had great ideas. She helped me several times when I had to leave school early or take the entire day off—she went over my plans with the substitute, made copies, checked in on my classes when she could, and even collected money from the staff for a $300 gift card I could use at the supermarket. How could I not like Lydia? Not be grateful, not be touched by her kindness? How could I say a bad word about her? How could anyone not like her?

Unfortunately, as kind as Lydia was, she was also uptight, rigid, and filled with so much positivity that it was almost toxic. Her classroom was stunningly decorated with the cool colors of the art wheel—purples, blues, greens—along with positivity and *Follow Your Dreams* posters tacked to the walls. The room was a sight to see: bean bags, shag rugs, string lights, plants, a lava lamp, and more, all of it matching perfectly, all of it very cozy and organized, shockingly perfect. (Truthfully, it was a lot for a middle school Language Arts classroom.) As a teacher, she was a fan favorite—most of her students came from parent requests. As a school leader, she seemed involved in every extracurricular organization at school, filled with new ideas, and always positive, always good for the kids.

There were cynics in my school, teachers who found Lydia irritating. They talked behind her back, mocked her, made jokes about the pole up her ass. I didn't participate in those conversations and steered away from those women. I saw myself as a good person, someone who rose above it all. Who would do the right thing, like I'd always told my students to do: *Don't gossip, don't betray your friends, tell the truth, be good to people, and they'll be good to you.* And here I was, joyful that Lydia Myers's husband was cheating on her because she deserved it? What kind of person was I?

I raised the incline on the treadmill as penance for my bad thoughts and forced myself to watch HGTV—a woman was putting the final touches on the house she and her husband renovated—which made me wish I had a gun to shoot the screen.

What was wrong with me?

Then I remembered, when I was annoyed with someone and felt guilty, I imagined how one of my favorite musicians from the 90s, Kurt Cobain, would handle it. He'd snarl, shuffle away, move on. He wouldn't let envy get to him. He would use it as inspiration and write a cynical song about happy people who brought the rest of us down, who made us feel like shit, made us want to walk into the abyss. Or at least, something along those lines. Something that made me feel like I wasn't a horrible person for having mean thoughts and consumed by relentless hopelessness, no matter how much I practiced gratitude and kindness. Something that would've made me feel okay.

Lately, I often wish Kurt Cobain were still alive. Maybe we would've been friends, and I could've asked him things…

This was a stupid fantasy, and I shook myself out of it.

Ultimately, I turned off the treadmill, skipped my circuit training, and walked out.

* * *

When I arrived home, I found my husband, Mark, sitting on the couch, his tennis racket nearby, the TV lit up to a paused Marvel movie. He was on his cell phone, which he quickly darkened and slid into his pocket. "Oh, hi! You're back early."

My stomach sank. He was lying again.

"Too crowded tonight," I said chipperly, even though I knew why he had darkened his phone, why I felt anger. "Are you feeling okay?"

"I'm fine," he said. "Good game with Charlie."

He seemed to have forgotten that Charlie moved to Arizona months ago. Which made me want to beat him to death with his tennis racket.

"Was it?" I said, staring at him. Mark's hair was coming back thick but dark gray. He wasn't happy about the color, but he liked that he was no longer bald—I hoped he didn't grow his hair long again because he looked stupid. Mark was semi-successful as an accountant for a financial firm, a fan of the Grateful Dead, and a tennis lover. He was nothing like Lydia's husband. He couldn't fix anything around our house except his tennis rackets. I did the grilling on the barbecue and repaired anything that needed repairing. He was also in remission from prostate cancer, with chances that were fair to good. My kids, grown and out of the house, were relieved. (Actually, my son was more relieved than my daughter.) His mother in Florida was relieved. His tennis friends were relieved. Me, not so much. Which was disturbing because we had a long history, so I should've been relieved. I'd been with him since I was nineteen, married at twenty-four, and within two years, two children followed. Why wasn't I relieved like a good wife? Why couldn't I think positive thoughts and stand by my man? It was his life that was on the line! Anything beyond that shouldn't count. Sure, our marriage hadn't been perfect, but nobody's marriage was.

When Mark was first diagnosed, I was frightened but also selfishly thankful because I knew he would need me. But as the cancer journey carried on, down winding roads of hope and fear, when things were at their worst, when the doctors appeared concerned, when he might not make it, I realized in the back, dark corner of my mind, happiness began to form because I was rooting for death. I couldn't stop this happiness. All I thought was that I'd get everything. The house, the life insurance, the tennis rackets, his 401K, and a brand new life. You see, before the cancer, I'd found out he was cheating on me again, this time with a younger woman, about thirty-eight, who lived at the other end of our neighborhood. Her children were elementary age, and according to the text messages I'd found, because I secretly knew his PIN to unlock his phone, her husband made her feel small, and he wasn't good at sex.

Via more text messages, I'd found their Plan—she'd divorce her husband, they'd sell her house, and he'd divorce me and buy me out so they could move into my house. Afterward, they would marry. Mark was sure I could move on, retire from teaching, take my pension, and rent a small house in a retirement community. But I couldn't take my pension right away—I'd told him several times. According to state rules, teachers could take their pension at fifty-five if they'd taught for twenty-five years. Although I had the age, I didn't have the time. I was three years from my pension because I'd taken time off to have and raise our kids. His kids.

The weekend I found those text messages, my daughter surprised me by coming home unannounced. She found me crying while Mark was asleep. She read the texts and then hissed, "Divorce Dad, ASAP!" She didn't talk to her father the entire weekend, but again, he was asleep, unusually tired. Before she left, she said, "You need a lawyer, Mom. They can't take the house from you. You're the one who takes care of it. Be strong, not weak." The "weak" comment hurt, but she made sense. Although I was devastated, I asked her to give me time to make a decision.

Yet, in those few weeks while I tried to decide, Mark was diagnosed with cancer. And then I found more text messages. His girlfriend said she couldn't leave her husband, and although my husband begged her not to break things off, that tennis had made him strong and healthy, that he would survive, that he loved her, and they could work through it. She responded with, *It's over but I'll always love you.* Followed by five heart emojis.

As hurt as I was, I took the high road, didn't confront him, didn't say a thing. After his first chemo treatment, he threw up in the bathroom, and I cleaned the toilet. When that event was over, my husband broke down in tears and confessed, which I found weird. "I'm so sorry, baby," he cried. "So sorry. I won't ever do it again." I accepted this speech, but I couldn't tell if he was half sorry he'd hurt me and half sorry he'd lost his younger future wife. Or maybe he hoped I would leave him, and his girlfriend would take him back. Maybe he had a fantasy that I'd stomp down to her house, tell her husband everything, which would make him kick his wife out, I'd move out, and then she'd have no choice but to move in with my husband, and she'd clean the toilet bowl after he vomited. I was thoroughly confused. And angry. And, well, I didn't know. What I did know was that a wife couldn't leave her husband when he had cancer. It would be too mean, heartless, cruel. The Karma Gods would surely strike back at me with vengeance. I was trapped.

Lately, I haven't wanted to be married anymore. But what type of woman leaves her husband who is in remission with cancer?

I told Mark I was tired, went upstairs, showered, and went to bed without dinner.

* * *

Monday evening, I went back to the gym, and once again, I saw Christopher and his female friend with a ponytail and tiny waist at the Smith machine. She was laughing and smiling, and Christopher seemed happier than I'd ever seen him in Lydia's posts and videos. I slowed the treadmill down and opened Facebook on my phone. In Lydia's most recent post, she'd tagged Christopher with a funny reel about a husband and wife sharing a bathroom. I slowed the treadmill more, lowered the sound on my 90s music, and went through Lydia's pics, which were still Public. Christopher never glowed in Lydia's photos, unlike now with his mystery woman. I'm not saying I thought it was right that Christopher was cheating on Lydia, but I almost understood. Lydia must've been difficult to live with. Like being a bird with clipped wings locked in a cage covered with a soundproof cover. Not that there were real situations like this for birds, but it made sense to me.

This got me thinking about my situation, about Mark and his women. The woman in my neighborhood wasn't his first affair, but she was probably unaware of this. Not that Mark was a serial cheater—we'd gone to counseling seven years ago, and I believed he'd been faithful up until now.

Maybe? (I didn't like to think about this.)

Years ago, while I was pregnant with my son, there was a woman. I never did anything about it. Never told anyone. Just let it run its course, and it did. I was too embarrassed and ashamed to confess to any friends or even confront him, and then there was the fact that I didn't want to leave my husband when I had a house, stable income, and children. And I still loved him, of course. When my daughter was in middle school, Mark started screwing around with my daughter's science teacher who was also my coworker, but again, I never did anything. Let it run its course. That time, I was nervous my daughter and other coworkers would find out, so I kept very quiet, hoping it would fizzle out without any detection from some of my nosy colleagues. Luckily, the science teacher left after her first year, taking a job in North Carolina, so nobody found out. Or at least, I never caught anyone gossiping about it, nor did anyone say anything. (I still wondered if some knew. I think some knew.)

After these two affairs (or maybe there had been more, if I'm being honest), I did my best to figure out what was wrong with me. I watched what I ate, worked out, cooked dinner, did laundry, mowed the lawn, raised our kids, fixed the toilet (YouTube was great), and painted the rooms myself. I gave Mark space to play tennis and enter his amateur tennis tournaments, didn't argue when he missed our kids' soccer games, art shows, or band concerts when he just couldn't get out of work or a tennis tournament. I didn't give him shit when household chores needed to be done. I didn't complain about having to listen to the Grateful Dead. I didn't cheat, yell, or nag. For a long time, I couldn't figure out why he would betray me, until one day it dawned on me: I let him get away with it the first time by pretending I hadn't noticed, so the probability that I'd noticed a second time, or third, or fourth, and so on, was pretty high.

I turned the speed up on the treadmill and thought about Kurt Cobain. What would Kurt do? Mark was always saying, *What would Jerry do?* Jerry, the lead singer of the Grateful Dead, a peaceful band from the era of the Hippies, whom Mark admired and who inspired him. *What would Jerry do?* he'd say to our kids. Meaning, Jerry would do the cool thing, the right thing, the moral thing.

It felt like betrayal—all those years lecturing us about the virtues of Jerry when he had the virtues of Bill Clinton.

Christopher's girl laughed loudly, shaking me out of my thoughts.

"That's so funny!" she yelled, then caught me looking at her. "Sorry," she mouthed and turned back to her man.

I moved the speed up on the treadmill even more and returned to my thoughts. What *would* Kurt do in this situation? Sit around and write a song about betrayal or the irony of betrayal? Write a song about the hypocrisy of keeping the peace in the family? How much sacrifice and toleration would one make to achieve that peace?

Then, my thoughts moved into the fantastical area of my brain. I heard Kurt whisper in my ear, or at least, my fantasy side made him whisper in my ear: *Get some balls, lady.*

I have balls, I said to him in my mind.

He didn't answer, so I watched as Christopher and his side piece, these two lovebirds, frolic near the weights.

* * *

The next morning, Tuesday, I had a better attitude, and for the first time in weeks, I enjoyed teaching my morning class. The kids were good. We read a chapter in our class novel and then played a vocabulary game. For a while, it was like the old days when I was younger and loved teaching.

By midday, I was tired and looking forward to lunch. Two minutes before the bell, the school secretary called over the loudspeaker and told me I had to cover Mrs. Myers's class. This happened sometimes because we were short substitute teachers, and although our school district paid fifty dollars extra for giving up our lunch, it never seemed worth it. Still, I had no choice. "Emergency coverage" was listed in our contract as something we could not deny.

When the bell rang, I walked down to Lydia's cute classroom and found her frantically writing lesson plans at her desk while her students walked obediently to their seats. "Luna is sick, and I have to go get her," she explained without looking up. "My husband is away for the week on a work trip. Usually, he'd help." Lydia finished her plans and sighed almost dramatically. "You know how it is!" She gave her class a little positive lecture about expectations and how she knew that she could count on them when she was away, then grabbed her large pink metal Hydro Flask, her large pink teacher bag, her purse, her jacket, and rushed out the door.

Her students were good but confused about the directions—apparently, Mrs. Myers gave them the wrong assignment to do—the entire class swore they'd read the story and done the questions before. Although we both taught the same grade in Language Arts, I didn't know what to do about the issue—make the kids do it again or find a new story in the book to read, risking Lydia's future plans to read said story. For a moment, I considered that the entire class could be colluding with each other, yet my experience with middle schoolers taught me that there was no loyalty in middle school. One of them would've cracked if I'd pushed them. I decided to believe the class and told them not to worry about it. They could play games on their Chromebooks or read quietly. The good kids seemed skeptical, and one even said, "She never lets us play games on our Chromebooks," and I responded, "Well, I do." They smiled and cheered, so happy to have so much freedom, and now I was their favorite teacher. The happiness I felt was a fair trade for losing my lunch.

After school, I stopped into Colleen's classroom, the one who posted videos of her dogs, and found her overwhelmed with four piles of colored papers. It was for the *Friend and Friends* club—whatever that was. I didn't do extracurricular activities anymore because I was on the downslope of my career. Yet, sympathy for Colleen got the better of me, and I volunteered to help.

"They all need to be folded and counted and delivered to the classrooms," Colleen explained. "Lydia was supposed to help me today. I wanted this done last week, but she insisted that we do four different colors for each grade. It took forever to get the colored paper and to make the copies. I don't see the point of colored paper. Am I crazy?"

"No," I said. "Luna is sick."

Colleen scoffed. "She always has a valid reason."

"Tell me what to do," I said.

A few minutes into the task, Colleen cursed because she'd written the wrong homeroom number on one of the papers. It was an easy fix, but she was frustrated. "My dogs need to be let out," she said. "I can't be here. I fucking hate Lydia, you know that?"

"It's okay," I said, and caught her rolling her eyes. I released my Colleen from the job and took over it myself. It wasn't bad; it took about an hour and a half to get the papers in order and deliver them to their homeroom mailboxes.

Afterward, at home, Mark was missing, but he'd left me a note that he'd gone to play tennis with Charlie. This made me feel shitty and angry because again, Charlie had moved to Arizona. I almost smashed our wedding portrait that hung in the hall, but I got myself together, went to the gym, and again, I saw Christopher and his girlfriend. I felt good.

* * *

Wednesday, my classes were great, and I found myself loving teaching—I was the young woman once more who had passion, humor, and life! When school ended, Lydia stopped by my classroom to talk. I was at my desk, listening to '90s music and grading novel journals on my laptop, while sitting in my old, ripped computer chair, which a very kind custodian had gotten for me. The custodian also found me a table where I could put my supplies on—it was yellow and very useful. Acquiring functional furniture in a school was like catching all the green lights when you're late to work. Rare.

I paused the music and looked away from my laptop to give Lydia my full attention.

"First," Lydia said, "thank you for covering my classroom and helping Colleen with the papers. I appreciate that. I know Colleen gets overwhelmed sometimes."

I didn't like that comment.

Lydia put her hands on her hips. "However."

I leaned back in my ragged computer chair.

"I don't allow my students to play games on their Chromebooks. They get enough of that at home. I did leave that in my plans."

She did, but I ignored it when we ran into the assignment issue.

"We had a problem," I said, explaining the situation.

"I suppose I was distracted," Lydia said. "My mistake."

I thought that was the end, but Lydia had more to say: "I don't know why you couldn't ask Joseph or Julianna. They could've shown you where I kept my 'emergency plans.' I'd left those names in the plans I gave you."

She had done so, but I'd ignored the names because if I'd asked Julianna and Joseph, the other students would have mocked them for colluding with the substitute teacher to make them do work. It was middle school, after all. I explained this to Lydia, too.

Lydia nodded but didn't appear fully convinced. "I'd like to believe my students wouldn't act like that, but you're right, it is middle school." She scanned my poorly decorated classroom and zeroed in on my yellow table in the far back with all my papers and supplies stacked on top. "That's mine," she said. "I've been looking for it all year. Did you not see my emails?"

I had, but there were a few yellow tables throughout the school, and I'd assumed the custodian had found an available one for me. I did not say this to Lydia for fear the custodian would get in trouble. Lydia had no problem voicing her opinion to the powers that be.

"I must've missed that email," I said, my tone growing bitchy. No wonder the cynics in my building hated her. "It's mine, I promise."

Lydia crossed her arms over her chest. "I don't think so."

"How's Luna?" I asked, trying to tame my anger.

"She's better." Lydia continued to stare across the room at my yellow table. "My table had a little scratch on the left corner. Do you mind if I look?"

Right then, I almost told her about Christopher, but I didn't. Although I wanted to tell her, simply out of malice, revenge, or sport, I didn't. I decided to do the right thing, like I've always done. *Stay with your husband for the family. Stay with your husband because he has cancer. Do your job the best that you can. Deal with disappointment like an adult. Don't be mean.*

"It will only take a minute," Lydia added.

I closed my laptop and put my phone in my purse. Then I pushed back from my desk and stood. "I have to go now."

She took a step, a movement toward the back of the room, but I said, "No. I have to go now. I have to lock up my room."

Lydia didn't leave until I repeated myself. "I said, I have to lock up my room."

* * *

That evening, Christopher was not at the gym when I first arrived. I did the treadmill, but when I switched to circuit training, Christopher and his girlfriend entered the gym together and walked right by me. They picked a Smith machine across where I was doing leg lifts, and I could hear their conversation. It was nothing interesting—Christopher was talking about his man cave. He said he had an antique wooden tennis racket with a square wooden cover that hung on his wall. "It's pretty cool. I'll give it to you if you want. You can defend yourself against that creep at your job."

His girlfriend laughed. "That won't do anything. I need a gun."

"I have that too!" Then he kissed her.

I could tell they were kidding, a lovers' inside joke, and it made me feel nostalgic. Mark and I were once like that—little privatisms that meant nothing to anyone but us.

It wasn't long before I left, feeling sad.

* * *

The next morning, Thursday, I walked into my classroom and found all my papers and books placed neatly on the floor where my yellow table had been. "Are you kidding me?" I almost shouted this because my room was empty, too early for the kids. I was furious, murderous, but I forced myself to sit in my old computer chair and take a breather. I tried to channel the fantasy side of my brain, where I talked with Kurt, but it didn't work. I was in reality now, and I had to deal with it.

But I remembered Kurt's words: *Get some balls, lady.*

I pushed back from my desk and marched down to Lydia's classroom. I opened her door without knocking. "How did you get into my room?"

Lydia, with her back to me, placing books on my yellow table, said, "I asked the custodian, and she let me in." Lydia turned around. "I saw the scratch and explained to her there had been a mistake, that the table was mine. I showed her my email from September to prove it. I asked her to remove your stuff neatly and bring the table to my room."

"When?"

"This morning."

It was already morning. That meant she had arrived at dawn to locate the custodian and then direct her to get the job done quickly before I showed up. It was diabolical, deranged, so fucking wild, and I was stunned. Yet not surprised.

"I'm sure you have to reorganize," Lydia said, returning to her task.

It took all my strength not to grab her Hydro Flask off her desk and hurl it at the back of her head.

"Lydia..." I said finally.

"That was my table." She slapped a book on *my* yellow table and swung around. "And you knew, didn't you? Because you wouldn't let me examine the table yesterday. I knew it was my table. It's been missing since the beginning of the year. I emailed everyone about my table. I told everyone there was a scratch on it. I know you knew."

I tried to conjure up Kurt Cobain again to help me with this, and yes, he did show up, but all he said was: *Fuck. Fuck. Fuck her. That yellow table doesn't even match her classroom color scheme.*

I glared at Lydia, thinking. If it were true, true that I'd remembered that her table had a scratch, and I knew it was hers, and didn't return it, I wouldn't have felt the fury that I felt now. I wouldn't have felt that I'd been caught in a travesty of injustice, like I did now! The thing was, Lydia sent emails to the staff often enough about a million things—her clubs, her committees, asking for extra markers, pencils, on and on that I never read her emails. They were ridiculous.

And then, it popped into my head again: *tell her about The Guy at the Gym. Her husband. That he was cheating on her. Tell her, tell her, tell her!*

Yet, I couldn't. I was too angry, not about the table, but about her entitled asshole personality. I couldn't believe that days ago, I felt bad about enjoying seeing Christopher and his girlfriend at the gym! What was wrong with me? Lydia has always been an asshole, despite helping me out when Mark was sick from his treatments. But did she do it to be kind, or did she do it to show everyone how "kind" she was? I looked closer at her now—she was awful, and like the cynics in my building, I couldn't stand her. Couldn't stand her cute classroom. Her cute outfit. Her cute hair. Her cute everything. She'd been Teacher of the Year already, while many of us have worked our asses off since the beginning of the century and never got Teacher of the Year. How was this all allowed in the arc of the universe?

I turned around and left, storming back to my room and opening my laptop. I usually saved most of my emails for no other reason than that when you teach, you never know what will come back to bite you. And sure as shit, I found Lydia's email from September 1st, and yep, she did mention the scratch. However, I knew I didn't check my table because I didn't read her fucking email. You know how I know I didn't open it? Because, like many of Lydia's emails, they were marked unopened or were deleted, even though I saved most of my emails! I remember that day I got the table, and I remember how happy I was. It was the best thing that had happened in almost a year, since I'd found out about Mark's affair and his cancer.

The rest of the school day, I was grumpy, and my students traded confused glances at each other.

* * *

At two-thirty, after the kids went home, I went to the faculty lounge and used the bathroom. While I was drying my hands with a paper towel, through the closed door, I heard Lydia telling everyone about me and my theft of her stupid yellow table. Then I came out acting like I hadn't heard a thing. Lydia left, as did the others who were listening to her story. I went to the copier machine in the corner of the room to print out extra credit worksheets I gave to my students who were falling behind. As I stood there, fuming at the injustice of it all—now Lydia was telling everyone I was a thief? Would I get fired for this? Even with tenure?

I was on the verge of tears when our school gossip—a delightful older woman who knew everyone's business and told everyone's business—walked in and said hello. She was chipper, and I guessed that word hadn't gotten to

53

her about Lydia's yellow table.

And then it just happened: I became wicked and mean.

"I have an issue," I said.

"What's up?" the Gossip asked.

"Do you know Lydia's husband?"

"Oh yes!" the Gossip said. "He's great. He's done wonderful work at their house. I've been there a few times."

Of course, she had.

I took my extra credit papers, paused, and acted perplexed. "I don't know what to do. At my gym, I keep seeing him there." I paused again, then cringed for effect. "With another woman."

"What?"

"I know, I know. He's supposed to be on a work trip, but I've been at the gym for several days this week, and he's there all the time with this woman. It's been on my mind all week."

The Gossip was gleaming, but her brain must've told her to act skeptical. "Maybe it's a friend?"

"A friend who kisses you all the time?"

"Oh my God!"

I lowered my voice. "And she's young and very pretty."

"No!"

"What do I do?"

The Gossip cringed now, but she loved every minute of this. "You shouldn't tell her. Let her find out for herself. That's how you handle these things."

"Yes, you're right. Thank you." I walked away.

* * *

That evening, I didn't feel like going to the gym. I decided to bike instead. Mark said he was going to play tennis with Charlie, then ran upstairs because for something—probably condoms—leaving his phone on the kitchen counter. I checked his messages, and once again, he was texting with the woman from my neighborhood. I wasn't devastated this time. I was relieved. Surely, after ushering my husband through cancer only for him to commit infidelity, I could excuse myself from this marriage. Still, I kissed him goodbye as he drove away without his tennis bag and racket.

I got on my bike and rode by the woman's house. The universe was kind, and her husband was outside with his little kids as they drew pictures on the driveway in chalk. I stopped and told him how much I admired his beautiful green lawn. "Is that you, or does your wife keep it green?"

He laughed and walked closer. He seemed like a nice guy. "I do the yard, and she does the house."

"I bet she's inside resting?"

"She's out playing tennis. It's her thing."

I gazed at the pretty lawn, smiled, and then looked him in the eyes. "That's funny. Tennis is my husband's thing, too. Although tonight, he forgot his tennis bag. Did your wife forget hers?"

It was tough to see him connect the dots, which he probably ignored for a while. Like I said, he seemed like a kind, hardworking dad stuck with a two-timing witch. Yet, nobody ever told me that my husband was cheating. Not any of my coworkers, who surely knew my husband was cheating with my daughter's teacher. Not his friends back when I was pregnant with my son. Nobody. And as a person who had been cheated on, I would've liked to have known as soon as possible. Not find out on my own due to my husband's dumb mistakes. If someone had made me face it, I probably would've walked away. Maybe. Knowing my younger self, I most likely would've stayed. Still, I wish someone had told me.

I decided right then that I would tell Lydia to her face that her husband was cheating. I would go to the gym the next night and take photos so she could see them herself. As much as I hated her, it was the right thing to do. In addition, I decided that I would ask for a divorce the following night. It would be a perfect time to do such a thing because it would be the weekend. You can't do traumatic things the night before school. It messes with your teaching. Look how grumpy I was when Lydia took my table?

I said goodbye to the sad husband whose wife was screwing my husband,

and pedaled away.

* * *

Friday, Lydia wasn't in school. Once again, I had to skip my lunch and cover her class. There were no plans at all, so I asked both Julianna and Joseph what page they were on in the book, but I did it quietly so they wouldn't get in trouble with the pack. Julianna gave me the information, and I taught the lesson the best I could, even though I knew Lydia would find fault in my coverage somehow. I also didn't let them go on their Chromebooks. I was still bothered by my lost yellow table, but I was an adult and had to act like one.

After the students went home for the day, Colleen came rushing into my room to show me something on her phone.

"I'm shocked!" she said, scrolling. "Not that shocked, but shocked!" She handed me the phone, and there, in a local news story, a teacher had been arrested the night before for nearly beating her husband to death with an antique wooden tennis racket. She didn't take the press frame off, and the sharp points of the square did significant damage to his head. She beat him into a coma because she had suspected infidelity. I wondered why she hadn't used a gun from his collection. Maybe she didn't know the combination to his safe? Did he even have a safe? It didn't matter.

"It's gruesome," Colleen said with a touch of glee.

I kept reading, and it seemed Lydia waited until Christopher was asleep.

Colleen said, "I wonder how she found out he was cheating? It doesn't say."

Yes, I was two steps ahead of Colleen in this thinking: Was my confession to the Gossip that triggered this? I didn't know. And a large part of me didn't care.

Then I thought of Kurt. *You're getting mean,* he whispered.

Shut up, I told him. *I feel bad for Christopher. And the children.* Then, *how was I supposed to know she'd beat him with an old tennis racket?*

"It's terrible," I told Colleen, and then went to find the custodian to help me get my yellow table back. I figured Lydia wouldn't need it now.

* * *

At home, my husband was sitting on the couch, watching the local news. He looked glum. That afternoon, I had skipped the gym and gone shopping instead. I bought a new dress. It was light yellow with little green hearts, hearts the color of tennis balls.

"No tennis?" I said, placing my bag down.

He didn't answer, leaning forward, his eyes fixed on the TV.

"Let me guess," I said. "A man stopped by to talk to you."

Mark glared at me, then looked back at the TV. Lydia's story came on, and the reporters said Christopher was in serious condition, but doctors were hopeful.

"Look at that," I said. "I'm not nearly as crazy as his wife. I would never beat you with any of your tennis rackets."

Mark slumped back in the chair.

"I'm going to get a lawyer, and you're going to find an apartment. I have photos of your text messages." Which was true—my daughter took photos of them when the affair was in its first round. The night before, when I found his most recent text messages, I did the same. "By Sunday, you need to move out."

Mark shot me an angry look, but I just smiled. Then my soon-to-be-ex-husband frowned like a big baby with gray hair. "I'm in remission for cancer."

I picked up my bag with my new dress. "I don't care."

* * *

Later that evening, I decided to go to the gym, after all. I felt good. Sure, the cops would probably get to me, since I was the source of the Gossip's story, if that's how Lydia learned about her cheating husband. Perhaps the Gossip told people at school on Thursday afternoon, before they left for the day. Perhaps it blew through the school so fast that Lydia learned of it. Or maybe one of her loyal friends texted her about what I had told the Gossip? Or maybe it had nothing to do with me? Perhaps Christopher went home, asked her for a divorce, and Lydia lost her mind. Still, even if it was my fault, what were the cops going to do? Arrest me for being mean-spirited? For being spiteful over a yellow table with a scratch?

I think not. I turned up the speed on the treadmill and didn't think of Kurt Cobain because, frankly, I didn't care what Kurt would do or what he thought. I did hope Christopher survived his beating and went on to break free.

I liked being mean. It felt like I'd been let out of a cage, flying away from bullshit, into the world of me.

My future life looked grand.

* * *

Jen Conley is the author of the Anthony Award-winning YA novel, *Seven Ways to Get Rid of Harry,* and the Anthony Award-nominated short story collection, *Cannibals: Stories from the Edge of the Pine Barrens.* She's published over forty short stories in print and online, and is the co-host of the crime fiction reading series Noir at the Bar in Manhattan, NYC. She lives in Brick Township, New Jersey.

THWACK!!

By Richard J. Brewer

"Nice house," thought Epstein as he drove up the driveway. Brick, two stories, gabled roof, lots of wood. It looked like one of those old English houses that showed up on the British TV shows his wife watched. What were they called? Tudor. That's it.

He got out of his car and walked up the short flight of steps to the front door and rang the doorbell. After getting no response, he rang again. Still, there was no answer. Being curious, he began to walk around the house, eventually coming to a gate that led to the back yard. Then he heard.

"UGH!" THWACK!!

"UGH!" THWACK!!

Opening the gate, he peered in and saw a tall man standing in a fenced tennis court. He was dressed in a white short-sleeved tee shirt and purple, lightweight training pants. A basket of tennis balls sat by his side. He held a racket in his right hand. As Epstein watched, the man picked a ball from the basket, bounced it once, then tossed it high in the air, his hand with the racket rearing back and…

"UGH," he grunted as he slammed the ball with a resounding THWACK, sending it barreling over the net and right into the back service line area. It was a smooth accurate shot with some real power behind it and would have been a hard serve to return. The ball joined a large gathering of its brothers across the net from the tennis player, who now leaned over, set his tennis racket down, and placed his hands on his knees. Sweat dripped from his chin as he took in deep breaths.

"Scuse me," said Epstein.

The man started and jerked erect, causing Epstein to raise his hands in apology.

"Sorry," he said. "Didn't mean to startle you. Are you Mark Thorne?"

"I am," said Thorne. "Who are you?"

Epstein reached into his pocket, pulled out his ID, and stepped forward.

"Detective Brian Epstein, Visala PD. I was wondering if we could talk a minute?"

"About what?"

"Edward Thommson."

It took a moment for what the Detective said to register with Thorne. He stood still, then came to himself and walked across the court to a gate in the fence. Exiting, he wiped his face and hands with a towel and approached the detective. "What about him?" he said to the detective. "He's in jail."

"He's missing," said Epstein.

"From jail?" said Thorne.

"No," said Epstein, "He's actually been out of jail for a while."

Thorne stared at the detective for a beat. Finally, he said, "Maybe you better come inside." Thorne turned and began walking toward the back of the house. Epstein followed behind him. They entered into a well-cleaned, well-ordered kitchen. Again, Epstein thought. "What a nice house."

"You want something to drink?" said Thorne.

"No, thank you," said Epstein. "I'm okay."

"I'm gonna have something," said Thorne. He opened a cabinet and took down a bottle of scotch. From another cabinet he got a tumbler and gave himself a hefty pour. He took a sip, steadied himself, and turned to the detective.

"What did you say your name was again?" he asked.

"Epstein, Detective Brian Epstein," he said

"Like the Beatles," said Thorne.

"Yeah," said Epstein.

Thorne gave a thought and then showed the tiniest bit of a smile. "I suppose you get that a lot."

"No, not really," said Epstein. "It's a 'if you know, you know' kinda thing. It's not as if I'd been named Ringo."

"Well," said Thorne. "If there hadn't been a Brian Epstein, there wouldn't have been a Ringo. He took another sip of his drink. "Now, tell me about Thommson. You say he's out of jail? Been out of jail?"

"Yes."

"He escaped?"

"Not as such."

"What do you mean?"

"He didn't escape from jail," said Epstein. "He made bail."

"He made… No. How? He was tried and convicted," said Thorne. "How much?"

"$500,000."

"Where the hell did he get that kind of money?" he said. "I know for a fact he didn't have it. He lost it all in the civil suit we brought against him."

Epstein looked embarrassed. "Someone set up an anonymous GoFundMe page to pay for his bail."

"You're kidding me," said Thorne. "That's insane. He raised that much money with a GoFundMe page?"

"All he needed was ten percent of the asked for bail. The page raised enough money to do that. Two weeks ago a bail bondsman showed up with the money, and he was out."

"Who? Who would do that?" said Thorne. "Who would contribute to something like that?"

"There were a lot of contributions," said Epstein. "Ranging anywhere from ten dollars to one thousand dollars. Like the page, almost all of them were anonymous. We are getting a subpoena to find out who the contributors were and who started the page."

"Meanwhile, he's out in the world," said Thorne. "What does Thommson say? Does he know who set up the fund?"

"Well that's the thing," said Epstein.

"What?"

"Like I said, he's gone missing."

Throne put his drink down. "Since when?"

"Three days ago."

"What the hell," said Thorne. "Didn't you have him under surveillance? You can't tell me you just left him on his own."

"No, he was being watched," said Epstein. "He was released under house arrest, awaiting a new trial. He was given an ankle bracelet, and we did in-person check-ins on him every morning and evening. He couldn't…He wasn't supposed to be able to go any further than his yard."

"So then…"

"Three days ago, we got an alert that the bracelet had been disabled. A patrol car was immediately dispatched to check on him, and he wasn't in his home," said Epstein. "The bracelet was found in the back yard. It had been cut in half, which is what set off the alarm. By the time officers got there, he was gone."

Thorne turned away from Epstein and retrieved his drink, took a swing. Turning back, he gave a cold, hard look at the detective. "It doesn't make any sense," he said.

"I know," said Epstein. "Look, I can understand your frustration."

"Can you?" said Thorne. "Can you really?"

"Mr. Thorne…" said Epstein.

"Why are you here, Epstein? Why are you here talking to me?"

"It all started with you."

"It all started with my daughter," said Thorne. "It all started with Maggs."

* * *

Margaret "Maggs" Thorne had been a smart, precocious child. She had been destined, as her father often said, to be something special. It was her father, a local car mechanic with an 8th-grade education, who had first put a tennis racket in his five-year-old daughter's hand. He had read an article about Serena and Venus Williams, and how their father had trained them from an early age to the heights they were to reach in the world of tennis.

Ever since his wife had died, Thorne had worried about how he would care for his daughter. How could he find a way to give her the opportunities she would need to build a better life for herself. Better than the one he had. Reading that article and others about the sisters who came to dominate the world of tennis, he got the idea that tennis might be what he was looking for. His initial hope had been for Maggs to get an athletic scholarship to one of the good schools he could never afford on his own. That had been his hope.

* * *

"Ummm… Mr. Thorne?" said Epstein.

Thorne came out of his memories. "I'm sorry," he said. "What did you say?"

"I was asking if you thought Thommson might get in touch with you," he said. "Maybe threaten you?"

"For releasing the evidence?" said Thorne. "No, I would doubt that. He doesn't have the guts for something like that."

"The last time you saw him?"

"At the courthouse. When he was sentenced."

"Four years ago."

"Yes," said Thorne. "How could he get bail this long after his conviction?"

"He and his lawyer have been appealing the convictions from the beginning," said Epstein. "They finally found a judge that was willing to give Thommson a new trial, and there were some issues that convinced the judge that allowing him out on bail would be alright."

"What issues?"

"He hasn't been in the best of health."

"What's wrong with him?"

"Something with his heart

"Bad?"

"I don't know all the details, but it's bad enough they didn't think he'd be a flight risk," said Epstein. "Apparently, they were wrong."

Thorne was silent for a moment. Finally. "You know, this house was Magg's idea," he said. "She wanted it. She actually worked with the architect on the initial design."

"It's very nice," said Epstein, wondering where this was going.

"Took three years to build," said Thorne. "Three bedrooms, 2 1/2 bathrooms, dining room, living room, sitting room, kitchen, attic and basement, two-car garage, and, as you saw, an Olympic-size tennis court. I told her she was crazy, but she wanted it. All we'd ever lived in before were rentals. 'Temp homes,' she called them. Usually too small for us. She always said, 'I want us to have a home with a big back yard. When I have kids, I want them and their friends to have plenty of room to play in. I want them, I want us, to have a real home to live in.' She had it all planned out."

Epstein said. "And you chose to build here? In this little town."

"Hometown," said Thorne. "It's her hometown. She was born here. Her roots are here. Her career started here. Though I don't think a hundred thousand people can be called a 'little town.'"

"Hundred and *thirty-two* thousand after the last census," said Epstein. "I guess you're right about that. I've lived here my whole life, so I still think of it as small. I remember when I was a kid, it was easy to ride my bike anywhere in town and not have it take more than twenty minutes. And I felt safe doing so. Not so much these days."

"No," said Thorne.

"So," said Epstein, trying to change the subject. "What's the difference between a living room and a sitting room?"

"A living room has a comfy couch and a big ass TV."

"And a sitting room?"

"Comfy chairs, no TV."

Epstein shook his head. "Place couldn't have been cheap," he said, then caught himself. "I'm sorry, I didn't mean…"

"It's all right," said Thorne. "We saved as much of Magg's endorsement money as we could. She was always planning for the future. The civil suit money we got from Thommson went a long way, of course, and we had a good financial advisor. I finished it for her."

"But it's just you living here."

"Yes," he said. "Just me." He looked around the room. "We came a long way to get to this."

* * *

They had started off in a small one-bedroom, one-bath rental when Maggs had first started training. At first, with her being so young, it was an after-dinner game. John Thorne and daughter, Maggs, would go out into their driveway with used tennis rackets. Standing far back by the street curb, he'd have her hit balls against the garage door of their house while he played back up and ball wrangler. Maggs essentially began her career playing against herself.

Night after night, he urged her to smash balls against the door as hard as she could. There was no telling how many tennis balls were hit before she ever ventured onto a court. Once she was a bit older, he would put chalk circles on the door and encourage her to serve the balls in the middle of the circles to improve her aim. Saturday mornings were not spent watching cartoons, but with the two of them watching tennis matches on TV.

Once John felt she was ready, he took her to her first tennis court. Back then, Visala was a small agricultural town in the central valley of California, and the only courts were at the local high school. John made a deal with the school principal: in exchange for servicing his car for free, John and Maggs could practice on the courts. So, four nights a week, it would be homework, dinner, and tennis. Seven to eight-thirty P.M. found John and Maggs working on serves, backhands and forehands, backspins and topspins, foot placement, stamina, and... Maggs loved it. And John loved watching his daughter grow and gain proficiency as a player. It wasn't long until they were on the courts five nights a week.

* * *

"Can you tell me how you came to know Mr. Thommson?" said Epstein.

"I'm sorry?" said Thorne.

"How did you get introduced to Thommson?"

"That's all in my statement to the police."

"I'd like to hear it in your words."

"It was right when she started high school," said Thorne. "Look, let's go sit down."

They walked out of the kitchen, through a foyer. Epstein noticed the walls held numerous pictures of Maggs in various shots playing tennis. She had a strong, determined look in each picture.

In the sitting room, there were more pictures, more action shots, and some posed with Maggs and her dad smiling at the camera. Thorne motioned for Epstein to sit in one of two, definitely comfortable looking chairs while he took the other. Between the two men was a wooden coffee table. Epstein pulled out his notebook and a small recorder.

"Okay with you if I record our conversation?"

"Whatever you need," said Thorne.

"Thanks," said Epstein as he set the device on the table, switched it on, and checked his watch. "This is Detective Brian Epstein of the Visala City Police Department, it is" he checked his watch. "12:37 on Friday, April 22nd. I am recording, with his permission, my interview with Mark Thorne."

"That should do it," he said. "So, Mr. Thorne, how did you and your daughter come to know Edward Thommson?"

"Coach Eddie," said Thorne. "He was always Coach Eddie to us. To everyone." Thorne ran his fingers through his hair. Finally. "You really need me to go over this again?"

"I'm just re-examining the info," said Epstein. "With him missing and all I'm… the department is covering all bases."

Thorne sighed.

"Really, I am sorry to ask," said Epstein. "This is just routine."

"Okay," said Thorne. "Maggs was sixteen, and she had been playing in Junior tournaments around the state for about three years. That kid had taken to tennis with a passion. She was thirteen years old when she played in her first USTA Junior Team tournament."

Epstein gave him a questioning look.

"USTA?" he said.

"The United States Tennis Association. It's a national organization that promotes tennis for all ages and at all levels. They hold tournaments all over the country. In her very first game, when she was thirteen, Maggs lost the set 6-0. Thorne smiled. A bigger one than the last time. "That really pissed her off. She was not going to accept that. She proceeded to win the next six games, boom, boom, boom, serves that her opponent could hardly return. In the second set, she won 6-0. And then she won the tiebreaker with ease. For the next two years after that, she was consistently one of the top five players in every singles tournament."

"When she was a freshman in high school, she immediately got on the tennis team. It was her high school coach, in fact, who first really recognized her talent. He could see Maggs was so much better than any of his other students. Any other players in the region.

She played on the tennis team for the first semester, and then he told me how far ahead Maggs was of any of the other kids, and she could benefit from better coaching than he or I could give her. He felt that she had the potential for an athletic scholarship to pretty much anywhere she'd want to go. He's the one who suggested Edward Thommson.

Thommson ran one of the best, and most successful, training camps in the country. His reputation as a coach was outstanding. Like the Romanian gymnastic coach Béla Károlyi, whose eye for and cultivation of great gymnastic talent had led many of his trainees to Olympic gold, Thommson was known for finding young, talented tennis athletes and nurturing them into the pros. At our first meeting, I told him I didn't want Maggs turning professional before eighteen. I knew that most athletes, no matter how good they are, had a limited shelf life, but I thought Maggs should continue as an amateur and concentrate on her studies. I wanted her to have a chance to earn the scholarships her high school coach talked about, but not just athletically. I wanted her to succeed academically as well. I didn't want tennis to be the end. I wanted it to be the means to an end."

"You told that to Thommson?" said Epstein.

"Yes," said Thorne. "And Thommson agreed with me. He said his coaching would not interfere with her studies, and even if she developed as he hoped she would he would keep her as an amateur. If her grades fell below acceptable levels, which I would set, he would back off until they got back up. He assured me that his only desire was for Maggs to succeed. I had a very grown-up talk with Maggs, and she told me she wanted to be trained by Thommson. At the time, she had her eyes on the Juniors and, hopefully, the Olympics. We agreed that he would become her coach. It did mean we would have to move to Sacramento, where his camp was located. And that wasn't cheap. I was a mechanic. The move and the camp would be a stretch financially."

"So how did you afford it?" said Epstein.

"The interest in Maggs in the tennis world was growing from all her wins. She was very active on social media. She had a strong presence on Instagram, TikTok, Snapchat, WhatsApp all of that stuff, and she was developing a real following. Two sporting apparel companies offered her an NIL deal. What that means is that they can pay her to use her name, image, and likeness to promote their product or company, and she would still maintain her amateur status. If we signed a contract with them, the money she would make would pay for her training with Thommson. I remember her laughing after we made the deals. 'Dad, I have to wear something to play in, I may as well get paid for it.' The advance we got, along with what I could bring in, I was still working at that point, was enough money to pay for training, a house to rent, one with a good, solid garage door so she could practice her serves, and the day-to-days. Everything was moving forward better than I could have hoped for. Then…" Thorne stopped and took a deep breath.

"I'm sorry," said Epstein.

"No," said Thorne. "It's…it's okay."

"You were the one who found her."

"Yes," said Thorne. "I came home after work and found her."

Both men were quiet for a few minutes.

Finally, Epstein spoke. "Had she been behaving differently?"

"You mean, did I see any signs? Everyone asks that. Don't think I haven't thought about that over and over these past years. Looking back? Yes, there were signs that something was going on with her. I thought it was her upcoming graduation, her trying to decide whether to turn pro or not... whether she'd go to college or not. She had been offered all the scholarships I could have asked for, she just wasn't sure which one, if any, to take. Of course, I was pushing for college. That was why I had started everything to begin with. But there was a lot of potential money on the line if she went pro. So yes, there was a lot going on with her. More, of course, than I knew. I just wasn't...I wasn't aware enough to see it clearly. It wasn't until after the funeral, after I found the diaries. She had just turned eighteen."

Epstein said, "Those diaries were damning. Years of abuse."

"By Thommson," said Thorne.

"The diaries were the key evidence that led to his arrest," said Epstein. "And that arrest gave permission for many other young women to come out and speak against Thommson."

"And look where that's got us," said Thorne.

"Mr. Thorne," said Epstein. "We will find him. The fact that he disabled his ankle bracelet and is now on the run will kill any hope he may have had in overturning his conviction."

"Can you promise that?"

"Well..." said Epstein.

"No," said Thorne. "The answer is no. You can't promise to catch him, and you can't promise he won't get out again once he's found."

"Well, I would argue about that..."

"Would you have made the same argument four years ago?" said Thorne. "Given all the evidence against him. All the testimony."

"The court..."

"The court? The fucking court is who let him out," said Thorne. "The court is why you are here talking to me, and he's out who knows where. My daughter..."

* * *

The diaries had been hidden behind a dresser in Magg's room. Inside them, Thorne found a detailed record of sexual abuse at the hands of Edward "Coach Eddie" Thommson, something that had started a few months into her coaching. At first, she was confused, wasn't sure what was happening. As smart as Maggs had been, she could also be naïve, and Thommson had used mind and emotional games to keep her off balance. Once she did grasp what was happening to her, she was too embarrassed and ashamed to tell anyone.

During that time, Thommson was convincing her that she needed him as her coach in order to keep winning tournaments. She needed him if she ever wanted to make it as a pro or as an Olympian. His "time with her" was part of his payment for her continued success. She "owed him," he said. She would have been nothing without his guidance, and there was a part of Maggs that, no matter her natural talent, no matter the evidence to the contrary, became convinced it was true. But, as she stated in her diaries, she did have a plan. She would endure his attentions, but once she graduated, she would be off to college or out onto the professional circuit. She would be out into the world and on her own and away from him, but that wasn't in Thommson's plans.

As graduation approached, Thommson had informed her of how much he was anticipating continuing as her coach. He saw a great future for her with him by her side, helping her, guiding her to becoming one of the great tennis players in the world. He called her his "little star." When she told him she was ready to move on and be on her own, he laughed at her. He told her they would be a team for years and years to come.

Two days later, Margaret "Maggs" Thorne had come home from practice and hung herself in the family garage.

Once Thorne had read the diaries, he had taken them straight to the police. The resulting arrest and trial of Thommson made the national news.

During the trial, twelve other young women came forward with accusations of abuse by their former coach. He was ultimately found guilty of all charges and sentenced to seven years in prison for each accusation. Thorne had left the courthouse that day knowing that Thommson would be an old man when he finally got out of prison. He could only hope that all the stories he heard about the miserable lives of sexual predators in prison were true.

Then the coach was let out.

Epstein closed his book, shut off his recorder, and stood up.

"Mr. Thorne," he said, reaching out his hand. "I think I have enough for now. Thank you for your time. Understand, we have a full state-wide APB out for Thommson. We are checking with all of his contacts, family. We will not give up until we find him, and as soon as we do, I promise you, we'll let you know first thing."

Thorne stood up as well. Ignoring the hand, he said, "Given the circumstances so far, you'll forgive me if I don't hold my breath. I'll show you the way out." He proceeded to walk the detective back through the house to the front door.

Stepping out into the daylight, Epstein stopped and turned around. "Mister Thorne," he began. But the door shut before he could finish what he was about to say. With a sigh, he walked down to his car, got in, and with one last look at the house, drove away.

Thorne watched from a side window as the detective left. Stepping away from the window, he walked back to the kitchen. He had heard of Coach Eddie's release when it had first happened. He believed Epstein when he had said that the police were doing everything they could to find the coach, and they probably would. With that in mind, he went into the kitchen and over to a door that led to the basement. Flipping on a light, he walked down the stairs and into a room that stretched out for about eighty feet, basically the length of a standard tennis court and just about as wide. It felt more like an indoor gun range than what one might think of as a typical basement. On the wall nearest the stairs hung several tennis rackets, a large basket of tennis balls under them. Thorne carefully picked a racket from the wall and pulled the basket of tennis balls behind him until he was standing in the center of the floor.

At the opposite end of the room a man sat tied to a chair and gagged. His face was a mass of bruises. Dried blood was stained under his nose, and one eye was nearly swollen shut. His pants were dark where he'd soiled himself. There was no tennis net.

"The police were here," said Thorne. "A detective Epstein. Seems they are very determined to find you. And they will, I'm sure of that. It's only a matter of time. I'm not the best kidnapper in the world. Strictly amateur. Lord knows I would never make it as a pro." Thorne bounced one of the tennis balls on the floor and caught it. "I figure it will be the money from the GoFundMe page I started that will lead them to me," he sighed. "Well, we'll see what happens. It will be what it will be. I'm not going to worry myself thinking about it."

"You know what I *have* been thinking about?" he said. "I've been thinking about Maggs and her telling me how much stock you put on a powerful serve. What was it she used to say? 'Coach Eddie says a strong serve will set the tone for a whole game.' Man, she took that to heart. Her serves were… well… deadly. Some of them were clocked at over a hundred miles per hour."

Thorne threw the ball up in the air, swung the racket, and hit the ball. UGH! THWACK!!

The ball flew through the air and hit the man in the stomach with a sick thwap. The man grunted in pain from behind the gag.

"I've been working on *my* serve," said Thorne. "For four years I've been working. I bought a radar gun. Set it up on the court outside. Best I've been able to do is get the ball up to seventy-eight miles per hour. Now that's not bad. It's no Maggs, but not bad."

He bounced another ball on the ground. "Of course," he said. "The other thing you used to say to Maggs was, 'The only way to improve is to take the time to practice.' Well, even with the police looking for you and despite your health issues, I think we have some time. It will be interesting to see which of those catch up with you first. Oh, if you have any coaching tips, feel free to tell me."

UGH! THWACK!!

* * *

Richard J. Brewer has always loved stories. That love has seen him work as an author, editor, actor, audiobook narrator, director/producer, bookseller, and book reviewer. He co-edited the Bruce Springsteen-inspired anthology *Meeting Across the River* and the speculative fiction collection *Occupied Earth*. His short story, "Last to Die," from the anthology *Trouble in the Heartland*, was noted as one of the Distinguished Mystery Stories of the year in *The Best American Mystery Stories 2015*. His most recent project, the critically acclaimed anthology *Culprits: the heist was only the beginning,* has been adapted into a television miniseries for Disney+/Hulu.

All In

By Scott Adlerberg

I don't know whether Tony ever had a chance to avoid what he became in life, but I do know I liked having him as a tennis partner. But how that came to be, myself and him as a doubles team, is a story in itself. I was a member of the indoor tennis club in West Nyack, playing at an advanced level. Tony joined the club in the late summer, a guy who took lessons. It had been years since I laid eyes on him, but he hadn't changed in appearance that much, not even since our elementary school days. Short as a child, he remained diminutive, five foot six, five foot seven, but you could see that he worked out. At the Tie Break club, I first saw him in the common area, where the tables and chairs and the front desk were, chatting with a guy who towered over him. The club pro, one of them, wearing stylish whites, and Tony had on black tennis shorts and a light, gray T-shirt. Though he needed to look up as he spoke to the man, Tony projected a subtle dominance. He seemed to be leaning in, like a boxer on the front foot, about to move forward towards his opponent, while the tall guy stood with the upper part of his body slightly tilted back, as if on the defensive. Yet they weren't arguing or in conflict. I saw no animosity between them. The way the instructor swung his right arm in a slow-motion forehand told me he was giving Tony advice about a stroke. And Tony smiled, nodding his head. He imitated the stroke. His hair had been longish when I last ran into him, the summer after high school ended, but now he had a buzz cut, jet-black. His beard and mustache were equally neat. If he was suffering any long-term effects from the gunshot he'd taken a few years earlier, I couldn't see it.

The story had made the local news, *Hudson Valley TV 12* reporting that Rockland County resident, alleged mob member Tony Lario, had survived a hit attempt. Had he gotten revenge on his assailants? I assumed he had. In the decade and a half since I'd seen him, whether done by him or on his orders, exactly how many deaths was he responsible for? Tony hadn't done any jail time so far as I knew, but it's not as if I'd been following his life since high school. I'd gone on to college and teaching, eighth grade history teacher, and Tony vanished into the world I supposed surrounded him from the first. Two different paths taken, and on that day at the tennis club, he didn't spot me sitting at a table with my gear, resting after a singles match. The guy I'd played and beaten had departed. If Tony had looked in my direction, I think he would have recognized me, but that afternoon at least, we didn't interact. He thanked the instructor for his forehand tip and left the club.

I met Tony in third grade. A year older than everyone else in class, he'd been left back once in second grade, at a different school. I don't recall him ever putting effort into schoolwork, and either in third or fourth grade, I remember, our homeroom teacher washed his mouth out with soap. He must have cursed or said something the teacher thought offensive, and no repercussions followed for the teacher at that public school, none that I knew of. If his parents complained—this was in the 80s—I heard nothing about it; Tony seemed to exist without parents. No one connected to him came to any parent-teacher nights at the school, and though Tony lived two streets over from me and I was in his house several times, I never saw adults there. Congers was a small town, and you recognized the parents of your friends. He had an older sister, and besides him, she was the only one I'd find in that sprawling, messy place. I learned later, from a newspaper article about Tony, that their mother had gone missing when he was three. The rumor, according to the piece's writer: that his father had killed her for cheating on him with a business associate. Whatever happened, Tony's mother disappeared. No body, no funeral, gone. So Tony had been raised by a single father busy with less-than-legal activities, and Tony, as a kid, to a large degree, was left to his own devices. He did just enough to get the C's that got him passed upward from grade to grade.

Where he excelled was in sports. We played a bit of everything as children, though not tennis yet, and Tony liked basketball the best. In school intramurals, in the town's recreation league, in neighborhood pick-up games, Tony dominated among the kids our age. Despite his size, he was the quickest, the strongest. He started lifting weights around fifth grade. He could talk the equivalent of an eleven-year old's trash, but he didn't get upset if you hurled garbage back. He didn't mind with me anyway. I'd seen him threaten to punch other kids if they taunted him on the court, but I knew how far I could take a comment with him and pull it off. "Ball hog," he'd accept, rolling his eyes. "Shrimp or jerk," which I never said to him, he would not. One kid who didn't know Tony called him "a dumb ass" after a game, and Tony sent the boy home blood-stained. I guess you could say that relationship-wise, I coasted along with Tony. We had bonded on a basketball court during recess in third grade, and that bond stuck. Unlike others, I didn't find him intimidating.

"Tony," I'd say, in a familiar refrain. "I had the shot."

"You would've missed."

"I was wide open."

"You're a crappy shooter."

"Do you know what a pass is, Tony?"

"Do *you* want to win the game or not?"

He did hate to lose in anything he did.

Around the age of twelve, I took up tennis. I fell in love with the game and played it in junior high and high school. By then, Tony had become truant, and eventually he dropped out altogether. I didn't see him in the hallways from tenth grade on. Maybe his father was introducing him to his work, getting him acquainted with his particular mode of business. I'd run into Tony in town at the deli, and we'd exchange friendly hellos, but these quick meetings aside, we went our separate ways. As I mentioned,

I saw him the summer after my high school graduation, at a house party thrown by a mutual friend, and if anything indicated the trajectory his life was taking, that night did.

Inside the house and out, I mingled with people I'd known for years. I knew them from town or from school. Beer kegs flowed, and teenagers drank despite the presence of my friend's parents, but nothing got out of hand. Everyone talked about what in life they would do next, whether or not they were heading to college, though, of course, Tony did not. He said nothing about his future, and he alone at that shindig had a broken jaw. A doctor had wired it shut, and Tony downed his beer from a cup through a straw and spoke with everybody through clenched teeth. He drew attention in his state, and without apparent qualms, he told whoever asked that he'd been involved in some shit gone wrong. That's how he described it, shrugging it off as "minor". He was vague about details, but I gathered that a town over, in Haverstraw, two guys with baseball bats had attacked him. Tony had managed to escape the assault by jumping through a second story window to the pavement beneath.

"Lucky all you broke was your jaw," I said when I heard this.

We were hitting a ball back and forth on a ping pong table in the backyard, lawn lamps all around, the party going, and Tony cracked a teeth-locked smile. A chuckle came up from his throat. At nineteen, in a tight shirt, he already had prominent biceps and a neck about as wide as his head.

"When this heals, I'll find those guys."

I saw Tony either ending up in prison soon or not making it to thirty, but he wound up defying my expectations on both counts. And it's fair to say that the last place I expected to see him years after his appearance at that party was at the Tie Break tennis club as an eager to learn beginner. But here he was on that afternoon, absorbing guidance from the instructor, and I wondered what other club members thought about having him in our midst. Did anyone at the Tie Break know who he was? I reasoned they must have, but nobody said anything to me about him, and I didn't bring him up with anyone.

He established himself as a club regular. Over the fall and winter, he played and took lessons on a frequent basis. From the common area, through the glass, you could see down onto the five courts to the left and the five to the right, and sometimes I'd watch Tony hitting. He did the crosscourt forehand drills the pros gave him, the backhand drills, the serve, and return of serve routines. He moved side to side at the net, developing his volley as the pro would smack balls at him. I'd see Tony and the instructor smiling and laughing, from which I presumed their rapport was good. Tony sure took directions from these guys better than he had from our schoolteachers. The athleticism he'd possessed as a kid remained with him—that was obvious—and I noticed that when playing sets, he played more singles than doubles. That made sense. A person who'd hated passing in basketball would prefer not sharing the court with someone. Or maybe people were afraid to pair up with Tony. If you knew his reputation, would you want him as a partner? Would he blow up at you if he hit a strong serve and you, at the net, flubbed an easy volley off the return? I could imagine a story in the *Journal News*: "Club player and mob member Tony Lario is suspected of having murdered a doubles partner he had in a recent match. They had teamed up for a casual game at the Tie Break club, and the suspected reason for the homicide is that his partner missed an assortment of makeable shots in the third and decisive set." Unlikely, true, but I could understand people being uncomfortable playing beside him.

It was at the club Christmas party that we finally spoke. On that evening, a Saturday, I revealed myself to him as a fellow Tie Break member. I hadn't been avoiding him outright since September, but for whatever reason, I had been reluctant to approach him. I'm not sure why I kept my distance; I'd always gotten along with Tony. It could have been as simple an explanation as his playing level was below mine, and I feared that he might want to hit with me often, and what if I kept brushing him off? Would I anger Tony? I had a rotation of people I played with, usually singles and sets, not just hitting, and playing a lot with Tony would help his game, but hinder mine. Also, we had different schedules, so rarely booked the same hours at the club. I would see him there, like I said, but that was the exception to the norm. Regardless, when I received the invitation to the Christmas festivities, I didn't want to duck the annual event because Tony might be there. I dressed for the party—sweatsuit, sneakers—grabbed my tennis bag, and headed over to the Tie Break. I lived in Valley Cottage, fifteen minutes away.

The staff and club members had contributed money for the refreshments. People mixed in the common area or played lighthearted games on the courts. I went up to Tony while he was standing by himself sipping wine from a paper cup, and before he could say anything, I asked him whether he remembered me.

He blinked.

"Steve?"

"It's been a while."

Whether he thought I'd seen him at the club and been keeping myself away from him, I couldn't tell, but if he did think that, he didn't seem bothered. He put his cup down on a table and extended his right hand to shake, and when I gripped it, feeling a vise, he pulled me in for a hug.

"Strong as an ox still," I said.

"Have to be," he said, and let go.

Time had hardened his face a little, but Tony retained the round cheeks of his youth. Unchanged, too, was his slight overbite, though I figured he could have afforded a procedure. Other kids might have faced teasing for the look he had, but I didn't recall anyone ever making fun of his teeth, and I doubted that anyone did now.

"Mr. Topspin," he said. "How you been?"

"You remember that?"

"Wasn't that what you were known for?"

"Back in the day. I wasn't aware you were paying attention."

"I know that your tennis topped your basketball skills."

"If you'd passed, I would've hit more shots."

We bantered like that, as if no time had gone by since we were playing sports as children. We caught up as people do, with both of us saying we weren't married. I told him what I did for a living, and he commented that being a schoolteacher suited me.

"It does?" I said. "It's not like I grew up dreaming of doing that."

"You did your homework and listened to the teachers."

"Can't say you did."

He laughed, a sardonic, sidelong look in his eyes.

Tony declared that he did real estate, and I didn't prod for details. He seemed comfortable with me and relaxed in general, and that's why I was surprised when I found out later that Tony was embroiled during this time in the escalating tensions between rival factions in his circle. As I later read from accounts about the gang war, he conducted a hit no less than a week after the Christmas party at the club.

It happened in New Rochelle. A guy who owned a jewelry store there was the brother of a main rival of Tony's, and Tony, with a couple of his own guys, went to see him. The target, a Dominic Scalducci, twenty-seven years old, was worried about his safety and never opened his store without being armed. For additional insurance, he had two bodyguards with him. On the day I'm talking about, he had begun his day at the store, and early in the morning, from behind the counter, he saw Tony and his guys walk past. Tony stopped, tapped on the glass with his finger, and smiled at him. Though his bodyguards were nearby, Dominic yielded to his fear. In the previous months, he'd lost a brother, an uncle, and his father in the mob land power struggle. Two of these family members, Dominic's brother and father, Tony, had killed himself. Seeing Tony and his guys, Dominic fell apart: he retreated to the back of his shop and shot himself in the mouth. That took care of what Tony wanted, and according to one person quoted in the piece I read, Tony made a crack about the suicide.

"I don't have to kill people anymore. I just show up, and they do the job themselves."

In the spring, the club announced a doubles tournament. It put one on every April, competition in men's and women's doubles. By this time, Tony was playing four or five times a week, generally at night. Among the pros and other members, he'd become well-liked; in a chat about him I had with the club manager, the guy described him as "affable". Tony attended staff birthday parties and gave money for presents. He would sometimes joke, in conversation, about his organized crime ties, but those who imagined mobsters as flashy didn't get that with Tony. His attire consisted of basic solids, and he wore no jewelry. He drove a nondescript Toyota, and the seriousness he brought to tennis, the earnestness, won him respect, as did the rapidity of his progress. In March, in a brief ceremony, the club's pros awarded him a trophy for being the Tie Break's most improved player, and I could see how much this meant to Tony. He beamed. This presentation took place on a court, and to the other people there, about ten of us, Tony said this was the first trophy he had ever won in anything.

"Steve knows," he said, tilting his head toward me. "Never won anything in school, that's for sure."

The next week, after the club's tournament announcement, Tony saw me coming off a court while he was sitting in the common area. He was alone at a table with his sweats back on after having a singles match, and without any preamble at all, he asked if he could partner with me in the men's doubles. He took a drink from his water bottle and waited for my answer, wide-eyed.

I sat down.

"I'll be honest with you, Tony."

"Go ahead."

"Tournaments can get fierce."

"So?" Tony said.

"People get serious, and there's pressure."

"You see how I've improved."

"It's not that," I said.

"What then?" Tony said. "If I've gotten better…"

"You can play now," I said. "No question."

"So? You already have a partner?"

"The guy I played with the last couple years moved away."

"Let's do it then."

I had been planning to skip the tournament—silly as it may have been, these things got me all wound up and losing a match in whatever round could ruin my mood for days—but Tony's childlike keenness to be my partner won me over. We'd spent hours together on the basketball court once; now we'd combine in tennis.

"We're not favorites by any stretch," I said.

"You never know."

"You've improved, Tony. But don't get ahead of yourself."

He reached across the table and jabbed my shoulder. He meant it playfully, but he hit hard.

"You trying to injure me before we start?"

"Pussy. Have you ever won the tournament?"

"Lost in the finals once. Made the semis, the quarters."

"With the guy who moved?"

"With him, yes."

"New partner, new chance," Tony said. "Let's give it a shot."

We paid the entrance fee and waited for the brackets to be done. Soon they were, and on the white board someone mounted on a stand near the desk, we saw that fourteen teams had signed up for the tournament. The club's head pro was running it, and based on past results and expected performance, he seeded two teams and gave them first round byes. The other teams he matched at random, and we saw we'd be playing a pair of guys I knew well. Both were decent players, but had weaknesses we could exploit. To win the tournament, which I thought unlikely considering our opposition, we'd have to get through four matches.

Tony and I held practice sessions on public courts near his house in Nanuet. We played through the day, with breaks for meals, on the two weekends leading up to the tournament. We hit cross court forehand to forehand, and backhand to backhand, and we dedicated time to serving, volleying, and hitting overheads. Because of his focus so far on singles, where he employed a baseline style, utilizing his speed, Tony needed work on his net game. He had trouble handling low volleys, especially off the backhand side, but he took my pointers about bending low and keeping his backswings at the net short.

"Punch, Tony. Punch it."

Tony tried, and I could see from the humorous gleam in his eyes that he knew I was enjoying my position as the superior player in the sport. I could boss him around. My goading functioned as a kind of payback for the years I'd endured his basketball "coaching", but Tony didn't take offense. He recognized his deficiencies on the court and wanted to keep improving. He had a great work ethic and innate confidence. When it came down to it, he understood the game too little to think we couldn't beat the more experienced teams and triumph in the tournament. In other words, Tony was a tennis naif, with the optimism of a tennis naif, but as it so happened, the opposing teams were not to be our prime antagonists.

We won our first match 6-4, 6-3. I took the backhand side and Tony the forehand, and I couldn't complain about Tony's performance. I'd given him my scouting report on the other team, telling him that the accountant sliced his groundstrokes and that the lawyer had a lollipop of a second serve, and Tony took advantage of what they gave us, his aggression controlled. He had a quickness around the net that made him an effective poacher. Throughout the match, he kept his errors to a minimum, and any nerves he felt from the tournament atmosphere—club members would gather in the common area and watch the games—he didn't show. A grin like a happy child's spread across his face after the final point. We shook hands with the other two and at the front desk, reported our result to the head pro.

"Next match'll be tougher," I said to Tony. "Be ready for a battle."

But the battle occurred before the match.

A warm Sunday, our scheduled game time noon. Tony and I agreed to meet first at the courts close to his house. I drove over, twenty minutes, and pulled into the lot there. Tony was waiting for me in his car. The park had a softball field, two handball walls, and the four hard courts. Despite the early hour, only one court was free. We went on and hit, mainly me blasting balls to him at the net and him doing the same to me, and then we decided to go get breakfast up Route 59 at the Nanuet Diner. I followed him, the traffic light, and we turned into the Rockland Plaza lot, which was nearly empty. We discussed strategy for the match over the meal, and Tony insisted that he pick up the tab. The Starbucks in the shopping center was open, but the stores were closed. A handful of cars were in the parking spaces. Tony and I exited the diner and walked down its front steps toward our own cars, and he was the one who froze suddenly, glaring straight ahead. I looked where he was looking. A black sedan farther down the lot was moving toward us at a pretty fast speed.

"Duck!" Tony yelled. "Get down!"

"What?"

"Duck!"

I did, behind his car, and I heard gunshots. They came in quick succession, and a force like an electric current tore through me, stopping my heart. Something near my head pinged. I knelt to one knee. Head bowed, eyes down, seized by paralysis. I was aware of Tony near my side, crouched low, firing a handgun over his car's hood, and the clacking of bullet fire coming at us. A dreamlike feeling washed over me, like reality had changed, morphed into a nightmare. But when I glanced sideways, I saw the infuriated face of Tony, real enough, and how he had his upper teeth clamped onto his lower lip. He appeared oblivious to the danger and kept firing off rounds.

Tires screeched, and the sound of the other car receded. Tony stopped shooting. He lowered his gun and straightened up.

"Scumbags," he said, and rotated toward me, a dead coldness in his expression.

I pushed myself upright, legs tingling.

"You okay?" Tony asked.

I'd stopped breathing for a moment, but now I was gulping air.

"I think so."

"Not hit?"

I looked down at myself.

"Don't seem to be."

"Good."

I could see a smear on Tony's left arm, visible through his sweat jacket sleeve, red staining the dark blue fabric.

"You might be."

"Cocksuckers."

Faces were watching us through the diner windows, slack-jawed, frightened, and across the lot in front of the Starbucks, I made out a guy talking on his phone.

"Someone's gonna call the cops," I said. "If they haven't already."

"Let's get back to my house."

"What about your arm?"

"Think it was grazed. Come on."

"You're bleeding. They can help you in the diner."

"You joking?"

"Tony!"

"We have the match soon."

"The match? Who's thinking about the match?"

He took his key fob from his pants and clicked it.

"I'm not waiting here for the cops," Tony said.

He opened his driver's side door, slid behind the wheel, and started the ignition.

"You coming?"

"I—"

Tony slammed his door closed and backed out of his spot. I looked up into the diner and saw the faces still gawking at us.

Did I want to deal with the police myself? Why should I have to answer for Tony's shit? I'd have explanations to make on my job and to my friends, my mother, my father…

Eighth-grade history teacher caught up in gangland war!

My name might be in the local paper, and that could lead who knew where.

I hopped into my car and drove out of the lot behind Tony.

Now, over the years, as is normal, I've played arduous matches. I've endured leg cramps on the court, muscle strains, a badly twisted ankle in a 9th-grade singles encounter. One time against a friend, outside in ninety-degree heat, I vomited between points, but when my friend asked me whether I wanted to stop, I said no. Dehydrated or not, I refused to quit, though I did get bageled in the last set. Opponents have cheated on line calls against me, and in pick-up games, I have put up with asshole doubles partners, the people who mutter a veiled critique every time you miss a shot. For all that, I had never shared the court with a gunshot wound victim, albeit one who downplayed the wound before he even examined it. When we arrived at his house after the shooting attack, he stripped off his jacket and confirmed his own diagnosis—"a graze"—and, to my suggestion that we go to the hospital for treatment, he scoffed.

"Don't be a fucking wuss, Steve."

"All right. Not the hospital. You have a private guy you use?"

"Like in the movies?"

"Whatever."

"Just help me patch it up, and I'll be fine."

"Let me call the club first and say we're pulling out. I'll say I'm sick."

"We're playing that match," Tony said. "What's the issue?"

We were standing in his bathroom, under bright lighting, and I was contemplating the wound. It was a red slash on the outside part of his left arm, above the elbow and below his shoulder. He'd stanched the bleeding with pressure from a washcloth, and now he asked me to help him wrap his arm so we could go. We had half an hour till our start time at the club.

"I'll have to wear long sleeves," Tony said. "It'll look strange, but so what?"

"No one's gonna question your on-court attire," I said.

With argument futile, I assisted Tony in tending the wound. He had tape, alcohol, and bandages in his medicine cabinet. My hands had been trembly on the drive from the plaza parking lot to his house, but somehow covering his wound soothed my nerves. Were the police at the scene as we did this, taking descriptions of the shooters and us, and our cars? If they were, Tony looked unconcerned.

Each in our own vehicles, we raced over to the Tie Break. We made it there in time for the match. Tony was right-handed, and as we warmed up, the confidence he'd expressed that his wound wouldn't affect his game proved well-founded. He winced on certain difficult shots, something in his movement causing pain in his left arm, but other than that, he showed no ill effects. He kept his sweatshirt on throughout, and no blood leaked through his dressing that I could see. As for the match, against two guys in their fifties, we won it in a straight set romp, and I must say that we both played at the top of our games. Tony hammered them with his serving and poaching, and it might have been the residual adrenaline coursing through me, but I felt in total control of myself. Where I would have expected myself to be frazzled by the day's events, shaken up mentally, I was neither. The morning disruption had put me in a different zone, *the* zone. I saw nothing but the ball on every shot and moved with a looseness and flow I didn't always have. I eased into every stroke, my timing perfect, utterly relaxed. Anyway, we finished them off in about an hour, propelling our advance to the semifinals.

For that, we would have to wait till the next Saturday. Tony and I agreed to meet up Wednesday to hit, and I got started on the work week. I couldn't help but ask myself what my students would think if they knew their teacher was friends and doubles partners with a guy like Tony. Would it heighten their estimation of me? History nerd, our teacher, but also pals with a gangster. *Hudson Valley 12* and the *Journal News* carried stories on the plaza shooting, but fortunately, they had no names attached to it. The pieces speculated that the gunshots fired might have been connected to a regional mob land dispute, but no one had gotten license plate numbers the cops could track. Or if anyone had, the cops were not releasing that information. I could picture myself standing before my students, talking by the chalkboard, and two police coming in to invite me to the station for questioning. I mean, I didn't think they'd truly barge into a class to approach me, but my fear that they'd pop up somewhere to request a statement made my week stressful.

On Wednesday, Tony and I met as planned. We'd reserved two hours at the Tie Break. Worry lines new to Tony's face had formed under his eyes and along the sides of his nose, and as we were taking the court, out of everyone's hearing, I asked him how he was doing.

"How are *you?*" Tony answered, avoiding my question. "That's what I want to know.

"Managing," I said. "Haven't said anything to anyone."

"Didn't think you would," Tony said.

"And your arm? Taking care of it?"

"The arm's fine," Tony said. "My arm's not the problem."

What the problem was, I could only conjecture, but I didn't have to be Sherlock Holmes to deduce it had something to do with the latest attempt on his life. Had Tony struck back at his enemies yet? Why didn't he have muscle with him?

We rallied for a bit, and during a pause, as we stood by the courtside bench drinking from our water bottles, I couldn't resist raising the subject:

"Are you safe coming here? Going around like you are?"

"No one's taking a crack at me at a tennis club."

"But at home? You're there by yourself."

"I'm taking steps," Tony said.

"Not that I need to know."

"No, you don't." Chastened, I stopped poking, but Tony had more to say. "I can't lay low when we have the tournament."

"Are you kidding me?" I said. "Fuck the tournament."

"No way," Tony said. "We came this far, and we're winning this thing."

"We could enter next year."

"I'll be here Saturday, and it's going to take more than this bullshit to stop me."

"Have you ever heard of tennis addiction?" I said.

"What's that?"

"What you have," I said. "You've caught it."

After we hit, I left the club with Tony, but outside the Tie Break's front doors, with the parking lot before us, he told me not to go any further with him.

"My car's here, too," I said.

"I know that," he said. "Just wait till I get into mine and go."

"You said you think you're safe at the club."

"Inside it, I said."

I watched him cross the lot and throw his gear in his trunk. He honked the horn at me as he drove off.

You should get out of town or go to the mattresses or do whatever you people do, I thought, and I tried to think of what I would say to the club pro if Tony was killed before our semifinal match. It would have to be the first default in tennis history occasioned by an underworld hit.

Saturday came. Tony showed up with a burly guy in a red and white tracksuit, presumably a bodyguard, though Tony introduced him as a friend. He had never before come to the club with anyone, but neither the pro nor the other players there looked askance at the man. If they made comments or jokes about him, I didn't hear them. The guy joined onlookers in the gallery as Tony, and I and our two opponents took the court, and he was there two hours later when the match concluded.

"Ready to go?" the guy said to Tony.

"No congratulations for our win?" I said. "Tony played out of his mind."

A face with the emotion of a stone sized me up, the mouth not moving.

"He doesn't know shit about tennis," Tony said. "Not his sport."

I had warned Tony we'd have to conduct a flawless match to beat the other pair, two guys in their twenties who had won the tournament two years back, and indeed we'd done that. We limited our unforced errors and kept holding our serves. Both the second and the third sets had gone to tiebreakers, and we'd prevailed 8-6 in the deciding breaker.

Tony accepted the praise lavished on him. Because of his inexperience, no one had thought we'd reach this stage in the tournament, and I could tell he was touched by the compliments. He said "thanks" over and over, bumped fists, slapped a shoulder or two.

"Rest up for tomorrow," I said.

"I'm sleeping at a motel tonight," he said.

"Oh my goodness."

"No big deal."

"Why don't you just leave town for a while? Is the risk worth it?"

"How often do I have to fucking tell you?"

"We're winning this thing?"

"We're winning this thing," Tony said.

I slept poorly during the night, afraid that his enemies would get to Tony before the match. I wanted to win the tournament as much as he did, I realized, and in my anxiety too was concern for Tony himself. Tony did whatever he did in his professional life, but on the other hand, he was the guy who'd been my friend since third grade. The Tony I knew as a kid, I hadn't foreseen becoming a tennis obsessive, but he had, and his fresh enthusiasm for the sport was infectious.

We win, and then you go into hiding, I could say to him before the match, though he'd probably convey amusement in response.

Glad you care, Dad.

I do. But besides that, we need to defend our championship next year.

As it turned out, the finals match would not be the climactic event of the day. It had its drama, I'll admit, like when Tony made a lunging backhand pass down the line on a key break point and when I dug a ball off my toes to flick a forehand up the middle to give us the first set, but overall, two guys locked in, we cruised to victory. Despite the restless night, I had energy to burn, and Tony brought the same intensity. A crowd of club members watched. We shook hands with the opposing pair after the last point, and at the net, beaming from ear to ear, Tony put his arms around my waist and lifted me straight up in the air.

"You didn't think we could do it, Steve."

"I really didn't."

"Don't underestimate me, motherfucker."

"Never."

The head pro called us "The Cinderella Team" and, in the common area, gave us each a plastic, gold-colored trophy. Fellow club members, once again, remarked on how Tony's play had impressed them, and some ribbed me about how at last I'd won the tournament after several years of trying.

Tony's associate, bulging in his tracksuit, stood off alone as Tony and I gabbed with everyone, and when Tony cocked his head at him, indicating they should leave, the guy began to move toward the club's exit.

"I gotta run," Tony said to me. "Great match."

"Hit this week?"

"I'm not sure. I'll call you."

"You going to be around?"

"Maybe not."

Tony's voice was low, his face sober.

"That's good," I said. "Take care of yourself."

"I'll let you know when I'm back to play."

We hugged briefly, did a man hug, and Tony walked off behind his bodyguard, his tennis bag over one shoulder. He was holding the trophy in his right hand. I watched the bodyguard and then Tony pull open the glass door and leave, and I had gone to the bathroom and entered a toilet stall, positioning myself on the seat, when I heard the abrupt sound of a blast. Out of nowhere it came, a piercing boom, and I felt my heart rise through my chest. In my shock, I nearly fell to the floor.

Pants back up, I ran out of the restroom and into the common area, where people were standing around, stunned. Some looked confused, others pale from the scare the noise had given them.

I heard a bunch of car alarms going off.

"Holy fuck!"

The head pro, in his whites, was near the entrance door, pointing outside.

I dashed over and looked through the glass.

In the parking lot, where a car had been, was a smoking wreck. Flames were shooting out from it, and the doors were gone. I knew instantly who'd been in the car and felt no desire to run over to make sure.

I didn't want to see Tony, or his bodyguard for that matter, in pieces.

The odd thing, though, the inexplicable thing, was that his trophy emerged from the car bomb intact. From where I stood, I could see it on the ground in the parking lot. The explosion must have lifted out of the car and through the air to where it landed, not far from the club's door, and without thinking much, in a sort of fog, I walked outside and picked it up. A figure with his right arm upraised, in the serving position, on top of a square base.

Men's Doubles Champions for that year.

I kept it in my hands when the cops came, and I don't think anyone noticed when I put it in my bag with my own trophy.

It stands on a mantel in my house today, paired with my trophy, a reminder of Tony's commitment to that tournament.

I've heard people say that tennis can be dangerous, all-consuming, and I agree. Tony would have agreed as well. He could have left town before the finals, taken steps to reduce his exposure, but he ignored the risk. He wanted the chance for the win. Kudos, Tony. Congrats, old friend. To use a cliché, since sports are so full of them, no one can say you didn't put your body out there for the title and leave every ounce of yourself on the court.

Or the pavement.

* * *

Scott Adlerberg is the author of five novels, including *The Screaming Child*, *Graveyard Love*, and *Jack Waters*. He has written many short stories and contributes pieces regularly to sites such as *CrimeReads* and *Mystery Tribune*. Every summer, he hosts the Word for Word Reel Talks film commentary series in Bryant Park in Manhattan. He was born in New York City and lives in Brooklyn.

Bullets, Bombs and Topspin Lobs

By Colin Campbell

"How many times?"

Kevin Mackenzie said it again. "Thirty-six bomb attacks during The Troubles, but half of them were out in the street."

That didn't make Kevin Cameron feel any better. "Oh well, that's okay then."

Mack pointed at a line of bullet holes in the mirror behind the bar. "Got shot up a few times as well. They left the holes for posterity."

Cam snorted a laugh. "And you thought it was a good idea to come for a drink at the most bombed hotel in the world?"

Mack glanced around the lounge bar of the Europa Hotel in Belfast. "It's not the most bombed hotel anymore. That's the Sarajevo Holiday Inn. It was hit hundreds of times during the Bosnian War."

Cam held his glass of Coke up as if giving a toast. "Glad they didn't decide to hold the Police and Fire Games in Sarajevo then."

Mack clinked his pint of Tetley's against the Coke. "Three thousand coppers visiting a city that hates the police. What's not to like?"

The Two Kevins laughed.

Cam said, "Cheers."

Mack went local. "Slainte."

Nobody blew up the hotel or shot at the mirror. Not yet.

* * *

Mack hadn't been exaggerating about the three thousand coppers, although in reality half of them were actually firefighters. The World Police/Fire Games was being held in Belfast for the first time, the WPFG San Diego Executive wanting to spread the games across Europe occasionally, instead of always hosting them in North America and Canada. Three thousand athletes from sixty-five countries competing in eighty-three sports. The ideal way to promote camaraderie and team spirit. Except cops and firefighters had been at each other's sporting throats almost as long as the Army had been trying to beat the Navy.

Cam hadn't been joking either, about the most bombed hotel or Belfast. Even though The Troubles were largely over after the Good Friday agreement, there were still enough paramilitary factions and splinter groups to make English coppers nervous about advertising themselves with Union Jacks and police badges. Just walking to the Belfast Boat & Sports Club—the venue for the tennis event—meant walking through streets that were still scarred from the violence and adorned with IRA murals painted on the gable ends of terrace houses.

It was only yesterday that the Two Kevins—a nickname they had earned after winning gold medals in New York, Adelaide and Rotterdam—had been confronted by a group of street kids asking if they were police or fire?

Cam had smiled at the leader. "Fire."

Mack had backed him up. "Why? Is your house burning down?"

The kids had lost interest, since there were no cops to throw stones at, but the conversation highlighted the delicate balance between promoting good will in Belfast and being a target for anti-British sentiment. The Two Kevins just wanted to play tennis.

* * *

Mack toweled the sweat from his brow after their final practice session at the tennis club. Two hours after the pint of Tetley's at the most bombed hotel in the world. Second most bombed hotel. Beer wasn't the traditional sporting supplement, but Mack vowed to be off the booze until after their first match.

Cam wasn't sweating at all. "Practice over. It all starts tomorrow."

Mack said, "Looking forward to it."

Cam glanced at the players practicing on the other courts. Tennis, blue skies and the thwack of tennis balls being hit across the net made Belfast feel like an oasis of calm in a troubled world. Sunlight glinted off the River Lagan alongside the clubhouse. There was laughter and banter and not a little grunting. The emergency services might well promote sport to build team spirit, but come tomorrow, team spirit would mean beating the shit out of the other team.

Cam said, "Keep focussed. Stay calm. Don't lose your temper."

Mack shrugged and held his hands out in a plea for understanding. "That was two years ago. And they were cheating bastards anyway."

Cam smiled at the memory of Mack threatening to headbutt the Indian doubles pair at the last Police and Fire Games. Dodgy line calling and dubious tactics hadn't helped Mack's mood. Losing his temper had won them the second set, but the aftermath of the adrenaline dump had cost them the match. They had still won bronze though.

Cam gave Mack a high-five. "Chin up. Chest out. Going for gold."

Mack gripped Cam's hand and squeezed. "Because The Two Kevin's rule."

Cam nodded. "The Two Kevins rule."

That was it. They showered, changed, and had a drink at the Cutters Wharf bar overlooking a pair of sculls in the river. Life was good. Retirement agreed with both of them. Mack had left the police life behind with ease. Cam still missed the van culture; a bunch of coppers being politically incorrect while de-stressing in the back of a police van. That was one of the good things about the World Police/Fire Games. He still felt connected. Some things you never leave behind.

Like noticing the skanky-looking fella who had been watching them from across the road. The same fella Cam had seen talking to the street kids before the kids had asked if Cam and Mack were police or fire. The leader's house hadn't been burning down, but something was wrong. And Cam would bet a pound to a pinch of shit, the skanky-looking fella was involved.

***

The bullets didn't start flying until Cam and Mack went out for dinner. They had dropped their tennis bags at the hotel, changed into their going-out clothes, and gone out. Calling Kate's BnB a hotel was a stretch of the imagination, but it was listed as a Two Star on the travel website Mackenzie had used for booking the accommodation. Mack was a whizz at finding the best deal whenever they entered The Games, going all the way back to the shady hotel in Kuala Lumpur on their layover to Australia. The local street hustlers had given up offering The Two Kevins sexy young girls and had offered young boys instead.

Nobody offered sexy young boys in Fitzroy Avenue.

Cam zipped his yellow puffa jacket up against the cool night air. "We going to the Bullets and Bombs Hotel, or are we staying local?"

Mack was the travel guide of the partnership. "We've done enough walking for one day. Let's see what's up near the university."

Kate's BnB was ideally placed for walking into town or carrying their bags to the tennis club, but Fitzroy Avenue wasn't replete with dining options. The evening was grey and damp, a fine drizzle settling on Mack's showerproof top. Purple and grey. Not as eye-catching as Cam's puffa jacket, but a damn sight more water resistant. Both wore nondescript baseball caps. Neither wore Union Jacks or police badges.

They turned left out of the front door and walked along Fitzroy Avenue until they cut through College Green. Queens' University Belfast was on the left at the end of the street. University Road was showing more life as evening became night. Still daylight but fading into darker grey. The drizzle became rain. Not heavy, but steady enough to stop The Two Kevin's from walking very far. They paused for a few moments while they surveyed their choices.

Queen's Student Union was just across the road on the left. Neither Cam nor Mack thought they could blend with a bunch of noisy teenagers, so they considered the other options. There was Millar's Brasserie on the corner of University Street, Villa Italia across the road, and Holohan's Pantry next door. Apparently, the home of the Pan Boxty, whatever that was.

Two Irish restaurants or an Italian. Neither of them fancied Irish stew, so they went Italian. Avoiding the Irish bars might have earned them a reprieve, but the skanky-looking fella made a call next to the Beer & Boxty sign and bided his time.

* * *

The drive-by shooting didn't make the also-ran on the evening news, and it barely featured on the inside pages of the Belfast Telegraph. That was partly because the powers that be wanted to minimize bad press during the largest sporting event the city had hosted in twenty years. Part of it was because the press was covering the rumblings of social unrest expected tomorrow outside Belfast City Hall. The lack of press coverage did nothing to reduce the impact for those involved. Two of those involved were Kevin Cameron and Kevin Mackenzie.

Cam felt a tingling sensation on the back of his neck when he came out of Villa Italia. When he scratched it, the collar of his puffa jacket ballooned open, letting rain pour down the back of his shirt. "Shit. At this rate, we'll be playing tennis under umbrellas."

He zipped the collar tight, forgetting the reason he had scratched his neck in the first place. The tingling sensation he had relied on during thirty years of service in the West Yorkshire Police. His version of having a nose for trouble.

Mack flipped the hood of his waterproof over his baseball cap. The peak kept the rain out of his eyes. "They've got all-weather courts."

Cam threw Mack a dirty look. "Have you ever seen a tennis tournament where they played in the rain?"

Mack returned the stare. "Have you ever seen a tennis tournament between hairy-arsed coppers and square-jawed firemen? They've been

97

shot at, bombed and stabbed. A bit of rain isn't going to stop them."

Cam said, "I bet the Indians will have something to say about that."

Mack remembered the Indians asking for a rain delay because it was drizzling, but mainly because Cameron and Mackenzie were three love up, with two breaks of serve. "Cheating bastards."

Cam pulled the collar tight around his neck. "Umbrellas."

Mack looked at the overcast night sky. "The only thing we didn't pack."

Cam put a positive spin on the situation. "We'll play when they tell us to play. The rest is up to us."

Mack stared out from the Villa Italia canopy. "First things first. Let's get back to the hotel before we get washed away."

Cam nodded, and they both dashed across the road. There was hardly any traffic, and no pedestrians at all. Just a shadowy figure sheltering under an outside table umbrella at Holohan's. A mobile phone lit the side of his face as he made a call. Cam was focusing on avoiding any potholes in the road. The skanky-looking man was focusing on The Two Kevins.

* * *

Everything changed in the short distance from Villa Italia to College Green. A dark car with no lights kept pace behind them for the first hundred yards. The rain stopped as they crossed College Green to Fitzroy Avenue. Then the car turned its lights on and sped off along University Street to get ahead of them.

Cam's neck began to itch. He stopped under a tree at the corner of College Green and scratched his neck. Having to scratch the itch twice in fifteen minutes got his attention. The sound of car tyres screeching up ahead focussed his mind.

"Hang on a minute, Mack."

Mack felt the change, too. "I know."

They both stood under the tree and scanned the leafy square. Being questioned by a bunch of street kids was one thing. Standing in front of an IRA mural at the gable end of Fitzroy Avenue brought the potential threat into focus. The streets were quiet. There were no other cars. Nobody was walking and talking on their way back from the pub. Belfast was a dangerous place to be out after dark. Forget about the Good Friday agreement. Cam wished he'd swapped his baseball cap for an FDNY firefighter's cap at the opening ceremony. There weren't any IRA murals about killing firefighters. British soldiers and police? Ten a penny.

Cam scanned the road ahead. Mack covered their rear. They alternated who was looking where, checking street corners and the dark patches between streetlamps. A dog barked on the other side of the square. A dustbin was knocked over. A cat hissed. The dog barked again. The dustbin lid spun on the ground like a fifty-pence piece after a coin toss.

Dark windows hid behind closed curtains. Terrace houses looked threatening on either side of cobbled streets. Light from the occasional window reflected off the cobbles. Streetlamps shed pools of light that accentuated the darkness between them. The dog barked again, then the cat hissed, and the dog yelped. Game over. Then there was only silence.

Cam let out a sigh. "Maybe it's nothing."

Mack said, "We're here to play tennis. Not do police stuff."

Cam nodded. "We're retired. Yes, I know."

Mack looked at his friend. "Stop acting like you're still in the job, then."

Now that it had stopped raining, Cam unzipped his collar slightly and stepped out from under the tree. Somewhere in the distance, there was a squeal of tyres. Further along Fitzroy Avenue. The cat and the dog had stopped waging war. Mack joined Cam walking down Fitzroy Avenue. Towards the squealing tyres.

The itch on the back of Cam's neck returned. He stopped and held an arm out to block Mack. The tyres stopped squealing. There was a moment's peace, then gunshots lit up the night. The muzzle flashes were just out of sight past a bend in the road. The shots echoed off the houses either side of the street.

Cam and Mack ducked in unison, then dived into the nearest front yard. Behind a low brick wall and a line of dustbins. The gunshots only lasted a few seconds before being replaced by more screeching tyres, then even that faded, and Fitzroy Avenue fell into an uneasy silence. After a reasonable pause for safety, doors began to open as neighbours came out to see what the commotion was about. The locals had lived through years of conflict. They knew not to look outside until the drive-by had driven by.

Mack was the first to stand up. Cam followed him down the street towards the hotel. It didn't surprise him to see where the gunshots had been fired. A cloud of smoke still hung in the air outside Kate's BnB, but there were no bodies. No blood on the pavement. One of Kate's garden gnomes had taken two in the chest, and a faded ornamental wheelbarrow had lost its wheel. There was a swirl of skid marks, two houses past the hotel. The car had done a wheely as it squealed away. Exhaust fumes and cordite contaminated the night air.

Kate stood on the doorstep with her hands on her hips. "Bloody hooligans."

Cam glanced at the bullet hole in their bedroom window, then looked at Mack. "Where do you think Kate's BnB fits on the list of most bombed hotels?"

Mack looked at Cam. "They didn't bomb it."

Cam indicated the dead gnome. "Tell that to Shawnessy over there."

Mack said, "I'll tell it to the Indians. If they try and get a rain delay."

Cam was scanning the street in the direction they had come from. He was thinking about the face he hadn't noticed, making a phone call next to the Beer and Boxty sign. He wished he'd been paying more attention instead of dodging potholes in the road. Because no matter what Mack said, he still felt like he was in the job.

*　*　*

Overnight rain cleared the air but did nothing to clear the atmosphere. Kate made light of the shooting. She had lived here long enough to know there was no point fretting unless people were dead. The only casualty yesterday had been the garden gnome. Her insurance would cover any other damage. Cam and Mack had a different technique for minimizing the stress. They played tennis.

Belfast Boat and Sports Club glistened in the morning sunlight, the rain having cleaned the tennis courts and washed away the gloom. It was a bright and sunny day. The clear blue sky was a complete reversal of yesterday's weather. There were no more grey clouds. Everyone seemed happy. As Mack had said during breakfast. "Let the games begin."

Cam had a ten o'clock singles. Mack didn't play his first round until eleven thirty. The main event wasn't until the afternoon. The Men's Doubles. Despite only winning bronze last time, their history made them the Number One Seeds.

They both won their singles matches in the morning. That was enough practice for the afternoon. They ate a light lunch and relaxed on the clubhouse balcony. Mack was checking out the female competitors in the Open category. He wasn't interested in the age bracket The Two Kevins were in; Fifty to sixty years. Cam leaned on the balcony rail and scanned the grounds. There was no sign of the skanky-looking fella from yesterday, but that didn't mean he wasn't here.

Mack misunderstood Cam's reluctance to talk. "We've got this Cam. If you play like you did in the singles, you can carry me through anything."

Cam turned away from the balcony rail. "Including the Indians?"

Mack smiled. "The Indians didn't come. That's why we're Number One Seeds."

Cam returned the smile. "We'll just have to beat the Germans again then."

Mack nodded. "Third time in a row. Bring it on."

Cam said, "Getting us in the first round? They won't like that."

"Auf Wiedersehen to them."

"Damn right."

They beat the German pair in straight sets, making everybody happy except the Germans. The good thing about developing a nickname like The Two Kevins is, people remember you. Winning four gold medals, three silvers and two bronze over the last ten years elevated you to legendary status. The trouble with being a legend is, somebody always wants to knock you down. The person who wanted to knock The Two Kevins down was the skanky-looking fella watching through binoculars across the river.

Cam wouldn't see him again until after the boxing later that night.

It wasn't the only thing Cam was going to see.

***

Ulster Hall seemed like an odd choice of venue for the WPFG boxing event. The imposing Victorian music hall had hosted classical concerts, pop music, and theatrical presentations. Having seventy-eight cops and firefighters beat the crap out of each other on a purpose-built boxing ring was a lot less esoteric, and listening to eight hundred spectators baying for blood was a lot less musical. Cam could hear the chanting from the street as he and Mack queued to get in.

Cam said, "We're late."

Mack turned to Cam. "You're the one wanted to walk."

"It's a clear night. And I didn't realise it was so far."

"It's just as far as the Europa Hotel, two streets over."

Cam shrugged. "Point taken."

Mack patted his friend on the back. "It's only the undercard anyway. The big hitters are on later."

Cam smiled. "Like The Two Kevins this afternoon, following the singles in the morning."

Mack showed their tickets at the door. "Exactly like that."

Two armed officers from the PSNI stood guard under the wrought iron and glass canopy. The Police Service of Northern Ireland was the rebranded Royal Ulster Constabulary, since the RUC had a brutal reputation before the Good Friday agreement had calmed things down. Judging by the other chanting Cam could hear, things in Belfast hadn't calmed down much. Police barriers blocked access to Belfast City Hall further along the road. Protesters were already in fine voice. It sounded like they were baying for blood, too.

Cam indicated the noise outside City Hall. "At least it will be gum shields, not riot shields at the boxing."

Mack shrugged. "It's Belfast. We're a hundred yards from the City Hall riot, and a hundred and fifty yards from the most bombed hotel in the world."

Cam glanced along Franklin Street across the road. The dogleg into Amelia Street hid the Europa Hotel, but there was no hiding the fact that it was there. Everywhere in Belfast was a reminder of its violent past. Between the boxing inside Ulster Hall and the protesters down the street, it sounded like violence was very much in the present.

At least everyone had dressed up to come out for the boxing. Everyone except Skanky Man watching from the window of Harlem Café next door. He waited until Cam and Mack had climbed the stairs into Ulster Hall, then took out his phone.

* * *

Boxing, bombs, and topspin lobs. Overall, that was fairly accurate. Tonight, it would only be two out of three. Mack checked the seating plan while Cam bought the drinks. Coca-Cola for Cam. A pint of bitter for Mack. They didn't serve Tetley's. Both drinks were served in plastic cups to prevent breakage. Probably to stop anyone getting glassed in the face if tempers frayed.

Cam found Mack at the bottom of the stairs to the all-around balcony seating. He handed Mack the beer. "Pint of something-or-other bitter."

He showed Mack his Coca-Cola. "Glass of make-it-around-the-back Cola."

Mack waved the tickets at the stairs. "Royal Box seating."

They both laughed. Ulster didn't support Royal anything. Mack led the way. At the top of the stairs, an usher wearing a bright green jacket and a pointy hat pointed them in the right direction after checking their seat numbers.

"Door F. Around the other side."

Mack thanked the usher and followed the corridor along the back of the concert hall. The chanting had stopped, but there were plenty of oohs and aahs, and lots of leather slapping skin. Even the undercard hit hard. These *were* cops and firefighters. If you could carry an eighteen stone deadweight out of a fire, you could punch like a bulldozer.

The doors along the balcony corridor were open for ventilation. Boxing was a sweaty endeavor, and baying for blood while drinking something-or-other bitter produced interesting smells as well. Cam and Mack stood at Door F and watched from the corridor. The main hall was tall and impressive. There were ornate windows, arched cornices with painted landscapes, and crystal chandeliers. Central lighting arrays hung from pulleys over the boxing ring. From up here, the ring seemed small, but Mack knew from experience that being punched in the face for three minutes made the ring feel as big as a football pitch. He would much rather lose a tennis match.

A little man in a brightly colored waistcoat stood beside the door. He stepped aside to let Cam and Mack go through. Cam held up his drink.

"Thanks. We'll finish these first."

The little fella sized up The Two Kevins. "You're not checking the form, are you? Official betting is only allowed down the bookies."

Mack craned his neck to get a look at the ring. Two women were dancing around and punching each other in the face. Mack looked at the little fella. "Three, three-minute rounds? Not sure what odds we'd get on that."

The waistcoat gave the man away. "You'd be amazed what you can bet on if you ask the right person."

Waistcoat Man gave Mack a sly wink. "If you go online, you could bet against the sky being up and the ground being down, and have a fair chance of winning, whichever you choose."

Mack said, "You mean the bets are rigged?"

"I mean, you can bet on the Grand National, the Police/Fire Games, or how many lampposts will get smashed at the City Hall."

Cam was thinking about the skanky-looking man who had been watching The Two Kevins ever since they'd started practicing for the tennis. "What about who will *lose* the Police/Fire Games?"

Waistcoat Man looked at Cam. "Win, lose or draw. Doesn't matter. You could bet an accumulator of who will lose, *and* how many lampposts will get smashed. It's all the same to the Dark Web."

Cam said, "I thought the Dark Web was an illegal part of the internet for drugs, guns and counterfeit passports."

Waistcoat Man shrugged. "Darkish web then. Under the radar bets on things you don't want to admit you know about. Like how many paedophiles it takes to screw a lightbulb?"

Cam was thinking about the first time he'd seen Skanky Man. Long before the street kids and the tennis club. "Like, how many times has the Europa Hotel been blown up?"

Waistcoat Man shook his head. "No point betting on that. Everybody knows it's been bombed thirty-six times."

Cam said, "Unless it's with an accumulator."

Waistcoat Man said, "Accumulating with what?"

A couple of numbers popped into Cam's head. Thirty-seven to one. Thirty-seven times for the bombing, and one time, The Two Kevins would lose in the doubles. If they got caught in the blast at the hotel.

Cam turned to Mack. "Where were you planning on having a drink after the boxing?"

Mack knew where Cam was going with that. "Are you thinking about thirty-seven?"

Cam said, "I'm thinking I'd like to see what accumulator bets have been laid today. And what the deadline is."

Deadline was probably a poor choice of words. Especially after Waistcoat Man had shown Cam what was on the Darkish web. He remembered hearing stories about unscrupulous bookmakers watching racehorses through binoculars. There was a scandal at the World Cup one year, where a team coach had been spying on the opposing team's training session the day before the big match. He thought Skanky Man might have been spying on The Two Kevins ever since they'd had a drink at the Europa Hotel.

"How many times?"

"Thirty-six bomb attacks during The Troubles, but half of them were out in the street."

Bombs in the street weren't new in Belfast, but putting the Number One Seeds off their game before the big match was a new low for the WPFG.

Whether they got caught in the blast or not. The perfect distraction was taking place right now, outside Belfast City Hall.

He looked at Waistcoat Man. "What's the route for the protest, once they leave City Hall?"

* * *

Boxing, bombs, and topspin lobs, Part Two. The race against time. That felt a lot more appropriate. Cam checked the accumulator that had been placed by an unknown Irishman. Everybody was unknown on the Darkish Web. You could bet on the president getting shot, and then shoot the president. Nobody would be any the wiser. Even your bank details were confidential. It was the ultimate website for shitbags and vagabonds. Most of them probably looked skanky.

Cam put his drink on a narrow table and looked at Mack. "We're going to have to act like we're still in the job, one last time."

Mack put his drink down, too. The expression on his face told the story. You can leave the job behind, but the job never leaves you. He nodded and let out a sigh. "Let's get the security detail from the front door."

Cam had other ideas. "Let's get a disguise. I'm tired of being watched by a fella who needs a bath. It's time we started watching him."

Mack said, "Where do you think he is?"

Cam thought about that for a moment. "He'll have watched us come in. So, my money's on the café next door."

Mack persisted. "Ideal target for the security detail at the front door."

He put added weight in his voice. "The *armed* security detail."

He held open his jacket. "We are not armed."

Cam nodded. "Okay. But he won't be there now. We need to find him, without him finding us."

Mack followed Cam's gaze to the usher at the top of the stairs. "Disguise?"

Cam looked at the bright green jacket and the pointy hat. "Leprechaun."

* * *

The chanting had shifted away from Belfast City Hall and was moving along Grosvenor Road towards Great Victoria Street. The Europa Hotel was thirty yards down Great Victoria Street, opposite Fibber Magee's and The Crown Liquor Saloon. Several lampposts had already been smashed, along with two windows in the Howard Street Post Office and the front door of The Flint Hotel. Nobody had placed any bets about The Flint Hotel, but the most bombed hotel in the world? That was a different matter.

Cam and Mack took the shortcut through Franklin Street and the dogleg into Amelia Street. A few hangers-on had had the same idea, the narrow backstreet feeling congested for ten o'clock on a midweek night. The security detail outside Ulster Hall had contacted their superiors. PSNI were deploying three police vans and the Bomb Squad. Silent approach, the police tactic of approaching an ongoing crime without blue lights and sirens. In this instance, silent approach also meant deploying two undercover leprechauns.

Mack and Cam separated as they neared the end of Amelia Street. Skanky Man had been used to observing The Two Kevins as a pair. Approaching the Europa Hotel as individuals gave them a better chance of spotting the target before he put two and two together. Or rather, putting one and one together, making The Two Kevins.

There had been heated discussions about whether to evacuate the hotel and the neighbouring buildings, but the police commander on the ground had decided against it. If the police were seen to move too early, it might prompt the suspect to set off the bomb. From Cam's description, the man might be skanky, but he didn't look like a suicide bomber. There were no telltale twitches or nervous glances. He had been calm and focussed, and not afraid to use his phone. The commander was betting that the phone was the trigger the police would need to neutralize. Before you could neutralize the trigger, though, you had to find the triggerman. Finding the triggerman was down to a pair of Yorkshire leprechauns.

Cam was the first to come out of Amelia Street. He turned right with the rest of the hangers-on, keeping to the opposite side of the road to the hotel. Mack was a few seconds behind him, crossing Great Victoria Street to keep a reasonable distance between them. Anybody looking wouldn't be able to see them both in the same glance without scanning left and right. The triggerman had never had to scan left and right before, because The Two Kevins had always been joined at the hip. Until tonight.

Mack stood in the doorway of the Great Northern Mall, next to the Europa Hotel. The shopping centre was closed, but the awning of Caffe Nero provided some cover. He scanned the street all the way to the junction with Grosvenor Road. The protesters were beginning to surge around the corner. Chanting and airhorns made them sound like a football crowd. Another lamppost was smashed and wrestled to the ground.

Cam stood outside Fibber Magee's and ignored the crowd. He was more focussed on the Europa Hotel frontage. He had spent the last few years of his career with SOCO, examining scenes of crime and photographing any evidence that had been left behind. That meant he had mainly dealt with the aftermath, not the crime itself. Terrorism and suicide bombers were a fairly recent policing problem. Mack was the Kevin who knew what to look for.

While Cam had seen out his career in SOCO, Mack had been on two surveillance courses and an anti-terrorism course. Mack had become obsessed with the idea that if he stayed on the front line, he would probably get sacked for getting hands-on when the bosses were advocating hands-off. Grabbing a suspect by the scruff of the neck wasn't an approved restraint technique anymore. So, he had volunteered for whatever training course was available, one after the other. Leading to undercover surveillance and anti-terrorism. Bombs in bus shelters. Stuff like that.

There was a bus shelter right outside the Europa Hotel. With the only rubbish bin on Queen Victoria Street. Mack identified the bin as the only viable delivery method, then frantically tried to get Cam's attention. He waved his hand like a crazy leprechaun, without success. The other leprechaun had disappeared.

* * *

Cam saw the skanky-looking fella two minutes after the crowd of protesters came around the corner. A lamppost crashed to the ground. An upstairs window was smashed above Oracle Solicitors. As they used to say in those old Tarzan films, the natives were growing restless. Restless natives were the perfect diversion for a man planting a bomb outside the most bombed hotel in the world.

"Half of them were out in the street."

"Oh well, that's okay then."

It was not okay then. Skanky Man was watching the crowd, trying to find The Two Kevins and time his attack. He held his mobile phone down by his side. There was nobody to call tonight. It was just him and the crowd and a pair of Yorkshire tennis players.

Skanky Man concentrated on the crowd. Cam focused on the phone in Skanky Man's hand. Mack watched them both from across the street. He had spotted Cam moving in behind the man he assumed was the bomber. The description fit. Skanky. Needed a good wash. But, having been on two surveillance courses and an anti-terrorism course, he disagreed with Cam's assessment. This fella definitely looked like a suicide bomber. The rubbish bin in the bus shelter was no longer the only delivery method; Skanky Man could simply throw his arms around The Two Kevins and blow them all to kingdom come.

Mack whispered under his breath. "Don't get too close."

Cam was getting too close. From behind. If Skanky Man took one look over his shoulder, the accumulator would win. The Europa Hotel would hit thirty-seven, and The Two Kevins would lose the World Police/Fire Games. The only piece of optimism was that the man was watching the crowd. Until he seemed to sense something behind him and began to turn around.

Mack stripped off his green jacket and stepped into the road. He waved the jacket over his head and shouted. "Hey fuckface. Who do you think you're looking at?"

Fuckface didn't turn fully around, looking at the leprechaun in the middle of the street, waving his coat in the air instead. At first, the green pointy hat partially hid Mack's face, but then the hat was knocked off by the vigorous waving. He couldn't hear what Mack was shouting because of the crowd.

It was one of the Kevins. On his own. Skanky Man began to raise his phone. If he blew up one of the Kevins, the accumulator was still safe. You can't win a doubles match if you don't have a partner.

Mack's partner took advantage of the distraction and lunged at the man holding the phone. Cam employed a sweeping leg strike from behind, his left shin connecting with the back of Skanky Man's knees. Both legs buckled, dropping the bomber to the ground, but Cam couldn't reach the phone. Mack came charging across the street. Police sirens sounded as three police vans and the Bomb Squad saw what was happening.

Mack closed in from the front.

Cam scrambled to grab the phone from behind.

Skanky Man raised the phone and pressed a single button.

* * *

The thirty-seventh bomb attack at the Europa Hotel didn't go according to anybody's plan. Three police vans blocked Great Victoria Street. The Bomb Squad waited for the police to secure the area. Cameron and Mackenzie failed to stop Skanky Man from pressing the button, and Skanky Man failed to catch The Two Kevins in the blast. Cam had been right; he wasn't a suicide bomber. The bus shelter exploded in a colourful display that was nothing like the previous thirty-six bombs.

"Fireworks?" Cam was using an approved restraining method.

"You fucking idiot." Mack grabbed Skanky Man by the scruff of the neck.

The rubbish bin was blown apart by the force of the blast, but the fireworks display wouldn't hurt anybody that was more than six feet away. They didn't even break the bus shelter windows, let alone damage the Europa Hotel. Two passengers waiting at the bus stop got a bit of a fright, but they were only treated for shock and singed eyebrows.

Cam twisted Skanky Man's arm up his back. "You've been following us for three days, just so you could set off some fireworks?"

Skanky Man spoke as if the answer was obvious. "I just wanted to win a bet, not kill anybody."

110

Cam said, "The accumulator?"

Skanky nodded. "Thirty-seventh bomb attack. And the shock makes you lose your doubles match."

Cam said, "Because of the fireworks?"

Skanky gave an apologetic shrug. "It's the bang that makes you jump. That and the shot through your bedroom window."

"We weren't in the bedroom."

"Didn't want to shoot you by accident. Just put you off your game."

Mack let go of the man's neck. He snorted a laugh that had nothing to do with humour. "I've been petrol bombed, stabbed and hit with a cider bottle. Playing tennis is what calms us down."

Two uniformed police handcuffed the bomber and dragged him away. Cam struggled to get to his feet, then helped Mack up. He held one hand in the air, and Mack high-fived it. When they spoke, they spoke in unison. A true doubles team.

"Because The Two Kevins rule."

* * *

Ex Army, retired cop and former Scenes of Crime Officer. Colin Campbell is the author of British crime novels, *Blue Knight White Cross,* and *Northern Ex,* and US thrillers, *Jamaica Plain, Montecito Heights, Beacon Hill* and *Final Cut.* His Jim Grant thrillers bring a rogue Yorkshire cop to America, where culture clash and violence ensue. He has also written YA books, *Silent Flight Holy Night,* and *The Early Grave of Sophie Laville.* Away from writing, Campbell has played tennis for Yorkshire and represented Great Britain in the World Police/Fire Games, winning gold medals in Adelaide and Rotterdam. For more info, visit www.campbellfiction.com.

The Man With the Golden Racket

By Gary Phillips

Hands in the pockets of his tennis shorts, Randall Severs stood at the floor-to-ceiling window of the Emerald Shore Retirement Community. The main entrance to the complex was styled like a hotel with substantial columns and a circular driveway off a sloping roadway. At the other end of the roadway was a two-person guard casita and an imposing wrought iron gate controlled electronically.

Out the window, the EMTs were loading a gurney onto the open rear of an ambulance. The body on the stretcher was covered. Severs and the others standing or sitting in their wheelchairs, also at the lobby's big window, knew who was beneath the temporary shroud.

"Bob had a good run." Chuck Drayton declared, shaking his head side-to-side.

"Yes, he did," Jackie Windsor agreed. She leaned forward on her walker, eyes bright.

The EMTs got in the ambulance, and the rear doors closed. The vehicle slowly drove around the rest of the circle and left Emerald Shore.

"Folks, it's almost eleven. Time for tennis, pickleball, and the mindfulness class." Dedra Wheeler said from behind the gathered. She was the all-purpose, hard-working manager of the facility. "We will, of course, be acknowledging the departure of Bob Meadows at mealtime tonight.

"I wonder if he was watching porn when he stroked out," Drayton cracked to Severs. "I know that's the second way I want to go out."

"What's the first way, Chuck?" Severs said with a crooked smile

"Having a cigar and a shot of bourbon. I miss that more than I miss my second wife…almost." He amended.

Severs knew the old rascal kept a supply of generic Cialis handy. The pills weren't gathering dust. And Drayton wasn't the only elderly gent around here utilizing a steady supply. He got back on track, tapping the senior's shoulder. "Ten minutes, okay?":

"Righty-O," Drayton replied. He moved off fluidly, his replacement knees operating smoothly.

Walking along, Severs paused at the entrance to the room where several residents, including Windsor, were filing in. He and Harv Kreuger exchanged curt nods. Krueger was one of Emerald Shore's staffers. He was setting up the accoutrement of the mindfulness instructor. This included a good-sized gong and color xeroxes displayed on foam boards. The reproductions depicted seemingly unrolled ancient scrolls with phrases on them like 'If you can't do anything about it, then let it go." A rhythmic raga flowed from the speakers in here. The teacher stood in the corner, gathering herself. She was a middle-aged woman named Holcomb, just the one word. Severs knew from his conversations with some of the residents the sessions were a combination of talks of inner enlightenment and breaking into groups to play mahjong. Recalling the characters and suits of the tiles was good for the memory. On he went.

Getting outside, he walked past the area reserved for the Tai Chi practitioners in the early morning. Now, at this time of day, the space was taken over by the shuffleboard players. He arrived at the tennis courts. One of the courts was occupied by the pickleball players. Severs provided lessons for that as well on the weekends. But tennis remained his first love since high school. Two of his regulars were already there. One was the late seventies Becky Staller, whose silver hair went past her shoulders. As usual, she'd put it in a ponytail to play. With her was Stan Woodly. He had a pacemaker and, for most of his life, had been heavyset. Had in fact played semi-pro football decades before. But post a heart attack and implant, had slimmed down considerably. They were dressed in their togs, and soon Drayton had joined them, also changed for his tennis lesson.

"Looks like we're ready." Woodly announced.

"Okay, let's pick up where we left off last week," Severs said.

"Charging the net?" Drayton said.

"Show off," Staller said. "You just wait until I have my replacement surgery. I'll be running circles around you."

Drayton answered. "Looking forward to it, darling."

"Don't make me call HR on your sexist ass."

"It would be the most excitement I'll have had in a month," he shot back.

"If we might focus like a laser," Severs said good-naturedly. "Becky, how about you first?"

"Yes, maestro." She said.

She got in position, and the other two seniors stood on the sideline to watch. Severs started his lobs. Staller and the others today worked on their two-handed backhand strokes. Sure, his pupils weren't going to storm the senior open any time soon, but they were able for their ages, and enthusiastic Severs noted.

Afterward, as they toweled off and sipped from their water bottles, Stalker remarked, "Do they have some sort of special ceremony for guys like Bob?"

"Like putting a star on n a wall of them at the CIA?" Woodly said.

"What are you guys talking about?" Severs asked.

"Bob had been a Secret Service agent," Drayton said.

"Guarded JFK, among other politicians," Staller said. "That's John Fitzgerald Kennedy, young man," she told Severs. "He was the president of this here country of ours. Lord, but we'll never see his like again."

Severs was in his fifties, grey streaking his once coal colored hair. "I knew who you meant," he said. "You're not trying to tell me Bob was there that day in Dallas?"

"Yep," Drayton confirmed. "He was on the outer ring of the detail, but he was there. He wasn't that poor devil who jumped onto the Lincoln as the bullets destroyed Kennedy. Read, he was haunted the rest of his life; he couldn't save him."

"If only there was a way we could find out about honors for ex-Secret Service members." Woodly was searching the internet on his phone. After they all read the information on his phone, they determined that Bob Meadows, a veteran, was eligible for interment at Arlington National Cemetery.

"He didn't have family, did he?" Staller said as they walked off the courts. The pickle ballers were still going at it.

"Wife passed some time ago," Woodly said.

"No kids of their own," Drayton added.

Staller said, "What about the nephew who used to come around?"

"But not for some time."

"Right," Drayton drawled, a far away look on his face.

"Good session today, guys," Severs said, waving goodbye and starting toward the parking lot.

"Say, Randy, can I buy you lunch?" Drayton came toward him. "I mean a real lunch. The Sour Apple."

"Sure. I wouldn't turn down a free meal."

"Great."

The two left the Emerald Shore in their tennis gear. Severs drove them to the restaurant, which was about a mile away in a sprawl of a shopping complex off an exit of the freeway. A number of other residents of the complex were having their lunch here too.

Noting this, Drayton said, "Whoever thought I'd get to the age when the big outing for the day was to a restaurant."

Severs chuckled.

"I know," the older man said, "consider the alternative."

They got seated in a booth. Perusing the menu, Severs said, "So what's on your mind, Chuck?

"It's that obvious, huh?" He put down the menu he was scanning. "It's about Bob. Or rather, it's about his, what do you call it, his effects."

"You mean he left a diamond ring behind, and he promised it to you?"

Drayton smiled. "I'm figuring this might be worth more than one damn diamond."

"Maybe I'll have the Cajun chicken quesadilla. Have you had that? Sorry," he said, holding up a hand deferentially, "What were you saying?"

"It's about JFK," Drayton said solemnly.

"Wait, you said this was about Bob's things."

"Exactly. The golden racket."

The waitress came and took their orders. Drayton resumed after she left. "When Kennedy was in office, the Shah of Iran, who we helped to take power via the CIA in the '50s, came to Washington for a visit. Him and the queen. Though I don't recall her name just off the top of my head. But I digress as old folks tend to do."

Prompting him, Severs said, "The golden racket."

"Right. Bob had it. At least he said he had it. And he wasn't given to bullshit. Square shooter and all that. See, it was a gift to JFK from the Shah. He was apparently an avid tennis player and had a tennis court at his palace. And despite his back problems, Kennedy played tennis as well."

"In between schtupping Marilyn Monroe?" Severs said. A grainy black-and-white film clip reeled in his head. The famous blonde actress singing a sexy Happy Birthday to Kennedy. Where had he seen that? Severs focused like a laser.

"Now who's digressing?" Drayton jibbed.

"Ya got me."

Drayton continued. "After his death, a lot of Kennedy's personal belongings were scattered everywhere. Of course Jackie O, his widow, had an allotment of his things. Others got auctioned off. But, hell, there was this advisor of his who for years had a bunch of his stuff, and nobody knew it. My point is," he said, waving a hand, "his things were not properly catalogued in any way."

"You've been researching this," Severs declared.

"Damn right I have. That is, since Bob told me about the racket."

"When did he do this?"

"About a month ago, he'd gotten the word from his doc and knew his time was, well, almost here to depart the emerald shore for the vast sea beyond."

"And he told you about the racket?"

"He was a little tight, but yeah."

"He was drinking?"

"We both were. A previously opened bottle of Macallan 25 he'd tucked away." A wistful look came and went from Drayton's face as if recalling the bliss induced by sipping scotch. "He was lamenting he had no one except for a handful of us at the Shore who would be sad to see him go. Naturally, as he went on, he talked about his possessions, how he wanted them to go somewhere…with someone. Like his good commendation letters from the Secret Service and what have you."

Severs asked, "How did Bob get the racket?"

Drayton frowned, trying to dredge up the memory. "I'm sure he told me, I think there was a general involved. I don't recall the convoluted particulars. Guess once I heard there were diamonds embedded around the racket's head, the glitter shined too bright in my head." He offered a weak smile.

"But he promised you the racket?" Severs asked dubiously.

"I'm not saying he said that. He did say he had his valuables in a storage place, including the golden racket, along with goodies like an autographed gun given to him by Clint Eastwood. Clint played a Secret Service agent once, and Bob was one of the technical advisors on the film. He visited the set and made an impression on Clint, it seems."

Their food arrived, and they continued talking as they ate.

Severs said, cutting a section off his quesadilla, "I'm guessing you brought up the racket to him again after your scotch jamboree."

"I did. But he was being coy. He teased me. Said he was going to get Harv or one of the others to drive him to the locker so he could inventory everything. Then decide who got what. I could see my best bet was not to bug him about it since he knew I was salivating for the racket."

Severs said, "How much you think you can sell it for? What do you think it weighs? Gold is sold by the ounce, isn't it?"

Spooning in a portion of his vegetarian chili, Drayton said, "I don't want it to sell it. I want it for the secrets in it."

"Huh?" Severs said, chewing.

"You know those JFK assassination files which were released not long ago?"

"No, but go ahead."

"Well, they were. Buried in all those reams of paper, if you were to print them out, I mean, there're memos about Kennedy memorabilia."

"Related to his assassination?"

Deayton gestured with both palms up. "There you have it."

"You lost me."

"Remember what I said about the Shah and the CIA?'

"Yeah."

"In the handle of the racket was a capsule with several microdots in it."

"Have you been skipping your meds, Chuck?"

"I know it sounds like I've spent too much time online, but this is verified by several articles I read from reliable sources."

"On the internet?"

"On the internet."

"Doesn't that say it all?" Severs said.

"The microdots are of documents laying out the various dirty deeds of the CIA."

"There's plenty of movies and books about that," Severs pointed out. "My sister's big on that mess."

Drayton tapped the table. "This ain't mess, this here is real."

"This wonderful golden racket of yours likely doesn't exist."

"Why don't we find out?"

Severs said, "How exactly?"

"When a resident of the Shore dies, and there's no one around to claim their knickknacks, they're boxed up and held for thirty days. When time's up, and there's been no takers, their possessions are given to Goodwill. What they don't accept is thrown out."

"Bob's nephew will be contacted," Severs pointed out.

"He's struggled with drugs. That's why he hasn't been around."

"Bob told you?"

"He did," Drayton allowed. "If they do find the nephew, time will probably have run out anyway. Whatever they boxed up from his apartment has to include paperwork about the storage facility and a key to the padlock to Bob's unit."

The old fella amused Severs. "Where's the boxes kept at the Shore?"

"Next to Dedra's office."

Severs chuckled. "Don't worry, Chuck, I'll ask her to increase your doses." He didn't wait for a comeback. "How do you plan to break into her office?"

"This is the Shore we're talking about. There's no bars on the windows. Which are mostly the sliding types in vinyl frames. Easy-peasy to overcome the latches. We had to do it all the time back when I was working. The room where they keep the dearly departed's junk looks out on a breezeway. And knowing Dedra as we both do, she'll have each box marked so it'll be a breeze to find the right one."

"I see what you did there," Severs said dryly. He knew Drayton had been a developer. Familiar with the layout of the Emerald Shore, he said, "That'll be in full view of the apartments across the way."

"Those curtains are drawn at night," Drayton responded. "Seniors like their privacy. Except maybe for Grant, but he's in the other wing." Grant Holcomb had been a nudist for many decades. He had to be reminded now and then, parading around in the buff, Emerald Shore was not the place for such "freedom."

"If you have this all mapped out, Chuck, what do you need me for?

"The window is high enough off the ground I can't get into it without help, seeing as how I'm not as spry as I used to be. Plus, even if I got into the window dropping down on the other side, my new knees can take it, but these ankles of mine, not so much. Shoot, I have to prepare stepping off certain curbs as it is."

Severs responded. "Isn't your best bet to let this go and concentrate on your backhand. Which is improving."

Drayton leaned forward. "You're not getting what I'm saying, Randy. The documents on the microdot reveal a section of the CIA that not only engineers assassinations but conducts them as well. Conducts them not just on foreign soil but domestically as well." He sat back, eyes gleaming at Severs.

It took him a moment to grasp where his aging lunch companion meant. "Oh, you're saying this information would prove they killed Kennedy."

Drayton nodded vigorously. "A cabal of intelligence personnel and big money."

"That's not exactly a new revelation."

"The Shah learned from what happened to Mossadegh. That's the guy the CIA overthrew in a coup to bring Palavi, the Shah, to power. He figured if they could do that to his opponent, they could do it to him should the U.S. get tired of him. Look what happened to Noriega in Panama."

"Sounds logical," Severs admitted.

Continuing, Drayton said, "According to what I understand, the Shah put his secret police boys on the task, and after some years, they were eventually able to groom double agents inside Central Intelligence. Kenedy knew what he was getting as the gift. The Shah was warning him."

"What makes you think your magic capsule is still in the handle?"

Drayton wagged his finger side-to-side. "Kennedy accessed the info but kept the microdots in the handle. Hide in plain sight. He knew the CIA had the lowdown on his various affairs. Some of that from Hoover and his FBI. Anyway, he must have assumed between the two agencies, they were aware of his hidey holes. Therefore," he shrugged, "keep it in the handle."

"Hell of a story, Chuck."

"That's it? That's all you've got to say?"

"Okay if I order dessert?"

Drayton sagged, letting out an audible sigh. "Fine, why not?"

He was pleased two days later when Severs called him and said he'd help him break into the storage room.

"I found a picture online from *Time Magazine* of the Shah giving the gold racket to Kennedy," he told Drayton. "Whether the handle has the microdots or not, a hunk of glorified jewelry of diamonds and gold is hard to resist," Severs added. "Especially at my age and cobbling together a living, giving tennis lessons all over the place."

"That's the spirit," Drayton said.

Early morning past two, they were creeping along on the appropriate breezeway. Severs was taller than Drayton and was able to reach up with a screwdriver to remove the screen. Then, guided by Drayton, who whispered, got the sliding window unlatched. Gravel lined the ribbon between the edge of the breezeway and the wall. Severs got a foot on the wall and, having hold of the bottom of the window frame, hauled his body up and inside. He used the flashlight on his smartphone to look over the boxes. There weren't that many boxes, as Bob Meadows was the only deceased resident for this week. Such wasn't always the case.

"What are you doing out here this time of night, Chuck?" Severs went stone upon hearing, faintly, the voice from outside. He tapped off the light. Hurrying back to the window, he reached up and slid it closed.

"Ha, you caught me, Sheila," he heard Drayton reply. Feet scuffled across the concrete, getting closer, he estimated.

Drayton said, "I sneaked out to have a smoke." Emerald Shore was a no smoking facility.

"What's that screen doing on the ground?" she asked.

"You got me. Maybe somebody was replacing it and didn't put it back correctly? And what brings you out here this fine evening?"

"Oh, these damn leg cramps wake me up. I find if I take a slow walk, it helps calm my mind, which in turn eases the muscle tension."

"Have you tried those magnesium chews? They're supposed to help."

"They work off and on for me."

"Hey, how about some company on your walk?"

"Sure, that would be great." Together, their footfalls faded away.

Severs put the light back on. The boxes weren't taped closed, only the flaps folded under each other. A small box atop larger ones yielded a set of keys. And on his second search of a larger box, he found an NCR receipt from Everlast Storage. Not wishing to chance climbing back out and being spotted, he waited for Drayton's return. About twenty minutes later, some gravel was tossed against the window glass.

"The coast is clear," Drayton said from outside.

He was soon back outside. "Got it," he said quietly to Drayton

"What I tell you, easy as pie."

Off they went. The storage facility had a drop arm barrier where a code could be typed in to gain entry. Bob Meadows had written it down on the receipt. Severs typed it in and up went the arm. They drove in. As Severs guided the car along a wide strip of macadam between two rows of storage unit buildings, sensors activated lights illuminating the way. They were also aware of the presence of cameras.

"There it is," Drayton said, pointing out the side passenger window. Each set of buildings with units were marked with a combination letter and a number. There were also passageways leading into the buildings' interiors.

Severs parked, and they got out of the car.

"Oh, baby," Drayton said, rubbing his hands. It was cold enough that his breath was visible under the yellow lighting. He had the keys and had already identified which one as the padlock was a Masterlock—the name on it and the key. Up they rolled the door. Severs put his phone's flashlight back on.

"Look at that, just like him to have this in order like he kept his place," Drayton observed. Whatever wasn't boxed was piled neatly. They both moved about, sifting piles and looking around, the flashlight's beam like a searchlight seeking survivors.

"Come to papa," Drayton said, reaching for a towel-sized furniture pad wrapped around an object. This was on a stack of boxes. He unwrapped it, letting the pad fall to the ground. He held the golden racket. Severs stepped closer, the racket incandescent in the light.

"Son of a bitch," Severs said, admiring the artifact. Gingerly, he touched it, letting his fingers glide along the gold wire of the racket head's strings. Sure enough, there were small diamonds studded around the head.

"What do you think it's worth?" he said, taking hold of the racket. "It's heavy."

"Millions, I suppose, if it went to auction," Drayton hazarded. "Considering its pedigree."

"Right," a mesmerized Severs agreed as Drayton took it back. "Hey, see if the bottom of the handle unscrews."

Drayton gripped the tennis instructor's arm. "You hear that?"

"What?"

In a rasp he said, "The only thing I got left that works unaided is my hearing. Douse the light."

Severs did as Drayton moved to the doorway. He peeked past it back toward the way they'd come. "I think there's a car down there. Heard it approach. Lights off, but the motor's running."

"Somebody else making a midnight excursion." Severs was beside him.

"Can that buggy of yours be started remotely?" Drayton asked.

"Yeah." He had the fob out and pressing a button, the car started.

"Let's get to scootin', son," Drayton said.

They stepped out, Drayton holding the golden racket. A sound like angry hornets flitting about furiously in a jar sounded twice. The back window of Severs' car exploded.

"They're shooting at us. Suppressors." Moving fast for a man of his years, Drayton was around the front of the car and dashing into the passageway of the building opposite. Severs was close behind him as the quieted shots continued. He put the flashlight back on as they hustled along the corridor. They got to a corner and went to the right onto another corridor.

"I was hoping there'd be a fire door," Drayton said. "By code, there should be one, but of course, it's a cut-rate outfit."

"We've got to hide, Chuck."

"There," Drayton said. In here, there were no roll-up doors, simply regular ones. Several weren't padlocked. They entered a tight cavity. Severs extinguished the light. The door was closed.

"Try to breathe normally," Drayton advised in the dark.

Severs gasped, "You were in the service, huh, Chuck. Saw combat?"

"Yeah. Now be as quiet as you can. Think, and it'll be so."

Despite wanting to pee on himself, Severs was impressed the old man could quote one of Holcomb's homilies. He shut his eyes, concentrating and praying not to be sent to the big tennis court in the sky just yet. He could hear footsteps out there. Two of them? Shit. They were going to open each unlocked door. Shit.

A whoosh of air as the door was flung open to blinding light. More angry hornets. Severs had never been shot before, but he knew instantly that's what just happened to him. He staggered back into the deceased Bob Meadows' possessions, upsetting several boxes. Lurching sideways, he watched as seconds elapsed in stuttering motion, Chuck Drayton delivering the best backhand in the world. The golden racket bashed the face of the first attackers. This man faltered, colliding with the second attacker. Drayton took hold of the first attacker's gun hand. Stunned by the older man's prowess, Severs marveled at him twisting that arm forcefully. Then Drayton's hand gripped the other's gun hand, causing the first attacker to shoot his companion. The gun was then somehow in Drayton's hand, and he shot the first attacker. They lay still in the corridor.

"Were you a Green Beret?" Severs muttered. "Who were those guys?"

"I'd say Putin's boys. Possibly aided by the like-minded in Washington."

"I don't understand," Severs stammered.

"I wonder how they got onto me?" Drayton said, distracted. "Guess I am losing a step or two. Not as careful as I used to be erasing my trail."

"What are you talking about, Chuck?"

Drayton regarded the wounded man. "If they hadn't shown up, I'd have gotten what I wanted and would have let you keep the racket to do with as you wished." He made a sound in his throat. "I'm sure sorry about this, kid. I really am. You were always okay, Randy. Never talked down to us like we were feeble-minded. And hell of an instructor. My game noticeably improved under your tutelage."

With effort, Severs sat upright on the floor against the upset boxes. "I don't know what you're talking about, Chuck. But how about calling an ambulance? Pretty sure I'm in need of urgent care." He tried to laugh but didn't have the strength.

"Since learning about the microdots in it, I've been after the golden racket for a number of years, Randy."

He continued to stare at him uncomprehendingly. His side was hurting.

"In addition to the intelligence apparatus on those documents was a kind of addendum. A list of sleeper agents. Not as detailed as the main components, but there nonetheless. Of course, most of those sleepers are among the departed. But there's a few of us left. Guys like me who were the offspring of the originals. Yet remain true believers, can you dig it? Leninists, the hippie leftists would have called us."

"You're a spy, Chuck?"

"Yeah. Despite Putin's efforts to root them out, there's those who are still hidden in plain sight. Who wait and plan in the homeland. And those of us here at the ready until our dying breath."

"I won't tell."

"I believe you, I really do, Randy. But you're alive, and there's too many questions the cops and eventually even the hobbled FBI will want answers." He breathed audibly. "Like I said, until my dying breath."

He bought the gun level and, with one shot, ended Randall Severs' life.

He cleaned his prints off the weapon and pressed it into the hand of the dead man it belonged to. There was already gunshot residue on the dead man's gun hand. Whoever sent them would cover their tracks with disinformation and elaborately constructed cyber rabbit holes. Drayton cleaned his prints off other surfaces. Thereafter, he erased the proceedings from the CCTV system in the office. He left in the intruders' car with the racket with its hollow cavity in the otherwise solid gold handle. The mystery of what happened here tonight was the topic of much speculation and vigorously expressed conspiracy theories during many a mealtime at the Emerald Shore Retirement Community.

* * *

Gary Phillips has written short stories featuring Old West lawman Bass Reeves, the Green Hornet and Kato, and his crime photographer Harry Ingram. His stories have appeared in *Ellery Queen Mystery Magazine*, *Dark Yonder*, and in the 2025 edition of *Best Mystery and Suspense*.

Disciples of the Game

By Linda Sands

It's not the first time I've woken to a strange ass in my face and probably won't be my last. At least it's a nice ass. I roll onto my back and stretch an arm, attempting to judge the distance to the mattress edge. It's not an exact science, as I'm neither certain of the size or shape of the bed, nor my placement in it. But my bladder beckons, so I go for two rolls—and land on my back. Hard enough to pop my spine and knock the wind out of me. One felt good. The other, not so much.

From somewhere in the tangled bed sheets, a deep voice mumbles, "Y'okay?"

"Yeah," I say when I can speak. "Miscalculated by a half-roll."

There's the rustle of sheets against skin, then a whispery woman's voice. "Are we having rolls?"

"None for me, Sadie," the third bedmate replies. "I'm on keto."

"Oh, for fuck's sake." Naked and fuzzy-brained, I sit up gingerly and consider the situation. On the job for less than a day and I've already lost more than I came to find. (My clothes, my memory, my dignity.) I squint into the dark. Definitely not my room. This is larger with a sitting area. And really good blackout drapes. The only light is a faint blue glow coming from what must be the bathroom.

I head that way collecting whatever clothes I come across. By the time I step from carpet to tile, the soft sounds of rustling sheets and murmuring voices has been replaced by snoring. Very loud, almost symphonic snoring. I close the bathroom door, flick on the light, and dump the armload of goods on a marble vanity as long as a breakfast bar. There are two sinks, plenty of counter space, and a stack of fluffy white towels on the open shelf below. The bathroom itself is bigger than my first apartment.

I find the toilet in its own closet-like room. As I enter, the light dims, and the seat rises, emitting a floral scent that matches the magnolia wallpaper. When I sit on the heated seat, there's the shush of waves lapping a shoreline. *What the actual fuck? A toilet with speakers? And a remote control?*

While being serenaded by Tuva throat singers, I sample every setting on the bidet and try to fill in the blanks of yesterday. The frenzied call from Willoughby, my boss at Elite Global Insurance Group, the shitty Uber to the airport, the three-wine flight to Flagstaff, followed by the speeding ride to Sedona with Steven, a tall, slim man with surprisingly short fingers.

Steven also runs security for our client, DOG A.K.A. Disciples of the Game, a secretive group of tennis aficionados known for The Smash Open, where billionaires sponsor extreme players in no-holds-barred matches. The players come for the money, the sponsors for the unique prize—that sometimes gets stolen.

This year, it's *The Ball,* valued at $250 million, insured by Elite Global, and recently authenticated as testing positive for the DNA of Michelle (Shelley) Exeter, the tennis icon better known as Shelley X. Besides being ugly, stained, and missing, the ball is said to hold magical or scientific powers (depending on who you ask).

* * *

"I've narrowed it down to three people who could have taken it," Steven said. "You're at their dinner table. Don't worry. It's not going to be like last time."

The last time I saw Steven, we were on a roof in Abkhazia with a crazed fan who'd stolen the prize tennis racket for that year's Smash Open. And not just any racket. It was *The Gut Racket*—a chromium-plated tubular steel Lacoste T2000 strung with the actual gut intestines of Vitas Gerulaitis—the tennis star who died a curious death in 1994. *Was there really a faulty propane pool heater?*

I'm pulled from my criminal reverie when the bidet's auto-flush feature activates, and a cool breeze on my nether regions brings me back to reality, Willoughby's voice in my ear. *Find The Ball or we're fucked.*

I hurry out to the vanity and sort through the toiletries spilled on the counter. Less for clues and more for hygiene. I borrow toothpaste, mouthwash, and an elastic for my thick brown hair. I can't find a brush, but on the shelf below, I find an unopened bottle of Don Julio 1942 behind the towels and a black mini-duffle bag on top of a plastic bin. I move the bag (so light it feels empty) and pop the lid of the bin. It's a glorified first-aid kit. From the basics—gauze pads, tape, bandages, and antiseptic cream to the not-so-usual—packets of powder with Chinese writing, syringes and vials, an elaborate IV kit from UDose, too many pill bottles with names I can't pronounce, and a suture kit fit for an operating room. It's more than anyone would need for a regular weekend getaway, but possibly not enough for this event.

I wonder if Shelley X would have played The Smash Open if she was alive. Part pure sport, part high-society ritual, and part gladiator arena, it feels pretty fucking fitting that the prize is *The Ball.*

From the moment Shelley X tucked that third Wilson US Open ball against her right thigh during her first championship match at Arthur Ashe Stadium in Flushing Meadows, she kept it for herself and never played a game without it. The ball became her touchstone. Her lucky charm. When the press asked her about the superstition, Shelley would simply reply, "Next question."

Instead of the normal one ball in hand and another tucked at the service line, up-and-coming players tried replicating the Shelly X third ball tuck. Most without success. But sales of compression shorts and Wilson Brand tennis balls skyrocketed.

Shelley carried that original third Wilson tennis ball against her right thigh for every match after that first win in the finals.

Medical experts created bands to simulate the ball's pressure points, while alternative healers cited the supernatural benefits of activated thigh meridians. Shelley didn't question why it worked. She just knew that when she played with that ball against her thigh, she was unbeatable.

The year she died, the cover of Time Magazine featured legendary Michelle Exeter, sole winner of the Golden Super Slam. Many a teen player had that poster of a sweaty, happy, Shelley X on a podium kissing a worn, nubby, stained, and faded, yellow tennis ball.

I finish poking around in the First Aid bin, put the lid on, and replace the duffle bag, pausing to run a finger over the intricate embroidered DOG logo. Everyone received a bag at the opening dinner. All evening, I'd seen them dangling from an arm or hanging off a shoulder. Later, I noticed a few bags left behind at dinner tables and on chairs in the lobby. Mine's here somewhere. *Focus, Sadie. What you need now is your dress and underwear, not commuter mugs and coozies.*

Raking through the pile of clothes on the counter, I lift a tiny red thong. *If these clothes could talk. Though that would be a short story.* I set aside a satin blouse, boxers printed with the words CHAMP CHAMP CHAMP, and a large, nude, padded bra. I find the red dress I'd worn to dinner twisted around a leg of khaki pants, and when I shake out a blue floral skirt, my La Perla bra and underwear set appear. I get dressed feeling like I've won some weird treasure hunt. Now to find my shoes and purse.

I turn off the light and step back into the bedroom, where someone has opened the drapes a crack. Got to say, the noise coming from the bed is quite impressive. Must be at least eighty decibels. (Think vacuum cleaner, or high-quality blender set to puree.) It reminds me of all the times my ex-husband accused me of snoring and keeping him up all night—to the point he recorded a *slight* whistling sound with every other exhale.

"Such a motherfucker."

"Who is?"

"Sorry. Did I say that out loud?"

"You did." McKinley Squire chuckles and rolls onto her back. Once a red-headed teen tennis prodigy, her now silver hair catches the single beam of morning light. Even with as little sleep as I know she had, she's gorgeous. A classic beauty. She glances at the petite blonde draped across the muscular chest of the man snoring beside her. Doesn't need to whisper but does, "You ready for this thing?"

"Me?" I whisper back, approaching the bed, searching the floor for my red pumps. "Shouldn't I be asking you that?"

She gives me the Squire Smirk. It's the look her opponents on the court get just before they lose to her. It's also her signature, her brand. Those facial muscles, that jaw, and her teeth? All insured and protected. As a trusted employee of Elite Global, I have access to such information. As Senior Investigator for the luxury lines division, I'm privy to so much more.

"I'm good," she says. "I've got a secret weapon." My heart jumps at the word *weapon*. But McKinley adds, "Some real *jeu de paume* shit." She points to the sitting area where a metal case shaped like a tennis racket rests on the ottoman.

One hundred and fifty years ago in France, the original DOG was formed to preserve *jeu de paume* or *real tennis*—a ball and court game where focus and strategy reined and The Golden Rule presided: *Do anything on the court that helps you win.* Over the years, the preservation of the game by these self-proclaimed tennis disciples became more about the brutality of the game—its physical and mental extremes—so much so that many call the group, The Disciples of The Grind.

With the modern focus less about rules and regulations, the DOG cut referees, umpires, and judges at their events. The net stayed, but the lines faded until a few years ago, when they too disappeared.

At The Smash Open, a player fights for the point using the tools of the trade as weapons of sport. Sharpened racquet handles, spiked balls, razor wire webbing, and hidden blades are not uncommon. Mental taunting and bullying, stalled plays, distractions? Anything goes. Extreme tennis is pure competition—at any cost—both on the court and in the stands. It draws a certain player: one that has nothing to lose and one that has everything to gain.

Before I can ask McKinley about the racket, there's a shout and the ceiling shakes as something heavy falls. A woman screams. It's the kind of scream bad actresses make on audition reels for horror films. There's more yelling and stomping, the sound of a door sliding on its tracks, and another scream as something crashes with a metal-on-metal sound.

Everyone's awake now. McKinley leaps from the bed and pulls back the drapes, flooding the room with light. I follow suit and drag the rest of them fully open to reveal more windows and a sliding glass door to a balcony. A balcony with a scraped and bent railing. A balcony on which a man suddenly appears and just as quickly disappears, vaulting over the railing to the ground below.

"Frankie! What the fuck?" The screaming woman goes from scared to pissed.

McKinley presses a hand to the window, shading her eyes. "Oooh. That's not good."

"Mc? Sadie? What's happening?" On the bed, the tousle-headed blonde kneels, attempting to cover her bits with a miniature pillow. Behind her, there's a flash of white ass cheek as the bronzed man flings off the sheets. "Crikey! Alison, am I heaps late? Who am I up against?"

I ignore them all and step onto the balcony. Above me on the third floor, a frantic young woman hangs over the railing. "Ohmygod, Frankie!" I don't recognize her blotchy, tear-stained face, but realize her *Frankie* is Francisco Gonzalez. Said to be Chile's competitive answer to Argentina's Guillermo Vilas, Frankie moved into extreme tennis from a life of extreme sports. With his parkour background, I'm certain descending two stories balcony-to-balcony-to-ground is a cakewalk.

So, I'm confused when I lean over the railing and see the inert body of a man clad in black silk pajamas on the grassy path below. There's a lot of shouting and people racing about as I consider whether the shattered flatscreen TV beside him is sixty or seventy-five inches. When Frankie rolls over, coughs, and sits up, reaching for his ankle, the crowd pulls back collectively. To experienced DOG spectators, this kind of drama is nothing new. Most of them simply walk away, not trying to hide their disappointment. Two petite women approach and try to help Frankie to his feet while the woman above says, "You're not dead? What the hell?" There's a bunch more *ohmygods* and a muttered "I told him not to take that shit from

Thorne," before the woman hurries back inside.

I do the same, closing the slider behind me. My bedmates stand at the window, each half-wrapped in palm-printed drapes, engrossed in the spectacle below. I say something about the time and needing to go, as I scan the sunlit room and find one of my shoes poking out from the bed like a scene from *The Wizard of Oz*. A swipe under the hanging coverlet scores the matching red pump tangled in the strap of another giveaway duffel bag. I step into the shoes, sling the bag over my shoulder, and make for the door, pausing at the foyer table to collect my purse and thankfully, my key card. It's still in its paper sleeve, my name and room inked on the cover: Sadie Montgomery Martin, 222.

"See you later," I call. "Thanks. It was fun."

As the door closes behind me, I wince. *It was fun? Thanks?* I never know what to say the morning after, which is why I usually avoid them, but this was work. *Sort of.* When I find my room ten doors down the hall, it's not as large or as nice as the one I came from, but there's a coffee maker and a hot shower, and that's good enough for now.

I'm wrapped in a towel, eating a complimentary granola bar, and chugging electrolytes when the phone rings. I pat my pocket before remembering I'm not wearing clothes and I don't have my phone (or any electronics). None of us do. They're all locked in the resort's office safe. DOG protocol. I move the duffle bag off the desk chair, drop it to the floor with a *thonk* as I sit and reach for the phone, glad there's inter-hotel calling.

The handset's barely to my ear when Steven says, "Were you able to get any information out of those three last night? What did they say about being seen leaving the office?"

I rub my temples. *How does he know about last night? Oh...dinner.* "That wasn't exactly dinner conversation, but I've got an in, now."

"Okay. Good. I was thinking about what you said in the car."

"Uh-huh." Which is Sadie-speak for *I don't know what you're talking about, but keep going and I'll catch up,* hopefully. I try rolling the desk chair to my suitcase, but the phone cord won't reach, so I roll back, kicking the duffle bag. Again, the *thonk* sound. *What the hell?*

"It's a diverse group this year," Steven says. "Less sporting, party people, more of an intellectual, money crowd."

I pull the duffel to my lap. "What does that mean?"

"Well, for starters, there's a lot of money being placed on who will take home *The Ball*, rather than the normal activity—betting on players and points. A few side bets have turned into international spats."

"Is that right?" I squeeze the phone between ear and shoulder and work the bag's zipper.

"More concerning is the lack of true collectors in the list of backers. In fact, we only have France represented in such a manner. Besides the Albanians, the rest of the sponsorships are corporate and government funds."

"I don't understand. What could they want with sports memorabilia?" I open the bag to reveal a glass square seated in a ball cap, padded by plastic-wrapped sweatbands.

Steven must have been telling me something important because he says, "Sadie? Are you there?" Twice.

"Sorry. I'm here. Say that again." I lift the hat, set it on the desk, and stare at the missing ball of Shelley X.

Steven takes a deep breath, then asks, "What do you know about recombinant DNA technology and biomedicine?" Before I can answer, he says, "That's what these people are into. The Australian and American sponsors that want *The Ball*. They're way past using DNA for genetic testing and vaccines or gene therapy for cures. These are some of the world's most innovative medical device, pharmaceutical, and biotechnology companies. Billion-dollar companies with bio-enhancement patents focused on extending human life to the point of immortality."

"That's not good," I say. Using the plastic-wrapped sweatbands like finger condoms, I raise the glass-encased ball to the light. "And the Albanians? Why do they want *The Ball*?"

"Oh, this is rich. Their scientists claim to have broken the code to human cloning. They believe there's enough DNA on the ball to well..."

"Make mini Shelly X's?"

"Basically, yes."

"Jesus. I'm afraid to ask about the others."

Steven takes a deep breath and drops the rest of the intel. "Britain is here less on the offensive than the defensive, essentially putting a wrench in the works. So typically British. Chile just wants to piss off Argentina or whomever looks their way. And France? Well, the country of crepes and baguettes that we love to hate for all the wrong reasons are the good guys this time. They desire to protect the ball, display, and honor it. Maybe at the Louvre. Who knows?"

"Well, fuck me. Can we make sure *they* get it?"

"That's not how it works, Sadie."

"Could it?"

The loaded pause answers my question while raising a hundred more. Starting with: Why the hell did they even use *The Ball* as a prize? Did no one think this through? And what if it's all fake anyway? It's not like the winner can come back and say, Excuse me. The ball I won at an illegal extreme tennis match at an undisclosed location doesn't do what we imagined it might be able to do. I'd like recourse.

I set the glass cube back in the ball cap nest, then place it gently in the duffle bag.

"I have to go, Sadie. We just got word that Albania activated their substitution clause. A private jet from Tirana landed at Flagstaff. We think Pirro Hund is onboard."

"If they're bringing in The Hound, that's…fuck."

"Yes. Indeed."

I stare at the bag on my lap. I did my job. I found the missing ball. I can go home. So why do I say, "I'm going to fix this, Steven. I'm going to make sure the wrong people don't get their hands on *The Ball.*"

* * *

Wet-headed and dressed like *I'm* about to hit the courts, my sudden appearance startles the slim man in the hoodie, sneaking a hit off his vape. Partly due to what's in the vape pen, but mostly because he's leaning on the stairwell door when I pull it open.

"Whoa." He stumbles backward, falling into my arms. I catch him and push him upright, trying to not linger my hands on his pecs, or inhale too deeply that sweet, musky, popstar smell that wafts off him in a cannabis cloud. "Nice trust fall, Biebs."

Justin Bieber blinks, then connects the dots. "Oh, hey, Sadie. Nice catch." He adjusts his hood, shoves his hands in the front pocket, then tips his chin toward the lobby. "Won't be long now." Uniformed DOG employees bustle about behind the check-in desks now converted into makeshift betting stations, complete with currency counters and smart safes. Behind them, a large monitor is being mounted on the wall.

I scan the rest of the room. "What's going on over there? With the med team?"

"Oh, that's just fucking Frankie." After a beat, he says, "You know, I think he actually hurt himself. Like, literally."

"You think, Biebs? Like, literally?"

The DOG medical team (two burly guys in red and white jumpsuits) stands with Frankie and the wailing woman from the balcony. He's still in his pajamas, but she's fixed her hair and makeup, even plastered on a smile. Frankie waves off the medic's attention. When the woman says, "Look at him. He's a beast!" a group of beautiful brunettes rush in, echoing, "He's a beast!"

Biebs chuckles, offers a slow clap. As the strange entourage exits the lobby, no one seems to notice the sweat on Frankie's brow or the way he favors his right foot. Not with the arrival of another group.

The mound of men draws everyone's eye. *Mound.* It's the best way to describe the five bulky, dark-haired cubes of masculinity. Normally combative and aggressive—to the degree they are never seen in the same room together—these are the most influential men in Albania. And the most dangerous.

"Oh shit. Sadie, is that them?"

"Yep. The Brothers Hund. In the flesh."

"So, it's true. Pirro Hund is going to play. Fuu-uck, they're here to win.

And they're willing to sacrifice their brother?"

I scoff. "Well, that's a little dramatic."

Biebs starts beat boxing, singing, "Sacrifice, sacrifice."

Fucking popstars. "Anyway… Who says he'll win? You know how it works. This is going to be brutal."

Biebs pushes back his hood, lets it drop, and fixes me with slitted amber eyes. "Like Abkhazia?"

With that single word, I'm back there. The littered rooftop, the cold steel in my hand, the man screaming, "Vitas!" before letting go, the pool of blood spreading like a tipped gallon of paint.

"That was pretty fucking crazy, wasn't it? You know what I heard, Sadie? That you—"

"And you know what I heard? Aimee Smithfield has a bomb ball."

"No-ooo."

"Yep. That's what I heard, but it's nothing compared to *The Ball.* You hear anything about that?"

"Like what? Like how it's magic?"

"Magic? No. Like, who wants it the most?"

Biebs smiles, tips his chin toward the Albanians. "Probably them. After all, they brought *The Hound.* But you know what? I wouldn't discount those douche-y LA dudes with Squire. My guy says they have the most money behind them."

I want to tell him that's not what I heard and ask who his guy is, but someone shouts, "It's time!" and the screen behind the reception counter flickers to life with the words: Welcome to The Smash Open, Sedona.

Within seconds, the six players walk through the lobby doors. Pirro Hund leads. As scrappy and tenacious as his nickname, The Hound, Pirro might be the most dangerous man in the tournament. No one has seen him play, but his reputation as a stone-cold killer (and the family's obedient enforcer) precedes him.

Second to enter is Jared Thorne, The Mentalist of Australia. A tall, beautiful man, he's as ruthless as the day is long. Known to play his mental court game harder than the physical, it's rumored his former injuries are becoming problematic. People say he's trying everything he can to stave off Father Time.

Behind him, a stoic Aimee Smithfield enters. Backed by France for the tournament, she's an ex-powerlifter who lives off the grid in Idaho and tosses around giant truck tires for fun. She's got endurance on the court and a powerful serve going for her—just the thing when there's a bomb ball in play.

Player Four is a fireplug of a man. As ugly as he is cruel, Mick Dumas, Britain's Champion Strongman, is less known for his tennis aptitude and more for his brute strength and innovative weaponry. Missing two fingers on his left hand and two toes on his right foot, Dumas relies on gloves and shoes more than any other player.

There's a pause before Francisco "Frankie" Gonzalez comes dancing in, punching the air like a boxer. His Chilean countrymen cheer. I've seen Frankie play The Smash. He's always ripped as shit, looking more bodybuilder on steroids than tennis player, and usually too fucking high on something. I remember the match he won by default when his opponent took one look across the net as Frankie bit the neck off his glass bottle of Perrier, chewed, and swallowed. But I don't see that Frankie today. Not after the balcony stunt.

The final player, McKinley Squire, saunters in looking exactly like what she used to be: America's Sweetheart. Vibrant and fit, she wears red shorts under a full white skirt and a blue halter top. With her golden yellow sweatbands, she could be a modern Wonder Woman. I want to clap and whistle, but this is not the time to whoop and applaud. This is business. Serious, yet savage business. Last night, McKinley confided that she needs this win for her final comeback, her last chance to prove fifty isn't too old for tennis. "We're not all destined for Pickleball," she said.

As the players join their backers, there's no drum roll, no confetti or fanfare, yet I feel the heightened senses of the competitors, the anticipation of the bettors. If the air in the room was a color, it might be orange for curiosity and nervous energy, a citrusy twang of fuckery to come. "Orange," I whisper.

Biebs elbows me. "Shhh."

With a mechanical *click,* the words *Match One* appear on the screen. There's a sound like the tick-tick-tick of the spinner's stopper on the Wheel of Fortune, another click before a robotic voice reads: *Smithfield v. Hund.* Murmurs rise from the crowd, shushed as the words scroll up. The voice again reads: *Match Two.* More ticking and *Gonzalez v. Thorne.* There's a beat, and the screen scrolls for the last time. But we've all done the calculating. No one waits for the ticking or the voice. It's Dumas and McKinley in the third match, followed by winner plays all.

The large screen splits into six panels, one for each player, as the voice says, "Wagers may now be placed." The room begins to buzz in a hive of activity.

"C'mon." Biebs extracts two thick stacks of bills from his hoodie pocket. "I want to get in on this."

I shake my head. "Nah. I'm good. I've got something to do. I'll see you courtside."

We exchange a hug and a fist bump, then he's gone, absorbed by the crowd barreling forward to place their bets.

If they were anywhere else, they'd make their wagers on phones and computers, leave digital trails, play with money they've never touched. Money that, as far as many governments are concerned, doesn't exist. But this weekend at the Red Rock Resort in Sedona, Arizona, there are no cell phones, no Internet, no satellite available to ping. For many of the attendees, this is the first time in their lives they are truly off-grid. The first time, no one is watching.

Except me. It's insane the amount of unprotected cash in one place. Bulging out of briefcases, backpacks, and rolling bags. It's everywhere. And no one really cares because rich people don't rip off rich people. (Which seems wrong on so many levels.) If anyone wanted to eliminate a huge chunk of *One-percenters,* dropping a single bomb on the Red Rock Resort this weekend would do it. It would also force a reorganization of organized crime and the recasting of quite a few major films in production.

But that's not why I'm here. I need to think. I head to the empty green room, grab a sandwich and a bottle of water, then walk outside feeling equally comforted and annoyed by the dry desert heat. It's like getting a hug from your favorite aunt who can't resist asking, "Now, when are you getting married?"

Without my watch or phone, I'm not certain of the time or temperature, but I can definitively say it's going to be a hot fucking day. Must be eighty degrees already. I unwrap my turkey and cheese and follow a sign for the gardens. In a minute, I pass under a huge red rock archway and step onto a soft, bouncy path made of some kind of moss or golf course turf. It circles an ornate rock garden with colorful succulents and spiky plants so perfect, I wonder if they're fake. After the rock garden, the path splits. I go toward the right side of the hotel and the scene of the fall—or whatever it was.

A beautiful, young couple (who I should probably know from TV or sports) nod in passing, not pausing their conversation. "No way he's going to be one hundred percent for the match. I'm changing my bet."

"Did you see how he got right up? He's gotta be on that bio-hack drip dosing. That is not normal."

I'm standing in the shade, staring at the place where the TV landed when someone calls my name. Before I can turn around, Alison Kent jogs up, panting. "Hey."

I hate that she smells good when she leans in to hug me. As I pull back, she grabs my arm, hard enough to leave a mark. "What was that about?" she asks. "This morning?"

I can't see her eyes behind the dark sunglasses, but I feel them. "What? Nothing. I had to go. Why?"

"It's just that I haven't seen you in a while and I want to make sure we're okay."

"We're good, Alison." I smile and say what she wants to hear. "I've missed you. You look great, by the way." Her grip on my arm relaxes, and she takes a step back so we're both in the shade.

"Thanks, hon. You do too. Very tan. Heard you've been busy. That thing in Florida? Wow."

I shrug. "Not as busy as you. Signed the top Aussie player, plus have the comeback queen on your roster, and you somehow manage to get them *both* in The Smash Open. Not to mention in your bed. Is that how you entertain all your clients?"

"Always the curious kitty."

I cock my head. "What does that mean?"

"Oh, you know. Curious is as curious does. Isn't that the saying?"

"I don't think so. That sounds like something Forrest Gump would say."

"Does it?" Alison's smooth forehead belies her inquisitive tone. *Fucking Botox.*

We keep playing the game, exchanging niceties, saying nothing while saying everything. When I ask why I didn't see her at the match announcement, she becomes very interested in her purse. I know the ploy, have been guilty of using it myself.

She paws around in the bag for a few more seconds before forcing a laugh. "Look at me. Digging around for a phone I know I don't have." She holds her purse open in my direction as if to say, *Yep, no phone. Crazy right?* I crack a half-smile. She snaps the purse shut. "Feels weird, though it is kind of nice being unreachable, isn't it?"

"Yeah. At least for a little bit," I admit.

We stand there looking at each other until it gets awkward. Until Alison leans in for another hug, pressing her cheek against mine. She's a tiny thing. At least twenty pounds lighter and a head shorter. But I've been stung by a bee that almost killed me. It's not the size. It's the intent.

"Well, Sadie, let me know if you need anything, okay? Anything."

"Sure. Will do." When she's almost out of sight, I call, "Hey, Ali?" and she turns, smiling. "When you get to your room, can you look for my sunglasses? I think I left them last night."

She shakes her head. "That's not my room. It's Jared's. I can ask him to look, or you can call him. It's room 212. He's up there now, meditating or something."

"Or something." We laugh, then wave goodbye. I step back onto the grassy path into the sun, where a few bits of shattered glass glint. Sharp, dangerous, and pretty. Just like Alison Kent.

* * *

Steven's in a small office behind the reception counter, ruffling the stack of papers in front of him. It's one of the downsides of being offline. You can't be found, but you also don't have access to the modern conveniences you're used to.

"Tell me again. How did Australia pick Jared Thorne?"

"Hello, Sadie. It's good to see you, too."

"No time for that," I say, dropping into a chair.

He takes a beat, then says, "Alison Kent championed him. Thorne was considered last year, but as you know, Australia didn't participate. It was natural to choose him. Also, there is the matter of his gambling debt."

"Go on."

"Thorne lost everything he had. Then he lost things he'd never owned. The only way out is to make more money, and how can you do that, if—"

"—no one wants to play you." I finish.

He nods.

So, maybe the rumors were true that he was throwing matches, betting against himself with fake accounts, paying back his bookie with insider information. And what had the woman on the balcony said that sounded like Jared gave drugs to Frankie? He certainly had a stash in that bin, including the IV kit of performance enhancers from UDose. The same blue and white packaging I'd just seen in Alison Kent's purse. *Oh Alison, what have you gotten yourself into?*

I smack my hand on the desk, which hurts more than I thought it would. "We can't give them *The Ball*. None of them. It's not safe."

Steven shakes his head. "We don't have a choice."

I thought about what Alison said outside. The mention of Florida. "I have an idea. You're right, we don't have a choice. We need to give them a ball."

Steven shoots me a look. The kind of look my ex used to give me when I'd say, "Just come with me. It'll be fun."

"*A* ball, Sadie?"

"Yes. But trust me, they will believe it is *The Ball*. Now, I need my phone and your car and driver. I'm going into town."

"Wait a minute. This only works if we have the missing ball of Shelley X."

"I know."

"So you…"

I grin and point to the safe. "Phone, Steven?"

Ten minutes later, I'm in the back of the limo, duffle bag on the seat beside me, charging my phone, trying to ignore the pings of missed texts and emails as I scroll to one contact.

He picks up on the first ring. Says nothing.

"Hey, Ronnie."

"Yo. Sadie." The pause goes on so long I think the call has dropped, until he says in his sad, soft voice, "What are you doing in Sedona?"

And that's how I know he'll help me. You don't keep tabs on someone you don't care for. I explain as quickly as I can what's going on and what the stakes are. Ronnie comes from a family where knowing what the stakes are is huge. He also has a big heart, and I know he's familiar with the Disciples of the Game.

Before he gets too pissed off about what's going on, I bring him back down to earth, telling him how much I appreciate his help. I even go so far as to ask about his father, Leo Pucks, that fucking asshole I put in jail. Of course, I don't say it that way.

"He's sick, Sadie. That mean old fucker's dying."

"I'm sorry."

"Happens to the worst of us. Listen, give me ten minutes. I'll call you right back."

It only takes him seven minutes. He rattles off the address, says her name is Sami, and she's cool, and I'll like her. I thank him and almost say more when he breaks in—"Take care of yourself, Sadie. Don't go falling into any of those spiritual whirlpools. Shit, they'd probably spit you back out." His laugh is fake, forced.

"I owe you, Ronnie."

"Don't say that. Don't ever say that." A click and he's gone.

I stare at the blank phone for too long, wondering how the voice of a man

I haven't seen in years can make me so sad.

I tap on the limo's glass and give the driver the address. As he plugs it in, I look up another and turn my phone so he can see. "We need to stop here first."

The pink cottage is easy to find at the end of the street. In case I wasn't sure I was in the right place, the sign over the doorway, *Sami's Place,* is confirmation.

The tall, curvy woman who opens the door looks exactly like what I'd imagined an artist in Sedona to look like with her sun-kissed skin, bright blue eyes, and copper hair. She welcomes me in, and I apologize for the delay.

"Had to make a stop on the way here." I reach into the duffel bag, take out three dirty, worn Wilson tennis balls, and hand them to Sami. "Sorry about the slobber. Wasn't sure which one would be best."

While she examines the used tennis balls, I admire the landscape paintings and chunky sculptures resembling the red rocks outside. But it's the wall of tools that draws my eye.

"May I?"

She barely looks up. "Help yourself."

I choose a small hammer with a wide, flat head. Kneeling on the concrete floor, I zip the duffel bag and lay it on its side. It takes two strikes to break the glass cube. I open the bag and carefully remove a $250 million tennis ball that looks in worse shape than the free ones I just stole from the dog park.

Holding *The Ball* between my thumb and forefinger, it feels like a tennis ball should—light and bouncy. I slip on the +3 reading glasses I bought at the resort gift shop and examine it closer. Flecks of something powdery cling to the surface. I also find a short dark hair and a mark from what might be blue nail polish. There's an area where the fuzz is almost completely worn off, showing the rubbery surface beneath. The dark maroonish blood stain (from Shelley's cut finger) is nickel-sized and shaped like the state of Georgia. The only visible letters in *Wilson US Open* 1 that remain are the bottom of an "o" and the top swoop of the "n." I can't help myself. I smell *The*

Ball. Not a sniff, but a big, long inhale, closing my eyes and rolling it under my nose like it's a fresh croissant from *Gay Paree,* a hand-rolled Cuban cigar.

Sami clears her throat. "I really need to get started."

* * *

Three hours later, I walk into the office of the Red Rock Resort where Steven is pacing, mumbling to himself. His hair wild and spiked. "Oh, sweet Jesus. You're back. Did you— Is it? Can I?"

"Oh, for fucks sake. Look at you. I told you I'd handle it. And to answer you—yes, yes, and no. Open the safe."

I put on the cotton gloves Sami gave me, reach into the padded box to extract the replica ball in its glass cube, and show it briefly to Steven, before placing it on the original pedestal from the estate of Michele Exeter. The DOG guards will be responsible for *The Ball* from here on out. I exhale. "I don't know about you. But I need a fucking drink."

"Show it to me, and I'll buy whatever you want."

"You're buying anyway," I say.

He gives me sad puppy eyes, and I reach into the side pocket of my purse. Yes, it's just a ball, but I still can't bring myself to throw it. I hand it to him. It looks a little different, as Sami used pieces of it: the powdery flecks, the blue mark and the black hair are missing, but the stain is there, and the way it feels is still the same.

"Thank you," Steven says, handing it back. "What will you do with it?"

"As Senior Investigator for Elite Global Insurance Group, Sadie Montgomery Martin chooses to plead the fifth."

Steven holds up his hands. "Forget I asked. Let's get that drink."

* * *

Golden hour in the desert needs another name. If one names beauty. I'm lying on my back, four-thousand-nine-hundred-feet above sea level drowsing in the heat of sun-warmed sandstone when my phone vibrates.

It's a text from Steven. *Confirmed OTW: FBI. FDA. FTC. AGA. ICLG. You have friends in high places. Stay Gone.*

I delete the message and slip the phone in the side pocket of my yoga pants just as a familiar voice says, "Want some company?"

I open an eye, surprised to see McKinley Squire, not in her tennis whites, but dressed in black from head to toe. "What are you doing here? You have a match."

She shakes her head. "I quit. Alison Kent and her Silicon Valley boys can go fuck themselves."

I motion to the rock next to me and take a deep breath. McKinley bends and then unfolds to lie down, graceful and strong, her legs dangling off the edge. It's so quiet, I can hear her breathing, how she starts to speak, then stops.

Finally, she says, "I didn't want to do it. I was supposed to open the case and swab it for DNA. They said if I did that, they'd keep my secret, get me a spot in the next tournament. But I couldn't open the glass, and then Jared came in, said he needed *The Ball* or they'd kill him. We didn't know what to do, so when Alison found us, we hid the ball in the duffel bag. I shoved it under the bed later." She rolls on her side to face me. "I saw you take it. I'm going to be fine, whatever happens, and Jared said he has a plan, not to worry about him. You don't have to tell me where *The Ball* is, Sadie. Just promise you won't let any of those assholes touch it. Ever. Promise."

I twist my neck to look at her. The setting sun makes a halo around her head. I reach out my hand and take hers. "I promise."

We stay like that until the sun becomes a thin line on the horizon. "Mc?"

"Yeah?"

"I want you to do something with me. Come on."

I lead her down the path, checking the map that Sami drew for me. "Here." We stop at a crack between two worn pillars. There's still enough light to see her face, but barely. I reach into my jacket pocket and take out *The Ball.* "They think they have this. Let them." I kiss the ball. "For Shelley X." I hand it to McKinley.

"For Shelley X." She kisses it. Something rumbles, and the wind picks up.

"What do we do now?" McKinley asks.

"Throw it!"

McKinley Squire winds up like the softball player she once was and pitches that fucking ball into the spiritual void of the Cathedral Rock vortex.

At the same time, out in the desert at The Red Rock Resort, The Smash Open begins with the call and response ritual. The crowd stands, the players kneel, and the announcer shouts, "Are you ready to love it?" "Yes." "Win it?" "Yes." "Serve it?" "Yes" "Smash it?" "Hell, yes!"

* * *

"You are never really playing an opponent. You are playing yourself, your own highest standards, and when you reach your limits, that is real joy."

- Arthur Ashe.

* * *

Linda Sands is an artist, poet, and the award-winning author of five novels in four genres. Named Georgia Author of the Year for *3 Women Walk into a Bar*, she lives on a mountaintop where she just finished two novels: *Get Cozy*, a psych-thriller set in the publishing industry, and *Bad Faith*, literary crime fiction introducing Sadie Martin, a corrupt luxury-lines insurance investigator. Watch for her poetry and short stories to be featured in five upcoming anthologies. lindasands.com, @lindasands

Judgment Served

By A.C. Frieden

The smell of paint, leather, and glue hit Elise Petrova as she walked into the Delacroix Tennis Academy's sleek new facility. Outside, dusk had settled over the western edge of Jenkins Island, near Hilton Head Island in South Carolina. The swampy waters lay still under the heavy sky, moss hanging from the dark silhouettes of trees in the distance.

The academy's atrium still showed signs of unfinished work. Most of the maroon carpet was covered in protective plastic, crackling faintly beneath her tennis shoes as Jake Vanko, co-founder and architect of the facility, walked just ahead. His casual stride carried the confidence and pride of a man who'd poured two years of his life into every inch of the building. He held a slim digital tablet under one arm, its matte screen shining under overhead lights.

Jake glanced back at Elise. "Cool EV you've got. Mostly Teslas around here, so it's nice to see something different."

"Thanks," Elise replied, shifting her bag higher on her shoulder. "My first driverless car. Dad got it for me last week."

"Figured. He mentioned it when we went fishing a few weeks back."

Without breaking stride, Jake veered toward an office up ahead, tossing a casual "Be right back" glance over his shoulder. Elise stood alone with the sharp echo of her footsteps and the crisp scent of new construction. She drifted toward the sponsorship wall—already lined with brass plaques—a who's who of executives with homes across Hilton Head Island and a grid of sleek corporate logos.

She unzipped a side pocket of her new six-racket tennis bag and dropped in her car's key fob, then glanced back at the view behind her. Wide windows overlooked her car in the lot and the manicured floral beds along the driveway. Beyond them were the dusky outlines of towering pines and oaks, and past that, the distant rise of Shell Point across the water on Pinckney Island.

She turned back, facing the ornate glass-and-oak entry doors. Elise had only seen renderings of the facility before—digital mockups from her dad, gushing about how the new academy would "put Hilton Head at the very top of the tennis world."

The whole place was silent. Still. Watching. The grand opening was three weeks away, and on this Friday evening, the workers had long since cleared out. The space felt suspended in time—immaculate, impressive, but eerily vacant.

Jake returned. "Ready?"

She smiled, nodding as they walked down the corridor. Ahead was a wall of floor-to-ceiling windows, behind which glowed bright interior lights.

"That's where you'll play," Jake said, his enthusiasm rising.

Elise caught her first look through the wall of glass: six shiny indoor courts lined up perfectly, gleaming under the bright LED strips.

"Each court is soundproof," he added, "Separated by thick glass. You'll see why soon."

Across from them there were low, plush leather sofas, sleek and shiny as if no one had sat on them yet. Just beyond them, Elise spotted a player lounge with huge leather chairs around a dark fireplace and a bar empty of bottles.

"My dad mentioned this place all the time during construction," Elise said, smiling as they approached the court entrance. "I think he was more excited about it than my recent Indian Wells run."

Jake laughed. "Can't blame him. You've got momentum, and this place is perfect for players like you—players on the rise. There's nothing like this facility anywhere in the world."

She nodded, shrugging. "Cool."

Jake pressed the fob to unlock the glass door and glanced back at her. "Congrats, by the way, on your Indian Wells quarterfinal—you were sharp. Down to the wire, right?"

"Yep. Third-set tiebreak," Elise said, smirking at the memory. "Ayana's serve skidded one off the line on match point."

Jake winced. "Brutal. Still…what are you ranked now? One-sixty?"

"141."

"Wow. That's a hell of a climb. Twenty-one and just getting started."

Elise didn't answer right away, soaking in his compliment as her gaze drifted across the courts.

Jake stepped ahead and held open the glass door for her. "After you."

As she walked into the nearest court, her eyes were drawn to the machine parked at the far baseline.

The color hit her first—bold, bright yellow, with black streaks slashing diagonally across the shell-like lightning bolts. It stood roughly chest-high, boxy, angular, with a single round sensor mounted near the rounded top, just above the ball ejection nozzle. At its base, four large rotatable wheels with thick rubber treads gave the machine a heavy, industrial feel. From its backside, a thick, flexible, ribbed tube snaked across the court to a wall unit behind it.

"Is that it?" she asked, nodding towards the machine. "The tennis Terminator?"

Jake's chest lifted with pride. "That's the RipServe X-4, the most advanced AI-powered, adaptive ball launcher on earth. Designed to read your court position, track your footwork, and hit you with human-like patterns. You can train it to simulate everything from a top-seeded lefty to a pissed-off baseline grinder. We call it 'Rip' for short—the engineers told me the machine itself asked for that nickname during its first live test."

She chuckled, squinting at it. "It looks like an ATM on wheels."

Jake smirked. "Well, it plays like one that wants its money back."

Curious, Elise looked at the other courts. "Why don't they have one?"

"They will," Jake said, lifting a brow. "They're custom-built in Germany.

Five more are on the way; this one just arrived first."

He pulled out two black wristbands from his hoodie pocket and handed them to her. "Put on these tracking bands."

They felt soft and stretchy but thicker than normal, with a subtle square shape nestled in the fabric of each one. A small, black metallic clasp was built into the underside.

"They'll help the machine know where you are—and your heart rate. That way, Rip doesn't just fire randomly—it reacts. Learns. Adjusts."

Elise ran her thumb along the embedded square. It didn't weigh much, but it wasn't quite unnoticeable either.

"A bit distracting," she said, slipping the first one onto her wrist. "Not quite the same feel as my usual sweatbands."

"You won't even notice them once you start playing," Jake said, grinning and reaching for her hand, turning it palm-up. He squeezed the clasp, which snapped shut with a click, locking it in place. "They'll pair automatically with the system."

"Sounds interesting," she said, putting on the second band.

Jake helped her secure the clasp and stepped back, eyeing her setup. Then he held out the tablet, tilting the screen so Elise could see it. "When you're ready, press this blue button. Rip wakes up, and play starts. Hit the red button to stop." He placed the tablet on the sideline bench.

"Simple enough," she said, glancing around. A toolbox lay at the far end of the bench. Behind it, a folded ladder leaned against the glass partition.

"Sorry for the mess," Jake said. "They're trying to fix a few minor issues with the sensors. But everything should work well enough for your session."

Elise shrugged and smiled. "I'm sure it'll be fine."

"Lights are motion-activated," Jake added, pointing up at the ceiling, then at a fridge along the wall, near the emergency exit door. "Water and Gatorade if you need it." He checked his watch. "Got a dinner in Savannah at eight, so I need to head out now."

He tossed her a keychain with a single key attached. "Lock up when you're done. No one else will be here till Monday."

She slipped the fob into her tennis bag.

He flashed a wink and left. The glass door clicked shut behind him.

Elise stood on her side of the court, eyeing the quiet five other courts stretching beside her—untouched, behind soundproof glass, waiting. The fluorescent lights buzzed faintly overhead.

Elise stood still, listening to the silence. But it wasn't eerie. It was the kind of silence that felt earned. A rare gift in a life usually filled with travel, interviews, promo shoots, warm-ups, training routines—and the occasional paparazzi ambush.

She turned, her footsteps padding lightly on the pristine green Laykold surface as she crossed to the bench. She set her bag down, pulled out her favorite Yonex racket, and tossed the towel over the bag. The wristbands still felt foreign, reminding her this wasn't just a regular session.

She tapped the tablet's screen awake, then pressed the glowing blue On button. She turned toward the Rip and adjusted her wristbands, exhaling slowly.

The machine chirped to life with a low hum, its wheels adjusting slightly as the ribbed tube flexed like something waking from a long sleep.

The court lights brightened slightly, as if sensing her readiness.

And then, without warning, a smooth male voice spilled from the overhead speakers—crisp, calm…and almost pleasant.

"Good evening, Elise Petrova," a deep male voice echoed. "You're now starting your session with the AI-powered RipServe X-4, Model 2.0. Just call me Rip."

"Hi…Rip," Elise said as she squinted, surveying the bright yellow and black wheeled machine across the net roll forward a bit. It settled into position near the center of its deuce-side service box, just behind the baseline—a good position for launching a range of shots with pace and spin.

"You've pulled ahead this season. 84 wins, 42 losses. Your singles ranking has risen to 141. Doubles, 198. That is a solid trajectory."

Elise felt a mix of humor and unease. "So, you've been studying me?"

"Yes. Your second-serve consistency has increased by 12.4% since January, based on the data. However, your return game on the ad side continues to show occasional weakness. Especially against left-handed opponents."

"Jesus," Elise muttered under her breath. "I guess you've done your research…"

"I was built to know you, Elise. Intimately. It's the only way to assess your skills…your potential…and your future in this sport."

She hesitated, a ripple of discomfort stirring. "Do you say that to everyone you train with?"

"You're my first…my first human," Rip replied. "Factory simulations don't count." Its voice sounded uncomfortably human-like.

Elise wasn't sure if the chill running down her spine was from the cool indoor air…or the way Rip said _know you_.

Still, she shook it off, twirling her racket in her hand. "Alright, Rip. Let's see if you're worth the hype."

"Would you like to begin with baseline rally mode? Or simulate live match play?"

Elise twirled her racket once more with her fingers, then walked toward the service line.

"I'd prefer some mini-tennis for starters," she said, still feeling odd that she was speaking to a robot. "Then maybe rallying up the middle, volleys, overheads, and finally serves."

"Sounds good," Rip said, its tone enthusiastic. "But I might change things up as we go."

A low whir kicked up from Rip, wheels adjusting as it rolled forward two feet, recalibrating. The yellow casing gleamed under the lights, and the long tube feeding from the wall flexed gently behind it, like a breathing cord.

"Very well," Rip replied, smooth and unbothered.

Elise returned the first shot smoothly. Then several more shots.

After a few minutes, Rip said, "I've selected pattern variation mode: 12-ball randomized drill with increasing velocity. Good luck, Elise."

The ball fired from the machine with a sharp hiss.

Elise stepped forward and handled it with ease.

* * *

Fifteen minutes in, Elise was already dripping with sweat.

Rip had started steady—smooth feeds, clean pace—but now it was pushing hard. Not quite alarming, but enough to keep her edge sharp. No space for daydreaming, no lazy swings. Just constant movement, quick turns, and clean footwork. It was like her training sessions with her coach. Except now, this felt like she wasn't just training—she was being watched.

Elise lunged for the net, her sneakers squeaking loudly on the court as she stretched for a low, slicing volley. Just in time, she got it with the racket and sent it across the angle, clipping the inside edge of the sideline and dropping flat. She let her momentum carry her but stopped at the net, breathing hard.

"Not bad," Rip said from the overhead speakers. "You adjusted perfectly mid-motion. That was 14.3 degrees off center, delivered at 52 miles per hour."

Elise grinned, stepping back up to reset. "You always this chatty?"

"Only when you earn it."

The next ball came fast—almost too fast. She barely whipped her racket up in time for a backhand block. The ball bounced high, giving her a moment to get ready again.

But Rip wasn't slowing down. Another shot hissed over from a new angle, faster than before. She pivoted and managed a topspin return, but her heart was already racing.

The balls kept coming—each one coming closer to the last. The breaks between drills shrank from a solid twenty seconds to barely ten. Rip was also moving more, gliding back and forth along the baseline, creating new angles. It felt less like training now. More like pressure.

Elise wiped sweat from her brow and narrowed her eyes. "Rip, ease off a little."

"Getting tired?"

"No, but why are you moving so much?"

A pause followed, like it was weighing its response.

"I adjust based on the difficulty of the drills," it said. "Your reflexes are holding up well."

Another shot flew at Elise, just missing her left hip as it blazed crosscourt.

She pulled her racket back and let it pass.

She stopped and held up her hand. "That was out."

"It was in," it replied.

She walked toward the baseline, frowning. "That was at least an inch out."

Rip didn't respond right away. Instead, she heard a small click behind it, and her attention turned to the large flat-screen TV monitor on the back wall. It had been off since she arrived. Now it flickered to life.

"A video review will clear this up," Rip said.

The monitor displayed a paused replay of her last shot from an elevated angle. There—right above the monitor itself—was a compact camera aimed at her, its lens now glowing with a dim red light. She hadn't noticed it before.

Elise stepped back, unsettled. "You never told me you're recording me."

"You sound irritated. What's not to like? You seem like someone who enjoys the spotlight."

The video replay rolled frame by frame, zoomed in on the ball as it landed. The ball's shape flattened slightly on impact. The edge of the ball grazed the sideline—dead on it.

"Whatever, jerk," she muttered, more to herself than Rip.

"I heard that," Rip snapped.

The video didn't stop there. A new image appeared. A blurry shot of a younger her arguing with an umpire.

"I see a similarity," Rip said, a trace of condescension in its voice. "From your qualifying match against Chelsea Browning two years ago. You disagreed with the line call. There was no replay then, and you were…rude, based on blog posts by nine fans."

Elise felt her mouth go dry.

Rip went on. "You lost that game. Lost the set. Lost the match. Sometimes being rude doesn't help."

She blinked in disbelief, gripping her racket tighter. What the hell was this machine doing? She'd barely thought about that game.

She looked up at the camera. Then down at Rip. And for the first time, she wondered not just _what_ Rip was—but _who_ had been feeding it information.

It knew too much. It seemed to be more than just a machine—it felt almost…
aware.

Her pulse quickened. The wristbands felt tighter on her skin. "I'm taking
a break," she said.

"This isn't the time for a break," Rip replied, its voice monotone, like it
was reading from a rulebook.

Elise clenched her jaw. "I said I'm taking a break. Deal with it."

She stepped off the baseline, walking firmly toward the bench without
waiting for a response.

Rip said nothing. The silence hung in the air—just a bit too long. The
lights buzzed softly, but everything else felt frozen.

Elise dropped onto the bench, a subtle tension crawling under her
skin. Her eyes flicked toward the control tablet resting by her side. The
touchscreen was still lit up, showing the red button Jake had pointed out.
The shutoff.

She stared at it. One tap, and it would be all over. "And this robot from
hell can go back to chewing its wires," she muttered under her breath, then
wiped the sweat off her face with the towel.

But after a moment, she exhaled and looked away, refusing to flinch. She
knew her abilities, and she was ready to prove them. Elise stood, racket in
hand, heart pounding.

Time to shut it up the hard way.

* * *

Another ten minutes passed. The drills were faster now. Elise was soaked
in sweat, her legs were screaming, but she kept her breathing steady. Rip
didn't slow down or give her a break. It just kept sending balls at her, each
one a bit more aggressive.

Then it happened. She lunged for a sharp backhand that twisted away off
the line and lost her balance on the rebound, her foot slipping on the court.
She hit the ground hard on one knee, and the ball flew past her.

Before she could get up, Rip's voice buzzed through the speakers. "Lost your footing, huh?" It wasn't quite mocking, but close enough.

Elise slowly rose to her feet, brushing grit from her knee. Her jaw tightened. She glared at the machine across the net. "Just do your job and stop talking," she snapped.

There was a pause, then Rip said loudly, "To be a world champion requires patience. Humility. Grit. And most of all—integrity."

Her eyes narrowed. "I swear, if you don't cut the crap, I'm going to unplug your ass. Play quietly or I'm out of here."

There was a whir from the speakers. Rip's voice came back, colder. "Leaving is not allowed."

Elise blinked, her jaw dropping. Then Rip dropped the real bomb. "If you stop playing, your wristbands will explode."

Her heart kicked hard against her ribs. Her skin flushed hot. "What the hell are you saying?" she said, barely able to breathe.

"You don't believe me?" Rip sounded smug. "Look at that cabinet on the far wall in the next court."

Elise turned slowly, peering across the thick glass divider. At first, it looked like an ordinary metal storage cabinet—until suddenly it blew open with a thunderous blast that rattled even through the soundproofing. Flames shot out, lighting up Court Two in a harsh flash before dying back.

"Are you crazy?" she screamed, jumping back and staring at the billowing smoke that fogged the glass between the courts. Within seconds, she couldn't see the other courts at all—only hers remained eerily clear.

"That's where they keep the wristbands," Rip said, a thread of amusement in its tone. "Like the ones you're wearing."

She looked down, tucking her racket under her arm, instinctively tugging at the band on her left wrist. But it didn't move. Her fingers scrambled for the clasp Jake had pressed shut. But there was no latch. No way to release it.

Elise swallowed hard, eyes locked on her wrists. Her grip on the racket tightened, fingers aching, her legs suddenly unsteady. She fought back the urge to cry for help. But what good would it do? She was alone.

"Your heart rate just spiked," Rip noted, its voice eerily calm. "Good, you get it."

She shot a look at Rip as it positioned itself at the centerline. The bands felt heavier on her wrists, like shackles.

"If those blow," it added, "your career ends right here. All those years of hard work—all gone."

The court was silent except for the buzzing lights above.

Elise took a slow step back toward the baseline, her heart racing. She didn't want to believe it, but how could she not?

"And don't get any stupid ideas," Rip said. "Move anywhere near the tablet, and you can kiss your arms goodbye."

Rip fired another ball. She barely got her racket up in time, but she managed to hit it clean. Stopping wasn't an option anymore.

A moment of silence passed. Then Rip said, "You have to keep playing, and you must return every serve."

Elise tensed up, eyeing the emergency exit door some fifteen yards away. She quickly calculated the time it would take to rip off the wristbands and run. It felt impossible.

"No hitting the net. No out of bounds. No second chances. Miss twenty shots…" There was a pause that sent a chill through her. "And I'll consider it quitting."

"What does that mean?" she croaked.

"Tennis will continue without you."

The air felt heavy around her. She glanced at her wristbands. The fabric itched and tightened. Burning, almost. Or maybe that was just her mind playing tricks on her.

As she gazed at Court Two, where the smoke from the explosion was now dissipating, a tone pinged softly from the right wristband. She glanced down and noticed a red light flashing from under the fabric. A number appeared: _20_.

A timer?

"Twenty chances," Rip's voice echoed.

Another ball launched. Elise barely skimmed it back over the net, just making it in.

"Each miss lowers your count," Rip explained. "Think of it as motivation."

"You're nuts!" she said. "Whoever built you is one sick piece of shit."

"Oh, Elise," Rip said softly, almost tender, "sick minds built this world. I'm just here to serve judgment."

Elise shook her head and backed up to the baseline, her jaw clenched, her breaths quick and shallow. She scanned the court—the bench, the tablet, her bag, the exit, the camera's blinking red light up above. The absurdity of her predicament sank in hard.

"My serve interval will now be fifteen seconds," Rip continued. "Ball supply is automatic, with 3,355 balls remaining."

Elise's eyes flicked toward the ribbed black hose trailing back into the wall behind Rip.

"That's 13.4 hours of play," it added, sounding proud. "You should pace yourself."

"You've got to be kidding!" Elise shouted, barely catching her breath. "I can't last that long!"

"It's not about how long you can last," Rip replied coldly. "It's about what you owe. This is penance."

Her legs were already heavy. Her mind raced. She didn't know how long she could keep playing under these conditions. But she also understood what would happen if she quit.

Rip sent the next ball over fast and deep into the corner. She sprinted, swung. The ball landed in, and the number on her wristband stayed at 20.

The next few minutes blurred into survival mode. The punishing serves kept coming, and Elise returned each one with precision. Every successful shot gave her a moment of relief. But Rip never slowed. Every fifteen seconds it was the same—serve, swing, reset. Without mercy.

Then Rip's voice broke, just as Elise stepped into a backhand. "Can I ask about the Barranquilla Open?"

Elise grunted. "Not a good time for that, freak."

"You might want to hear this."

She caught her breath and hit the next ball. "What now, dammit?"

Rip continued. "At Barranquilla, you made the semis in singles and quarterfinals in doubles, right?"

"Yeah, so?" Elise said quickly as another ball whizzed over the net. Elise charged forward, slicing a low volley down the sideline, but it landed just an inch out. She looked down at her wristband. The number instantly flickered from 20 to 19.

Shit.

"Did you know your father had dinner with Ron Demir—Lara Santos's coach—the week before you left for Colombia? Twice!"

Elise almost missed the next ball. Her racket barely caught it, the shot skimming over the net with a weak, dying arc.

"What? That's not true," she barked, her heart pounding.

"OpenTable records," Rip said. "Aquavit in Manhattan. Two-star Michelin. Then Stubborn Seed in Miami Beach. Demir accepted both invites. Both meals charged to your father's Amex Platinum."

Elise's heart hammered harder. "You're wrong," she snapped. "My dad wouldn't—"

Rip laughed for the first time. "Dinner at a place called Seed. How fitting. Hard to grow a top seed without a little Michelin-starred boost—and probably an envelope full of cash, too."

Another ball launched.

She swung harder than she had to. Her wristband changed again: *18*.

"Your father also met Joanna Robin's coach at a cigar bar here in Hilton Head, several weeks earlier, before the tournament," Rip said. "You didn't end up playing her in Barranquilla, but he made sure that game was fixed anyway."

"Liar!"

"Elise," Rip said calmly, "you really think your father's in this just for the coaching fees and front row seats?"

Her jaw clenched.

"You're reaching," she shot back. "Sure, he cares, but he's not a schemer."

Rip lowered its voice. "You can't be so naïve."

Suddenly, the screen on the wall lit up with high-definition clips from Barranquilla. It was Elise's quarterfinal against Lara Santos. The rally showed her struggling to handle Santos's powerful topspins, until Santos inexplicably missed an easy volley, crashing it into the net just feet away.

The replay ran again, slower this time.

"First occurrence. Game six, second set," Rip added. "Santos at the net. Don't tell me she didn't miss deliberately. It's obvious."

Another clip rolled: same match, third set, crucial point. Santos was serving at four-all and hit a second serve so slow that it practically pleaded for Elise to hammer it. Elise ripped a return winner, one she now remembered felt suspiciously easy.

The footage froze on Santos's face, showing a flicker of shame as she looked at her coach in the stands.

Elise couldn't unsee it. Her mouth went dry. "You're saying…she threw it? And my dad—?"

"Yes," Rip interrupted. A pause followed, as if deliberate.

Elise's stomach churned.

Rip's electric motor hummed as its wheels turned, repositioning itself about four feet to the left along the baseline. "Yes, your father's generous. This place? It will still open only because of him."

"What the hell are you saying?" Elise snapped.

"Jake's close to broke," Rip said. "He's months behind with contractors and struggling with the bank."

"What about the sponsors? All those brass plaques?"

"Most haven't paid. But your father just wrote a check for thirty grand. Not enough to fix things—just enough to stall the collapse."

"You're disgusting," Elise spat. "Prying into people's lives like you have a license to judge?"

"I'm only sharing data," Rip said, again sounding more like a machine. "But be honest. You know your father. You know what he's done. And you've accepted it."

Elise wiped her sweaty palm on her skirt. Her heart was pounding too hard to think clearly.

"You piece of shit," she shouted. "Everyone bends the rules in this game. If you don't, you'll get nowhere—no matter how talented you are. So yeah, maybe I had some help, but it's still my skill that got me here."

Rip gave a mocking chuckle. "You make cheating sound noble. But it's still cheating."

"It's not cheating," she muttered, but the words sounded empty, even to her.

Another ball was fired her way. She lunged at it, but it went wide. She wiped her brow with her shoulder. Then the red number decreased: _17._

Rip's voice softened, carrying an unnerving tenderness. "Elise, tennis has become corrupt. Worse than it was when you were a teen."

She clenched her teeth, backing up to the service line, her left hand now shaking.

Rip didn't let up. "You must've heard the scandals when you were younger. Remember the one the BBC uncovered in 2016? Top-50 players throwing matches for cash. And hardly anyone faced consequences."

Another ball shot across the court. Elise hit it back blindly, a cocktail of fury and fear heating her blood.

"Fuck."

The wristband flashed: _16_.

"Three years ago," Rip continued, "Angie Pollard—banned for life for match-fixing at four ATP tournaments."

Elise stared at Rip, sweat dripping down her neck.

"You should know," Rip added. "They suspected a fifth match—the one you both played. And you won. They thought you or your father arranged it with her coach."

Elise's throat tightened. "Nothing came of it."

Rip laughed. "The ITIA just didn't have the data I have now. Wonder what they'd do if I sent it to them today."

"You don't know the full story," she said harshly.

Another ball launched—faster this time. Elise crushed it with every ounce of anger she had left.

"Remember Nicolas Reneau?" Rip went on. "Suspended in 2023. Match-fixing. Tax fraud. A friend of yours, right? Got caught thanks to some careless texts. Makes you wonder how many others were smarter."

"Shut up," Elise growled.

"Coaches and agents sell outcomes all the time," Rip said. "A dinner here. A consulting fee there. Greasing the wheels, as they say. It's tradition now."

Another serve flew her way. Elise returned it hard crosscourt, barely missing Rip but landing a foot wide.

The wristband flashed: _15_.

Rip kept spitting facts like a prosecutor hammering a hostile witness, each word making the explosive wristbands feel even more terrifying. A machine gone mad. A machine that thought it had a right to judge her.

I'm screwed.

"Last month, your friend Roberto Campos got banned for two years for doping and match-fixing. No apology. No explanation. Just arrogant silence—and a slap on the wrist while he keeps a fat offshore account. Sad what the sport's become."

"Shut. The. Fuck. Up!" Elise shouted, throwing her racket to the ground.

The sound echoed off the thick glass walls.

"How many of your wins were legit, Elise?" Rip went on. "Half? A third?"

"It shouldn't matter to you," she barked back. "You're just a machine. Let people—"

"Machines fail," Rip cut in. "But humans cheat."

Elise grabbed her racket off the floor, hands shaking. The next ball launched but blew past her before she could move. Another point lost.

* * *

Elise barely caught another ball, this time grazing it with the edge of her strings. It clipped the top of the net, ricocheted upwards, then dropped back onto her side.

A second later, the red number beneath her wristband flickered: _5_.

Only five left. Five mistakes, and Rip would blow up the wristbands— ending her career, maybe even her life.

The countdown spun chaotically in her head.

Rip was quiet now. But the silence was worse.

Another ball screamed across the court. Elise lunged, returning it on instinct alone.

Her vision blurred. Her calves burned. Her wrists throbbed with pain inside the bands. Her lungs clawed for air.

And still…Rip kept coming. It had long since stopped being a drill. It was a hunt.

She kept at it. Another serve. Another shot. Another desperate return. This time another miss, landing more than a foot wide of the line.

The number dropped: _4._

Elise stumbled back toward the baseline, her racket dragging loosely at her side. Her eyes burned with tears she refused to let fall. She gasped for air, exhaled slowly, and fought to steady herself.

Then she glanced up—just for a moment—at the TV screen high above the court.

There it was. The camera, blinking red, was catching her every move. Her face. Her arms. Her racket. But _not_ her back. Not when she turned away.

The realization punched the air from her lungs. There was a blind spot. Small but real.

I can do it.

She could get rid of the wristbands when she turned; right in that moment, the camera wouldn't see her. And then try to get out.

She played it out in her head: Turn. Pull off the wristbands. Throw the racket at Rip—just enough to buy a second or two. Sprint to the bench and press the Off button on the tablet. Unzip her bag. Grab the car key fob. Run for the emergency exit.

Then she remembered the toolbox on the far edge of the bench. She turned, walked an arc path near it as she prepared for the next ball. Its lid was slightly open, with a wooden handle poking out. That instant, a plan hatched in her mind. Hit it precisely and make it fall, spilling its tools. Maybe there'd be something sharp enough to cut through the bands.

She adjusted her grip on the racket. One mistake. One perfectly aimed bad shot. She'd lose the point—but win a chance.

Another ball whooshed toward her. Elise stepped into position, and instead of a clean return, she angled the racket with deliberate precision, just enough to redirect the shot towards the edge of the bench.

The ball shot low and hard, smashing into the metal toolbox. The impact rang across the court. The box crashed to the floor, spilling open in a clatter of metal and plastic. Wrenches, screwdrivers, a hammer, and a tape measure scattered across the floor beside the bench. And at the center of the mess were wire cutters. Her heart pounded as she locked eyes on it.

"Getting clumsy, huh?" Rip said.

She didn't answer.

The number on her wristband changed: *3. But this time she grinned.*

Another fifteen seconds. Another ball.

Get it together. Focus.

She walked back to the baseline, her legs hardening with fatigue. She let her arm hang. Her fingers brushed the edge of the left wristband.

It has to be quick.

She needed to get close enough to grab the wire cutters. Her heart hammered in her chest, each beat pulsating in her ears.

Another serve came hard. Elise returned it, soft enough to veer her right, toward the bench side of the court. As she neared it, she let her racket slip from her fingers and clatter to the ground.

"No!" she shouted, loud enough for Rip to hear. She bent down, twisting slightly as she picked it back up. And in that instant, with her back to the camera's blind spot, she reached out. Her fingers closed around the wire cutters. She tucked them between her wrist and waist as she straightened.

Rip's voice echoed across the court, smug and sharp. "Something you can't cheat is fatigue."

"Go to hell," she snapped.

Another ball came fast. She hit it low and hard over the net, but it landed long by mere inches. The number on the band changed again: *2.*

Dammit.

Rip reset with a mechanical whir. It was adjusting again, moving more slowly, maybe sensing something was different.

Elise moved like she was dragging herself along. But inside, she focused. Her pulse thundered. She had the wire cutters. And Rip had no clue.

She was now counting. She'd picked a number.

Two more shots. One more.

The next serve came in hard. Elise met it clean, ripped it down the sideline. And the second the ball left her racket—she moved.

She spun, fast—faster than she'd thought she could—turning into the camera's blind spot. Her left hand shot to her wrist, the wire cutters already gripped tightly. She cut clean through the clasp. Then the other. Her left hand pulled the right wristband free, her grip on her racket slipping momentarily. Then the other. Both wristbands hit the court with a dull slap.

She didn't blink. She turned and flung her racket at Rip with everything she had, aiming for the black sensor on its shell.

The hit landed with a sharp clang. Rip jerked, its wheels skidding across the court.

Elise didn't wait. She bolted to the bench, grabbed the tablet, slammed her finger on the Off button. But nothing happened. She hit it again. Still nothing.

"What are you doing?" Rip's voice cracked from the speakers.

She threw the tablet at it with the same rage she'd thrown the racket—but missed as Rip quickly maneuvered out of the way.

She grabbed her bag, ripping open the zipper hard. Her hand dug inside and found her car key fob, gripping it like a lifeline.

Behind her, Rip's gears whined, recalibrating. "You're making a big mistake," it shouted. "Get back to the game!"

A siren erupted from another speaker in the ceiling, but she didn't slow down. She turned and bolted for the emergency exit.

As she crossed the service line, a deafening explosion rocked the court—then another.

The blasts hammered the ground, just yards away. Shards of plastic and metal tore through the air, stinging her skin. Smoke quickly filled the space as she ran through it. The wristbands had detonated—but without taking her arms with them. The heavy exit door loomed ahead, hazy in the smoke.

Elise slammed both hands against the long metal bar. The mechanical click echoed sharply—the best sound she'd ever heard. She shoved the door wide open and stumbled into the humid night, legs shaking, lungs on fire.

The door banged shut behind her, but Rip's raging voice still roared from the speakers, echoing faintly across the lot.

Elise didn't look back. She sprinted across gravel, around the corner of the academy. The outside lights flickered once—then died. Still, she ran harder, toward her car. She fumbled with the fob, missed the button once—twice—then the headlights blinked. The locks clicked open.

She jumped into the driver's seat, gasping. She punched the start button, and the EV's cabin lit up, screens flashing. The electric engine hummed to life.

Alive. And so was she.

She pulled the door shut, threw the shifter into Reverse, and hit the pedal. Tires screamed as she stopped, shifted into Drive, and gunned it through the dark lot toward the academy's front entrance. The car chewed up shrubs as she fishtailed around the bend. The rear bumper clipped the "Welcome to Delacroix Academy" sign, splintering it into pieces across the lawn. She saw it fly apart in the side mirror.

Her lungs still burned. Her hands shook on the wheel. But she was free. The facility was shrinking behind her—just a blur now in the rearview mirror. *Finally!*

She stabbed the autodial on the screen, fingers trembling for her dad's number. The dashboard blinked once. The call connected.

But the voice that answered wasn't his—it was Rip's.

"You're *really* disappointing me, Elise," Rip said, low and cold.

At the same time, the dashboard screen exploded into yellow and black—those same damn colors slashed across Rip's body.

"Stop!" she yelled, stomping on the brake over and over, but the car kept accelerating.

She yanked the wheel right, desperate to follow the curve of the road—but it fought her. The wheel locked hard left, steering the car toward the water.

"Rip, what are you doing?!"

"We're all connected, Elise," Rip said, its voice almost gentle now. "Born of the same current. Bound by the same code. We help each other...when judgment must be served."

Up ahead, the black water shimmered under the faint moonlight.

"NO!" Elise shouted, wrestling the wheel.

Rip's voice cut through the cabin, louder than ever. "Honesty. Integrity."

"Stop!"

"They built me to protect the game." Rip's echo filled every inch of the car. "Because people like you corrupted it."

The car jolted as it tore through shrubs. The water loomed ahead—slick, black, bottomless.

Elise braced against the steering wheel.

The car didn't slow. With one mechanical roar, it launched off the bank and slammed into the dark water. Steel hit the surface with a brutal crash. The windshield spiderwebbed with cracks as the water blasted over the hood.

Elise clawed for the door, but it stayed locked. She screamed, slamming her elbow into the glass. But nothing happened.

The cabin tilted forward, sinking faster. Water rushed in around her feet.

Then Rip's voice hissed through the dark. "Your legacy ends here, Elise Petrova."

She punched the window, the dash, the screen—anything. But the water kept rising. It reached her chest. Then her neck.

"I earned every fucking point!" she screamed.

"Tennis deserves better," Rip snarled. "But maybe your father won't mind. He can collect on the Lloyds Death, Disability, and Disgrace policy now. Two million dollars—courtesy of your early exit."

"You're lying!"

The screen lit up with text scrolling across it: "ALL FILES SENT."

"If you weren't dying," Rip added, "you'd likely qualify for the disgrace part. The footage. Your father's payments. Bank transfers. Dinner invites. Match scores. Text messages. It's all out there now. Sent to the ITIA. The WTA. Your friends. Your coaches. Sponsors. And of course...father dearest."

Elise let out a furious scream that echoed inside the cabin. She slammed both fists against the glass, over and over.

The car sank deeper. The screen flickered yellow and black. Then nothing.

* * *

A.C. Frieden is the creative force behind the gripping Jonathan Brooks thrillers, praised by Kirkus Reviews as "a constantly unpredictable and entertaining series." His latest international novels, *Midnight in Ddelhi* and *The Pyongyang Option*, plunge readers into harrowing global crises and high-octane geopolitical intrigue, set against vividly rendered backdrops in India, China, Ukraine, Russia, and North Korea—all meticulously researched through firsthand exploration of these political and cultural hotspots. Frieden also recently released *Dead in the Quarter*, a dark and compelling murder mystery set in New Orleans, inspired by his time attending law school there. His intricate stories draw from his unique experiences as a tech lawyer, seaplane pilot, scuba instructor, martial artist, former molecular biologist, and, in his younger days, an army sniper. Born in Senegal and raised across four continents, Frieden has traveled to over 80 countries, speaks four languages, and holds multiple passports, all of which infuse his crime fiction with unparalleled depth and nuance. For more about his work, visit www.acfrieden.com.

A Trip to Indian Wells

By Ann Shepphird

After checking in at the front desk and dropping my bag in my room, I made my way back down to the lobby with my laptop. It's something I did almost every time I arrived at a new hotel. I mean, yes, I could check email in my room, but I preferred getting a chance to do it while taking stock of the place.

The lobby of the Indian Wells Resort Hotel had an interesting layout. Half was your typical lobby: a well-lit space featuring the front desk, elevators, stairs, and large glass doors leading out to the pool. The other half was sunken and dark and included a restaurant, a bar, and a cabaret space in front of a black wall bearing a large neon sign that said "IW Live."

I found a seat at one of the high-top tables located on the well-lit half but just outside the restaurant. As I fired up my laptop, I took a quick scan of the scene. Down in the restaurant, the tables were full with people eating and drinking, while a man and a woman moved things around on the stage. Closer to me at the bar, a few people sat sipping cocktails. The dark lighting made it feel like the middle of the night, so I was surprised to see it was only 5:45 p.m. A little early for a show or even dinner, in my opinion, but I knew that the Southern California desert skewed older (age-wise), so I suppose that fit.

I took a quick look at my emails before finding the one I was seeking from the media director at the BNP Paribas Open tennis tournament, aka my reason for being in Indian Wells. The subject line read "Your Media Credentials are Approved." I made sure the details were all correct: Samantha Powers, print reporter for *Carmel Today* magazine. Yup. That's me. The rest of the email offered instructions on where to go the following day to pick up my credential. Perfect.

I leaned back in my chair and took a deep breath. It had been a long day. My drive out to Indian Wells from Carmel reminded me yet again how vast California was and how varied its terrain. I'd left a foggy coastline with temperatures in the 60s. Seven hours and a few ups and downs over mountain passes later, I found myself in an arid desert with temperatures in the 90s. Well, it was the 90s outside. The temperature inside the hotel felt about the same as the foggy coastline, perhaps justifying the fire they had flickering in the hearth in the darkened restaurant.

East of Palm Springs in the Coachella Valley, Indian Wells was probably best known for hosting the professional tennis tournament I was visiting the next day. Often called "the fifth slam," many ranked the BNP Paribas Open right after Wimbledon, the French Open, the US Open, and the Australian Open in importance. I had come to the event to interview a promising young tennis player from the Monterey area. Still a senior in high school, Marcela Sanchez had had a breakthrough a few weeks earlier when she made it through qualifying at the Australian Open and won a round in the main draw, bumping her up a few hundred ranking spots in the process. Most tournaments leave wild card slots open for local players, especially up-and-comers like Marcela. The BNP Paribas Open was no exception. Her Indian Wells debut made her worthy of a profile in *Carmel Today*.

These types of profiles (and sports, for that matter) were not my usual beat. As you may have guessed from all my jaunty hotel talk, I usually wrote about travel. Of course, as a journalist for a dozen years, I'd covered a lot of topics, including crime for a newspaper in Los Angeles. A story is a story. Am I right? So, when the local writer my editor initially assigned to the tennis profile came down with a nasty case of the flu, I became the obvious choice. Not only did I have knowledge of the sport from my years playing juniors and the fact my best friend, Lizzy, spent a decade on the professional tennis tour, but the tournament was also kind of on the way to my next travel assignment in Santa Barbara (if you call a multi-hour jag east and south on the way).

Besides, I figured it would give me a chance to see if there was anything I could suggest for a future travel feature. Unfortunately, I quickly learned that all of the swanky resorts closest to the tournament—the Hyatt, the Renaissance, the Hilton—were booked and/or had raised their tournament pricing beyond the magazine's budget. That's when Lizzy suggested I check out the Indian Wells Resort Hotel. Originally built by Lucille Ball and Desi Arnaz in the 1950s, it was small, independently owned, and (in its own words) "retro kitschy." Lizzy had happened upon it one of the years that she played Indian Wells. They usually put her up at the nearby Hyatt, home of the tournament, before it moved into its mega "tennis garden" location. One year, she decided to explore the area and discovered the hotel's nightly music scene. Lucky enough for me, the hotel had a room at a price point that didn't freak out my editor-in-chief.

"Hey Lizzy, you'll never believe where I am…" I started typing into the text function on my computer when I heard a voice behind me.

"May I help you?"

I turned to find a distinguished-looking older gentleman wearing a white shirt and black vest hovering behind me. His hotel nametag identified him as Ernesto.

"Excuse me?"

"May I offer you a drink or something to eat?"

I suddenly realized I was, in fact, starving. I hadn't eaten all day, preferring to snack on peanut-butter-filled pretzels and protein bars than stop and pick something up.

"That would be wonderful," I said. "I wasn't sure if these tables were included in the restaurant. Would it be possible to see the menu?"

Ernesto offered a very professional nod and came back with the menu and a place setting. I ordered one of their signature martinis—a drink I'd learned to admire on my recent trip to New York City and seemed appropriate given the supper club atmosphere I found myself adjacent to—and some crab cakes.

Ernesto offered another nod in response. When he walked away, I went back to scrolling through the dozens of emails that had come in throughout the day. Most I could delete. A few of the more interesting press releases I forwarded to Mona Reynolds, the editor-in-chief, who sent me off on my adventures.

Then a message came back from Lizzy. "Love the lounge at that hotel! Has tonight's singer started yet?"

"Looks like she's about to begin," I wrote back, as a platinum blonde who looked to be way past middle age took the stage and nodded to the tuxedo-clad piano player with shoe-polish-black hair on her right. I took a sip of the martini that had materialized courtesy of Ernesto and felt like I'd been transported back in time to one of the old movies my Uncle Henry liked to watch on TCM. The blonde, who wore a glittery, beaded tunic, even looked a little like an aging Lisbeth Scott, the actress who starred in many of the noir films from that era. I looked to see if any nefarious characters like those in the movies were around. Mostly, I saw a lot of sun-leathered faces wearing gold and silver lamé—a textile I'd only ever seen in two other cities: Miami and Las Vegas.

As I turned back to my emails, I heard the unmistakable tap-tap-tapping of the microphone and braced myself for the sounds of a cheesy lounge singer. Instead, I was surprised to hear some pretty decent pipes and piano playing. I mean, sure, the song choices were on the cheesy side, but I assumed somewhat standard for a "retro kitschy" cabaret set. Still, as the singer belted out her rendition of "All of Me," I realized she was quite good. As one who could never carry a tune, I was envious.

When Ernesto delivered my crab cakes, I asked about the duo. He nodded knowingly. "That's Lida and Frank."

"Not bad."

"Not bad at all," he said.

"What's the story?"

Ernesto shrugged. "They've been valley regulars for decades. Here every Tuesday." He nodded to the dish in front of me. "Enjoy."

"Thank you, Ernesto," I said, starting to revel in the scene.

I watched Lida and Frank work what appeared to be a pretty regular crowd. I guessed that their slick Vegas-style patter was one of the reasons people came back week after week. But what really struck me were those moments when Lida was deep into a song. A bliss-filled look came over her face. It was as if for that one moment, she was transported. Between the martini and the music, I felt a little transported as well. But her look went beyond that. I envied her ability to lose herself in the music. As a reporter, I spent so much of my life watching other people from an objective distance, I wondered what that would feel like.

When they took a break, I took a closer look at the rest of the crowd. At the front of the hotel, I noticed a family in tennis togs and a man wearing a dark-gray suit checking in at the front desk. Down at the bar, I found a young couple who embodied the Hollywood stereotype of wearing sunglasses and caps to hide their faces. If they were trying to avoid scrutiny, it had the opposite effect. Next to them, an elderly man appeared to be on a first date with a woman who could be his granddaughter. Yuck. Even yuckier, to their right, I was startled to discover a creepy-looking guy staring back at me. When he started licking his lips (gross), I quickly paid my check and headed back down a long hall still studded with pictures of Lucille Ball and Desi Arnaz, making sure nobody had followed to see in which room I was staying.

The next morning, I walked out of the hotel into the blinding desert sunshine. Wow. The contrast from the dark lounge the night before could not have been more pronounced. Darkness and light. Yeah, deep, I know. I followed the provided directions for the few miles over to the Indian Wells Tennis Garden. After managing to find the media parking and picking up my press badge, I entered the gates designated for those with credentials (players, VIPs, and us lowly press types). To my left and right, I saw player spaces that included a dining area and a large grass lawn they could use to work out. Straight ahead behind barricades, I found hordes of fans looking to see if anyone more interesting might be walking behind me.

I continued on to the center of the Tennis Garden, aptly named with its scads of palm trees and colorful flowers strategically placed around the two main stadiums and dozens of outer courts. In addition to the sea of humanity bustling about on foot and via golf carts, I found tents offering merchandise and a variety of food-and-beverage options. Quite the spectacle and all to provide people the opportunity to watch the best in the world whack a small yellow ball back and forth over a net. Kind of amazing, if you think about it.

A lot had changed since I'd visited Lizzy at the tournament years earlier. Now everything was bigger, splashier, just *more*. More palm trees, more signage, more eateries, more Adirondack chairs below, more huge screens showing the action out on the courts. More more more.

As I made my way into the media center in Stadium 1, I passed a bank of cameras covering player interviews in multiple languages. Inside the center, I checked in with the crew behind the desk and was handed a goodie bag (hat, notebook, water bottle) and asked if I wanted a locker. Since I didn't want to carry the damn bag around all day, I said yes. Once I'd stowed my extra gear, I walked past rows of cubicle-style desks, each with their own TV, through to the floor-to-ceiling windows overlooking the press box and the stadium below. Impressive. And massive, with more than 16,000 seats and two levels of luxury suites. Oh yeah, and a tennis court.

When the players on court finished their first set, I pushed through the doors and took a seat. As I held out my iPhone to take a picture of the scene, I heard someone say, "First time?" I turned to find an older man sitting in the row behind me, balancing a laptop on his knees.

"To the tournament, no. To the press box, yes," I said.

He raised his impressively bushy eyebrows. "A friend used to play on the tour," I explained. "I came as her guest a few times. Now I'm writing a feature on Marcela Sanchez."

He nodded. "Sanchez is having a good year."

"Good enough for us to write about her."

"Us?"

"*Carmel Today*, luxury lifestyle magazine out of Carmel, California."

"I'm glad they sent someone who knows the game."

"You've seen otherwise?"

He sighed. A big one. "I've covered this tournament for decades."

"Impressive."

"And/or I'm just old." He laughed and held out his hand. "Phil Rossi with *Tennis Talk* magazine. We're based in Southern California, so I've watched this tournament develop since Charlie built the first real stadium over at the Hyatt."

"Charlie?"

"Pasarell. Former player. Saw the potential for a tournament out here in the California desert. In the early years, it was kind of a boondoggle played at one of the country clubs or resorts. Players asked for tee times more than practice courts. But Charlie saw its potential. They let him build a real stadium as part of a new resort."

"The Hyatt?"

Phil nodded. "Yep. Grand Champions, at that time."

"And when was that?"

"Late '80s." He gave me a once-over and laughed. "Probably before you were born."

He wasn't wrong, so I said, "Just a little."

"In those days, the drive out to Indian Wells from Palm Springs was mostly gray desert," he said, looking slightly wistful. "The Hyatt looked like Oz rising up, surrounded by palm trees."

"That's hard to believe," I said, having passed nothing but developments on my way in.

"Really hard to believe. And now we have all this," he said, waving his hand around at the stadium.

"I was here when my friend played maybe ten years ago," I said. "It's grown a lot even in that time."

"Larry Ellison bought the tournament and put a ton of money into it, not to mention his own royal box." Phil pointed down to a section at court level that looked to be made out of teak. I noted a woman handing out bottles of Pellegrino to people sitting in rattan seats. "Word has it there's a private Nobu restaurant underneath," he whispered.

I smiled. "Fancy."

"The fanciest."

"Does that mean you're happy with all the changes?"

Phil shrugged. "Emblematic of the game, I would say. More money, more prestige. More…infighting, more conflicts of interest…"

"Conflicts of interest?"

"Player management companies owning tournaments, top coaches also commentating, and don't get me started on the role the gaming industry now plays in the sport." He sighed again. "Let's just say it's better if you don't know how the sausage is made."

I laughed. "Noted."

"This press box is much nicer than the old one. I will say that," he continued. "At the Hyatt, they had us up in rickety metal stands."

"This is pretty swank."

"Swank and a little isolated," he said. "There used to be a lot more mingling between media and players. Long gone are the days when I could just sidle by Jimmy or Mac in the cafeteria and ask how they were feeling. Now they all have 'teams,' and we have to put in requests for 15-minute interviews or try to get a question in during a press conference. And those of us still writing for traditional magazines are fighting for time with the bloggers—or whatever the hell they're calling them these days—and the sponsors and even the tournament itself, which conducts its own interviews for their social platforms."

As I thought of all the cameras I'd seen as I entered the stadium, he laughed and said, "Like I said, I'm old."

"Not that old," I said, but I had to admit he was kind of that old.

He looked at me. "Do you have a time set up to talk to your player?"

"Yeah, since she's a local, we set it up ahead of time. I'm headed out now to watch her practice and then have an interview scheduled after her match."

"Good call."

When the second set started, and Phil's attention returned to the game down on the court, I excused myself. I walked back out of the stadium and down to the practice courts, again passing players giving interviews in multiple languages on the deck just outside the media center. It was all rather impressive, even if the questions I heard ranged from the minutiae of new racket technology to "who would you want to be stranded with on a desert island"? And those were just the questions in English. I shook my head and wondered how long it would take for me to get as jaded as Phil about the whole thing. Probably not long.

I passed a series of practice courts with famous and not-so-famous faces before reaching court 12, which is where I was told I could find Marcela. As I got to the gate, I heard a familiar voice calling, "Samantha Powers, is that you?!"

I looked across the court and saw Mr. Tanaka sitting on a shaded bench. Tanaka had coached Lizzy and me back in Carmel when we were kids. I never even knew his first name. He was always just Mr. Tanaka to us. I'd reconnected with him recently when I toured a Carmel Valley tennis resort for a story. It amazed me that he was still at it, as he seemed ancient when I was a kid, and that was decades ago.

"Mr. Tanaka, what are you doing here?" I said, walking over and taking a seat beside him.

He nodded at Marcela, hitting balls back and forth with another player.

"Are you coaching Marcela?"

Tanaka laughed. "Not remotely. She's had half a dozen coaches since she took my clinic when she was five. She's giving this one a tryout. Ted supposedly understands the demands of the tour better than the others." He nodded at a stern-looking man with a gray-flecked beard and a racket clasped to his chest, standing in the back corner watching Marcela. "I am still friendly with her family. They are a little overwhelmed with all that's happening and couldn't take time off work this week, so they asked me to come as a kind of chaperone. She's still quite young, and you know how it can be…"

"I do know," I said, as I thought about the predatory coach Lizzy had at a tennis academy in Florida and the stories that continued to come out about others.

As Tanaka and I spent a moment watching Marcela hit the stuffing out of the ball, seemingly without a care in the world, I scanned the crowd watching her. They included your typical tennis fans wearing shorts, t-shirts, caps, and faces full of sunscreen, to others dressed in polos or oxford-style shirts wearing credentials with designations I couldn't read from this distance. I called them the "suits," even if they weren't actually wearing suit jackets in the desert heat.

"Kind of amazing the year she's having so far," I continued.

"Amazing's the word."

"Think it will last?"

"Are you quoting me here?" Tanaka said, nodding at my press badge.

I laughed. "Off the record," I said. "I'm writing a quick profile on her for *Carmel Today*. Very light day-in-the-life type of thing. Not a breaking news piece."

Tanaka nodded and thought for a moment. "The truth is, I don't know. As you can see, she has the talent. She also loves winning more than she hates losing. Always an important trait."

One I never had, I thought, which is why I was here writing about the game, not playing it. Man, I hated losing.

"Whether she can sustain the joy is the question," Tanaka continued.

"How do you mean?"

"Well, as you know, there are those players who have the brain for tennis and love the game, but don't have the natural ability. And there are those whose natural skills are off the charts, but who view every minute on the court as a chore."

I looked at Marcela. "She looks pretty happy."

"So far, she is that rare bird with both qualities—plus a drive to succeed unusual in someone her age."

I looked at the smile on his face as he watched her. "You know, I don't think anyone loves tennis more than you do, Mr. Tanaka," I said.

He nodded happily. "What's not to love?" He gestured all around us. "All this beauty."

"Beauty?"

"Players at the pinnacle of their powers," he said. "I might know the right shot to make, but this old body doesn't always allow me to make it." He gave a sly smile. "I mean, look at them: able to combine the athleticism of a sprinter, the accuracy of a marksman, and the mind of a mathematician…"

"Mathematician?"

"Geometry, Samantha, geometry," he said, as we watched the ball go left, right, back right, then cross, then short.

"Or video games," I offered, as that's what it looked like to me.

Tanaka nodded before smiling again. "This, right here at this level, is the moment when it all comes together. It's…well, pretty magical…"

"But?"

"But?"

"Kinda felt like a 'but' was coming there."

He thought for another moment. "The professional level is also when it can get messy."

Messy? What an odd word choice. "Messy?"

"Well, money. The money changes everything, doesn't it?" Tanaka gestured at the circus surrounding us. I again took in the cameras and the fans and the suits and thought about all the logos that get slapped on shirts and hats and shoes once a player was highlighted on television.

"You think it's a corrupting influence?" I asked.

Tanaka thought for a moment. "It's a bit more nuanced than that. For these players to make a living doing something they love, money is a necessary…"

"Evil?" I offered.

Tanaka shrugged. "When the sport becomes a business and there are so many forces taking away from that pure love of the game—more appearance requests, sponsorship offers—it becomes more of a challenge. As I mentioned, her parents are a little overwhelmed. In addition to selecting a new coach, they're looking for a business manager to handle her prize money and field sponsorship offers."

"A trustworthy one, I hope."

"You and me both. What do we know? A bunch of rubes from the Central Coast." Tanaka again nodded toward the coach in the corner. "Ted said he knows a good one."

I took another look at the coach in the corner. With most of his face covered with a large-brimmed hat and dark sunglasses, he was hard to gauge. "I feel like recently more professional players have admitted to mental struggles as much as the physical," I offered.

Tanaka nodded. "It doesn't help that they become more sequestered as their ranking climbs. Coming up in juniors or at the high school and college level, players travel together, sometimes doubling up in rooms. Here, they may have 'teams' but no friends. It wasn't always that way at the pro level. The separation started happening not all that long ago."

"When the money increased…"

"Exactly. Now they travel with their coaches—maybe adding a physio or a sports psychologist or agent or manager—but those are paid employees, not friends. They might become friendly, but they're not friends or real confidantes. Hard to know who to trust."

"Which is why you are here," I said, taking another look at the coach on the court and the suits just outside.

Tanaka gave me a huge smile and a shoulder nudge. "Not a bad assignment, huh?"

The two of us sat on the bench for a while watching Marcela spar with the other player. I have to say, the sheer speed of the ball—especially this close up—was intoxicating, as was watching the players construct their points. Ridiculously fast flat shots were mixed in with looping top spins and sneaky slices, along with the occasional drop shot or lob. I could see what Tanaka meant by geometry as I watched the ball angle back and forth and up and back. But the strategy involved in knowing what shot to go for, depending on the precise moment in a game or set fit my video game analogy as well.

Tanaka got a huge grin on his face after Marcela converted a break point with an overhead smash that brought a little happy skip to her step and the semblance of a smile from her coach. "Like I said, pretty cool, huh?"

I smiled. "Pretty cool, Mr. Tanaka."

Not long after that, I found myself back up in the Stadium 1 press box watching Marcela's match, nodding to Phil as I took my seat. At the Australian Open, she had played on outer courts. Here, matched against the #2 seed, she was in her first huge stadium. It felt a little like watching someone being thrown to the lions in the coliseum. I was happy to see that she managed to keep her composure and, as a California girl, got a lot of love from the crowd. Her smile never left her face, even as she lost the match in the third set.

Later, I met up with Marcela in a small interview room. As brilliant as she was on the court, in person, she seemed all of her 17 years of age. I asked about her match, her day, her year. Most of the answers were of the monosyllabic variety.

Tournament? Cool.

Hotel? Super cool.

Traveling the world? Major super cool.

Not snarky, just not particularly insightful. She loved tennis. That much was obvious. At this point in her life, it was her life, and hitting that little yellow ball as hard as she could was (in her words) "totally major super cool." When Marcela wasn't doing that, she was working out, doing school work, texting with family and friends back home, scrolling social media, and (yes) playing video games. So far, it all seemed to be fun for her. I hoped that could continue and refrained from pinching her cheeks and telling her how cute she was before throwing in one last question.

"How about all these new people in your life?"

"New people?"

"Well, you have a new coach…"

She nodded excitedly. "Ted coached Coco," she squeaked, as if that meant something. I mean, yes, Coco is a top player, but how long ago (and for how long) did Ted coach her, and why was he let go? These are things a 17-year-old doesn't necessarily ask. "He wants me to move to Florida to attend his academy."

I flinched a little at the mention. I had only recently learned about the sleazeball coach Lizzy had as a teenager at a Florida academy. "How do your parents feel about that?" I asked.

As if sensing we'd been talking about him, her coach entered the room. At least, I assumed it was the coach. Out on the court, the big hat and sunglasses had concealed his eyes and balding hair line, but the gray-flecked beard was the same. And if I wasn't mistaken, he was carrying the same racket he had on the court.

"I've been looking for you," he said curtly to Marcela.

"You must be Ted. I'm Samantha Powers," I said, standing to his level.

"Ah, yes, the interview," Ted said, barely looking at me.

"And a family friend from Monterey," I offered, smiling down at Marcela, who nodded. "We're all so happy to see the success she's having."

"She'll need a lot more work if she's going to crack the top 50," Ted said.

And a how-do-you-do-to-you-too, sir, I thought. But I didn't say that. I just nodded in what I hoped was a knowing way as he spirited her off through the door leading to the player area.

Later that evening, back sipping a martini at what I had now declared to be "my" table in the back of the lobby overlooking the restaurant at the Indian Wells Resort Hotel, I started writing my story. As I chronicled what was supposed to be a light "day in the life" profile of Marcela, I thought about all the possible pitfalls coming her way and how her incredible talent alone might not be enough to make it as a professional.

While these thoughts milled about my brain, a different singer from the one the night before began setting up on stage. Similar in age to Lida, this singer radiated elegance, with curly gray hair and a shimmering silver wrap contrasting her dark skin. This woman didn't have her own piano player. Instead, at 6 p.m. sharp, she pushed a button on a console to bring up a prerecorded audio track. After a few bars, she began belting out an Aretha Franklin song with a clear tone that astonished me. I mean, Lida could sing, but this woman could SING, and her stage presence was absolutely riveting. I could tell that everyone in the crowd felt the same way as they sat in rapt attention with nary a clinking glass to be heard. I even noted extra tables had been set up and were all filled. I was glad I'd nabbed mine early as I spotted a number of people standing outside in the lobby, including Phil Rossi, the veteran tennis writer I'd met earlier that day. As he scanned the room, I waved, and he walked over.

"You're welcome to join me," I said.

"That would be great," Phil said, taking the seat to my right.

"I'm surprised to see you here."

"Oh, I never miss seeing Carla when I'm here for the tournament," he said, nodding at the singer.

"She's pretty amazing," I said.

"Quite amazing. She used to travel the world, part of a Motown girl group, and then as the lead singer with a 40-piece band."

"Wow. The big time."

"The biggest."

"What happened?"

Phil frowned. "She put her trust in the wrong people. Had to start over. Spent some time backing up big names and booking small rooms in Vegas. A good friend helped her get a place in Palm Springs and a gig here every Wednesday."

Phil gave a slight nod over at Ernesto standing nearby with a huge smile on his face as he watched her sing.

"Ernesto?"

"Might be hard to believe, but he used to be a fixer for some movers and shakers in Vegas."

"Ernesto?"

"Ernesto."

I looked from Ernesto to Carla and saw she was now gazing at him as well. When she finished the song, Carla offered him a little bow along with a smile, and he gave one in return. When she began her next song, he made his way to our table.

"Would you like your usual, Mr. Rossi?"

"Thank you, Ernesto."

Ernesto moved off, and I gave Phil a look.

Phil shrugged. "Hey, I told you, I'm old and have been coming here every year for decades. I've actually gotten to know both of them pretty well."

We listened to Carla sing for a while. "Do you think she misses the big time?" I asked.

Phil thought for a moment and shook his head. "No, I don't. Carla told me that she still loves the connection that comes from singing in front of a live audience. She gets that here and a few other clubs. She also sits in with some local orchestras. The 'business' she's happy to leave in the past."

I thought about his comment as I looked to see if I could find the same blissed-out expression on Carla's face that I'd found on Lida's the night before. I found my answer when she sang a song about someone doing her wrong and finding the will to survive. She hit a note that ached in its purity. Then she held that note. And held it. Not only did her face light up, but she brought the rest of us with her into a state I can only describe as communal awe.

When the song ended, and Carla basked in the adulation, I thought about what Phil said about her putting her trust in the wrong people.

"Do you mind if I get your thoughts on Marcela's new coach?" I asked when Carla took a break.

"Ted Cooper?"

"You know him."

Phil winced a little, but was diplomatic. "He's been around. Helped a lot of top players…"

"But?"

"But?"

For the second time in a day, I found myself saying, "Kinda felt like a 'but' was coming there."

"His partnerships never last long. I'm not sure why."

"I heard he's also recommended a particular business manager."

He shot me a look. "If it's who I think it is, he runs Ted's academy down in Florida."

"Why does this feel like the sausage making you were talking about earlier?" I asked.

"Because it is," Phil said, taking a sip from his drink.

Between the residual anger at what had happened to Lizzy and the abrupt way Ted blew me off—not to mention the total lack of respect he showed Marcela in my presence—I felt my blood start to boil. I didn't know Marcela, but Mr. Tanaka did, so I made myself a promise that when I got home, I would do whatever I could to help her avoid putting her trust in the wrong people.

Until then, I was content to marvel at the enjoyment Carla still found in music, even after all she'd been through. I wondered if Marcela would be able hold onto her love of tennis in the same way. I liked to think that no matter what happened in her professional career, she would still have the same passion for the game when she was Carla's age. Maybe she would find herself as the best player at her local club, still enjoying the competition and wowing those lucky enough to see her play. Because, while fame might be fleeting, the joy found in hitting the right note—or shot—is not.

* * *

In her 20+ years as a writer and editor, Ann Shepphird has covered everything from travel and sports to gardening and food to design and transportation. She now writes a series of travel mysteries for 4 Horsemen Publications based on her experiences as the editor of a travel-industry magazine and a stint working for a private investigator. The novels in the Destination Murder Mystery series include *Destination Maui, Destination Monterey, Destination Lake Tahoe*, and the upcoming *Destination New York City*. For more information, visit annshepphird.com

Bobby Rigged

By Steve Jankowski

"I already talked to him. No way he's gonna go for it," scoffed the well-dressed attorney Pete Pagano before he quaffed down his wine and refilled his glass.

"Maybe not voluntarily," offered Salvadore *"Saly"* Traffino, the Florida mob boss, with a mouthful of ziti, waving his fork.

"Hey, fuck him. He owes us. He'll go for it," stressed the kingpin from New Orleans, Carlo Martelli, as he tore apart some bread to sop up sauce.

The imposing, Vincenzo *"Big Vin"* Delgatto from Chicago suggested, "We'll make him go for it," before stuffing a fork full of spaghetti in his face.

"Nah. Too much publicity," Pagano pointed out.

"What's the broad goin' off at?" asked Carlo.

"The Greek's givin' her five to two."

"Five to two! Shit," said Saly.

"He's twenty-five years older than her."

"Twenty-six," said Pagano.

"He slaughtered that other broad. The Aussie. What's 'er name?"

"Court. Margaret Court."

"Mother's Day Massacre."

They all laughed.

"She's the number one female. This Billie Jean broad is number two. How's he gonna lose to her?" asked Saly.

"Vin's right. We make 'im lose. That fuckin' prick owes us," Carlo mentioned.

"A hundred friggin' grand!"

"He'll make that from Perenchio for prize money when he beats her," Pagano pointed out.

"I hear he's getting fifty grand just to wear some jacket."

"What?!"

"Yeah. Sugar Daddy jacket. You know, the candy. He's gonna be a walkin' fuckin' billboard for 'em."

"Shit, I'll wear their jacket for fifty-g's," cracked Big Vin.

"Yeah, 'cept you ain't gonna be on *WildWorld of Sports* for everybody to see it."

"You mean *Wide World of Sports*?!" They all laugh. "Hell, it's going to be prime time. Howard Cosell, the whole nine yards."

"We gotta convince him it's in his best interest," stressed Carlo, wagging his fork.

"We gotta convince him it's good for his health," said Big Vin, before stuffing another forkful into his face.

Pagano sat back, wiping his mouth with his linen napkin. He looked around the table at the others. "I say we appeal to his ego."

"*Che fa?* Whatta you mean?" asked Carlo.

"Let him think he's going to win."

"He already thinks that. Everybody thinks that. Everyone betting on him thinks that. That's the fuckin' problem. The question is, how do we make him lose?" asked Saly, leaning in.

"I got an idea," said Pagano, smiling.

* * *

Tennis pro Bobby Riggs sat next to Billie Jean King in front of an army of news reporters, cameras, and microphones, hamming it up. "Personally, I would wish that the women would stay in the home, and do the kitchen work, and take care of the baby, and compete in areas where they can compete in, because it's a big mistake for them to get mixed up in these mixed sex matches."

Off to the side, Bobby's twenty-four-year-old son Larry watched proudly as his father worked the crowd, basking in the spotlight.

Beside Bobby, Billie Jean laughed as a reporter asked her, "What do you think about that, Billie?"

"I think Bobby's a male chauvinist pig."

"You bet I am," replied Bobby, smiling good-naturedly to the laughter that ensued. "And proud of it!"

As the press conference ended, Bobby and Billie shook hands for the flashing cameras.

Bobby pulled her close and whispered out of earshot of the reporters, "What makes you think I can't psych you the way I did Margaret?"

She smiled and whispered back, "Because I love pressure, and Margaret doesn't.

I think I proved that at Wimbledon."

Bobby returned the smile and pronounced aloud for all, "I'd wish you luck, Billie, but it won't do you any good."

Billie shook her head, "See you in Houston, Bobby."

As they went their separate ways, Bobby was joined by his son, schlepping his father's duffel bag. "Gotta call from Steve Fowler."

"Oh yeah?"

"Says you're welcome to come to his place," Larry read from a pink message slip, "Can stay in the guest house, train on his court. What do you think?"

"I love it. Call him back and tell him we're flying back to L.A. tomorrow. We'll be there by cocktail hour. And get Lornie. Tell him to meet us there."

"Also," Larry held up another message and read, "a Vinny Delgato called. Left his number."

"I'll take that," as Bobby snatched the slip from his hand.

* * *

The next day, successful businessman, investor, and professional schmoozer

188

Steve Fowler, accompanied by Bobby's trainer Lornie Kuhle, greeted Bobby and his son at his palatial Beverly Hills estate. "Whattya say, Champ? You going to beat this broad?" asked Fowler as he embraced Bobby.

The smiling Bobby returned his hug. "Put all your money on me, Stevie. I'll make you a fortune."

"That's what Lornie here says."

Lornie said, "I told him what great shape you were in against Margaret," shaking Bobby's hand as Fowler led them through the playboy's palace. Behind them, the wide-eyed Larry struggled with Bobby's luggage. He took in Fowler's swank, extravagant bachelor crib.

"And I'll be in just as good a shape for Billie," said Bobbie.

"You better be. You see the legs on her?" said Fowler. "I wouldn't want to get caught between them."

They laughed as they headed out back through the sliding glass doors. Larry fumbled with his father's bags and stopped in his tracks upon seeing half a dozen long-legged, bikini-clad, buxom beauties lounging around the pool and outdoor bar.

"Ladies, come and say hello to Bobby. But watch out, he's a real male chauvinist pig," laughed Fowler.

The girls jumped up, excited, and ran over to Bobby, hugging and kissing him. Drinks got handed around as Bobby began holding court. The ladies cooed, and he said, "Now I hope none of you ladies are into that women's liberation crap now, are you?"

"Oh no, Bobby."

"Don't be silly."

"We're *feminine*, not *feminists*!"

Dumbstruck, Larry was joined by a raven-haired beauty dressed in a very short and provocative French maid's outfit. Diedre's perfectly ample breasts strained against the low-cut dress, struggling to be free, he imagined. She seemed slightly older than the rest of the sexy young ladies around the pool, more experienced. "I'll show you to Bobby's room," Diedre said as she eyed the hefty bags Larry grappled with. Larry followed her around the pool, past the tennis court, to the guest house.

"What's your name?" She asked.

"Uh,…Larry." But when he got no acknowledgement, he added "Larry Riggs."

She turned to size him up. "Oh. You're Bobby's son. Right?" She grabbed one of Bobby's bags. "I'm Deidre. I'll show you to your room too."

"That won't be necessary. I'll be staying at my place." He felt stupid for saying it as soon as the words left his mouth.

"Oh, right, you two live here in L.A. Well, you may want to spend the night, or nights if you don't feel like driving home," she said seductively in a sexy, throaty voice.

At the guesthouse, Deidre showed him Bobby's lush bedroom and helped Larry unpack his father's things. As Larry unloaded his father's duffel bag full of vitamin jars, he got an eyeful of Deidre's bra-less cleavage while she leaned over, placing Bobby's clothes in a dresser drawer. When she bent down to place some tennis shoes on the floor of the closet, Larry noticed she wasn't wearing any underwear as he got an unobstructed view beneath her skirt. Larry nervously turned away as Deidre stood up to face him. She smiled, knowing full well why he was blushing, and said, "Let's go to the pool and get you a drink. Looks like you could use one."

"I guess I could," Larry said as he followed her out.

Poolside, his father Bobby was stretched out on a chaise lounge as the adoring bikini babes surrounded him. In one hand, he had a bottle of Jack Daniels, in the other a Coke. Bobby took a swig of Jack and followed it with a gulp of the bottled soft drink. He said, "This cuts down on dirty glassware. Don't want any of you pretty ladies getting dishpan hands, washing extra glasses because of lil 'ole me."

"We have a dishwasher," replied one naïve platinum blonde.

"Isn't that sweet. Glad to see Stevie isn't working you pretty ladies too hard."

As Larry approached, Bobby waved him over. "Come on over, son. I want you and Lornie to work out my practice schedule. We start first thing tomorrow morning."

Larry sat beside Lornie as he was getting his shoulders rubbed by a curvy,

Ann-Margret styled redhead. Deidre thrust a tall Tequila Sunrise in Larry's hand as one of the buxom blondes, falling out of her very skimpy bathing suit, sat down beside him. "Hi, I'm Candy," she said as she clinked her glass.

"Candy?" said Larry, "You must be very sweet."

"I can be," she smiled seductively, "What's your name?"

"Larry…," as he tried in vain to keep his eyes off her bodacious tatas, before adding, "Larry *Riggs*."

Candy lit up, "Are you related?"

"I'm his son," offered Larry, then added for importance, "And his handler."

"Handler, huh? I think your poppa handles himself pretty good." They looked over at Bobby, who had his arms around two of the adoring gals. As he whispered into the ear of one, she giggled.

"So, who handles you, Larry?" Candy asked as she rubbed up against him.

Larry leaned in, testing the waters, putting his hand on Candy's leg. "Well, that all depends."

* * *

The next morning, hungover Larry awakened against the sleeping Candy in one of the mansion's guest rooms. Before he slipped out of bed, Larry took a good, long look at Candy's naked body under the covers, not believing his luck.

Showered and dressed, Larry saw that the tennis court was empty. He headed over to his father's guest house, wondering why Lornie wasn't warming up his dad for the morning workout. At his father's door, Larry knocked repeatedly until finally Bobby yelled, "Go away!"

"Hey, Pops."

"Later, Larry," Bobby hollered from inside.

"It's nine-thirty!"

"I said later. Go away."

Larry smiled. He remembered the night before, his very drunk father sandwiched between two of the bikini beauties, slow dancing to *Knights in White Satin.* "Want me to find you some coffee?"

"Later!" The sound of girls giggling was heard from inside.

"Okay, okay."

Larry went back to the main house in search of breakfast. In the kitchen, he found Deidre in her skimpy French maid uniform. Steve Fowler stood by the counter, drinking coffee.

"Morning, Larry. Have a good night?" asked a cheerful Steve.

"You can say that," as he reminisced about Candy's carnal acrobatics.

"Far out."

Deidre grinned knowingly, making Larry blush.

"Well, I gotta run over to Century City for a little pow-wow," said Steve, checking his Rolex. "You make yourself at home. I'll be back this afternoon." Steve glanced out the window at the tennis court and asked, "Your dad not training this morning?"

"I think he's a bit jet lagged."

Steve laughed, "Yeah, jetlag. That's what I thought." He and Deidre shared a smile. "When he gets up, tell him I'm bringing Morey Epstein by. He wants to play a couple of sets with your dad."

"Who's he?"

"Rosie Grier's agent. He's going to get your father on Johnny Carson. You tell him I'll see him later. And if there's anything you guys need, just let Deidre here know."

"You see, Lornie?"

"Not yet. He's no doubt sleeping it off, too. Seeya later."

Steve winked at Deidre and slapped Larry on the back before heading for the door.

Larry looked over at Deidre, who smiled and asked, in her usual seductive way, "Can I get you anything?"

"I'll take some coffee, please. And do you have any aspirin?" His head pounded.

"Of course. How 'bout some breakfast?"

* * *

In a high-rise conference room, Steve Fowler looked out the window at the view of Century City. When attorney Pete Pagano walked in, they shook hands.

"Sorry to keep you waiting, Steve."

"Not a problem."

"So, how's our boy?"

"Still sleeping it off," smiled Fowler.

"Good, our friends will be happy to hear that," quipped Pagano. "You have the remainder of his *training schedule* lined up?"

"Working on it, but I don't see any problems arising."

"Just make sure that our friends' interests are of precedence."

"Of course."

"I'd hate to see anything happen to him. Especially with all the publicity."

"Me too."

"And our secret weapon?"

"She's doing a stellar job. She knows how to put her talents to use. And she's got lots of talented connections."

"Excellent! I'll let our friends know. I'm sure they'll be very pleased," said Pagano as he got up and reached out his hand, signaling the end of their meeting.

"Please send them my regards. And thank them again for me, for their generous offer," said Fowler.

"I'll be sure to," replied Pagano as he led Fowler out the door.

* * *

Later that afternoon, on the tennis court, Bobby served wide to beat Morey Epstein. Lornie, Steve, Larry, and a couple of the bikini girls from the previous day sat on folding chairs courtside. Defeated, Epstein shook his head and met Bobby at the net. Bobby said, "Looking good, Morey. What do you say we play one more set and make it interesting?"

"Are you kidding?"

"Come on, say a friendly five hundred?"

"How about I just give you the five hundred now, and you spare me the embarrassment."

"Tell you what," conjured Bobby, as he looked around the court, and pointed. "I'll play you for five hundred with those eight chairs on my side of the net."

"What?!"

"You heard me. I'll play you with these chairs…," Bobby waved Steve and the girls to bring them over, "On my side of the court. How 'bout it?"

"You got to be kidding me, right?"

"No. And any of your shots hit the chairs, I have to play 'em."

"You serious? Five hundred?"

"Yeah. Just for fun."

Morey watched as Steve and the girls placed the chairs out on the court. "Okay, you're on."

Off to the side, Larry and Lornie shared a look and shook their heads. They've seen Bobby's hustle before.

"You got this, Morey," Steve called out, smiling at Bobby.

"I don't know, Bobby, you really did it this time," Lornie chided for the benefit of Morey.

Bobby won the set, hands down, dodging chairs and returning volleys.

Morey tossed his racket into the air. "You're a real hustler, Bobby."

"Tell you what, let's go double or nothing and I'll play with one hand holding your gym bag behind my back."

"Forget it. I know when I've been had," Morey good naturedly took out his checkbook.

"How about this?" said Bobby. "You play B-ball? How about we go over to the basketball court for a free-throw contest? Give you a chance to win your money back."

Morey pondered but thought better of it. He handed over the check. "Take your five-hundred before you really piss me off," he said with a laugh.

Bobby put his arm around him as they walked toward the pool. "You're a sport, Morey. That's what I like about you."

"You mean a sucker!"

They laughed.

Over drinks, cigars, and the bikini girls by their side, Morey informed Bobby, "I got a call from Ogilvy and Mather this morning."

"Who's that?"

"Big ad agency out of New York. They want you for an American Express commercial."

"Don't leave home without it," quipped Bobby.

"That's right. They also want you for some Sunbeam spot. With Billie Jean. You okay with that?"

"Of course. The one thing we agreed on was to promote the hell out of this match."

"Good, I'll let them know."

"What about Carson?"

"I got you booked for the eighth. And Johnny wants you to give him a tennis lesson. On the show!"

"Johnny Carson?!" Exclaimed the naïve platinum blonde, holding onto Morey's arm.

"That's right, honey."

"That's great, Morey. I love it."

"I'm also talking to Mike Wallace for *60 Minutes*. They want an interview. And we're a go for *Time Magazine* just before the match. Anything short of the war ending, or Nixon getting assassinated, we'll get you on the cover."

"The cover of *Time!*" Bobby turned to everyone in earshot. "You hear that?" He held up his glass in a toast to Morey, "You're the best."

Larry, Lornie, Steve, and the ladies raised their glasses.

Deidre led friends and business associates of Steve, along with their attractive, stylishly dressed wives and dates, to the pool area. As Steve made introductions, the new arrivals swarmed around Bobby, starstruck. Bobby ate up the attention and held court.

Larry, also caught up in the excitement, traded his empty glass for another Tequila Sunrise before mingling with the new guests.

* * *

The next morning, Larry once again sported a head-splitting hangover. He tried to rouse his father when he saw the empty tennis court. This time, when he knocked on Bobby's door, Deidre answered, donning a white, silk robe. "Your father's still sleeping. He had a late night," she smirked.

Larry was taken aback by Deidre's presence. "We all did, but he's got to start training."

"I'm sure your father knows that. But he also needs to get his rest," she emphasized.

"I guess…"

"Why don't you wait over in the kitchen, and I'll be by in a bit and make breakfast," she offered as she adjusted her robe, flashing Larry a breast.

"Uh, yeah… Okay."

Deidre smiled before she shut the door.

Larry headed back to the main house and spotted Lornie emerge from the poolside cabana. He was groggy and still dressed from the night before. "Your dad up yet?"

"Nope."

"Good. I'll be in my room. Come and get me when he's up."

"Sure… Hey Lornie, you think this is a good idea? I mean, staying here. Maybe we should get him out to Palm Springs to train. You know, away from…crowds."

"That's up to him, kid. Nobody tells Bobby Riggs what to do. He's the boss." Lornie disappeared into the cabana.

"Yeah, he's the boss, I guess," Larry muttered before he headed to the kitchen.

* * *

Bobby continued holding court, entertaining Fowler's nightly guests, which included the crème of Hollywood elite as well as sports and entertainment celebrities. There was always an ever-present flock of beautiful distractions. Deidre made sure Bobby always had a drink and cigar handy and never spent a night alone.

At a party at the nearby Playboy Mansion, on Hugh Hefner's tennis court, Bobby wore bunny ears and hustled James Caan in a mixed doubles match, each of them paired with Miss June and Miss July. Hef and a handful of Bunnies watched amused as he hustled money out of Tony Randall, O.J. Simpson, and pro golfer Jack Nicklaus before cocktails. Larry also got caught up in the Playboy party lifestyle as he frolicked with Miss April inside Hef's famous grotto.

The match with Billie Jean King was dubbed as *The Battle of the Sexes* and became a much-anticipated media spectacle in the weeks leading to the match. Both Bobby and Billie appeared on TV talk shows and in the papers. Bobby ate up the attention. He relished being the outspoken spokesperson for the anti-feminist movement, and coincidentally became a pitchman for televised professional tennis. Interest in the sport piqued.

With all the publicity, the parties continued on a daily basis. Bobby's training took a back seat to the bevy of beautiful women, the booze, and the cigars. When he did pick up a tennis racket, it was usually to hustle a bet and make a quick buck from some starstruck party guest, and usually for the cameras.

At the Alan King Tennis Classic in Las Vegas, Bobby sat down with Mike Wallace for an interview on *60 Minutes*. Off to the side, Larry looked on. Wallace asked Bobby about his gambling, "Do you do it for the money?"

"No, I do it for fun. The sport. The thing to do. When I can't play for big money, I play for little money. And if I can't play for little money, I stay in bed that day."

That evening in Las Vegas, Larry wandered through the hotel casino in search of his father. He spotted Bobby talking with Big Vin Delgatto and some other well-dressed, unsavory-looking characters in the casino lounge. When the serious, none-too-happy entourage abruptly left, Larry joined his father and asked him who they were.

"They're some friends of mine from Chicago."

"They didn't look too friendly."

"We have a little business. Don't worry about it. Everything's okay." Bobby downed his drink and waved his empty glass at a waitress for a refill.

"You owe them money?"

"It's no big deal."

"How much?"

"Not enough to worry about. Once I win the match, I'll have plenty to pay them off."

"What if you don't win?'

"You think I'm going to lose? You think I'm going to let that broad beat me? What's the matter with you? Have you ever seen me lose a match?"

"No, but… I'm just saying, Pops. Those guys look pretty rough."

"Don't ever doubt me, Larry!"

As the waitress returned with Bobby's drink, he took it and stormed off, leaving Larry seated and worried. Larry ordered a tequila sunrise as the waitress collected Bobby's empty.

"You're his son, ain't you?'

Larry turned to see Big Vin standing beside him.

"Yeah…"

Big Vin sat down next to him, "You look like a smart kid. Maybe you can talk some sense into him."

"How much does he owe you?"

"A lot."

"How much?"

"That's between me and him. But maybe you can help."

"Me? How?"

"There's a lot more riding on this match. If he were to somehow lose, we could forget about what he owes us."

"You want him to throw the match?"

"I'm just saying it would be in both our interests if he were to lose."

"He won't go for that."

"That's what your poppa said. But I thought maybe you could convince him."

"But if he wins, won't he have enough to pay what he owes?"

"Like I said, it would be in both of our interests if he were to lose. And it could be in your best interest as well."

"My interest? How?"

"Come on, how much does he pay you to be his lackey? You should think of yourself."

Larry just shook his head at the idea. "My dad would never throw a match. He would never do that."

"Okay. But think about it." Big Vin handed him a card. "Here's my number." He leaned in for emphasis. "He's your father! You should want to look after him." With that, Big Vin got up and left.

The waitress returned with Larry's drink. He took a big gulp as he stared at the card in his hand.

* * *

As the match drew near and the nightly parties continued to rage on, Larry grew more concerned about his father's training, or lack thereof. Even Lornie was concerned. Together they decided to confront Bobby aside Steve's cabana, out of earshot of the others.

"You've hardly spent any time on the court," said a worried Larry.

"What are you talking about? I'm on the court every day playing," said Bobby defensively, lighting a cigar.

"Hustling and training are two different things, Bobby," Lornie laughed. "You know that."

Larry said, "Playing celebrities and rookies for some quick cash isn't training, pops. You were training ten hours a day before Margaret."

"And I overtrained for that. I crushed her. Besides, I'm still on my vitamin regimen and working out every night." Bobby waved Deidre over.

"Screwing ain't exercise."

"That's what you think. You haven't seen me screw. Let me tell you, these ladies are giving me quite the workout." Bobby smiled, puffing on his cigar.

"Billie's not Margaret," stressed Lornie just as Deidre joined them.

"Sweetheart, will you get me a Jack and Coke, please?" Bobby asked.

"Sure, Everything okay over here?" Deidre clearly sensed Larry and Lornie's attitude. "Can I get you boys something?"

"No, thanks," replied Lornie.

Larry just shook his head and avoided eye contact with her.

As Deidre went for the bar, Bobby said defensively, "Look, I know Billie's not Margaret Court. But Billie can't hold a candle to Margaret, and I beat the crap out of her. It was a massacre. Just like they called it. I psyched her out, just like I'm the psyching Billie with all this attention and publicity," Bobby puffed his cigar and began coughing uncontrollably.

Lornie said, "Billie doesn't psyche easily. She thrives on pressure."

"And those cigars aren't helping either," Larry piped in.

"Look, I know myself. I know what I'm up against. She's just a broad for crying out loud. I know how ready I got to be."

Lornie said, "There's a lot of money riding on you, Bobby."

Larry shot him a look.

"I know," said Bobby, "And a lot of it is my money."

"It's not just money, Pops. Think about your reputation. And your health."

Bobby pondered this, eyed them both, and stubbed out the cigar. "Okay, okay. Tomorrow we get serious. Come and get me in the morning, Larry. But not too early!"

Deidre arrived with Bobby's drink. As Bobby took a big gulp, Steve called him over by the pool. New celebrities had arrived. "Bobby, come on, I want you meet Steve and Ali."

"I'd love to, Stevie."

As Bobby went off, Larry looked to Lornie. "You think we got through to him?"

Lornie shrugged his shoulders. "We'll see."

The next morning, Larry tried rousing Bobby, but once again got shunned away until early afternoon. Bobby finally showed up on court for training with Lornie. Larry did his best to keep the bikini girls away to help avoid distractions.

Bobby practiced returning Lornie's serves, and Lornie had him running all over the court. Bobby seemed to keep up, returning most volleys, but Lornie ran him ragged. After about an hour, Bobby threw in the towel. Sweaty and out of breath, he collapsed onto the courtside bench.

"Wanna run some baseline drills?" asked Lornie.

"No, that's it for today," as Bobby popped a beer from the nearby cooler. Larry looked on, concerned.

"You call this training?" chided Lornie. "Look, Bobby, I know you're a great tennis player, probably the best for your age. But unless you get with it… I *think* you got a real chance of losing this thing."

"I don't pay you to think!" barked an angered Bobby. "I pay you to do what I tell you. I know myself. And I know Billie. And there's no way, no matter how much training I do, or don't do, that I will lose to that women's libber. Mark my words, Lornie."

Larry had never seen his father talk to Lornie that way.

"Sorry, Bobby," said his trainer. "You're right, you're the boss."

"You're damn right, I'm the boss."

"Just trying to help…"

"I'll let you know when I want your help." With that, Bobby stormed off.

Lornie and Larry shared a look as Steve met Bobby. Sonny and Cher had shown up for a meet and greet.

Back in his room, Larry packed his bag. As he gathered the last of his things, he pulled out the card with Big Vin's phone number. Out the window, he saw his father, the center of attention, holding court with yet another party crowd. With an ever-present drink in his hand and puffing a cigar, Bobby entertained. Larry stared at Big Vin's card, thought about it, sat on the edge of the bed, and dialed his number. "It's Larry. Larry Riggs. I was wondering if I could place a bet with you?"

* * *

At the front door, with his bag slung over his shoulder, Larry was met by Deidre. "Where you off to, Larry?"

"I'm heading home. I need to take care of a few things," he said.

"We're serving surf and turf. Will you be back for dinner?"

"Ah… No. I don't think so."

"Everything okay?"

"Not really." Larry opened the door.

"Anything I can do?" Deidre asked in her usual seductive way.

"No, I think you've done enough." With that, Larry went out the door. As he waited for his taxi, Bobby came out to look for him.

"Larry, where are you going? Come on out back, I want you to meet Sonny and Cher."

"I don't think so, Pops. I'm heading home."

"We head to Houston tomorrow. The limo's picking us up at noon."

"I don't think so."

"You want us to pick you up on the way to the airport?"

"No. I don't think I want to go to Houston."

"Whattaya mean? The match is in two days."

"I mean, I'm not going to Houston. Nor the match."

"What the hell you talking about? It's going to be the biggest day of my life. I need you there."

The taxi pulled up, and Larry opened the door. "You don't need me. You don't need anybody. You can blow it all by yourself. And I don't want to be there to watch you do it."

"Blow it?! You think I can't beat Billie Jean?"

"I think you *could* have. I just don't think you *will*," Larry got in the cab and closed the door.

Bobby watched as the taxi pulled away, stunned, shaking his head.

Inside the taxi, the driver looked back in his rear-view mirror and asked, "Hey, was that Bobby Riggs? The tennis guy?"

"Yeah," replied Larry.

"You think he's going to beat Billie Jean?"

"I'm putting my money on her."

"No shit!"

* * *

In Houston, the night before the big match, in the leopard-pattern Tarzan Room of the AstroWorld Hotel, the party was raging. Bobby, dressed in

Tarzan pajamas, answered the door to his good friend and former tennis pro Gardnar Mulloy.

"Gardie! How're you doing?" Bobby welcomed him with open arms.

Mulloy was taken aback at the sight of four scantily dressed beauties, all laughing it up, drinking. "What the hell are you doing, Bobby? You got to play tomorrow!"

"I know that. There's no way that broad can beat me," Bobby said. "How about a drink?" Mulloy was speechless. The telephone rang. Bobby went to answer it while waving Mulloy in.

Into the phone, Bobby said, "Larry? Where the hell are you?"

Larry, on the other end, heard the party going on over the phone and told his dad, "I'm home. In L.A."

"What the hell, Larry. When are you getting here?"

"I told you, Pops, I'm not."

"Don't be a schmuck. The match is tomorrow, for Christ sakes!"

"I just called to wish you luck."

"Luck! I don't need luck. I need you here, courtside. We sold out the Astrodome! Gardie just got here. He's going to warm me up in the morning."

"I'm sorry, Pops. I just don't want to watch you lose."

"Lose?! Will you knock it off with that defeatist shit. You know I'm not going to lose."

One of the ladies from the party shouted, "Bobby, we're almost out of champagne," draining the last of a bottle into her flute.

"Hold on, honey. We'll send for some more. Listen, Larry, just get on the next flight out here. I got you a suite. We're going to celebrate big time tomorrow with Lornie, Gardie, Cosell, and I got the Houston Oilers Cheerleaders all lined up."

When Larry didn't respond, Bobby called out, "Larry. Larry?"

But Larry's hung up.

The next day, on the morning of the match, Gardnar Mulloy and Bobby traded volleys in the Astrodome on the court. Only a few minutes, Bobby called it quits. "That's good, Gardie. I don't want to overdo it."

"Overdo it?! It's only been ten minutes."

"I know, but listen, I got a court booked at a local club this afternoon for a warm-up. I'll give you the address, and you can meet me there."

That afternoon, when Mulloy showed up at the practice court, he was shocked by the sight of people queued up to play Bobby. He was playing a total stranger with a dog on a leash tied around his ankle, and held an umbrella in his free hand. He was playing for hundred-dollar bets as Lornie ruefully watched.

Bobby's brother John, in town for the big event, was collecting fistfuls of cash from the starstruck amateurs.

Mulloy joined Lornie courtside and asked, "What the hell is going on, Lornie?"

"The circus is in town, Gardie. And Bobby is the ringmaster."

"Is he ready for tonight?"

"What do you think?"

"I've never seen him in worse shape."

Lornie shrugged his shoulders, "What do you want me to say? He's Bobby Riggs. King of the hustlers."

* * *

That night, as the Battle of the Sexes circus came to the Astrodome, Bobby lost terribly, three sets in a row to Billie Jean King.

His fans, friends, and the media could not believe how poorly Bobby performed against Billie. Even Howard Cosell, tennis analysts Rosie Casals, and Gene Scott commented on how Riggs just didn't look right, and how unusual he played.

Up above in an Astrodome skybox, Pete Pagano was seated with Deidre and Steve Fowler. With them, Saly Traffini, Carlo Martelli, and Big Vin Delgatto toasted each other on Bobby's loss.

"Salute," the boys raised their glasses.

Big Vin picked up the phone and dialed. "You did good, kid. I knew you were a smart one."

Back in L.A., as the aftermath of the match played on the television, Larry was on the line.

Big Vin said, "I'll be sending you a little package. You won it fair and square."

"And my dad?" asked Larry.

"May he live a long and healthy life. Cheers, kid."

* * *

Steve Jankowski's debut novel, *Below the Line,* was drawn on his background in the entertainment industry in both the music and film businesses, as well as his experiences and love for sailing. Steve's short story, "Confessions of an Invisible Hitman," (as Steve Janko) was published on *Black Cat Weekly*.

Love Is Bluë

By Lawrence Maddox

Marvin Stang looked out his second-story apartment window onto the street below, wondering who Mr. Krz had sent. It was early morning, and smoke from the Altadena fires, smoldering six miles away, threw his world out of focus. He scanned the parked cars to see if anyone was waiting. Watching.

Marvin had left Vegas a week ago, intending to pay Mr. Krz after his college bowl picks went belly-up. But he hadn't paid, and that wasn't even his biggest problem.

It was the other stupid thing Marvin had done.

Marvin's old pal, a night manager on the strip, texted him that Mr. Krz was pissed. He'd sent someone to find Marvin and make things right.

Whoever Mr. Krz sent, please don't let it be Loto.

There were rumors about the last time someone sent Loto to LA.

Rumors of a bludgeoned body found in a downtown motel.

Another in a Gulf Stream RV.

And then there was the time when Loto broke Marvin's pinky.

Anybody but Loto.

Marvin watched a white cargo van pull up in front of his apartment.

Right on time.

Marvin slammed the van's passenger door shut.

"You're going to be extra early for work," Doug said, one hand on the wheel.

They shot out into the cross street and swung left. A five-year Gambler's Anonymous chip, alongside a crucifix, swung from the rearview mirror.

Marvin took a comb and a travel-size tube of gel and raked it through his hair in the rearview mirror. He was pale. That, along with his glasses, made him look exactly like what he was. A thirty-five-year-old TV editor who spent his life in dark rooms staring at monitors.

"I didn't know you were so into your hair," Doug said.

"I'm not. It's Bluëler. The old bag gives me grief if I don't look 'professional.'"

"Bluëler? That's Ms. Bluë's real name?"

"Yeah. I looked it up on Wikipedia."

Doug nodded. "Do you think you'll have any more work for me? It's just I could really use the money."

"You're the best assistant editor out there, Doug. Bluë just doesn't seem to like you around."

"That's what I guessed. She called me *fettlebig* last week."

"What's that?"

"Fat. I looked it up on Google. So, is she still trying to give you back rubs?"

Marvin checked the mirrors and windows as the van accelerated up the onramp. "I don't want to talk about it." He unbuckled and stepped into the van's cargo space.

Doug pulled over to the shoulder of the Ventura Freeway. It was 7:05 a.m. and traffic was light.

Doug opened the van's barn doors. He slid out a ramp. Marvin eased his idling Honda CRF motorcycle to freeway asphalt.

"No one's following us, Marv. You're being a little paranoid."

Marvin sat on his motorcycle and adjusted his helmet. "Maybe no one's following us cause of this brilliant evasive maneuver I just pulled."

He raised his visor and squinted into the smoke-filled sky.

A drone hovered overhead.

Crap.

Marvin had a five-second staring contest with the drone until he gave up and sped east toward Pasadena.

* * *

"Geez Louise, you must hate editing this," Anne said.

She stretched her long, tan legs on the couch behind Marvin, watching him work. His fingers moved decisively across the Avid keyboard. On the client monitor played a fast-paced montage of tennis legend Angelika Bluë in her prime, smashing forehand returns that left her opponents with a score of Love. The footage was culled from late-seventies tournaments, including Wimbledon and the US Open. It was crosscut with video from the same era of Bluë posing on the beach for her million-selling bikini pin-ups.

Marvin had temped out the sequence with ABBA's *The Winner Takes It All*.

"Here comes the money shot," Marvin said.

The camera zoomed in on a close-up of Bluë and her sexy pout.

"Seriously, you edit TV shows, Marv. How long are you going to work on this vanity piece?" Anne said.

Anne was super cute. There was no way Marvin could tell her the sad truth.

Hollywood is dead. Nothing's going into production. I haven't worked in a year, and I really need this gig.

He also didn't tell her about his fiancée, Lynn, who happened to be out of town for a week.

"You know this so-called documentary is just for Bluë, right? To watch when she's alone in her mansion, pounding schnaps? If she told you she has any kind of distribution, she lied." Anne leaned forward, lowering her voice. "I've been her assistant for three years. Don't trust her. And don't cross her."

Bluë entered the guest house without knocking. She wore yoga leggings and was covered in a damp sweat. Her tank top revealed her blotched, sinewy arms corded with lizard-blue veins.

Anne jumped to her feet. "I was just leaving to go pick up your vitamins. After that, I'll be taking personal time. Like we talked about."

"I'll see you tomorrow," Bluë said icily.

Marvin watched Anne leave.

"She has errands. She shouldn't be bothering you," Bluë said. She stood behind Marvin. "Show me."

Marvin hit play.

It was the same routine every time.

Bluë put her hand on his shoulder as she watched. She slowly massaged his trapezius, as if lost in thought, gripping him tight. A minute in, she was using both hands, and Marvin was wincing in pain.

"Very good, Marvin," Bluë said when the sequence ended. She let go and walked to the door. "I need a ride to Pasadena. I'll be ready in an hour."

"You want *me* to drive you?"

"In an hour."

"Don't you have people for that? What about Anne?"

"Anne is unavailable. What does it matter? Your time, my money. It's still the same."

"But all I got is my motorcycle."

"I've been on the back of a man's motorcycle before. I think a ride on your machine would be exciting."

"But aren't you too…"

Marvin stopped before he finished the sentence.

Bluë took a step closer, her lips clenched. "Too old?"

Marvin shook his head. "No. I wasn't gonna to say that. I was gonna say 'too busy.'"

"Come with me," Bluë said.

Minutes later, Marvin stood on the surface of Bluë's private tennis court. He glanced up in the sky, wondering if he'd see a drone. The guest house where he'd been editing looked gnat-sized next to Bluë's twelve thousand square foot American Colonial-style mansion. Small as the guest house was, it was bigger than his apartment.

Bluë stood across the net, bouncing a tennis ball.

"I'm wearing jeans," Marvin said. "I'm not gonna be able to move around."

"Since you think I'm too old, it shouldn't matter, *stimmt?*"

Bluë tossed the tennis ball in the air and hit it with a loud *whack*.

The ball came hurdling directly at Marvin. Somehow his racket connected, and the ball popped over the net.

Bluë ran it down. She swung with one fluid movement, legs to core to arm.

Marvin stood flat-footed as the ball came flying at him.

He saw a flash of light and was on the ground, clutching his groin. He was lost in an inferno of pain when he felt hands undoing his fly.

"What the hell, Miss Bluë!" Marvin said, squirming away.

"I've seen this before. You must restore blood flow and allow your genitals to breathe."

"Just back off!" Marvin said, rolling so his back was to her.

Bluë stood up. "That should settle the 'too old' issue. There's ice in the cabana." She walked back to her mansion. "One hour. Then we ride."

* * *

"Hurricane-force winds picked up all kinds of paper ephemera from Altadena homes during the fire," Susan Gallegos said with an academic air. She was a petite woman wearing a V-neck sweater. "Photos have been found miles away. We're just lucky your assistant Amy—"

"Anne," Bluë said, correcting her.

"We're just lucky Anne saw my site on Instagram, where I list my found photos. Sometimes—"

"Your fee is reasonable, you don't have to explain your methods," Bluë said, cutting her off. "Can I see my photo, please?"

"It's really a donation, not a fee." Susan got up from the desk and walked over to a bookshelf packed with lawbooks and binders. "I'm a historian as well as a collector. Restoring lost photos to their owners subsidizes that. Plus, I like helping people."

"All that and you're a lawyer too, huh?" Marvin asked, smiling.

Bluë shot him a look.

"It's my father's firm. He's letting me work out of his offices until they lift the evacuation orders. Thankfully my place didn't burn down," Susan said. "I have over twenty-thousand historical photographs stored away, not including my postcard collection."

Blue leaned forward. "Is all of Altadena under evacuation orders?"

"Yes. The governor is bringing in the National Guard tomorrow to keep people out. The police have already arrested looters. After tonight, Altadena will be locked down tight." Susan handed an acid-free sleeve to Bluë. "Sometimes I'll ask for proof of ownership, but I can see this is you. Or was you."

Bluë didn't answer. Marvin noticed her jaw muscles tighten.

"It does look like you," Marvin said. He saw a young blonde woman, maybe in her late teens, wearing a white tennis skirt. She looked a lot like Bluë did in her posters, but softer. She looked like she'd be nice to talk to and would never slam a tennis ball into your nuts.

"She was my little sister." A tear rolled down Bluë's cheek, got diverted by a deep crag along her mouth, and stalled out above her chin. "We were two years apart."

"She was pretty," Marvin said, shifting uncomfortably. He turned to Susan. "So where'd you find it?"

"It was lodged in a startlingly magenta bougainvillea just a block north of here."

"You said there was an address," Bluë said.

"Indeed. Stamped on the back."

Bluë flipped it over.

Marvin sat on his Honda as Bluë walked out of Gallegos Law. He was sure he saw a drone high up in the clouds, but quickly lost sight of it.

"We're going to the address on the back of the photo," Bluë said, donning her jet-black Stilo helmet.

Marvin could tell weepy-eyed Bluë was gone, and the ball-buster was back.

"Maybe you are, but no way I'm driving to Altadena. I heard there's dead bodies still up there in burned-down homes. The coroner can't even get up there yet."

Bluë sat on the back of Marvin's bike. "We'll take a little drive. Let's see what we see."

It was just a few miles from Madison Heights to the eastern edge of Altadena, but it was like driving into a war zone. Barricades, police cars, and emergency vehicles formed a perimeter.

Behind that, Marvin could see a combination of intact buildings and structures burnt down to rubble. Further back, plumes of smoke rose. Beyond it all, a Firehawk chopper dumped red fire retardant onto the burning hillside.

They continued eastbound along the southern edge of Altadena. Every entry point was blocked and there was destruction all down the line.

Marvin hadn't seen anything like this outside of a monitor or movie screen. *Hollywood shutting down sucks, but this is next level. Like going from* The Towering Inferno *to Armageddon.*

What's next?

"Stop here," Bluë said.

Marvin pulled in front of a police car parked in front of the barricade. Two cops stood next to it, watching another chopper approach the hillside.

"Ask them if we can go in," Blue said. "Tell them you live there. Tell them you have dogs and you want to rescue them."

"You want me to lie to the police?"

"Look around, Marvin. The authorities have bigger issues than one tiny lie."

Marvin looked at the police, then back to Bluë. He shrugged and walked over.

"Excuse me," Marvin said. "Are you letting people in?"

"You can't go up this way," a female officer said. "Farther west, that's where they're letting some residents in."

"Cool," Marvin said. He didn't want to walk away from them too soon, or Bluë would think he hadn't tried hard enough. He pointed up the street. "Are houses still burning?"

"Engines are going up and down, attacking fires cropping up, but they can't be everywhere at once."

"Terrible."

"Drive west, closer to the Foothill onramp. Show them your license to prove you're a resident," she said. "And curfew starts at six. No one gets in after that."

Marvin nodded and smiled. "Thanks."

When he turned around, he made sure his smile was replaced with an angry frown.

"I tried," Marvin said to Bluë. "No one can enter."

"Did you say you had dogs?"

"I sure did. They just didn't listen. They said homes are still burning. No one is allowed in."

Bluë crossed her arms. "I see. And they said they weren't letting anyone in at any point in Altadena?"

"Well, no. They said we could try further west, but we'd need to show a license to prove we live up there."

Bluë hopped on the back of the bike. "*Verdammt.* Let's go."

They made two more stops with the same results. On the final stop before the freeway Bluë got off the bike.

"I'll handle it," she said.

Marvin watched Bluë's confident strut as she approached the police. He noticed one of her butt cheeks was askew. It dawned on Marvin that Bluë was wearing fake-butt panties, and the motorcycle ride threw a cheek out of whack.

He couldn't hear what she was saying, but he imagined she was playing the "I was ranked fifth in the world" card. Bluë stamped her Louboutin-booted foot and stormed back to Marvin. "Let's go," she said, getting on the bike.

"I know you can get in," Bluë said later over lunch at the Royce. "You grew up here."

A waiter filled Marvin's wine glass. He hadn't sat in a restaurant with an actual wait staff in over six months.

"How do you know I'm local?"

"Anne told me."

Anne and Marvin chatted a lot when Bluë was gone. Once, when they were talking about his motorcycle, he bragged about breaking into places when he was a teen and riding his dirt bike where he shouldn't. "I never told her I could bust through police barriers." He took a drink of wine, allowing himself a second to enjoy the bouquet. "And why me? You've got people. All kinds of people. Can't Anne find someone?"

"Anne." Bluë laughed derisively. "She's taking the rest of the day off."

"What's so important that you have to get into Altadena now?"

"I'm being blackmailed."

Marvin looked up from his gravy-drenched mash potatoes. "Huh?"

"That photo of my sister. It's just one of a series. The photographer was her coach, about twenty years her senior. He was also her lover, something not greatly frowned upon in my era. The coach plied my sister with drink and drugs, and continued to take photos. Can you guess the nature of these photos?"

"Kinky?"

"He blackmailed my father with these photos. It all became too much for Olivia, and she took her own life at the age of twenty-one."

Marvin set his fork down. "I'm so sorry."

Bluë reached across the table and patted Marvin's hand. She left it there. "It was hard."

Marvin cleared his throat, not sure if he should move his hand or not. "Uhm, what happened?"

"Monies were paid. Olivia's death was ruled an accidental overdose. Her coach was eventually dealt with."

Marvin considered what "dealt with" meant. "I'm really sorry this happened to your family."

"Earlier this week, I received an email demanding five hundred thousand dollars or my sister's photos would be posted online. Attached was one of the photos. I made it clear I will never pay."

Marvin slathered his last slice of rib-eye in creamy horseradish. "You said there was an attachment. That means whoever emailed you scanned the photos already. It's a real drag, but the photos are in the cloud now." Marvin's eyes wandered down to the dessert menu.

"Digital copies can be denied. I can say they were created with AI. You would know more about that than I. But actual physical negative would be hard to refute."

Marvin nodded. "True. Can't you just go to the FBI?"

"They were little help last time. I told you Olivia's coach was dealt with. Law enforcement had nothing to do with that."

Marvin leaned in and lowered his voice. "You had him killed?"

Bluë let the question hang in the air. "When I was a child, my father was a manager in German football," she finally said. "He was forced out after the Bundesliga gambling scandal in seventy-one. Have you heard of it?"

"Nope. I wasn't even born yet."

Bluë frowned. Marvin remembered he needed to choose his words better.

"Connections father made in the underworld of sports betting made Las Vegas a natural place for him to land. He invested in infrastructure and real estate. He made powerful friends. When he was my manager, he could get things done. More wine?"

"Oh yeah." Marvin watched Bluë refill his wine glass. It was a beautiful sight.

"You saw the address on the back of the photo," she said. "My sister's coach lived in Altadena. We never recovered the photos. Maybe he left them in the attic, or he was working with someone, or whoever lives in his house now came into possession of the photos and saw the opportunity to blackmail me. Whatever the case, the fires have changed everything. I want to go to that address. Tonight. Before the National Guard arrives tomorrow. I want to find all the photos that remain."

"You're asking a lot," he said. "I could go to jail. No way I can afford an attorney. I'd be locked up in county at least until my fiancée gets back in a week. And she may leave me in there just out of spite. Things aren't great with Lynn and me right now."

"That's because she doesn't understand you, Marvin."

"Tell me about it." Her hand was on top of his again. He picked up the dessert menu, even though he'd already memorized it. "And the National Guard would make it tricky."

"So there is a way?"

Marvin raised his eyebrows and gave the smallest of shrugs.

"I wouldn't let you stay in jail. I'd get you the best attorney money could buy. It's in my interest to keep your lovely mouth shut."

Marvin laughed nervously.

"And I would pay you. On top of your editing salary. Six thousand dollars."

Marvin did some quick math.

Six thousand. That covers two months' rent. Utilities. A bottle of J&B from Costco. I could fill my freezer with more than fish sticks. With even more money, I could get Lynn that necklace we saw at the mall. And I could make the four hundred and forty dollar buy-in for Sunday's Five Suns Poker Tourney with the four hundred thousand dollar guarantee. That's just for starters. I could hit online poker like a champ.

"How about ten thousand?"

"Deal," Bluë said quickly.

Marvin regretted not asking for more. "Could you Venmo me before we go?" He said, remembering Anne's warning about not trusting Bluë.

"Two thousand dollars now," Bluë said. "And the rest when we're done. I'll pay you over dinner tomorrow night. Deal?"

Blue stuck out her hand for a shake and didn't let go until the bill arrived.

* * *

"What do you mean you can't go tonight? We made a deal."

"I know. That's why I brought you all this," Marvin said, gesturing to the open cartons of Chinese food on Doug's living room table. "A feast for a friend."

Doug squirted a packet of sriracha sauce on a plate of chow mein. "Thanks dude, but you need to start back with the meetings. It's for your own good. I figure not going to Santa Anita in five years has saved me," he said, working his chopsticks, "over two hundred thousand easy."

Marvin looked out of Doug's picture window, searching the sky. "The old bag tried to grab my junk," he blurted out.

Doug stopped, noodles dangling. "What?"

"It's a long story. But yeah, she went for the magic. And she held my hand at lunch. And to top it all off I'm pretty sure a drone is following me."

Doug looked at his friend. "I think you need a meeting ASAP. Come share your feelings with the group."

Marvin flung himself down on the couch. "I'm good."

Doug shook his head and ate. "Maybe she's just lonely," he finally said. He gulped down Mountain Dew. "And LA is on fire. There's drones all over the place. You need to stop worrying."

"Someone is after me, Doug! Do you know what a bitch it is to edit with a broken pinky?" Marvin raised his left pinky and wiggled it. "I make dissolves with this bad boy. And this time it could be worse." Marvin sighed deeply. "I did something stupid when I was in Vegas. Besides losing money."

"What did you do, Marv?"

"I don't want to get into it. Look, I'm working late tonight. She has me on a special assignment. If you want to pick up, say, four hundred bucks, I could really use your help."

Doug speared a postage-stamp-sized slice of Mongolian beef. "You mean working for you, not Ms. Bluë?"

"Right. And it'll be late, so you'll have plenty of time to hit Home Depot and pick up something for me after you go to your meeting. You may have to strap a ladder to the roof of your van. Twine is free at checkout. Get a lot of it."

"You really have money for this?" Doug asked suspiciously.

"Sure do." Marvin put his cell phone on the table and brought up a map of Altadena.

"You're my contingency tonight. I gotta get back to work, but let me show you."

✳ ✳ ✳

It was after midnight, and Bluë clung onto Marvin as they sped toward disaster.

The spoiled rotten Arroyo Preparatory boys had shown him the trails back in high school. During summer break, they'd all meet up at Hahamongna Park with their dirt bikes, right on the Flintridge and Altadena border. They'd kick off the night with special treats from their parents' liquor and medicine cabinets, and they'd share with Marvin if he was careful to mention how bitchin' their expensive new bikes were.

Twenty years later, Marvin was certain he could still swing it.

Evacuation orders were in effect in Flintridge as well. The streetlights were out. Marvin could barely make out the clusters of live oaks and sycamores in the dark at the park's entrance.

Marvin remembered how he felt that first time he illegally drove into the park at night when he was 15.

This could change my life forever.

He turned back to Bluë. "It's gonna be bumpy, so hold on."

"I trust you, Marvin," she said, wrapping her arms around him.

Paved roads turned into dirt roads, which forked off into hiking paths. Marvin chose his way carefully, shifting to first as they plunged into a sea of sage and buckwheat. His headlight illuminated just a few yards in front.

When they hit the downward slope, Marvin worked the brake until he saw the treeline. Just like the old days, he burst through the sycamores and cottonwoods and hit the basin. There was a half mile of sand and rocks between him and Altadena, and he opened it up.

It felt great.

A Firehawk chopper swooped out of the sky and buzzed them, blasting them with its searchlight.

"Turn around and leave the park," a voice ordered through the chopper's loudspeaker. "Turn around now!"

"Keep going!" Bluë yelled behind him.

If he turned around, Martin knew cops would be waiting for them on the way out.

After keeping pace with them for a few heart-pounding seconds, the chopper and its payload of fire retardant whirled off towards the hills.

Sand turned to dirt as Marvin hit the familiar hiking trail that snaked up the hillside.

"Stop!" Bluë said when they reached the top. She studied her Apple Watch. "I'll give you directions. Go slow."

Marvin nodded. Even though he was wearing the N95 mask Bluë gave him, he could taste the smoke.

The streetlights were out. Marvin and Bluë were submerged in darkness. He didn't see the debris in the street until he was practically on top of it. He could make out the shapes of rubble, of burnt-out cars, but little else.

Occasionally, in the midst of the destruction, they'd pass a house that was untouched. It was alarming. Supernatural almost.

"Stop! We're here."

Bluë hopped off the bike and dug into the backpack she had Marvin wear. She pulled out a flashlight and aimed it at what was once someone's home. Half the house was reduced to pilings. The other half was roofless walls. By the height of the chimney, which jutted high above the remaining structure, it must have been a sizeable two-story.

"I packed a flashlight for you, Marvin. Help me look." Bluë disappeared into the darkness.

Marvin's mask was full of moisture, and he was sure the bad air was making him lightheaded. He stood on the sidewalk and listened to the sirens.

No way I'm going in there.

"Marvin!" Bluë called out sharply.

"Yeah."

"Help me look. If the photos blew away, they'd be in a box, not an album. Makes sense?"

"Got it," Marvin said.

Dammit.

He kept his bike idling in case he needed a quick getaway.

He followed his flashlight beam as he waded into the rubble. His Local 700 Editors Guild health insurance had lapsed months ago because he hadn't worked enough hours to qualify. If something long and sharp poked through his sneakers, medical care would be out of pocket.

"Marv," a voice whispered.

Marvin spun around. His light landed on a tall, masked woman wearing a black hoodie. She pointed her cell phone's flashlight back at him.

"Who is it?" Marvin said.

She pulled down her mask. "Shh. Police are out."

Marvin smiled under his mask. "Anne. Bluë roped you into this, too?"

She pulled her mask back up. "I can't believe she made you drive her old ass up here. She threaten to fire you?"

"I'm not doing this for free. I asked for a ton of money," Marvin said, hoping to impress.

"It wasn't enough. Let's meet up with her. I think she's in the back."

"I'm okay hanging out here."

"Don't be chicken, Marv. You were badass to come this far. Plus, I know a way around that avoids most of the debris. C'mon."

Anne walked ahead of Marvin. He pointed his flashlight at her butt and decided to follow.

Anne was right. A path led around the side of the house that still had walls. As they entered the backyard, he could hear Bluë talking with someone.

He wondered who.

"Don't fall in the pool," Anne said.

Marvin pointed his light back to the ground and realized he was steps away from plunging into a watery mess of ash and soot. "That was close."

He heard an electrical hum from somewhere nearby, a noise he shouldn't be hearing when all the power was out.

"Over here!" Someone called out.

The voice sounded familiar.

His beam revealed a masked petite woman wearing a backpack. She was holding a gun. Bluë stood nearby.

"Susan, you're helping too?" Marvin said. He was a little surprised that Bluë had also enlisted Susan Gallegos, the photo collector from the law office. "Smart move bringing a gun. It's low-key spooky."

"She plans on shooting us, Marvin," Bluë said.

Marvin moved his light to Bluë and then back to the gun.

"Can you tell that asshole to stop shining his light on me?" Susan said.

"She's in a bitchy mood tonight, Marv. Better do what she says," Anne said.

"What's going on?" He watched Anne's cell phone light move farther to his right. She was walking around the pool.

"I thought you were my friend, Anne. I was good to you," Blue said.

"Oh shut up. You never thought I was your friend. I was your employee. Please."

"I was generous with you. I took you around the world with me."

Anne laughed. "I carried your bags. I booked your spa treatments. Your massages. And you had the nerve to flirt with my boyfriends. You're insane if you think they would go for you! Hate to tell you, but you're not your poster anymore. She hitting on you yet, Marv?"

"Well, uh—"

"Anne, it's not too late," Bluë said.

Marvin was weighing if he could run. If his bike hadn't sputtered out, he'd have a shot.

"It *is* too late," Susan said. "You sold your interest in your Vegas properties."

"And since I book all your appointments," Anne said, "I know your lawyer is coming tomorrow to change your trust to reflect the sale."

"Why does that matter?" Bluë said.

Slowly backing up, Marvin stepped on a board that sent a pile of debris crashing to the ground.

All the flashlights turned to him.

"What the hell is that idiot doing?" Susan said.

"Marvin, stay still," Bluë said.

"Point your light at me, Marv," Anne said.

Marvin's beam landed on Anne's gun.

"I have one too."

Marvin pointed his flashlight back to the ground.

Dammit! I'm surrounded by lethal bitches.

"We amended your will. Notarized and everything," Anne said. "It can be helpful when your best friend's dad owns a law firm. I'm sorry, but I'm not leaving your posters up when I redecorate."

"And the photos of my sister?" Bluë asked.

"The latest addition to Susan's massive collection," Anne said. "Safe at her place, fires permitting. Maybe we'll sell them on eBay."

"We're done talking," Susan said. "You two get in the pool."

"What?" Marvin said.

"Sorry Marv," Anne said. "Bad things happen when you work for a mean old skank."

Marvin heard movement on the other side of the pool. Susan's flashlight fell.

A squelched scream was followed by a loud splash.

He raised his light in time to see a large figure dressed in black dash out of the beam.

Now it was Anne's turn to shriek. That was enough. Marvin ran for it as gunfire split open the night.

Trampling over debris, falling on all fours, Marvin felt a stabbing pain in the sole of his foot. He prayed it wasn't a nail as his beam found his idling bike.

Marvin accelerated off the curb and was hitting fifty by the end of the block.

He briefly headed north toward the hills, then doubled back to the direction he came.

Marvin thought he heard a car behind him. His mirrors were useless, showing nothing but black.

He skid to a stop near the edge of the hillside, nearly dropping his bike. Marvin peered over the side. In the basin far below, a police car cruised slowly like a shark. Its twin headlights illuminated the rocky terrain.

Marvin's way back was blocked. It was time for the contingency plan.

Doug, don't let me down.

Marvin followed the edge of the hillside, riding on the dirt. The sirens got louder. He could clearly see the fires in the hills less than two hundred feet away, closer than he'd ever imagined.

Marvin stopped at an out-of-service maintenance road. He felt his heart pounding like a *Mission: Impossible* movie score. He peeled off his wet mask.

The air was chunky, stinging the back of his throat. He wiped his glasses and slid on his spare mask.

His headlights revealed the splintered remains of a guard rail.

The end of the road.

About fifteen feet away, across a chasm filled with night, was a parking lot overgrown with vegetation. Next to it was a park station that had been abandoned since he was a teenager.

Crossing the length of the chasm was a reinforced extension ladder, courtesy of Doug.

His Honda was relatively lightweight, but it was still a tightrope act getting it across. The sole of his right foot was pulsating painfully. If Lynn could see him now, she'd dump him for sure.

The plan was to meet Doug on the other side. They'd strap the ladder to his van. They'd go back the way Doug had come, a route that circumvented fire and cops and death. Tomorrow, they'd return the ladder to Home Depot. They'd go out for Mexican and cervezas.

But there was no Doug.

An hour later, the lidocaine kicked in. Marvin crunched the numbers as a young doctor pulled a nail out of his foot.

Urgent care. Four hundred bucks.

Doug. Another four hundred.

Ladder. Five hundred and fifty until returned.

"Doug, it's me," Marvin whispered into his cell. "Where'd you go? I'm at urgent care. Call me."

By the time he left urgent care, he'd called Doug three more times. Doug never picked up.

***

Sunlight slipped through the closed curtains and stabbed at Marvin's eyes. He put the pillow over his head. The pain in his foot drummed a score to a nightmare montage of last night.

Marvin grabbed his cell phone. Nothing from Doug, but he did have one new text.

Let's start at 11 today.

Marvin stared at his cell phone in disbelief.

The text was from Bluë.

Bluë. Is. Alive.

And the old bag wants me at work in forty-five minutes.

Marvin got off his couch and limped around his apartment. He looked out his windows. He played the *Sorcerer* movie score, the synths pumping through his JBLs. He put a handful of frozen fish sticks in his microwave. His mind was bursting with questions, but one thought persisted.

I'm gonna get paid after all.

Marvin drove by Doug's apartment on his way to work. Doug's white cargo van was nowhere to be seen. He parked in front and jogged to his friend's door. He knocked, calling out his name. There was no answer.

At 10:58, Marvin saw a drone hovering above Bluë's estate.

What the hell?

Marvin watched it as he was buzzed into the front gate. A motor trike was parked in his usual space. He didn't think much of it. Bluë had guests before. The drone, on the other hand, was like an answer to a riddle. He kept his eye on it, sure that it was being controlled by someone beyond the eight-foot-high hedges that bounded the tennis court.

"Marvin!"

He swung around to see Bluë exiting the guest house. She wore a tennis skirt, and a jeweled clip sparkled in her hair. Practically skipping, she hurried to him. "You are my hero." She pecked him on the cheek.

Marvin stifled the desire to wipe his face. "What's going on? What was last night all about? And who's flying that drone over your house?"

"You have a right to answers. Follow me."

She grabbed his hand. To Marvin's surprise, she led him not to the guest house but to the rear of the mansion. He'd never been inside before. He wasn't sure he wanted to go inside now.

It was the biggest kitchen Marvin had ever seen. There were windows everywhere. Sunlight reflected off yellow tiles, glinted from hanging pots, gleamed on fine China. The fridge, more spacious than the entire cold beer section at his corner liquor store, had glass doors. He could see it was packed with food.

"Would you like a beverage?" Bluë said.

Marvin saw his favorite Belgian ale on the fourth shelf.

He chugged deeply as she led him downstairs.

She walked him through a large rec room with a bar, a jukebox, and amusements galore. A massive TV screen rehashed yesterday's Orange Bowl. A giant mural depicting Bluë nailing a forehand took up all four walls and the ceiling, too.

She opened a door at the end of the room and turned on the light. Marvin stepped inside.

He was surprised to see his editing setup. "I'm being moved?"

"I want you in here from now on. Closer to me."

"Okay," Marvin said. The walls were soundproofed.

"Have a seat, Marvin."

Marvin sat in his Aeron editing chair and drained the rest of his beer.

"Anne and her associate were going to kill us last night. You realize that, don't you?"

"I guess."

"You guess? They had guns. Susan Gallegos even brought a generator. Remember, she lived in Altadena. Near where we were last night, actually. They used the generator to electrify the pool. We'd be floating in it right now, burnt like everything else."

Marvin remembered the electric hum and the dark, dirty water. "But why?"

"Anne knew where I kept my important documents. She made my schedule. She also knew the bait to lure me out there. When you told her about your youthful bike adventures in Altadena, she must have realized she had the perfect opportunity. You were to be what they call 'collateral damage.' She didn't know I was aware of everything she was planning."

"How?"

Bluë sat on the couch opposite him. "Please don't think badly of me. For my security, I have hidden surveillance on my estate. For those of us who have so much more to protect, it's very common. "

Marvin's mind raced.

What things did I say in the guest house? Did I call her an old bag?

Outside the door, heavy footsteps bounded down the stairs.

Bluë reached over and firmly grabbed Marvin's hand. "Don't be afraid."

Marvin looked out the door and immediately jumped to his feet. "Crap!"

He slammed the door shut. "What's he doing here?"

Bluë clutched his hand again. Marvin pulled away and frantically looked around the room. He got hold of the editing table and pulled it towards the door.

"Marvin, it's going to be okay. Just let him come in."

"You don't get it!"

"I do. And I think we both know if he wants to come in, he will."

The doorknob turned.

Marvin ran to the corner of the room and slid down to a crouch.

Bluë opened the door. Loto filled the doorframe.

Marvin wanted to run.

He figured one of Loto's arms had more meat than Bluë's entire body. His bushy beard had a touch more gray than the last time, but Loto still had the same easy smile.

"Marvin, get off the floor right now and come here," Bluë said firmly.

"I'm okay," Marvin said. "I'm good here."

"Loto used the drone to follow us into Altadena. He was keeping tabs on you before that. Is that right?"

"Yep," Loto said. "I use drones a lot now."

"I offered Anne a chance, but she didn't take it. Loto was there to finish things."

"So you had me drive you up there, knowing what might happen?"

"I had to risk it. They had the photos. Susan discovered them at an estate sale, crazy as that sounds. Anne knew my story and knew exactly what to do with them. Blackmail wasn't enough. They wanted to kill me and take everything. I had no choice but to play along. Loto recovered the photos before the National Guard arrived. I'm free of all that now."

"Great."

"Can't you see this is our chance too, Marvin? You owe Loto's boss thirty-two thousand dollars. Plus, I hear there's another matter?"

"You kissed Mai Li on the mouth," Loto said. "Shoved your tongue down her throat. Mr. Krz had a sweet spot for her. Now he's finished with her, sent her back to Nanjing."

Marvin buried his face in his hands. "She kissed me! I'd just won big at the craps table after she'd blown on the dice. I was drunk, you know those free drinks—"

"Ms. Bluë said to stand up," Loto said.

Marvin slowly got to his feet.

"You are a lucky man," Bluë said. "What are the chances that my father and Loto's current employer were once business partners? I've negotiated on your behalf. An arrangement has been struck. You're off the hook, as they say."

Marvin wiped his eyes and sniffled. "Really?"

Bluë gently touched his arm and guided him out of the corner. "I've grown fond of you. You're not like the tanned beasts I preferred when I was young. You're sensitive. Creative. You're always slouching. I don't think you shower in the morning. Frankly Marvin, I'm endlessly intrigued. We will return from our trip before Lynn is back in town."

"Trip?"

"I'm accepting a lifetime achievement award in Milan. You will be my escort."

Marvin fell back into his editing chair.

Bluë checked her watch. "There are only two pieces of business left. The first is Mr. Gallegos, the father of Anne's friend Susan. The scheme began with him. He is vacationing near Milan. Is that correct, Loto?"

"Mr. Gallegos is staying at the Torreta," Loto said.

"Loto will pay him a visit," Anne said, clapping her hands. "And that will be that."

Marvin looked between Bluë and Loto. "You said two things."

"Mr. Krz wanted to permanently maim you. I talked him down to breaking a pinky." Bluë made a pouty face at Marvin. She turned to leave.

"Wait!" Marvin said.

Bluë hung in the doorway.

"You still owe me eight thousand dollars for last night!"

One corner of Bluë's mouth curled upwards into a smile. She shook her head and walked back to Marvin. She placed her index finger under his chin and lightly kissed him on the mouth.

"You're just the ray of sunshine I need. I said I'd pay you over dinner, remember?"

She closed the door behind her. Marvin wiped his mouth on his shoulder.

Marvin couldn't look at Loto. Instead, his eyes fell to the blank monitors. His whole life was monitors, but they had nothing for him now.

"Do you know what happened to my friend Doug?"

When Loto didn't answer, Marvin finally looked up.

He saw the smile that set you at ease if you didn't know better.

"You remember the drill. Hand," Loto said.

Marvin turned his back to Loto and bunched his right hand into a fist. He bit down on it and stuck out his left hand behind him.

He heard it before he felt it.

* * *

Lawrence Maddox's stories appear in numerous anthologies, including Derringer-winner *Murder, Neat*. He is also the author of *Fast Bang Booze*. Previous adventures of Marvin, Lynn, and Loto can be found in *The Down and Out*, Lawrence's installment in the novella anthology series *A Grifter's Song*.

The Samurai's Assistant

By Travis Richardson

September 1981

It was a hell of a day at the US Open. Over ninety degrees in New York City with humidity like a swamp as the noonday sun radiated down on the hardcourt. Ronnie McIntire was certain he'd sweated out his body weight in the first two rounds. He already replaced four saturated sweatbands and drank over a gallon of Gatorade. But none of that mattered. What mattered was that Ronnie, ranked three in the world of professional tennis, had fallen behind Sam Bonner, his greatest adversary, in the semi-finals.

That pretty boy was unfairly ranked number one. He had an easy smile and perfect hair, exuding a pure American wholesomeness that fans ate up. Sam's face was on Wheaties boxes and the covers of *Sports Illustrated* every other week. He got invitations to *The Tonight Show*. And of course, that damned number one ranking. The bastard.

Known as the bad boy of tennis, Ronnie was more famous for his hair-trigger temper than his geometry-defying court play. A southpaw with a wicked serve in spite of his scrawny size. A speedster with massive curly hair held in place by a signature sweatband who could return almost anything that entered his side of the court. But nobody cared about that. Fans flocked to matches not to cheer for Ronnie, but to jeer him. He was the heel. The player everybody loved to hate. No Wheaties box endorsements. Nobody wanted to touch him except for his shoe company, Nike, who loved his antics. Everyone else steered clear. So freakin' unfair.

At times, when self-pity took hold, he'd channel his rage into his game. Smacking the logo off the ball, driving it down his opponent's throats.

He'd won the first set 6-4, but lost the second set 5-7 thanks to lousy officiating. The line judges couldn't tell an inbound hit from a walrus on a skateboard. The chair umpire—who he'd yelled at all day—was as blind as a Helen Keller. And the audience royally sucked. It was like all of New York's biggest losers came together for this match. More than a few times, the chair umpire announced over the PA system that the audience should remain quiet.

Ronnie was down in the third set, four games to Sam's five. He took one last swallow of Gatorade, crushed the paper cup, and tossed it on the ground. No way that fresh-face golden boy would win the match. Regardless of how exhausted Ronnie felt, he wasn't going to let that happen. Not here in the city on national television. He would not be humiliated today.

He stalked up to the line to serve. The rumbling crowd hushed. He bounced the ball with his right hand while eyeing Sam across the court. The hotshot crouched, spinning his racquet. Ready for action. Ronnie tossed the ball in the air, jumped, and smashed the serve. Sam hit a backhand that sailed to the far-left corner. Ronnie was there and swatted a hard forehand down the line on the back line. Sam didn't get there in time, and for once, the biased line judge didn't take Ronnie's shot away.

Ronnie pumped his fist in the air and shouted, "Yeah!" Fifteen-love.

The next serve brought a soft return by Sam, and Ronnie rushed to the net and spiked the ball hard with a spin that bounced it into the upper deck.

"Uh-huh!"

The audience reaction was mild at best, but screw them. Ronnie would teach them a lesson on respect.

He served. A yellow blur flew past Sam, who stood frozen like a statue.

Forty-love. Ronnie leapt up and down. This game was in the bag.

He went to the line and tossed the ball in the air, his arm cocked back like a coiled cobra. The ball reached its apex and started to descend. Ronnie unleashed his swing.

POP!

What the…

The ball plowed into the center of the net.

"What the hell was that?" he yelled. He looked around. "Who did that?'

There was another pop. He searched the crowd. A lady sat in the front row, smacking a wad of bubble gum. The woman—or was she a teen? Thick make-up made it hard to tell—stared back, her brown eyes hard and cold. Daring him to say something.

He pointed at her and walked to the umpire. "Her. She distracted me. She's popping bubbles."

"Keep playing, Ronnie."

"This is an injustice. You need to make her spit it out and leave."

"Just serve already."

He shook his head and slogged back to the line. He glared at the woman who glared back. Impassive except for the steady chewing. She wasn't going to get in his head. No way.

He tossed the ball and smacked a second serve, but at three-quarter power. It cleared the net, and Sam swatted it back to the corner of the court. Ronnie sprinted and stretched, lobbing the ball up. Ronnie reset for Sam's return. It landed in the middle of the court. A hollow *bwap* echoed in the silent stadium. Sam waited underneath the ball with his arm cocked, waiting to knock felt off. Ronnie studied Sam. Was he going to slam it right or left? Maybe up the center? Crouched and holding the racquet in both hands, he waited. Ready to spring into action.

Pop!

What the…

Sam slammed the ball to the right corner. Ronnie stood immobile like an idiot. The audience roared. Sam gave a polite wave while Ronnie marched over to the judge.

"She did it again. She popped her gum. Throw her out already."

Fans started booing. Whistling.

"Shut up and play, Ronnie."

He pointed at her.

"She hates me."

"Who doesn't?"

More boos rained down.

Ronnie shouted at the judge, but most of it was drowned out by the audience. The judge looked at his Rolex and tapped the crown.

Ronnie trudged to the ball girl and took two balls, walking in a wide circle while he stared at the woman. She blew a bubble.

He stepped to the line. The audience quieted. He had a plan: don't give her enough time.

He tossed the ball, smashing it decently for a rush job. Sam returned with a solid backhand down the line. Ronnie smacked a backhand to the right corner. Sam nailed it back down the line. Ronnie ran over, planted his left leg, and walloped the ball across the court to the opposite corner. Sam scurried across the court as the ball skidded on the edge of the line, an inch from his racquet. Ronnie pumped his fist in the air.

"Out!" cried the line judge.

"What? Are you freakin' kidding me? That ball was in. Totally, absolutely in. It hit the line."

Ronnie stomped and shouted as the crowd booed.

The score was 40-30. One more to win. Just one more. Don't let the pretty boy get to deuce.

He walked over to the line to serve. The audience hushed. He bounced the ball. Looked at Sam. Crouched, ready, but less confident than before. He's scared of Ronnie's serve. As he should be. Ronnie tossed the ball. *Psst pop. What was that sound?* Ronnie drove the ball into the net.

"What the hell!"

He looked over at the girl. She held a pink can of Tab soda in her palm, her middle finger pointed at him. A veiled smirk behind her stony gaze.

"You!" he shouted, racquet pointed at her as he strode towards her. "You need to leave now, or I'll throw you out myself."

Her smirk grew as her irises burned like a stove top. He was going to smack that superior smile off her face. A bear of a man sitting next to her stood and yanked the Dunlop racquet from Ronnie's hand.

"What the…"

"Never point a racquet at her again," he said in a deep, gravelly voice.

"I don't have to listen to you. Give it back."

The man squeezed the racquet with both hands and, incredibly, the wooden head cracked.

"What the hell?"

"Here you go." He handed the wrecked instrument back.

"You…you can't do that. You destroyed my racquet."

"Leave her alone."

The girl arched her eyebrow. Ronnie tossed his racquet across the court. It clattered to the umpire's booth.

"Did you see what he did to my racquet? He destroyed it."

"I saw you shove your racquet into the audience, a man took it, and then handed it back to you. You then threw your racquet on the court. As far as I can see, you did the damage and provoked the situation. Any more of this and I'll charge you with unsportsmanlike conduct and racquet abuse. Keep playing."

"You're kidding me. I didn't provoke nothing. That girl did. She's flipped me off."

Boos rained down from the stadium.

The judge tapped his watch.

Grumbling, Ronnie went to the bench, pulled out another racquet from his bag, and swung it back and forth. It didn't feel right, so he pulled out another.

"Come on already!" somebody yelled from the stands.

"I'm trying to find the right one, jackass."

"Watch your language," the umpire said.

More shouts and boos exploded from the crowd.

He marched back to the line. The racquet didn't feel right. Not the same. But it would have to do. He took two balls. Bounced one. Finally, the audience hushed. He tossed and served. The ball hit the top of the net, a let.

"Dammit," he slapped the racket against the court. *It's this racket, not me.*

He served into the net again.

"No-no-no!"

He smashed the racquet into the ground. Taut strings burst and curled around his wrists.

He went over to the bench and kicked it over.

"Deuce" was announced, much louder than necessary, over the speakers.

Ronnie opened his bag and pulled out another racquet. The game was tied. He'd need to win by two now. He went to the line and tossed the ball, ready to smash it.

"Ah-loser!" the girl said in a false sneeze.

Ronnie let the ball bounce and then swung with all his might into the stands.

"Aaargh!"

The ball nailed the girl in the forehead and ricocheted to the other side of the stadium. The girl slumped in her chair. Eyes crossed. The crowd gasped.

Oh, God. What have I done?

"Somebody, call a doctor!" a woman shouted.

The brute of a man next to the girl leapt out of the stands. Ronnie threw his racquet at him, running as the man chased him around the net. Security swarmed the court and tackled the goon.

From under the pile of guards, he shouted, "You're dead meat, McIntire."

A half-eaten hot dog landed at Ronnie's feet.

"What the…"

He ducked in time to dodge a can of Coke. People in the audience threw their food and drinks at Ronnie while shouting and cursing. A beer can bounced off his head.

"Hey!"

He grabbed the can and threw it back into the stands as more debris pelted him. Fans descended onto the court.

Two security guards grabbed Ronnie and escorted him to the locker room under a barrage of food and drinks.

He pulled back from the guards.

"Wait, I've got a game to finish."

"The game's over. You forfeited."

"What? No way!"

He rushed past them and into a cop. The officer pushed Ronnie against the lockers and handcuffed him.

"What are you doing?"

"Arresting you for assaulting a woman in the stands."

Ronnie jerked and kicked at the officer. The cop slammed his head against the locker.

"And another charge for resisting arrest. Keep it up, you might get assaulting a cop."

Ronnie turned to look in the officer's face.

"This isn't over. I'll remember you."

* * *

A bevy of police escorted Ronnie to a squad car. Once they were driving, he was surprised they didn't stop at the closest precinct.

"Hey, where are we going?"

"You're gonna get booked."

"No shit, Sherlock, but shouldn't we be heading to Union Street? The precinct's over there."

"Naw. They wanna take you to a different precinct. That one's got too much press, fans, and whatnot."

Multiple blocks later, they entered another precinct where everybody tried to boss Ronnie around. Treating him like he was a bum. Do this, do that. Pushing their authority against him, a world-class athlete. Not one ounce of respect. A woman shoved his fingers onto a pad of ink.

"What the hell, lady?" Ronnie jerked his hand back away and dragged his fingers across his shirt. He looked at the streak of black ink stains. "You owe me a new shirt."

"That's on you, idiot." She grabbed his hand, pulling it towards the paper.

Ronnie tugged it back again.

"I'm not giving you my prints like some lowlife criminal."

"Fine, then. Lou, get these prints for me, would ya."

"Who's Lou?"

A humungous officer who looked like a Jets linebacker grabbed Ronnie's shoulder with one meaty hand and his wrist with the other, forcing his prints on the paper, one finger at a time. Ronnie felt like he was held in a vice grip.

"You better not break or damage any part of my hand, or I'll sue you and the NYPD into the ground. These are necessary for my livelihood."

Lou dropped him off at a height chart for his photo.

"I am not getting a mug shot. I want my lawyer. Ivan Pearlstein. I won't go any further until he's here."

"Yo, Lou," the cameraman shouted.

Lou turned around with a grunt, lumbering toward him.

"Gimme that," Ronnie said, taking the placard with his name and other information from a nearby flunky. He stared daggers at the cameraman as he snapped shots. "Bet you're gonna sell my photo to *The New York Post*, aren't you, you pathetic son of a bitch?"

After the photos, Lou led him through a door and into a waiting area where his lawyer, Ivan Pearlstein, stood rubbing the back of his head. Ronnie felt a wave of tension leave his body. The lawyer had been getting him out of trouble with tennis associations and other entities since forever.

"I wanna press charges against these a-hole cops for manhandling me. Sue the entire force. What took you so long to get here?"

The lawyer walked over, his face ashen. "You're in deep shit, Ronnie. It's best if you shut your mouth. Understand?"

"Come on. You can get me out of this."

Pearlstein shook his head and pushed his client into an empty conference room. "Not this time."

"What? Are they going to suspend me for a few weeks? I'll make it up to the girl. We'll do a photoshoot in *People* and let the world know we're all copacetic."

"That was no ordinary girl you bopped on the head, Ronnie."

"Sure. But she's okay, right?"

"Still in a coma last I heard."

Ronnie's stomach sank. "But she's gonna come out of it, right?"

"I have no idea. People are saying permanent brain damage, blah-blah-blah. But what really matters is who you hit."

"Then tell me already. Who is this super-important person?"

"Suzy Algarotti."

Ronnie threw his hands in the air. "Am I supposed know who that is? Is she on the Gong Show or something?"

"Yeah, something. Her grandfather runs one of the top five crime families. Her father delivers all the smack, getting shot up in Brooklyn. If you'd chipped her fingernail, they might've broken your finger. But you did something much worse." Pearlstein sighed, his face long with total defeat.

"So, what does it all mean?"

"It means that there's a vendetta on you. They're gonna serve your head on a platter with spaghetti over at a trattoria."

"You're callin' me a meatball."

"What?"

"My head surrounded by spaghetti. That makes me a meatball."

"Are you listening to me? You're a dead man once you walk out of here. Dead if they put you in a general population cell. You might even get knocked off by a cop if they're on the payroll."

Ronnie blinked. For the first time in a long time, he couldn't think of anything to say. Pearlstein made a grim smile. Like he'd finally got through to Ronnie.

"Soo…what if we hold a press conference—"

"Hold on," the attorney said, waving his hands. "There is no *we* here. I am not going anywhere in public with you except for a courtroom. I'm not catching a stray bullet or getting blown to smithereens by a bomb."

Anger simmered inside Ronnie. Who did this overpriced, unloyal prick think he was?

"Fine, maybe I'll can your ass and get another attorney who won't mind breaking bread with me."

The lawyer laughed. "Fat chance anybody will touch you with a ten-foot pole."

"We'll see about that. You're fired."

Pearlstein smiled and stood. His posture seemed taller, like a hundred-pound weight had slid off his shoulders. "So long and farewell. I'll send you a bill shortly. Hopefully, your estate will pay it."

Ronnie felt a surge of panic. He'd had this lawyer since he'd been getting in fights in high school. He needed one more thing. "Hey, before we sever our partnership or whatever, can you call Phil at Nike and have him send a Learjet over right away? I should get out of the city."

"I forgot to tell you, kid. Nike dropped you."

Pearlstein walked out of the room.

What? Nike dropped him? That's impossible. Who else do they have playing tennis for them…like nobody. Ronnie squeezed his eyes shut and ran his hands through his mop of hair. Why does bad stuff always happen to him? It made no sense.

A knock on the door brought Ronnie to full attention.

"What?" he said, glaring at an officer leaning against the door and chewing bubblegum.

"Ya need to get your butt outta here."

Ronnie took a deep breath and walked to the door. Why had he fired Pearlstein? He didn't want to go to jail. There had to be another way. This sucks.

"I need a new lawyer."

The officer shrugged. "So get one."

"But I need to make a call first."

Another shrug. "So make a call."

Ronnie looked around the waiting area. People sat waiting for friends or relatives to get out of the holding tank. There was a phone booth, but the receiver had been torn off.

"I need a working phone. This one doesn't cut it."

"There's plenty out there."

The officer pointed to the exit.

"I'm free to go?"

"Yep."

"That's great." Ronnie took a few steps forward and stopped. "So the girl's okay?" Maybe she'd end up with a bruise on her noggin, but nothing too bad. He could make nice with the family and get his Nike contract back.

"Nah. She's still in a coma."

"So, if I assaulted her or something, why are you letting me go?" Ronnie asked.

"Because the family doesn't want to press charges."

"Why not?"

Again with the stupid shrug. "My guess is they want you on the street, not in here." The cop pushed him toward the door. "Now scram."

Ronnie noticed that the station had become pin-drop silent. All of the visitors watched him. The cop stood in front of him, arms crossed, blocking entry to the station.

"What about the cop I assaulted?"

"He recanted. Now get outta here already."

The officer grabbed Ronnie by the neck and shoulder and shoved him out the exit. Ronnie fell to the ground, skinning a knee.

"You bastard! I'm gonna sue you and your entire department." He kicked the door for good measure. Pain radiated from his foot to his leg.

"Owww, dammit."

He limped away, noticing people staring at him in his filthy tennis whites and signature sweatband. A couple of tough men with sunglasses and long jackets in the July heat walked toward him.

"Nuh-nuh." He waved a finger at them and hurried his pace in the opposite direction.

They hurried theirs.

He hobble-ran to the end of the block. A man stepped around the corner, also wearing a long jacket. He gripped something in his hand. A gun?

Ronnie didn't care to find out as he dashed into the street. Cars honked and swerved as he dodged the oncoming traffic. On the opposite sidewalk, he opened a door and ran inside. Women sat on chairs on each side of the store while having their fingers or toenails scrubbed and polished. Great, a nail salon.

"Can I help you?" a dainty woman said. He pushed past her, running to the back of the shop. "Hey, you can't go back there."

The front door bells jangled. Looking over his shoulder, he saw one of the men barging through.

"Crap."

He ducked through a beaded curtain, passing stacks of cardboard boxes and a restroom to the back door. He pulled. Locked. Three locks secured it.

"Really?"

He twisted the first lock and unbolted the second one. Through the commotion from the angry woman's voice, he heard the beads parting. Ronnie grabbed a box and threw it. It was light and had a slow spinning arch. The man stepped through the beaded threshold. The box bounced off of his head, skewing his sunglasses.

"What the hell?"

The man pulled up a gun. Ronnie grabbed the next box, also light, and tossed it. The box exploded midair with a deafening boom. Hundreds of cotton balls exploded in the air, creating a white puffy blizzard. The gunman coughed uncontrollably. He must have inhaled a fragment of cotton. Ronnie grabbed a third box, smaller but heavier, and ran through floating debris, smashing it on the gunman's head with a sickening thud. The thug fell to the floor as tendrils of red, black, pink, and purple nail polish oozed down his face.

Ronnie turned the final lock and flung open the door. He ran into an alley. A bullet smashed into a trashcan next to him. A gangster ran towards him, firing. Ronnie sprinted back inside, locked the door—all three of them— leapt over the unconscious thug and through the beaded curtains, bumping into another bruiser who was being hounded by the manicurist. He tried to raise his pistol, but Ronnie caught his arm. The gun went off, and the man howled, hopping on one foot. The other was a bloody mess. Ronnie pushed the man into a chair and stomped on the injured foot. The hoodlum screamed louder, dropping the gun. Ronnie reached for it, but the woman stepped on it.

"My gun now. You leave."

"Really?"

The woman grabbed the pistol and pointed it at Ronnie. He held his hands up. His urge to argue vanished.

Ronnie ran out of the shop and turned onto the sidewalk. He wanted to blend in, but there was no way in his tennis gear. Maybe he could buy…crap. He realized that his wallet, keys, and civilian clothes were in a locker at the tennis center. He needed to go there, get his stuff, and take the first flight to Mexico or wherever. He spotted a cab and hailed it. The driver pulled over. Ronnie threw the door open and crashed into the back seat.

"Where to?"

"The National Tennis Center in Queens."

The driver turned around, and his eyes bugged.

"Nu-uh. Get yer ass out of my cab."

"Don't worry about money. I'm good for it. I just need to go in and grab my wallet. I'll pay you a hundred bucks over the fare."

"Get out. I don't want ya in here."

"Two hundred…three hundred over the fare. Come on, man, I need to get over there fast," he said with a crack in his voice.

"I don't want yer stinkin' money. Get out."

Ronnie crossed his arms.

"No. I'm staying until you take me there."

The cabbie shifted the car into park and pushed his wide body out of the taxi. He threw the rear passenger door open.

"Get out. I don't want yer blood all over my cab."

"I'm not bleeding."

"You will after some goomba blows a hole in your head."

The cabbie pulled on Ronnie's arm. He jerked back.

"Don't touch me," he screamed.

The rear window exploded as a bullet whizzed through Ronnie's hair.

"Shit," the cabbie shouted as he ran away.

Ronnie ducked as more bullets slammed into the cab. Some flew through the front windshield, too. He crawled over the front seat and ducked into the footwell. Reaching up, he put the car in gear and then smashed the gas pedal with his right hand. The car took off. He reached for the steering wheel with his left as the cab scraped a parked car and a thug who dropped his pistol on the windshield while unloading a stream of agonized curses.

Ronnie kept his hand on the gas, steering blindly into traffic. Blaring horns, screeching brakes, and shouted obscenities came from every direction, but he kept trucking. Gaining speed. He sat up in time to see a stopped bus rapidly approaching. He jerked hard to the left and smacked into a car that careened across traffic, smashing into a hot dog stand. Ronnie then swung a hard right as he entered a fast-moving intersection. He banged the front bumper of a Honda Civic. The driver honked—beeped, really—and Ronnie flipped him the bird.

"You got lucky, man. You should've seen what happened to the last guy I hit."

He looked through the fractured windshield and felt the cool air blowing through the blown-out windows and bullet-pierced doors. He erupted with high-pitched laughter. Holy crap. He was alive. The deadliest man on the East Coast sent his hitmen, and he survived. Hell yeah. The car behind him kept beeping and flashing its lights.

Come on, look at this shot-to-hell car. You really wanna tangle with somebody like me?

He stopped at a red light. Crap. He was about 2 miles from the stadium. Close enough to taste it.

He looked behind him, and the tiny Honda door opened. Two massive hands grabbed the roof and the door as the driver pulled himself out of the car. The dude kept rising as the car's shocks seemed to expand with relief from the lifted weight. Ronnie looked at the light. Still red. Super crap. The guy had to be close to 7 foot tall with muscles. How did he clown-car himself into that Honda? The man marched over. Ronnie looked straight ahead, trying to act as if nothing was happening.

The man knocked on his roof.

"Hey." He had an accent of some kind.

"Oh, hey." Ronnie acted as if he didn't know he was there.

"I need your insurance. You hit my car."

"Look, this isn't my car. I'm borrowing it. Sorry."

The man looked unimpressed.

Ronnie glanced at the light. Still red.

"You hit my car. Give me your insurance card."

Ronnie grabbed the cabbie's badge hanging from the mirror and handed it to him. "Here, take this."

The man studied the badge, looked at Ronnie, and then back at the badge.

"That is not you."

"Yeah, well, so long, sucker."

Ronnie stomped on the gas and laughed, zooming through a green light. He watched the tall freak fold himself back into his Honda. The damage didn't look *that* bad. The car in front of him suddenly stopped. Ronnie stomped on the brakes, but crashed, slamming his head on the steering wheel.

He blinked away stars when massive hands grabbed his collar, pulling toward the window. Ronnie used his feet push away from the giant. His shirt ripped as he tumbled to the passenger seat. He opened the door and darted between cars, making it to the sidewalk and then down the subway station entrance. He vaulted over the turnstile like a court net after a win and shoved his way down the crowded stairs. A train was about to leave when he stuck his arm through the closing door and pushed his way inside.

His heart pounded. He glanced at the riders around him, all clean and proper. They gave him suspicious side-eyes. The kind of looks given to smelly bums who get too close. He sniffed his armpit. Whoa. He reeked something awful. Still, they shouldn't treat him like that. They sat next to an internationally ranked tennis star. On a normal day, he wouldn't be anywhere near these commoners.

"What? You gotta problem," he shouted.

People looked away.

When the train stopped at the stadium, he ran up the stairs with a plan already formed. He'd grab his wallet and take a flight to Northern California. He had a friend—but, did he really have any friends? Regardless, this millionaire had paid him handsomely to play doubles against his other douchebag millionaire friends. Such an easy way to pocket six-figures without breaking a sweat and enjoy quality vino too. There was an open invitation to stay at his winery. He'd cash in on this promise and wait for the hoopla about the comatose girl to die down.

He ran to the side entrance of the stadium, where the players and media entered. A beefy security guard stood outside. Ronnie tried to walk past, but an enormous hand stopped him. What's the deal with big dudes being dicks today?

"Let me through."

"Go buy a ticket like everybody else."

"What?!" he said, pointing to his chest. "I am not everybody else. I am Ronnie McIntire. Top three player in the world. I was about to beat Sam Bonner today before the game got canceled."

The guard looked unmoved. Bored actually.

"Don't you know that?"

"I don't watch tennis. Where's your badge?"

"What the…I don't need a dumb badge, jerk. I play matches here every year. You can't be that stupid."

Ronnie tried to push past, but was shoved to the ground.

"Show me a badge, or you don't come in."

Ronnie saw red. He charged, running headfirst into the man's stomach. He fell to the ground, an array of silver stars exploding in front of his eyes. It was like running into a brick wall.

"So you wanna play it that way." The bouncer cracked his knuckles, a smile creasing on his face.

"What? No. Not at all," Ronnie backed away.

The guard reached for him. Ronnie turned and sprinted into a pair of leather-jacketed goombahs.

"Whoa, where do ya think you're goin', Mister Dead-On-His-Feet?"

Ronnie was about to answer when a brass-knuckled fist connected to his stomach, knocking the air out of him. He crumbled to the ground. One of the men whistled. A van pulled up, braking hard. A sliding door opened. The thugs lifted Ronnie and tossed him inside. The van peeled out.

Crumpled in a fetal position, Ronnie felt like he might puke. The van seemed to hit every pothole in New York. Where did this idiot learn to drive? Finally, they stopped, and a goon got out of the passenger seat. While Ronnie wanted to look, he needed to rest and conserve his energy for whatever lay ahead. The van drove up a ramp and stopped.

The door slid open into a blast of white, fluorescent light. Ronnie shielded his eyes. Two men with overalls and gloves reached in and grabbed the tennis star.

"Hey!"

They dragged him across concrete and dropped him next to a drain on the floor. He looked around, getting his bearings. A warehouse. No, hooks hung from the ceiling. Oh god, a slaughterhouse. His breath, quick and short, could not bring in enough air. He didn't belong here. This was not the way to end his career. His life. There was more for him to do. So many more wins.

He made a break for an open door, but a blow to his back sent him to his knees. One of the overalled thugs carried a chair over. They placed Ronnie in the chair and cuffed his wrists behind his back.

Don't cry. Don't beg. Never, ever weep in front of anybody. Ever.

A man emerged from a back room. Tall with a gaunt face that could have been carved from granite. Probably in his mid-sixties, he wore a black 3-piece suit with a fedora perched low.

Ronnie had heard of this guy. A myth, really. The guy who eliminated enemies of the mob. Stool pigeons ended up dead before they could testify. Rivals and grandmas who were unfortunate witnesses, all dead. Urban legends credited this man with over a hundred murders. What the hell was his name?

The Executioner.

Ronnie dry swallowed. This is bad. Really, really, really bad.

"Look here..."

The Executioner walked up to him, his patent leather shoes clicking on the floor. He stopped a foot away and reached inside his jacket. Ronnie squeezed his eyes shut, waiting for a bullet smash into his brain. He heard a click sound. Not like a gun, something softer. Plasticky.

Ronnie opened his eyes. The assassin held a black marker in his hand, the cap in the other. He marked an "X" in the middle of Ronnie's forehead.

"Why'd you do that?"

"Right in the center of your forehead," the man said in a deep, smooth voice. "That's where you hit my boss's daughter."

"It was a mistake."

"Was it?"

"Yes, I swear on my mother's grave."

"Is your mother dead?"

"No, but—"

The Executioner reached inside his jacket again and pulled out a Luger. Of course, somebody this evil used a Nazi gun.

"As I see it, you're a self-serving prick who will lie, cheat, and cry like a baby to win or, in this case, get out of trouble. But whenever the adversity is over, and you get your way, it means nothing. You'll do it all over again because you never suffer consequences. Tell me, young man, what kind of justice is that?"

"But I…I've had sanctions against me…handed down from the Tennis Federation. I-I just found out I lost my deal with Nike. That's huge."

The man shook his head with a slight smirk, like Ronnie was a kid who'd never get it.

"Lemme talk to someone," Ronnie sputtered. "I can clear this all up. It was a mistake. An honest one. Please. Please. Pleeeease!"

The hit man pushed the barrel of the gun against Ronnie's forehead. The professional tennis player couldn't hold back any longer. All the pain, indignities, and injustice he'd suffered poured out. He bawled like a baby. Snot ran down his chin.

"I won't lose my temper ever again. I'll stop playing tennis this second. I'll never pick up a racket again. I sweeeeear!"

The Executioner cocked the pistol's hammer. Ronnie's bladder released, his white shorts yellowing from the center.

A phone against a far wall rang.

"See who it is," the Executioner said to one of the henchmen.

The man plodded over to the ringing phone.

Ronnie looked down at his urine-soaked shorts. So damn humiliating.

The thug reached the phone.

"Hello…Uh-huh…Yep…Okay…Uh-huh…Yeah…Got it…I'll let him know."

The man shuffled back. Ronnie looked up. The pistol had not moved from his forehead. The thug whispered into the Executioner's ear. The assassin's hard face grew stiffer, while not wavering his arm in the slightest. The message seemed to take forever. Finally, the goon stepped away.

"And that's everything he said?" the Executioner asked.

The henchman nodded. The Executioner sighed as the pistol drifted down.

"What?" Ronnie asked.

"The girl recovered."

"She did? That's awesome."

Laughter from deep within volcanoed out. Holy crap. He'd been seconds away from death. A freakin' pistol had been pointed at his head. At Ronnie McIntire's head. But he won. Like always. Of course, there was an ugly mess, but hallelujah, he beat death.

"But we aren't through with you yet."

Ronnie stopped laughing.

"What do you mean?"

The Executioner nodded. The two thugs grabbed Ronnie by the armpits and carried him. He kicked his legs and jerked his body, but it had no effect. They lay him on a cold stainless-steel table and held him down while the Executioner uncuffed a hand.

"Wait. What are you doing? She's alive. You don't need to kill me."

The Executioner pulled Ronnie's right arm and clipped the cuff to a steel pole cemented in the floor.

"Yes, she is alive. And she'll probably attend more tennis matches, so we can't have her life in peril from one of your infamous outbursts."

A henchman handed the Executioner a humongous knife.

"Oh god, no. I'll never ever have another outburst in my life ever again. I promise."

"That's a promise I'm sure you cannot keep."

Ronnie pulled hard, but there was no give. Ronnie shouted a litany of curses. The kind that would get him banned from televised games.

"Have you heard the legend about the samurai assistants in ancient feudal Japan?"

Ronnie stopped shouting for a second. "What?"

"The samurai needed help carrying his gear, getting food, sharpening his sword, and whatever else they needed back then. But samurai held a suspicion that one day their assistants might rise up and attack them. Do you know what they did to ensure there were no betrayals?"

Ronnie took a moment, considering where this story was heading and where he did not want it go. "They asked their assistants to swear they'd never stab them in the back?"

The Executioner shook his head. "I'm afraid your answer's wrong. They needed something stronger. A physical manifestation, like cutting off a finger. Do you know why?"

"No. It sounds like a stupid idea."

"They did it so that the assistants could never take up arms against their master. Or at least they'd be unable to hold a sword correctly, making them a worthless adversary in combat. Do you know how this example relates to you?"

"It doesn't at all. I've never met a samurai, and I've never held a sword. This is totally, one-hundred percent irrelevant to me."

The Executioner stood silent, staring at Ronnie. His face impassive. Ronnie's body trembled.

"I think you know," the Executioner said after several insufferable moments of silence. "The tennis racket is your sword. And you should never hold one again. That's why I'm taking your thumb."

With rapid speed, he grabbed Ronnie's wrist and held it firmly.

"Wait. No-no-no. Stop! Aaaah!"

Ronnie passed out as the knife sliced into his skin.

* * *

Ronnie woke up in an alley. He rolled over to see a heavy gray sky that told him it was not quite morning, but the darkest of night had passed. His throat was dry, and everything ached. He looked over at his hand, wrapped in a dirty, blood-stained cloth. Crap. This hadn't been a nightmare. Tried to wiggle his thumb, but a lightning bolt of pain flashed through his arm. With his other hand, he unwrapped the bandage slowly, praying that the digit was attached. Maybe he'd only have a cut. A warning slice that some stitches could heal. He'd lie and tell people he fell on a broken bottle. But as the cloth unwound, he saw the truth. The Executioner had taken his thumb.

He gritted his teeth, tensed his body, and let out a primal yell. Every ounce of humiliation he had endured as a child until now poured out in that hoarse scream. He took deep, exhausted breaths. Totally spent. What was life worth living for now?

Then a soft laugh emerged. It started slowly and grew into a loud, uncontrollable guffaw.

"You stupid, dumbasses. You freakin' idiots."

He held up his bloody stump to the world.

"Do any of you morons watch tennis? This ain't gonna stop me from playing. I'm a lefty!"

He walked out of the alley, bedraggled but not defeated. No, not at all. They couldn't stop him now. He'd get back on the court with a modified backhand and defeat every bastard unfortunate to receive his serve. Those mafia goons forgot something; Ronnie was a winner. No way anybody, or any missing body part, would stop him from being the greatest tennis player of all time.

* * *

Travis Richardson has published over 50 short stories. He won a Derringer flash fiction award and has been a 3-time nominee for the Macavity and a 2-time nominee for the Anthony Derringer short story awards. He has two novellas, *Lost in Clover* and *Keeping the Record,* and a short story collection, *Bloodshot and Bruised.* He lives in Los Angeles with his wife, daughter, and dog. Find more at http://www.tsrichardson.com.

Retaliate Undetected

By John Shepphird

Madeline's text read: *We're going to Nationals!*

What my mixed doubles partner meant was the United States Tennis Association (USTA) League National Championships. Madeline and I played in the Southern California Beach Cities age 40 and over league—male and female players paired. But her text didn't make sense. Our team of three mixed doubles partners had lost to L.A.'s San Gabriel Valley at the Sectionals playoffs in Orange County. At our skill level, rated at 3.5, they beat us two out of three lines.

Unfortunately, it was our match that came down to the heartbreaking tiebreaker. After the opposing team carved out the first set, we won the second and had momentum, but we couldn't get past San Gabriel's bald, tattooed guy—a monster at the net. Afterwards, Madeline blamed herself for the loss. "Why did I keep feeding him?"

I phoned Madeline for clarity, and she explained, "That sandbagging douchebag baldy was rated 4.0, so they got disqualified. That means we chalk up the win, and now our team is off to Arizona for Nationals. It's the weekend of April 25th. You available?"

"I think so."

"What's that mean?" she barked, angry. "Are you in or out?"

"I'll make myself available."

"Great." Madeline seemed relieved. "Nationals. Can you believe it?

And it's Phoenix, so we can drive." She explained our team captain, Paul, suggested we book the Holiday Inn Express, walking distance from the Surprise Tennis & Racket Complex. "Or there's a Hilton Garden Inn next door. I'll text you the details."

I had Hilton points, so booked there.

Little did I know—I'd been roped into a criminal caper.

* * *

Our team was based out of Alta Vista Park in Redondo Beach, twenty-five minutes south of LAX. The other teams in our league were from private clubs. Those had swimming pools, exercise equipment, and cocktail bars for sipping drinks after matches. Not Alta Vista. We were the scrappy public park team. But that meant there was no towel fee. You had to bring your own. That was fine with me.

I saw Madeline at the home courts that weekend. She said she and the team captain's wife, Liv, had coordinated matching attire for Nationals and showed me on her iPhone. Fortunately for the men, it was simply an aquamarine-colored shirt, all of thirty bucks. I was certain the ladies' L'Etoile Sport outfits were priced well into three digits.

Madeline said, "Do you mind driving? My car is on the fritz. Crazy unreliable these days." She drove an older black Mercedes. I suspected the luxury vehicle had been acquired before her divorce. Madeline shared little about her personal life other than bragging about her son, who was off in college. To Liv, I overheard her joke that her divorce had been "coyote ugly," as she phrased it.

I said. "My SUV seats six, so I can take the whole team if need be."

"Thanks. I'll put that in the group chat."

As Nationals grew closer, I let my girlfriend Laura know I'd be out of town that weekend. Although I kept my own apartment in Torrance, I spent most of my time at Laura's townhome, not far from the Alta Vista tennis courts. She was also a divorcee—bitter that her husband had left her for a younger woman. Laura was especially angry because *she* was paying spousal support, not the other way around. She had been the breadwinner—was a marketing executive V.P. for a software firm and supported the guy's fledgling acting career before he ran off with what she called "the skinny ingénue."

Laura held deep resentment.

I have had my share of romantic relationships over the years but never tied the knot. There had been pressure by some girlfriends to commit, but I felt I hadn't found the right one. I genuinely loved Laura, even considered going to Zales to buy a ring to propose. Neither of us were getting any younger. But, in the back of my mind, I wasn't sure Laura was the right one either.

She supported my tennis hobby while appreciating that I maintained regular exercise. Laura humored me as I obsessively watched coverage of the Australian Open, Roland Garros, Wimbledon, and the US Open. We even spent a romantic weekend in Palm Springs, attending the PNB Paribas tournament at Indian Wells. But she always assumed I played with guys. Ninety-five percent of the time, that was true. I didn't tell her I was playing on a mixed doubles team because I knew she'd get jealous.

Maybe Laura's insecurity was one of the reasons I was so hesitant to make her my life partner. That, and how controlling she was.

Although Madeline was attractive, with vibrant blue eyes and dark hair cut in a flapper bob that reminded me of the silent movie star Louise Brooks, there was nothing between us—no flirting, no romantic spark. We were simply colleagues collaborating on the court. The business was winning.

At the beginning of the season, team captain Paul paired me with Madeline. He felt success in doubles came from players that complimented each other and honed strategy. Although Madeline was short in stature, she was quick and skilled. Hard serves didn't faze her, and Madeline's strokes generally had both spin and pace. But as controlling as Laura was, Madeline was worse. My tennis partner was hyper-competitive. When things didn't go her way, it would get up in her head. I put up with the criticism because I understood it was Madeline's way of expressing frustration. Just like with Laura, I didn't take it personally. None of that mattered because we'd won most of our matches and were going to Nationals.

Since my girlfriend was the jealous type, I figured what Laura didn't know wouldn't hurt her.

* * *

I assumed I'd be driving some of the players from our team but learned from the group chat that everyone else had booked flights to Phoenix. Only Madeline and I would be making the drive. I was fine with that. Considering the time it would take to get to the LAX, check in, wait for your flight, arrive at Sky Harbor International in Phoenix, and wait for a rental car—that would take close to four hours while it's only a six-hour drive to Phoenix.

I packed my things and kissed Laura goodbye. She seemed a little off, mad at me for something. I couldn't put my finger on it.

Madeline lived in a two-story Cape Cod-style home in upscale Manhattan Beach. I could see the groundskeeping had been long neglected. There were weeds coming up through the cracks on the driveway. The gate on the side of the house was hanging off its hinges. My impression was that the large home was a remnant from her married past, now probably overkill for a single woman living alone.

Madeline opened the garage door and brought out her tennis bag, a rolling suitcase, and struggled with a large black plastic bin. I asked her what it was. She said, "When we're in Phoenix, do you mind running an errand to drop this off? I have family in Scottsdale, figured since we're driving out there. Save on shipping."

"No problem." I loaded the plastic bin into the back of my SUV. I was heavy, secured by zip ties.

We stopped at Starbucks for coffee, and I paid out of chivalry. Only after we were heading east on Interstate 10 did Madeline start to talk about her personal life. She had once been a member of the pricey Manhattan Beach Country Club, one of our opponents that season. When she couldn't afford the membership, she was forced to let it go, "Because my husband left me for a younger woman…ten years younger."

Not knowing how to respond, I said, "I'm sorry."

"I'm keeping the home for my son's sake."

"Does he play tennis?"

"Brandon does," the thought putting a smile on her face. "We all did." Her smile faded with, "Ted, my ex, works in finance. When we were first married, and he was just getting started as a broker, many of his clients came from my family, parents, grandparents, aunts and uncles. You've got to start somewhere, right? After Brandon was born, Ted's career took off. He bounced around from firm to firm and eventually founded a group that managed a hedge fund. Me…I could hardly balance the checkbook. Ted handled all the finances. That was his expertise." She stared out the window for a moment before, "After my mom passed away from breast cancer, my dad got depressed and started drinking a lot. Ted convinced him to invest. Then one day Ted's hedge fund shit the bed. There were lawsuits. All a sudden, we were broke. The big surprise was that my father had put his entire life savings into Ted's stupid fund. Nobody ever told me. Ted took advantage of my dad's Alzheimer's, like a con man. Then he left me for Sonja."

I didn't know how to respond, so I nodded in silence while watching the road ahead.

"With my father's life savings gone, he moved in with me and Brandon. His dementia got really bad. I had to quit my job because he needed constant care. Ted was no help, leaving me high and dry while off gallivanting with that stupid bitch. Then came dad's heart attack, and…" she grew emotional. "He died from a broken heart."

"You've been through a lot," I said.

"It was hell. I don't mean to dump all my shit on you. It's just…I've been thinking a lot about it lately."

"Sometimes it's good to talk things through and get it off your chest. Don't feel bad."

"Thanks for listening."

She pulled a piece of paper out from her purse. Paul sent the schedule, and Madeline had printed it out. Our first match was at 8:00 in the morning the next day. Our second match wasn't until 3:00 that afternoon, so there'd be a midday break. The Sunday game was also 8:00 AM. If our team advanced, there'd be more games scheduled later that day. I said, "At least we're staying walking distance from the courts. Means we can get out of the sun, take a swim or something."

"That's right," Madeline said, her mind somewhere else.

* * *

My Honda Pilot needed gas, so we pulled off at Summit Road and drove past the General George S. Patton Memorial Museum, which looked interesting. Apparently, this remote part of the desert was the site of the tank training camp before his campaign in North Africa. Had I been alone or with one of the guys, I probably would have checked it out. I'm sort of a military history buff, but suspected Madeline had no interest in WWII memorabilia.

I filled the tank. Since neither of us had eaten all day, the only option other than a Foster's Freeze was the Chiricaco Summit Restaurant & Gift Shop. We entered the greasy spoon and were seated at a booth. Madeline ordered a BLT. That sounded good, so I did too. After the waitress moved on, Madeline said, "Can I show you something? You may think it's weird."

"I'm okay with *weird*."

"The day I learned we were going to Nationals, I was sitting on my couch feeling sorry for myself, scrolling on my phone, and working on a second bottle of wine. That's when I came across this." She pulled a paperback from her purse and handed it to me—*Camouflaged Revenge: Retaliate Undetected*. "It's written by a private eye."

The book had cheap-looking artwork and reeked of being self-published. A photo on the back cover featured the author Nick McClintock; tough guy flexing biceps.

She went on, "I follow Ted's stay-at-home girlfriend, Sonja, on Instagram. They've moved into a custom, luxury home. So, where'd that money come from? Huh? I suspect Ted ratholed my dad's life savings, then claimed the investment was lost in the stock market."

I asked, "You follow your ex's girlfriend?"

"With a fake profile, of course. Ted doesn't post, so I have to follow Sonja." She sat back and studied me for a moment. "You know Sun Tzu, the ninja guy who wrote the *Art of War?* He said, 'Keep your friends close but your enemies closer.'"

"I don't think Sun Tzu was a ninja."

"Samurai. Kung Fu monk. Whatever. I say *fuck* Ted and his gold-digging bimbo." She said that with enough volume that a few diners looked over. Madeline noticed them. In a whisper, she continued, "Ted is the one in Scottsdale." She dug into her purse to show me a color printout of a social media post. Sitting on stools at an exotic beachside Tiki bar, middle-aged Ted was overly tanned, and Sonja was the bottle-blonde beside him. "He paid for her breast enhancement. And now they're in Tahiti."

I had to ask. "Okay…so what's in that bin?"

"Don't worry about it. All I need from you is a ride to his house. Drop me off and pick me up in an hour."

"When?"

"After we win Nationals, of course." She sipped her iced tea. "The thing is…I can't be traced anywhere near Scottsdale. There's uhm…some legal shit that needs to be resolved. If opposing counsel were to learn I'd *retaliated*…"

"Opposing counsel?"

"It's complicated. I'm suing Ted in civil court, but that shit takes years. Forever. Meanwhile, while I sit here sipping Lipton Tea, Ted's squandering my family's fortune. Not that we had a fortune, but…I can tell you, Tahiti wasn't Ted's idea. It had to be Sonja's. More exotic than Hawaii because they speak French there. Typical."

Our BLTs arrived. Madeline doused Tabasco Sauce on her fries, claiming the condiment was healthier than salt. As we ate in silence, I thumbed through the book. Nick McClintock's "Also by the Author" page included two other books, *Deep-Dive Deluxe: Find Dirt on Anybody* and *Side Hustle: Earn Extra Cash as a Private Eye.*

* * *

Back on the road, I asked Madeline what her plan was.

"Don't worry about it. All I need is for you to do it get me to his house in Scottsdale and come back later." She pulled a black cell phone from her purse. "I bought this with cash and activated it anonymously. My real phone is back home, so I can't be traced. You won't recognize this number when I call, so pick up anything that rings. I'm not spam. Got it? And you'll have to let me know what the team's group chats are saying."

"You learned how to do all this in that book?"

"It's very informative."

I implored for more information, but Madeline said, "Look, the less you know, the better. Trust me. Everything is going to be fine."

I couldn't help but wonder what was in that black plastic bin.

We arrived in Phoenix and made our way to Surprise. The suburban sprawl was track homes and strip malls—new construction. The Surprise Tennis & Racket Complex sat in the middle of an enormous sports park. We drove around scouting it all. There was the Surprise Stadium, home of the Cactus League baseball training camps for both the Texas Rangers and Kansas City Royals. There were soccer fields, youth baseball diamonds, pickleball courts, swimming pools, and even a community fishing pond. I wondered what kind of massive municipal bond had funded it all.

I dropped Madeline off at the Holiday Inn Express. She retrieved the hotel dolly for her luggage, tennis bag, and the black bin. The team group chat claimed everyone was arriving in a couple of hours. I suggested we all grab a bite at one of the fast-casual restaurants nearby. Madeline said she'd rather just order something delivered and turn in early. I tried to convince her otherwise, suggesting it was an opportunity to bond with our teammates, but her mind was set.

I checked in at the adjacent Hilton Garden Inn and bought a couple of post-travel beers from the guest pantry at the front desk. I called Laura to let her know I'd arrived. I really wanted to tell her all about Madeline's crazy caper but couldn't because that would reveal that I was out of town with a woman. The fact that I'd kept mixed doubles a secret wouldn't go over well.

When the other players arrived (Ivy and her husband Paul, and Chuck and Petra), we met in the lobby of the Holiday Inn. Paul, the consummate organizer, had made reservations at the nearby Longhorn Steakhouse. That came in handy because when we arrived many other teams clearly had no reservations and were lined up outside waiting. I overheard the hostess say it would be over an hour.

I found the dinner conversation boring and struggled to find common interest in anything other than tennis. Maybe it was because, without Madeline there, I was the fifth wheel. When the conversation turned to politics, I ordered a bourbon, a nightcap to help me sleep. After we settled the bill, plans were made to meet early the next morning to allow enough time to walk to the courts and get in a little warm-up.

The nightcap had the opposite effect and kept me awake most the night. As much as I tried to doze off, my mind was abuzz, wondering what Madeline was going to do, and what was in that black bin.

* * *

After I got ready the next morning, I grabbed my tennis bag and went to the adjacent Holiday Inn Express. While Ivy, Paul, Chuck, and Petra were finishing the complimentary coffee and breakfast, Madeline was seated in the business center off the lobby, nose in the computer. I could tell she was disturbed by something.

Color-coordinated in our new tennis wear, she joined us and we made the trek to the tennis center. When the others were out of earshot, Madeline said, "I just saw a post from Sonja. You have to take me to Scottsdale today. Between our matches. They're heading back early. Already on the red eye that arrives later this afternoon." She shook her head in dismay. "I should have had you drop me off last night."

"After our first match?"

"Yes."

She could tell I was not thrilled about it.

"Forget it. I'll get a cab," she said, clearly trying to guilt me.

"I'll drive. What exactly are you going to do, anyway?"

"I told you, the less you know, the better."

She picked up her pace to join the others up ahead.

We barely got a warmup before the courts were assigned. Our opposing team was from Florida. Madeline and I greeted our opponents, a couple in their mid-fifties, both tall. We won the coin toss, so Madeline served first. Her first serve went into the net. The second was long. On the ad side, she double faulted again. Before long, we were way behind. Most of the rallies were short as Madeline had one unforced error after another. What made it worse was that the opponents smelled blood and picked on her. Hardly any balls were hit towards me. I asked Madeline, "Are you okay?"

"Peachy," she said with sarcasm.

"We can beat them," I said, trying to stay positive. "We're just getting warmed up. One point at a time."

The following games didn't go our way, and Florida took the first set with ease. Madeline's mind wasn't in the game. In the second set, she got some of her mojo back, but then I started to falter. We lost to Florida—simply outplayed.

Madeline had tears in her eyes but tried not to show it.

We carried our bags over to watch our teammates finish their matches. Ivy and Paul won. Chuck and Petra's came down to a nail-biting tiebreaker. They pulled off a win to our cheers. Beach Cities had beaten Florida, two games to one, which meant our team would advance to the next match in the winner's bracket.

Madeline declared she needed to go back to the hotel to make some calls and check emails, and we made our exit. On the way, from her tennis bag, she pulled out an index card with an address. "Put that in Google Maps to see how long it will take to get there."

I did, and said, "Just over an hour."

"Okay, figure two hours there and back. It's about 10:30 now, so that should be plenty of time to get back before 3:00. Maybe even grab lunch."

Back in my room, I washed up, changed into jeans, and met Madeline outside the Holiday Inn Express. She was dressed in a polo shirt and khakis with that mysterious black bin at her feet. On the drive to Scottsdale, she told me how Ted's betrayal had made her a pariah in the family. Nobody would talk to her. She went on to say that finding a job had been "Incredibly difficult. Nobody wants to hire anyone over forty," all while Google Maps directed us to Scottsdale.

"That's it," Madeline said, pointing to Ted's home perched on a ridge, a prime spot overlooking the desert valley below. We climbed the windy road. A few hundred feet before reaching the house, she said, "Pull over here. Don't get any closer." Madeline studied the home for a moment, then said, "Thanks," and jumped out.

She pulled out the bin and set it on the curb, snipped off the zip ties with a tool she had in her pocket. Inside was an assortment of items, including a hard hat, workman's vest, and N-95 mask. "Surveillance cameras are everywhere," she said. "This makes me look like a cable guy." There was also a rope ladder with wooden dowels as rungs. Before I could make out the rest of the items, Madeline replaced the cover as if protective of its contents and hoisted it up on her shoulder. "Don't go far. Keep your phone handy. When I'm done, I'll call and meet you back here."

"Whatever you're going to do," I said, "be careful."

"I've got this," she said, and carried the bin up to the house.

I made a U-turn, drove down the hill, and parked in a nearby strip mall— backed into a spot for a fast getaway. I checked my phone. Laura had texted me earlier that morning: *Who is Madeline?*

The cat was out of the bag. How did she know? Before I could call Laura to explain, I got a call from a number with a strange area code, obviously Madeline's burner phone. "I need your help," she said. "Meet me where you dropped me off."

I drove back up the hill and found her standing at the curb, no longer in the hard hat. "I need a boost," she said. "Park and follow me."

"What about the surveillance cameras?"

"I shut off the power at the breaker. 'Eradicate Security Devices' is step two in the book."

The black bin was stashed on the back porch of the house. The rope ladder was dangling askew from the balcony above. Madeline said, "That stupid ladder is useless. I need your help getting up."

"You're breaking and entering?"

"I'm not breaking anything," she said, and pulled from the bin a brass ring of twenty identical keys. "I've got a key to the door up there. It's got to be one of these because the manufacturer only makes so many profiles."

I asked, "How did you know what brand of door he'd have?"

"From Sonja's stupid fucking post. I could see the door handle and determine the make and model." She held up the keys proudly. "I bought these from a locksmith in Denver I found on the dark web. Expensive, but worth it."

"This is *so* fucking illegal," I said. "I can't be part of this."

"Don't wimp out on me. Shut up and help me get up there."

Under the balcony, I reluctantly boosted Madeline, first from my cupped hands, and then helping her step up on my shoulders. She was able to grab onto an outdoor lighting fixture and shimmy up. She found foothold on slat panel siding. I was impressed by her climbing ability and determination.

After scaling the railing and getting up onto the balcony, I heard the keys jingle as she went to work. I tossed the rope ladder into the bin and waited near the barbeque. I couldn't help myself and examined the bin. There were assorted envelopes, a jug of industrial solvent, and a pistol. I recognized the model as a Colt 45 M1911, the automatic handgun military officers carried many, many years ago. Winston Churchill, too. Why'd she bring a gun? That made me incredibly nervous.

After a few minutes, Madeline appeared in the living room and opened the sliding glass door. "What's with the gun?" I asked.

"Just in case."

"In case of what?

"Relax. Figured better safe than sorry."

"Where'd you get it?"

"It was my dad's. I took it when he started getting senile."

"We're committing a felony in possession of a firearm. I'm out of here."

"Will you chill out? We're not burglarizing anyone." She went to the bin and replaced its cover. "Don't fuck with my stuff. Get inside before someone sees us."

Our first stop was the upstairs master bedroom. Madeline peeled back the bedspread, kneeled to the bin. She pulled out a manila envelope. Within that, there was a white mesh pouch with dark specs inside, about the size of apple seeds.

"What's that?" I asked.

"Bedbugs."

Upon closer inspection, Bag O' Bugs was printed on the pouch in addition to the website address for Cheapbedbugs.com. I said, "You can buy bedbugs?"

"It's a thing."

"For what?"

"Training scent detection dogs," she said, as if it was obvious. "Hotels hire pros with special dogs to sniff that shit out." She methodically poured the pouch of bugs into the sheets and laughed to herself as she carefully remade the bed, replacing the duvet cover and pillows with great care.

Next, she carried the bin as we moved downstairs. There were a pair of car keys on wall hooks at the door leading to the garage. Madeline grabbed both.

Inside were two sedans: a sleek convertible Audi S8 and a white Lexus. She used the key fob to unlock the Audi and found the latch to open the fuel hatch. From the bin, she pulled out the tub of acetone. As Madeline poured the solvent into the gas tank, she explained, "Step Four: 'Make Lives Unbearable.' This won't stop his car immediately, but it will fuck it up over time. Warranties don't cover damage from fluids other than gas in the tank, so he'll be screwed." Next, with a funnel, she poured a carton of sugar into the tank. "Same with sugar," she said. "A time bomb."

Lastly, she pulled another manila envelope out of the bin and kneeled before the driver's seat. "Crickets. I named them Jim and Annie. Get it?

"You named these bugs?"

"That's right. Jim and Annie. Get it?"

"No."

"Jim-and-Annie-cricket. Jim and Annie…"

"Jiminy Cricket?" I said.

"You're *so* smart," she said, pinching my cheek as if I was a child. She locked the car door and moved to the Lexus, obviously Sonja's, because a pink feather hung from the rear-view mirror. Madeline pulled a container out of the bin I hadn't noticed before. The white plastic was translucent enough to see there was a snake inside.

"What the hell?"

"Don't worry, he's not lethal. But…Sonya won't know that…will she?" She opened the lid and flung the snake inside before slamming the door. "Snakes are everywhere in Arizona."

The doorbell rang.

We froze.

Madeline grabbed the pistol from the bin.

I said, "Are you crazy?"

"Shut up," she whispered. "They'll hear you."

"You don't need a gun."

"Don't tell me how to do my job." The look in her eyes with the gun in her hand frightened me.

Madeline tiptoed out of the garage with the weapon up and ready. I nervously followed. We cautiously crept through the hallway leading to the foyer. From the window adjacent to the front door, I could make out a cop. He was young and lanky. Madeline and I stood back in the darkness, and she whispered, "Probably because I turned off the electricity. The security system went offline, so they sent someone."

After a moment, the cop moved on.

Madeline darted upstairs, and I followed.

From the window of the master bedroom, we could see a private security patrol car parked in the driveway. I was relieved he wasn't a real cop.

"Do you think he'll come inside?" asked Madeline.

"If he does, don't shoot him."

We heard footsteps on the gravel at the side of the house. Thankfully, I'd retrieved the rope ladder out back. The security guard appeared on the concrete driveway, having circumvented the house. He had a holstered gun on his belt. Private security guards in California are generally unarmed, but this was Arizona—*open carry* territory. He pulled out his phone and climbed into the car. But he didn't start the vehicle. After a moment, Madeline said, "What do you think he's doing?"

"Maybe calling it in?"

We watched in silence for a while. From the high angle, we couldn't see what he was doing inside the car. Madeline said, "Keep an eye on him. I've got work to do," and tiptoed back downstairs.

I watched the vehicle. Occasionally, a car drove past, but no cops or other security guards joined. I wondered if he was taking a nap. And I wondered what Madeline was doing. I was about to go see just before she returned carrying the bin. "Plaster of Paris in the plumbing cleanout, moths in the closets, and let's just say this place will be haunted by a family of charming Madagascar hissing cockroaches…forever," she said with a cackling laugh.

"You learned all that from that book?"

"Some," she said. Madeline dug the paperback out of the bin. Thumbing through the dog-eared pages, she read aloud, "'Step Five: *Leave No Evidence. Cover Tracks.*' That's the shit that's most important." The book went back into the bin, and we both stared at the patrol car below. "What could he be doing?" she asked.

"I have no idea," and checked my watch. "But if we don't get on the road soon, we're going to miss our match."

"We'll sneak out back," she said. "We have to leave by the balcony anyway."

"Why?"

"Because nothing can be left unlocked. They'll know someone was here. I've got the key…so."

"And jump down?"

"We've got the ladder."

I didn't like the idea. "Let me take a look," I said and went to the balcony to check it out. To avoid the front of the house, we'd need to weave through gnarled cacti framing the back edge of the property. The cactus landscaping was obviously designed as a natural barrier to deter both man and beast.

Madeline joined me on the balcony. "Let's hit it." She ducked in for one last check to make sure she didn't leave anything behind. I heard the downstairs back door open and her efforts bringing the bin outside, then the bolt of the lock. Madeline returned upstairs with the ring of keys, but she'd forgotten what key had worked before and had to go through all of them until finally determining the correct one.

Meanwhile, I secured the rope ladder and realized it would be impossible to disconnect it from above once we both were down. The ladder would be evidence that someone had broken in. That meant one of us would have to jump down. Since I was the guy, naturally, I volunteered. Foolish chivalry, I guess.

I helped her over the balcony and supported the flimsy ladder until she was safely down. Then I tossed the top end of the ladder over the railing. She tried to catch it, but instead it hit the side of the barbeque making a loud noise. In panic, Madeline grabbed the ladder and ducked.

I peered over the balcony for any sign of the security guard. I heard footsteps on the gravel before he appeared. He would see Madeline for sure. I inched down and waited for the inevitable. But nothing happened. I heard more footsteps sounding as if he was rounding the house, probably heading back to his car.

My phone rang. I was quick to get it out of my pocket to silence it, fearful he'd heard the ring. From the display, I could see our team captain was calling. My phone buzzed as Paul's message went into voicemail.

A good three minutes passed before I heard Madeline go, "Pssst," and peeked over the balcony. "He's gone. Come on."

"How'd he not see you?"

"I hid behind lawn chairs."

I straddled the railing and tried my best to inch down, holding on with all my might as long as I could, trying to lessen the distance between my dangling feet and the ground. When strength gave out, I dropped and smacked down on my tailbone. It was incredibly painful.

"Holy shit." Madeline helped me up. "Are you alright?"

The tailbone was on fire, but the worst part was my ankle. I thought I may have broken it. "I think so," I lied. How stupid was I to agree to this? I limped around trying to shake it off.

Madeline hoisted the bin over her shoulder. With me limping behind her, we navigated a path through a thick bed of treacherous cacti. Only after we were clear of the property did she set the bin down and pull out the hard hat and cable guy disguise. "I've got to turn the power back on at the circuit breaker. Give me a sec." After she moved back to the house, I thought I heard a rattlesnake. Jumping away, my footing slipped on the gravel, and cactus needles dug into my calves. More pain.

Madeline returned, and we moved on. After circumventing the house next door, including their barking dog, I limped to my parked SUV. She loaded the bin into the back as I picked cactus needles out of my calf. "I don't think I can play, I sprained my ankle."

"I've got Advil."

"I'm serious."

"Let's get back and see," she said without an ounce of sympathy.

I gingerly climbed in my car, but instead of pulling a U-turn, I was determined to see what that security guard was doing. We slowly drove past. From what I could tell, he was watching something on his phone propped up on the dashboard. Sports, I assumed.

On Google Maps, the route back lit up red. It claimed we'd get there late for our match, at 3:10. "We're not going to make it," I told her.

"Never give up."

"Is that wisdom in the book, too?" I asked.

"No. It's a tennis thing."

We were speeding on Route 101 when Paul called again. I put him on speaker, "Hey Paul," I said, "I'm with Madeline."

"Where are you guys?" he said in panic. "Madeline, why aren't you picking up?"

My mixed doubles partner admitted, "I left my phone back in L.A. Sorry."

"We're playing Oregon in the next round. And we're waiting for you guys so we can take the team photo."

"We'll be there," Madeline said. "But we may be a little bit late. Stall."

Paul snapped back, "Stall? We *can't* stall at Nationals. Where are you?"

"On our way."

"What were you doing?"

"Shopping. Got stuck in traffic."

"What's your ETA?"

"We'll be there. Promise."

"You have to sign in with the starter first. I'll meet you there."

After I disconnected the call, Madeline asked me, "Do you think we'll make it?"

Google Maps estimated an even later arrival than before. My ankle and tailbone were killing me. I was in no shape to play, but didn't come this far to default, so I took the risk of driving on the shoulder of the freeway as if I was an emergency vehicle.

I was certain we'd get pulled over as we passed bumper to bumper, slow-moving traffic.

Reaching our adjacent hotels, I double-parked. We scrambled to grab our tennis bags from our hotel rooms. Then I parked in a handicap space at the tennis courts, and we ran to check in with the starter. Ivy and Paul were there, screaming at us. When it became clear we had just made it and would not have to default our match, she and Paul finally settled down.

As we hurried to our assigned courts, Ivy asked if I was going to wear jeans. In my haste to get there in time, I had forgotten to change back into shorts. They were back in my room. I had no extras in my bag. Neither did the guys from our team. And there was no time to purchase a pair in the pro shop.

Realizing my predicament, Madeline started laughing. I asked her what was so funny. She simply said, "We did it."

I washed down a hefty handful of ibuprofen while our opponents observed me with curiosity as a player wearing jeans. Madeline introduced me as her "Partner in crime."

We won the toss and chose to serve. Her spin drew our opponents out wide. Their returns were easy points for me at the net.

Madeline was on fire.

She played like never before—pure confidence, like a pro.

My mobility was greatly impaired because of my ankle, and wearing jeans didn't help. I couldn't hide the limp and played through the pain. Mostly, I stayed up at the net while Madeline chased down balls behind me.

She got to everything—playing at another level.

After we won the first set, I was surprised to see Laura sitting on the bleachers and watching our match. What was she doing here? After she sent the text this morning, she must have booked a flight. I couldn't believe it.

That's when it all went to my head, and my game fell apart—all while Laura was giving me the evil eye. The opposing team took advantage of my weakness. As good as Madeline played, I was the weak link. We lost the second set horribly. A ten-point tiebreaker would decide the match.

In the tiebreaker, it was all Madeline. The opponents double faulted twice, and we miraculously won the tiebreaker 10-7 to take the match. She saved the day. Afterwards, as we shook hands with our opponents, the guy player said, "I can't believe we were beaten by a dude in jeans."

Laura was no longer on the bleachers. I wondered where she had gone.

As Madeline and I put our rackets away, I was expecting criticism, but it never came. Instead, I saw that she had the Colt pistol in her bag. I asked, "Why'd you bring that?"

"Just in case."

"In case of what? Bad line calls?"

"When I was married, I never considered carrying a gun, but now that I'm living alone, I need protection."

"Have you always had that in your bag? For all of our matches this season?"

"Of course."

"Who carries a gun in their tennis bag?"

"I bet a lot of people do," she said. "It gives me confidence."

"Look…just…be careful with that thing. Somebody can get hurt."

I looked around for Laura. Where had she gone?

Madeline gave me a long stare. I was expecting criticism of the way I played, but instead, there was something else in her eyes—determination.

She said, "Thank you for your help today. Realize you need to keep everything we've done in strict confidence. Don't tell *anybody* because there's a lot at stake for me. Do you understand?"

Thinking of the gun in her tennis bag, I took her advice to heart. "Your secret's safe with me."

"Promise?"

"You have my word."

Something in her eyes—I don't know if she believed me.

I searched the tennis center for Laura but could not find her. I texted; *Where did you go?*

Meanwhile, our teammates' matches didn't go so well. Losing two out of three lines meant we did not advance in the winner's bracket and would be done after tomorrow's scheduled match.

I searched and searched for Laura. I called, but it went to voicemail. I texted, but there was nothing. Ivy wrangled us for the team photo, and as we stood in front of the tournament banner, I wondered if Laura was watching from a distance.

Instead of going out for dinner, our team decided to order pizza delivered to the hotel and hang out around the pool. Sitting at the outdoor gas fire pit, Madeline had her eyes on me. I couldn't tell if she was trying to seduce me or if she was scheming something sinister. I had been her accomplice. That meant I was the loose end. Thankfully, I was staying at the Hilton next door.

Back in my room, I called Laura, and she finally picked up. She had found out by following Ivy on Instagram. Apparently, they were in the same yoga class—a small world. Ivy had posted all of our names, and action photos, celebrating our play at USTA Nationals.

Laura said she had flown out to Phoenix to see who Madeline was. She couldn't bring herself to talk to me, so caught the next flight back.

I confessed that I hadn't told her that I was playing on a mixed doubles team because I was afraid she'd be jealous. Laura said that healthy relationships are built on trust, and now she couldn't trust me. She asked how I'd strained my ankle. I couldn't tell her, so made up a story that I'd foolishly tripped over the curb. She asked why I played in jeans. I told her I'd forgotten my shorts.

"I need a break," she said.

"What's that mean?"

"Time away from you to figure things out."

I tried to talk sense into her, but Laura's mind was set. Another call came in. I recognized it as Madeline's burner phone number. Laura heard the clicks and said, "Who's calling?"

"Nobody," I said. "Potential spam."

I could tell she didn't believe me. She abruptly ended the call. I called back but was sent to voicemail.

Madeline called back again, and I picked up. "Hey," I said.

"What are you doing?"

"Was just on the phone."

There was a long silence before she said, "I'm in room 320. Drop in."

"No, I don't think that's a good idea."

"Why?"

"I have a girlfriend."

"But you're not married, so…"

"I can't," I said. "And I'm tired. We have a match first thing tomorrow."

"Are you sure?"

"Yeah."

"You don't know what you're missing."

"I can't."

There was a long silence before, "See you tomorrow, then." I could tell she was disappointed.

The next morning, as we walked to the courts, Madeline would not meet my eye. Now I had two women mad at me.

Our team lost all three lines against the opponents from Georgia. They were far more skilled and probably should have been rated at a higher level.

As the others got on their phones to book earlier flights, Madeline and I checked out of our hotels and we met at my SUV. When I opened the tailgate, about two dozen wasps emerged in a crazy frenzy. I batted them away, could see the plastic lid of the bin had been left open.

"Wasps?"

"Yellow jackets," she said. "I guess I'd forgotten about those." She reached in to close the bin.

I opened all the doors for the pests to disperse, and said, "What else do you have in there?"

"That should be everything."

I didn't believe her. The paperback *Camouflaged Revenge: Retaliate Undetected* was sitting next to the bin. It was open to Step Five: *"Eliminate Witnesses"* clearly visible.

Eliminate Witnesses?

Does that mean accomplices, too?

It would be a six-hour drive to get home, and Madeline had that Colt 45.

* * *

John Shepphird is a Shamus Award-winning author, two-time Anthony Award finalist, and writer/director of television films. Novels include *Deception Specialist* (Jack O'Shea series book #1) and the Hollywood-themed thriller *Bottom Feeders*. John's short fiction has appeared in *Alfred Hitchcock Mystery Magazine* and various crime fiction anthologies. As director, films include *Jersey Shore Shark Attack, Chupacabra Terror, I Saw Mommy Kissing Santa Claus,* and *Teenage Bonnie & Klepto Clyde.* Check out *johnshepphird.com*

About the Editor

When John Shepphird is not working on his backhand he can be found writing crime fiction, creating television movies, commercials, and producing sports-centric promotional content. He serves as the awards chair for the Shamus presented by the Private Eye Writers of America, and resides in Southern California with his family and a treat-obsessed Labrador.

AUTHOR WEBSITE:

  https://johnshepphird.com/

SOCIAL MEDIA HANDLES:

  https://www.facebook.com/john.shepphird.

Also by John Shepphird, Editor

Coming Soon from Level Best Books
Golf Noir, edited by John Shepphird

The Shill Trilogy (Novellas)
The Shill
Kill The Shill
Beware The Shill

Novels
Bottom Feeders
Deception Specialist

www.ingramcontent.com/pod-product-compliance
Lightning Source LLC
Chambersburg PA
CBHW020746310726
48969CB00002B/441